By the same author

A Regency Holiday

False Pretenses

The Runaway Heart

Double Masquerade

The Perfect Fiancée

The Grey Fox Wagers

Divided Loyalty (as Jean Paxton)

Gazebo Rendezvous

Proxy Bride

SUNFLOWER

A Novel

Martha Powers

Simon & Schuster

SIMON & SCHUSTER
Rockefeller Center
1230 Avenue of the Americas
New York, NY 10020

SIMON & SCHUSTER and colophon are registered trademarks of
Simon & Schuster Inc.

Designed by Meryl Levavi

Manufactured in the United States of America

10   9   8   7   6   5   4   3   2   1

Library of Congress Cataloging-in-Publication Data
Powers, Martha.
Sunflower : a novel / Martha Powers
p.   cm.
I. Title
PS3566.0888S8   1998
813'.54—dc21   98-17853   CIP
ISBN 0-684-83767-6

Acknowledgments

To Senior Editor Chuck Adams, for his gentle edit, even though he took out some of my favorite lines. To my agent, Karen Solem, for putting up with a writer's angst and guiding me through this venture. To George E. Carpenter, Chief of Police, Wilmette, Illinois, for clarifying law enforcement procedures and convincing me that a bakery is not worth robbing. To Margaret Watson, DVM, for answering my veterinary inquiries without openly questioning my sanity. To Joanne Strecker, RN, for describing the goriest wounds so that I could understand them. And especially to Sharon DeVita, for offering laughter and support at all the appropriate times during our long friendship.

To Bill Powers
who took a chance on an unknown
and to
Michael V. Korda
who did the same thing twenty-five years later

Where Roses Fade

With rue my heart is laden
    For golden friends I had
For many a rose-lipt maiden
    And many a lightfoot lad.

By brooks too broad for leaping
    The lightfoot boys are laid
The rose-lipt girls are sleeping
    In fields where roses fade.

A. E. HOUSMAN,
A Shropshire Lad, LIV

Sunflower

Ah, sun-flower! weary of time,
    Who countest the steps of the Sun;
Seeking after that sweet golden clime,
    Where the traveller's journey is done;

Where the Youth pined away with desire,
    And the pale Virgin shrouded in snow,
Arise from their graves, and aspire
    Where my sun-flower wishes to go.

WILLIAM BLAKE,
Songs of Experience

Prologue

To the east of River Oaks, Wisconsin, the light from the rising sun overlay the blackness of the sky with a widening veil of luminescence. The woods to the south of town clung to the night, trees harboring pockets of shadow as if afraid of giving up their secrets to the day. Slanted shafts of sunlight broke through the cloud cover, pulling objects out of the surrounding darkness. The trails and the open areas were the first to gather the light, lines and patches of bleached color surrounded by a gray mist that shrouded everything beyond the fringes of the woods. The silence of the night still dominated, challenged only by the stirring of insects beneath the cover of last fall's leaves.

Timmie Schneider stood perfectly still in the middle of the track, eyes closed, head cocked to the side as he strained to hear above the beating of his heart. His breathing was so rapid that he couldn't get enough air through his nose. He opened his mouth to relieve the feeling of suffocation.

It was going to be hot today. A muggy Fourth of July. Perfect for the picnic and fireworks at the high school tonight. He remembered last year when he lay on his back, oohing and aahing as each new color burst, filling the sky with snow glitters that burned out before they touched the ground. His sister Alice was such a baby that she'd hidden under Mom's skirt and wailed.

He heard the rustle of leaves up ahead and edged his foot forward on the path.

His father had shown him how to walk soundlessly in the woods. Dad had been in the army and knew about the need for silence. He'd been shot up in 'Nam. Timmie'd seen the puckered scars on his side and his leg. His dad said it had happened one time when he hadn't been quiet enough.

Timmie touched the ground with the toe of one shoe, testing for dry twigs or loose gravel before he shifted his weight. He inched forward with such slow deliberation that he didn't appear to be moving at all. His mouth stretched wide in silent laughter as a squirrel bounced across the path, not even noting his presence.

Holygod was heading toward the open field.

The big deer had gotten his nickname when Timmie and his dad first spotted him last fall. "Holy God! I never saw a rack that size," his dad had said. Timmie knew how much his dad wanted that big old buck, and if he could help he would. He'd thought about it since then and finally come up with the perfect plan.

He'd been stalking the buck for the last two weeks. He planned to keep at it right through July and August. When hunting season started, he'd be so familiar with the movements of the big deer that he'd be able to tell his father exactly where to set up his stand. His dad had promised he could come along on the first day of hunting, even though Mom said he wasn't old enough, at ten, to shoot. It didn't matter. He'd act as his father's scout. The kill would be as much his as his dad's.

It was tough getting up before sunrise, but the excitement of sneaking out the bedroom window and crawling across the front porch roof right beneath his parents' window made it worth the loss of sleep. In the last couple of days he'd seen his father watching him at the breakfast table. His eyes were narrowed and his nostrils flared as if he could smell the outdoors on Timmie's clothing and in his hair. Timmie didn't want his dad to find out where he'd been.

He'd been forbidden to enter Worley Woods.

All the adults in town were spooked. Two dead kids had been found in Worley Woods. And now, with Lindy Pottinger missing, his mom would go ballistic if she found out where he was going every morning.

He wasn't afraid. The area had been searched yesterday. He'd seen all the people standing around the parking lot when he'd gone grocery shopping with his mom, and he'd hurried over to the edge of the crowd in time to hear Police Chief Harker explaining how they were going to do the search.

It was just getting exciting when his mom grabbed him by the arm and dragged him into Sandrik's grocery store. He didn't argue. She had that look in her eye that he knew meant things weren't negotiable. She'd plunked Alice in the grocery cart and ignored her squawking. Lately Mom had kept his sister practically under house arrest.

Timmie didn't think anybody'd snatch Alice. The dead girls were eleven and twelve. Alice was only four and a real nuisance. A born whiner, Dad said. And her nose was always running. Alice wouldn't be his choice for the next victim.

Besides, his family had lived in River Oaks forever. All the dead girls were from the Estates, the new development east of town. He'd heard his mom and dad whispering about it when he got up one night to go to the bathroom. His dad had said, "First Janette, then Tiffany and Meredith. Maybe the guy has a thing against yuppie names."

A twig snapped, up ahead and to the left.

Timmie's heart pounded hard in his ears, but he forced himself to keep to his slow, steady pace along the trail. He heard the sound of leaves sweeping across the ground. He grinned. Maybe he'd catch Holygod making a scraping. That'd be something to tell Reed Whitney. And while he wasn't sure what a "yuppie" was, he knew what "yucky" meant. Even though he was Timmie's best friend, Reed had a stupid yucky name.

The light was getting stronger. Through the tangle of bushes, Timmie spotted a small clearing and saw a flash of movement. He hunkered down on the edge of the path, scanning ahead for an animal trail that would lead into the woods. The rustle of leaves and branches cut through the silence of the morning as the deer scuffed the ground. Keeping low, Timmie crept forward, using the animal sounds to cover his own movements.

A narrow trail slanted in toward the clearing. The wind was in his face, so Holygod wouldn't smell him. His beating heart practically deafened him as he eased his way into the woods. It was awkward walking crouched over, but he wanted to get as close as possible before the deer spotted him.

Three feet to go. Two. Almost to the opening.

The clearing was fifty feet across. The light held a bluish cast against the darkness of the woods that closed in around the small open space. A movement caught Timmie's attention.

On the far side, a dark creature was silhouetted against the trees. Not the buck.

Human.

Timmie sucked air in a sharp sibilant breath. The figure whirled, facing him for one split second, then turned and plunged into the woods. Despite the roaring of blood in his ears, Timmie heard the slap of branches as whoever it was fled in panic. The noise faded into the distance. Finally the woods were quiet.

Even as he sagged in relief, he felt a prickle of sensation down his spine. He'd been in the woods so often that he knew when something was wrong. The silence was artificial. The normal sounds of bugs and small animals were absent as if the wildlife, instincts alert to danger, were frozen in place.

He shivered. Still hunched over on the path, his view of the clearing was blocked by waist-high bushes, and he couldn't see the whole area until he stood up and took several steps forward.

A girl was lying on a brown blanket in the center of the open space.

"Oh shit! Oh shit!" he chanted under his breath.

It was the missing kid. He recognized Lindy from school. She was just a year older than he was, and she was in the class ahead of him. She'd been gone for two days. Without knowing how, he knew she was dead.

Fear rooted him to the ground. His mouth was open, his breath coming in gasps. His heartbeat pulsed in his neck, and he blinked several times to clear his vision, his eyelids stretched wide as he searched the fringe of trees for any hovering presence.

Worley Woods felt empty.

Timmie's breathing eased. Curiosity touched him. He'd never seen a dead body, except on television—and that didn't count. With one more lightning glance around the clearing, he took a step forward, then another, stopping beside the body of the little girl.

Lindy Pottinger looked so peaceful she might have been asleep. She was lying on her back, eyes closed, arms crossed over her chest.

She was naked.

Timmie took in the details only as impressions of color. White-blond curls, lifeless against blue-white skin. Lips slightly parted, painted with red lipstick. Stiff fingers holding four red roses.

Behind him a branch broke and fell to the ground. The sound cut through his rigidity, and his feet scrambled to find purchase on the dew-slick grass.

Lindy Pottinger, the fourth victim of the River Oaks Killer, had come home.

Chapter One

Friday, September 6th

Lieutenant Sheila Brady picked up the glossy photographs and fanned them out like a deck of cards. Four children had been murdered in River Oaks, Wisconsin, in the last two years. Blond, blue-eyed, preteen girls. Sheila's eyes registered and identified each face: Janette Davis, Tiffany Chastain, Meredith Whitford.

And now the most recent victim, Lindy Pottinger.

It had been two months since Lindy's death, and they still were unable to identify the killer.

Sheila leaned back in the swivel chair. It was a hot day for early September, and the conference room of the police station was stuffy. She unbuttoned the collar of her uniform shirt. As a detective she wasn't required to wear a uniform, but she usually did. It helped her blend in with the other officers.

She'd have to watch her time. Meg got out of school at three-thirty. Staring down at the photos in her hand, Sheila tried to block out the image of her daughter. Lindy Pottinger and Meg had been in the same class at River Oaks Elementary.

Since the murders, most River Oaks parents had become overly protective. Unfortunately for Meg, Sheila was already paranoid. After seven years of police work in Milwaukee, she'd seen too much to be indifferent to her daughter's safety.

With her index finger, she touched the small raised scar close to the outside corner of her right eye. The cut had given her the impetus to join the police force. Along with working for a more ordered world, she would be able to protect herself and Meg.

Meg was growing up so fast, she thought. Eleven now. Physically, she resembled her father. The same high cheekbones. The same thick brown hair and dark eyes. The same wide mouth. Only in an occasional hand gesture or body motion, a tilt of the head or a cocked eyebrow, could Sheila see her own influence on her daughter.

"I'll keep Meg safe," Sheila said. She repeated the words, a trusted totem against evil.

She'd jumped at the opportunity to leave Milwaukee and move to a small town. She had known there had been two unsolved murders but accepted the job on the basis that she wouldn't be working on the murder cases.

In December she and Meg had moved to River Oaks. The third child was killed in January.

She'd questioned whether she'd made the right decision, but the murderer's pattern of targeting blond, blue-eyed girls reassured her that her daughter was not in any immediate danger.

There were no guarantees in life, though. The killer could change his pattern at any time. Ultimately, the only way to protect Meg and the other children of River Oaks was to find the killer.

Originally, she had been relieved that she wouldn't be involved in the murder investigations. Lindy Pottinger's death changed her perspective. When her daughter's friend had been killed, she couldn't remain on the sidelines. Knowing Lindy, Sheila felt she had an edge and might be able to make a difference. Besides, she had found a clue.

She'd gone to the Chief of Police, Hank Harker, with her suspicions. Harker had listened without comment, then told her to pursue the theory and give him a report. She'd given it to him last week but had heard nothing since then.

If her instincts proved correct, she planned to ask him to allow her more involvement in the investigation. Until then, she continued reading through the files to familiarize herself with the individual cases. She reached for the next folder with new resolution and opened the cover to the page of summary notes.

The first child had been murdered two years earlier. Janette Davis was ten, blond, and blue-eyed and was living in the new development east of town called the Estates. Two months before her disappearance, she and her mother had moved to River Oaks from Green Bay, Wisconsin.

Janette had been reported missing late in the afternoon. The following morning, her body was discovered, partially buried, in a strip of woods between the road and an open field. The little girl's skull had been crushed by repeated blows from a rock found in the woods near the body. After she was dead, she had been raped.

It had rained heavily the day of the girl's death, wiping out most of the evidence at the crime scene. It was concluded that someone had given her a ride. Whether he had intended to attack her was uncertain, but the murder had been committed out of panic rather than premeditation. Months of investigation had produced no solid clue to the identity of the killer.

Ten months after Janette's death, another child had been kidnapped and killed. The body of twelve-year-old Tiffany Chastain had been found south of town in Worley Woods. The girl had been missing for several days.

No attempt had been made to hide Tiffany's body. The child had been laid on a blanket with her arms crossed over her chest. She held two red roses in her right hand, her lips had been painted with red lipstick, and she was naked.

Once the autopsy reports were in, Chief Harker had been convinced the two children had been killed by the same person. Although the presentation of the body had been different, Tiffany, like Janette, had been raped after she was dead. It was highly unlikely that two killers with the same obscene tastes were preying on the children of River Oaks.

The autopsy revealed she had not been bludgeoned like Janette. The cause of death was asphyxiation. Synthetic fibers had been found in her mouth, trachea, and lungs. Something had been pressed over her nose and mouth until she stopped breathing.

Poor Tiffany, Sheila thought, staring at the girl's picture. Her death had occurred around midnight, thirty-four hours after she had been reported missing.

Eight months later, Meredith Whitford had been killed, and six months after that, Lindy Pottinger. Meredith had been eleven, Lindy ten. Like Tiffany, each girl had been missing for several days and had been found naked in the woods.

Meredith, the third victim, had held three red roses in her right hand, and Lindy, the fourth, had held four red roses. Each childish mouth had been painted with lipstick.

Sheila brushed her fingertips across the comparison chart of the four murdered children. She shoved the summary aside. Staring up at the calendar, she checked the dates she'd jotted on a yellow-lined tablet.

Ten months. Eight months. Six months. The intervals between murders had been shortening, and if the pattern continued, four months would be the next logical progression. It had already been two months since Lindy Pottinger's death.

Time was running out. The cycle was beginning again. From the moment of Lindy's murder, the killer had begun the hunt for a new victim.

Sheila glanced up at the clock. It was close to three. Meg would be out of school in half an hour. Putting her briefcase on the desk, she dumped a pile of folders inside, returning the others to the file cabinets.

Downstairs in the locker room, she pulled out her purse and reached inside for her makeup bag. A touch of lipstick and some blush was all she ever used. She put on gold dangling earrings, checked herself in the mirror, and piled everything back in her purse.

She removed her gun, checked it, and placed it on the top shelf of her locker. She was relieved that she wasn't required to carry it twenty-four hours a day. With Meg and other children around, she considered it too dangerous to keep it in the house.

Guns weren't standard issue in River Oaks; every officer bought his or her own. Chief Harker had recommended the .40-caliber Beretta, only on the market four or five years. The reports had indicated it was well worth the higher price tag. After trying it at the range, Sheila bought one.

Upstairs, the bullpen was nearly empty. Sergeant Kinkelaar stood at the coffee machine and looked up as she hurried to her desk.

"I thought you'd gone home, Sheila."

"Just finishing up. Looks like you're in for a quiet night," she said.

"On a Friday? You've got to be kidding." Paul snorted when he saw her grin. "We just got a tip on a keg party over in the woods behind the high school. Most of them underage."

"Going to bust 'em?"

"Bet your ass." He flushed at his words. "No offense meant, Sheila."

"None taken," she said.

It was hard for the older cops to learn the new rules about sexual harassment. At fifty, Paul was always worried that he'd crossed some invisible line.

"Don't forget to throw some towels in the back seat of the car," she reminded him.

"Already took care of that. I don't want some punk who can't hold his liquor puking on the upholstery."

"I learned the hard way."

Chuckling, Sheila sat down and sorted through the papers on her desk.

"I never seen you with any jewelry on." Head tipped to the side, Paul eyed her. "I like the dangling sunflowers. They look good. You should wear them more often."

Sheila touched her ears. "Glad you like them. I had a trainer at the police academy who described a perp grabbing her hoop earrings and ripping them out. That kind of thing puts you off jewelry on the job."

"I guess so," he said with a shudder. He finished his coffee and crushed the cup before throwing it in the trash. "I better get my butt moving. See you later."

After locking her desk, she picked up her purse and her briefcase. Heading for the door leading to the parking lot, she said goodbye to the others in the open room. Her head was down and her thoughts were on dinner preparations as she opened the back door of the police station. She jerked back when a microphone was shoved in front of her, and she raised her head only to be blinded by the bright lights of a camera.

Automatically, she thrust her arm up, palm outward as if to ward off a physical assault. She was so stunned by the appearance of the reporter and cameraman that for a moment she couldn't do anything but stare at the lens and blink. Stepping back, she spotted the call letters of one of the Madison TV stations painted on the side of a news van in the parking lot.

"Get that damn thing out of my face," she said between clenched teeth.

"Turn the camera off, Julio."

The glaring lights disappeared, and Sheila blinked to clear her vision. Able to see once more, she glared at the crooked smile of Melinda Lawson, one of the Madison reporters she'd gotten to know since moving to River Oaks.

"Sorry to jump out at you like that, Sheila," Melinda said. "I usually don't sneak up on people, but my boss is on my back for a different slant on the murders. Wants it for the six o'clock news. Can you do a quick interview?"

Over Melinda's shoulder, the cameraman twisted the settings on his shoulder camera, preparing to tape. The enormous lens drew Sheila's gaze and made it difficult for her to talk with any ease.

Shaking her head, she said, "Another time."

"It'll only take two minutes. Three at the most."

Sheila shook her head again, and Melinda reached out, fingers grasping her sleeve in a desperate grip.

"Give me a break, Sheila." She lowered her voice. "You know how tough it is for a woman in a man's world."

Sheila was annoyed at the emotional blackmail, because in general she liked Melinda. She heaved a sigh and gave a quick nod of her head.

Melinda's flashing eyes were the only evidence of victory. She turned and positioned Sheila so that the two of them stood in a V to facilitate the taping.

"I really appreciate this," Melinda said. "We won't even do a setup. I'll ask a couple questions, and later we'll splice the tape together with an intro by yours truly. Now take a breath and relax."

When the lights came on again, Sheila tried to focus on Melinda but was far too aware of the camera. Her lips felt stiff, so she made no attempt to smile.

"It's been two months since the last child died. Chief Harker has announced no new developments in the murders, Lieutenant Brady. Would you say that the entire investigation is stalled?"

The abrupt question sounded like an accusation to Sheila.

"In real life," she said, "crimes aren't solved with the speed and drama of televised cop shows. No one element is the key to discovering the killer. Every day we resolve another aspect of the cases. It's the painstaking examination of every detail that leads to an arrest."

Melinda's eyes widened in excitement. "Are you suggesting that the police are close to making an arrest?"

"I'm not suggesting anything. Such a statement would be premature," Sheila said, hoping she didn't look as annoyed as she felt. "Police work depends on building a strong enough case so that when we make an arrest we will be assured of a conviction."

"How long do you think that will take?"

"As long as necessary."

"Before another child is killed?"

Sheila could feel her temper rising at the woman's baiting. The questions had little substance, and the tone was clearly antagonistic.

"There's not a police officer who's not obsessed with the desire to apprehend the murderer and prevent another death."

Melinda gave a solemn nod of agreement, then her expression hardened, eyes narrowed and mouth pursed in disapproval. Sheila braced for the next comment.

"Were you aware that some of the River Oaks police are referring to the murderer as the Goldilocks Killer?"

"That's ridiculous." Sheila could feel the heat of anger rise to her cheeks. "The media might use such a frivolous tag, but never a police officer. Such a nickname trivializes the crimes. This is no fairy tale. Four children are dead. Killed by some lowlife scumbag. Call the man what he is. The man is a pervert. Committing heinous crimes against helpless little girls."

The interview was over. Sheila felt her heartbeat in her ears. She pushed forward, using her briefcase as a battering ram to force a path past Melinda and the onlookers who had been drawn by the lights.

She was shaking as she unlocked her car. Only when she was inside with the doors closed did she feel any measure of composure. She was furious at her own reaction to the reporter. Under pressure, she'd lost her temper.

A psychopath was loose in River Oaks. She had no idea how he would select his next target or what would set him off on his next murderous attack. It could be anything. A look. A glare. A word.

She drove home, pledging to be careful of everything she said until the murderer was caught. "Please God, let it be soon," she prayed.

•

He sat in darkness, illuminated by the cone of cold blue light from the television set.

Impatient, he forced himself to sit still, pressing the heels of his hands against the overstuffed arms of the chair. The six o'clock news started. His breathing quickened as he waited for any mention of the murders.

Restlessness overcame him, and he reached for the glass bowl of sunflower kernels on the mahogany table beside his chair. He grasped a handful and raised them to his open mouth. Small roasted nuggets spilled down the front of his shirt, and he brushed them away as he reached for more. His hand moved mechanically back and forth between his mouth and the dish until his craving subsided.

He chewed the last handful slowly, savoring the sharp crunching of the seeds and the nutty aftertaste. He licked the salt and the oil on his lips, then methodically sucked each of his fingers.

Little-girl faces flashed on the TV screen. They all looked alike with their golden hair and their blue eyes. They were so like Donna, but they never laughed. There was awe and fear on the little faces turned up beseechingly toward him. They had asked him to teach them, and he had. In their eyes he had seen his own power.

His face was reflected on the screen. It appeared as flat white planes and black hollows in the harsh light from the television. He sat motionless, but there was no respite from the uneasiness of his spirit.

Suddenly Sheila Brady's face appeared, and he was instantly alert. She looked so young, almost childlike as she faced the camera. A grown-up little girl. Her blond hair shimmered behind the glass, and he could imagine the texture. It would slide silkily through his fingers.

Her hand was raised, blue eyes wide with fear above the splayed fingers. He leaned forward and reached out to touch the screen. His fingers trailed across the glass image of her cheek. He breathed through his mouth, a low rasp of sound, as he traced the movement of her lips. Oil from the sunflower kernels smeared on the lighted glass.

Her hair was pulled back in a braid, and he was dazzled by the flash of gold when she turned sideways. A single gold chain hung from her earlobe, and at the end was a golden sunflower, glittering and dancing against her neck.

She was a golden girl. Just like Donna.

When the news was over, he rewound the tape, then fast-forwarded to the interview. Suddenly he blinked his eyes and stared at Sheila's face. He grabbed the remote control and rewound, then pressed play. When he came to the closeup, he pushed the pause button.

It was there. A small raised scar at the outside corner of her right eye.

He remembered when Donna got the scar. She had fallen the week before the last day of school. They had been racing each other home. She usually beat him. He could have run faster, but he loved to watch her hair lift and fall, flowing like a golden waterfall across her shoulders and back.

Her heels kicked up, almost touching the roundness of her buttocks. He could feel his privates expanding as he fantasized how the two globes of flesh would fill his cupped hands.

He was so mesmerized by the rise and fall of her buttcheeks that he sprinted forward, intent on touching her. Closer and closer he moved until he was just a foot away. Obsessed with the need to caress her, he stretched out his hand.

On contact, his body exploded with a jolt of pleasure.

Donna was so startled that she jerked around to stare at him. She didn't even see the stone on the path. She tripped. He reached out to grab her, catching a wad of her skirt in his hand. He jerked backward. She lurched against him, and they both tumbled into the field beside the path.

He lay on his back, Donna pressed against the length of his body. Winded but excited by the feel of her, he closed his eyes, then groggily opened them. At the sight of the blood on her face, he gasped for air, breathless with horror.

The zipper tab on his windbreaker had jabbed her close to her eye. He shivered to think what could have happened.

Donna started to whimper, and he rolled up to a sitting position, grateful for the freshly ironed handkerchief his mother made him carry. Blood seeped from the trough of the wound, but he could see that it was only a small cut.

She sobbed when she saw the blood, terrified that she'd be disfigured. He reassured her by saying it would only be a little mark on her cheek that would probably resemble a beauty mark like they'd seen on the French queen in the history book. She stopped crying and wiggled against him in her delight.

They lay together in the grass while Donna blotted the blood with his handkerchief. She rested her head on his chest, and her groin pressed against his. He patted her back, then relaxed his fingers to massage her shoulders and neck.

His fingers kneaded the muscles of her neck, then slowly moved downward. He ached to touch the flesh beneath her clothes and feel the naked skin against the sensitive pads of his fingers.

She stiffened when he reached her waist.

As if against his will, his hands slid across the twin mounds of her buttocks. He stroked in rhythmic circles, waiting in suspense for her reaction. She began to tremble. Barely perceptibly at first, then as the movement increased, she squirmed against him, her breath coming in short little pants.

The sound of gravel slipping underfoot brought him to his

senses. He twisted out from under her and jumped to his feet. Seeing other children coming along the path, he pulled her up and they continued walking. He left her at her house, trudging on to his own place and spending the evening worrying about the cut beside her right eye.

It had left a scar. The mark gave him a curious feeling of possession.

The scar was still there, high on her cheek. He stared at Sheila Brady's face, her image held captive on the television. She could use the name "Sheila," but he knew she was Donna all grown up.

Tightness began to build in his groin. He was grateful that he'd found her. She had always belonged to him. The others had been merely pupils.

Now it was time to teach Donna all the things he'd learned.

•

"Mom! Mom! Come quick!"

Hearing the cry, Sheila dropped the papers on her desk and ran to the patio doors. Her heart thudded until she spotted Meg waving to her from the back of the yard. She slid open the screen door and stepped outside.

"Look, Mom. It's a mourning dove," Meg said. She was bent over, hands braced on her knees, her eyes intent on the ground. "It's hurt."

Sheila bent down, moving a few branches of the boxwood in order to see the bird huddled at the base of the shrub. The long pointed tail stirred the dust in the garden as it struggled to get to its feet. Black eyes glistened against the pink-tinted down on head and breast. The bird flapped its wings, falling awkwardly on its side.

"I think it's his leg." Meg shifted from foot to foot in her anxiety. "Can we help it? Please?"

Sheila reached out her hand, grasping the plump body of the bird, clucking under her breath to reassure the quivering thing. She turned it over and had little difficulty seeing the cause of the injury. One spindly leg was bent at an awkward angle.

"Is it broken?" Meg asked.

"Looks like it. I don't see any blood, so maybe that's all that's wrong with it." Upside down, the bird had quieted, lying limp across her hand with only an occasional flicker of motion to indicate it was alive.

"We could put a splint on it, couldn't we? And I could feed it until it got better."

Sheila could see that Meg was already envisioning her role as Florence Nightingale to the injured dove. For the first time since Lindy's murder, Meg's face was animated. Perhaps tending to a wounded bird would give her an opportunity to focus on something other than the death of her friend.

"Tell you what. If the bird lasts overnight, we'll take it to the vet tomorrow and see what he has to say. In the meantime we'll do what we can."

Sheila rose with the bird. Even at a distance she could see Meg's cat staring out the screen door, ears forward and eyes intent.

"Check Elmo," she said. "You'll have to keep the bird outside or he'll think it's his dinner."

"I've got a shoebox in my closet."

"It can't be cardboard or some animal will get it. And you'll need a cover so it won't hurt itself further trying to fly."

"How 'bout that old aquarium we found in the garage when we moved here? It's even got a top. It'll be perfect, Mom."

"Sounds good to me. You can put the bird in a wastebasket until the aquarium is cleaned out. Rip up some newspaper for the bottom. It'll make a soft nest for him."

Meg hurried ahead to open the kitchen door. Putting the bird in the kitchen sink, Sheila went in search of towels and additional supplies. Back in the kitchen, she wrapped the bird's body in a hand towel, holding it steady while she instructed Meg to cut up Q-Tips for splints.

"You better do it, Mom," Meg said, as she stared at the crooked leg of the mourning dove.

"You can handle it, honey. First, cut some strips of the adhesive tape. Good. Now wrap his leg with gauze."

Meg, face screwed up in concentration, tentatively touched the sticklike leg. She jerked back when the bird twitched. Biting her lip, she grasped the leg, binding it with gauze.

"Now what?" she asked.

"Lay one of the splints along the leg and see if you can straighten out the bend in it. Then a little more gauze to hold it in position. After that the second Q-Tip and some tape."

Meg fumbled in her nervousness, but with Sheila's encouragement, she eventually had both splints in place. She wrapped tape around the whole leg as Sheila held the Q-Tips steady. The bandage was bulky but secure.

"Nicely done. You make a first-rate doctor," Sheila said.

Meg beamed with pride and reached out a finger to stroke the head of the towel-wrapped bird.

"Is your stuff all ready for Beth's sleepover?"

"It's all set and Mrs. L. is picking me up."

"Good. Then you'll have enough time to get the cage set up. You can put him in a wastebasket until it's ready."

Meg raced off down the hall. Returning with the bathroom wastebasket, she carefully lowered her patient inside, then took it out to the patio.

Sheila cleaned up the kitchen, spraying disinfectant on the countertop. Standing in the archway leading to the family room, she watched as Meg bustled between the garage and the patio. At the brush of fur against her leg, Sheila jumped.

"Damn it, Elmo! One of these days you're going to give me a heart attack, you miserable ball of fluff!"

Leaning over, she scratched the cat under his chin and felt the throaty tremors beneath her fingers.

"Go ahead. Suck up to me when Meg's not around. I'll remember that when it's time for your dinner."

The cat pressed against her leg, the tip of his thick tiger-striped tail flicking back and forth. Sheila rubbed behind his ears, then pushed him toward the screened patio doors.

"Go keep an eye on Meg," she said.

As if Elmo understood her words, he ambled across the family room and sat down in front of the screen door. His head jutted forward, his eyes intent on the wastebasket as if he sensed the bird inside.

Beyond the screen door, the Indian summer evening beckoned. Sighing, Sheila headed back to her desk, her mind still on her daughter.

She was pleased with how well Meg had done in ministering to the injured bird. It was important that her daughter learn to be self-reliant.

Too bad she hadn't been more prepared for life as a single parent.

The summer before her senior year at Marquette University, Sheila had discovered she was pregnant. She was engaged to Robbie Brady, but they wanted to wait until they graduated to marry. For Sheila, abortion was not even a consideration, and besides, she'd wanted the baby. She and Robbie were married a month before classes started.

For a while Robbie thought it was fun playing house, but he wasn't ready for the responsibilities of marriage, let alone fatherhood. Sheila remembered how often she had caught him staring into the mirror, a forlorn expression etched on his face. It was as if he watched his carefree life fading away in the reflection.

Robbie changed after they were married. He no longer laughed with the abandon that had drawn her to him in the first place. He'd taken a job after his classes, and as her pregnancy advanced he sank deeper into gloom.

At first Sheila thought it was fear for her health that had him so depressed. Throughout much of the pregnancy, she had been sick. She was desperate to keep up with her studies, knowing that if she dropped out she would probably never graduate.

Meg obliged them by being born during Christmas break. Sheila hadn't even missed a class. She had a circle of friends, willing surrogates, who fought over the privilege of taking care of Meg. Even Robbie seemed to be delighted, frequently coming home with toys or other presents for the baby.

And now that baby was nearly grown, Sheila thought as she stared outside at her daughter. The girl sat on the flagstones, holding the injured dove in her lap, her dark head bobbing as she sang to the bird.

It made Sheila sad to remember that Robbie rarely held Meg. He used to gaze down at her in the crib or watch as Sheila rocked her. His initial joy in becoming a father had faded with the day-to-day realities of taking care of a baby.

When Meg was five months old, Robbie and Sheila graduated. In the middle of the graduation party, Robbie walked out. The last time Sheila'd heard from him since the divorce was five years ago. He was in California, working on the fringes of the movie business.

She was so deep in her own thoughts that she jumped when Meg slid open the screen door.

"Don't worry, Elmo, I still love you best," the girl said, scooping up the cat and rubbing her nose in the soft fur at his neck. "I think the bird might get better, Mom. He flopped around when I put him in, but then he snugged up in a corner. What should I feed him?"

"Don't birds eat worms?" Sheila chuckled at the small nose, wrinkled in distaste. "And maybe a bug or two."

"Ugh. That's really sick! Come on, Elmo. Let's look in the fridge. We'll find something he'll like." Talking softly to the cat, Meg strolled into the kitchen.

Sheila wondered if the mourning dove would survive Meg's loving care. The aquarium was set against the patio doors, and through the glass she could see the plump bird nestled in the shredded newspaper.

A gust of wind swirled the first leaves of autumn across the patio. Despite the balmy weather, summer was over. She'd never liked the fall. The colorful flowers died, leaving behind the golds and bronzes and browns. As the sun lost its warmth the bright hues faded. Soon the rich pigments of the landscape would be gone, dead until spring.

Turning back to the work on her desk, Sheila opened the next file and began to read. She continued working until Meg was ready to leave. When a horn honked outside, Sheila carried the sleeping bag to the car, said a few words to Beth's mother, and then gave Meg a kiss and a hug. She stood on the front doorstep waving as the car pulled out of sight.

After Meg left, the house seemed unnaturally silent. Sheila forced herself to go back to work, but as the evening wore on she found it hard to concentrate.

She should keep working, but she was restless. She reached for the beeper clipped to her waistband. No messages. She checked the batteries. It was September sixth. She put fresh batteries in on the first of every month.

She rose and walked into the living room to stand at the front window, staring out into the night. The great elms used to be lovely, but since murder had come to town, the wooded neighborhood seemed dark with sinister shadows.

Reviewing the four cases had brought the murders closer. She tried to keep her personal life separate from the grim realities of police work, but after reading over the files, she had the distinct feeling that evil had slipped into the house.

"Good God! What's wrong with me tonight?" Sheila muttered.

She rolled her shoulders to release the tension in her back and neck as she walked back down the hall. She stopped in the archway between the kitchen and the family room.

The cat was motionless in the center of the room. Head extended forward, his eyes were riveted on the patio doors. Sheila thought he was watching the mourning dove in the cage outside, but looking closer, she could see that his gaze was fixed beyond the patio into the back yard.

Goosebumps rose on her arms, and she shivered as she looked out the glass doors.

Blackness. Only shiny, flat blackness. As a child she'd been afraid of the dark, afraid of being pulled into the void beyond her bedroom windows. She had cried when her night-light was taken away. To Sheila, it was the ultimate punishment.

As she grew older, her phobia changed. She preferred to be inside the dark. She drew it around her, clothing her fears in the safety of the black. In the lamplit room, she was surrounded by the shadows of night. It pushed against the windows, searching for a crack to press through and fill the room.

"Pssst. Elmo."

Her voice sounded inordinately loud, but the cat remained attentive to his watch. Determined to ignore her attack of nerves, she crossed the room and flipped on the outside light. The umbrella table and patio chairs sprang into view, the brightly colored cushions garish in the yellow light. Sheila could see nothing in the back yard that might have caught his interest.

"Satisfied?" she asked as she turned to the cat.

One of Elmo's legs stretched upright, and he was busy washing his fur. With a final lick of his tongue, he raised his head and stared up at Sheila with unblinking gold eyes. She suspected he was smirking at how easily he had frightened her.

"Stuff it," she said.

She snapped off the outside lights, but knowing she wouldn't be able to concentrate with the void beyond the glass doors, she yanked the cord, and the draperies slid across with a soft shushing sound.

The doorbell rang.

She jumped at the sudden sound. Elmo had been right. Someone had been outside. Her pulse leaped with the rush of adrenaline. Meg uppermost in her mind, Sheila hurried toward the door.

Elmo, cat radar intact, was already waiting on the rug in the front hall. Sheila looked through the peephole. No one was on the front porch. Cautiously she opened the door.

On the stoop was a cardboard box.

She looked up and down the street but could see nothing to indicate who had left the package on the doorstep. She shook her head as she shifted her glance to the object at her feet.

The box was a brown shipping carton large enough to hold a small appliance. The top wasn't sealed. The four sides had been folded in on each other. Sheila's name and address were printed with a black marking pen in block letters on one of the flaps.

Despite the way it was delivered, it looked harmless enough. Sooner or later, she'd have to deal with it, so she might as well bring it inside. She leaned over to pick up the box.

Beside her, Elmo let out a low, guttural moan.

Chapter Two

"Stop that," Sheila snapped as the cat continued to wail.

Elmo's reaction unnerved her. She scanned the empty street. The box didn't look threatening, but the fact that it had been delivered in such a surreptitious fashion made her extremely cautious.

She nudged the carton with her foot. Nothing inside moved. With Elmo's reaction, she half expected to hear the scurrying of some animal. Gingerly, she picked it up. The box wasn't heavy. No more than a pound or two. Bringing it inside, she set it on the throw rug in the front hall, closed the door, and locked it.

Elmo had retreated to the kitchen archway. His body was close to the floor, his shoulder blades sticking out as his head jutted forward, ears flat against his head. His cry was replaced by a higher pitched keening sound.

"For God's sake, shut up."

At her sharp command, the cat fell silent.

She stared down at the shipping box, debating whether to call Chief Harker before she opened it. She could almost see the expressionless moonface staring back at her with a single raised eyebrow. In her infrequent dealings with the chief, she had tried to convince him she was a cop first, not a woman. Calling him would be a definite show of weakness.

"Well, Elmo. It's up to us guys."

She blew out her breath in three quick puffs of air and then, before she could lose her nerve, leaned over and grasped the corner of one of the flaps with her first finger and thumb. As the edge rose, it pulled the other sides away from the center. Using the tips of her index fingers, she pushed back the flaps, exposing the contents.

In the bottom of the box was a doll.

It was about a foot tall, one of a series of fairy-tale dolls Sheila had seen in the toy stores. The doll was wearing a yellow dress. The skirt and sleeves were trimmed with a white lace ruffle. A matching bonnet covered the head of curly yellow hair. The front of the doll's dress was splattered with blood.

Fastened to the doll's wrist was a tag in the shape of a book. The title was *Goldilocks and the Three Bears.*

A shudder ran through Sheila's body. Who could have sent her something so nasty?

Carefully, she leaned over and used her fingertips to close the flaps on the box. The cat edged forward, nose twitching as he sniffed the air.

"Sorry, Elmo, I need to take this package into the lab in the morning. Cat hair will only confuse them."

She picked him up and closed him up in Meg's room, then returned to the kitchen. Checking the emergency list on the side of the refrigerator, she dialed Chief Harker's beeper. While she waited for his return call, she stood in the archway staring at the box in the front hall. When the phone rang, she whirled around to pick up the receiver.

"Problem, Lieutenant?"

Harker's greeting was typical. After nine months, he still treated her with polite formality, never using her first name, only her rank.

"Sorry for disturbing you so late, Chief."

Briefly she told him about the arrival of the package and described the contents. He listened without interruption until she completed her report.

"Was your daughter there when the package arrived?" he asked.

"No. I was here by myself. Meg's staying overnight with a friend."

"Good. Kids shouldn't have to see stuff like this." She heard anger in his voice and could picture his blond eyebrows lowered over narrowed brown eyes. "Probably spooked you though. You OK?"

"Yes. I'm fine. It was a bit of a jolt."

"It was meant to shock you. Be thankful that it wasn't anything worse." He didn't give her time to dwell on his words. "Take the box to the crime lab in Madison."

"Now?"

"You have something better to do?"

"No. I-I just didn't think the lab was open this late," she stammered, her hand tightening on the receiver.

"It's not, but I'll put a call in to the head of the lab and ask if someone can come in for a rush job," he said. "Tell them to fax a preliminary report first thing tomorrow. I've got a meeting with Mayor Perkins in the morning, and I want to talk to you after that. Let's say eleven o'clock. In the meantime, get the box to the lab."

Without another word, he hung up. On the verge of asking a question, Sheila's mouth remained open as she listened to the dial tone. She pulled the receiver away from her ear and glared at it before she replaced it.

Dealing with Harker was never easy. He always made her feel slightly off balance.

She wondered if he was at home. Harker was divorced and lived in a white clapboard house several blocks from the center of town. When she'd first moved to River Oaks, she'd driven past the place. Expecting brick, unyielding and cold, she'd been surprised to find the house inviting with its green shutters, window boxes, and a porch across the front.

Would she ever be comfortable working for Henry Harker? He was forty-three, eleven years her senior; average height, maybe five feet ten; yet, he radiated a sense of power that was intimidating. His body was hard, well-muscled from daily workouts. She couldn't imagine him sprawled in an easy chair in front of the television. He probably sat in a wooden straight chair.

On her first day at work she'd learned he hadn't wanted to hire her.

His attitude was similar to that of a lot of the instructors at the police academy and most unit heads. The "It's OK for women to be cops but not in my department" type of response.

Ever since her arrival in River Oaks she'd been on probation, and she wondered if that was why Harker wanted to see her. Maybe he had a reply to the report she'd given him. If her theory panned out, she'd been planning to request further involvement in the murders. She bit her lip, wondering if the arrival of the mystery package would affect his decision.

•

Police Chief Hank Harker leaned his shoulder against the window casing in Mayor Perkins's office, staring down at Hodges Park. One side of the park faced City Hall, an imposing stone building, a monument to cheap labor and Old World craftsmen. Dotted along the other three sides were small clothing stores, an old-fashioned pharmacy, a movie theater, a bookstore, and other local businesses. With its small playground, walking track, flower gardens, and plenty of park benches, it still looked much the way it had when he was a kid, but much had changed.

River Oaks had been a sleepy Wisconsin farm town when he was growing up. It had been about a hard hour's drive to Madison until five years earlier, when the new freeway made for a quick commute to the capital. In five years the population of the town had shot from three thousand to ten thousand.

The character of the town had changed with the boost in population. The merchants were the only original residents who appreciated the expansion. There were shopping malls and fast-food places and stores that sold cutesy crap. The old movie theater had been gutted and rebuilt into two sterile little boxes so that two movies could be shown at the same time. Some called it progress; he called it a shame.

Hank looked down at his watch. The mayor was ten minutes late. One more reason to dislike the man, Hank thought.

Dick Perkins had decided to run for mayor after the second child was kidnapped and murdered. He'd exploited the parents' fear by promising to set up a citizens' patrol after his election.

He'd been elected, and Parent Watch was formed.

The organization reminded Hank of cops and robbers, grown-up style. The patrols rode around in four-wheel-drive vehicles and talked into their radios. He wondered if they had a secret handshake and maybe even a song. That sort of stuff would appeal to Dick Perkins.

If the patrols had been able to keep the killer from taking another child, Hank would have been grateful for the help. But none of those sporty cars with their fancy technical equipment had done a damn bit of good for either Meredith Whitford or Lindy Pottinger.

"Sorry I'm late," Dick Perkins said as he strode into the room and shook Hank's hand. "Grab a chair."

Perkins set his briefcase on the corner of the teak desk, then sat down in the high-backed red leather chair, his fingers rubbing the soft upholstery on the arm. The way the mayor was stroking it, Hank thought, he either had a leather fetish or suffered from a nervous twitch.

"How do you like what my decorator did in here? Mayor Grange's style was a lot different than mine."

"I never spent a lot of time up here with Patrick. We usually met across the park at the Duck Inn," Hank said. "I'd say the changes are pretty impressive."

"Your office could use some updating." Perkins swiveled around to indicate the abstract explosion of red and black paint behind his desk. "You know, Hank, a little artwork really sets the tone."

"I've got just the thing at home. It's a woodcut that says 'Fish, Fight, or Fuck Off.'"

For a moment Hank thought he might have gone too far. Perkins's face went blank, then suddenly his mouth stretched in a grin and he chuckled.

"You're quite the kidder, Harker."

Hank sighed. He really didn't want to antagonize Perkins. He might feel contempt for the man, but that didn't mean he couldn't work with him. After fifteen years, he was enough of a political animal to know it wouldn't do to piss off the mayor.

"I wanted to talk to you, Dick, because we've got a problem brewing with Parent Watch. In my book, citizen patrols rank right up there with vigilante justice. For the most part, I've had no cause to complain. God knows, help would be appreciated—my officers are doing double duty. But now the group's getting into some deep shit."

A pained look crossed Perkins's face. "I don't know as I'd say that, Hank. The purpose of Parent Watch is to add to the protection of the children of River Oaks. I've cautioned the members that they are merely an adjunct to the police force."

Spoken like a true politician, Hank thought. Rumor had it that Perkins had his sights set on a pond bigger than a small Wisconsin town. Some said he was angling to be the next state senator. After that, governor, and maybe eventually Washington.

It was possible, Hank thought. He had the look. A Harvard lawyer in his late thirties, he was at the top of his form with his fashionably styled hair starting to gray at the temples, handsome features, and tanned face. He was a good speaker, jumping on all the trendy buzzwords to elicit the right reaction. Too bad the guy was such a mealy-mouthed jerk.

Hank cleared his throat.

"Word is that some of your patrols are talking about doing a little more than driving around the streets."

"Technically, Hank, they're not my patrols. Ruth O'Brien is the head of Parent Watch."

"That's just a load of bull crap, Dick," Hank said. "Everyone knows Parent Watch is your baby. It's mostly folks from the Estates. Your neighbors. They'll listen to what you tell them to do."

Perkins shifted in his chair, recrossed his legs, and smoothed the chino material over his knees. "Everyone's got the best interest of the children at heart, and some think it wouldn't be such a terrible idea to carry weapons."

"Parent Watch exists because I permit it, and I can disband it tomorrow if I have good reason." Hank spoke slowly so that later there would be no question over what he had said. "If any patrol member is found with a gun, I will personally arrest him and charge him with disorderly conduct. No excuses. No exceptions. Do I make my position clear?"

"Perfectly clear," Dick said. Other than a slight tightening of his mouth, the mayor showed little outward reaction to Hank's words.

"We've received complaints that the patrols are more frequent in the Estates than they are in the old section of town."

Dick shrugged, spreading his hands wide. "It's only logical. The four children who were killed were all from the Estates. It seems like the children there are the most at risk."

"When you're dealing with a killer like this, every child is at risk."

"You don't have to tell me that, Hank. I've got two kids of my own." He motioned to the picture of his wife and children, prominently displayed on the corner of his desk.

Hank rubbed his hand across the top and down the back of his head, massaging the tight muscles of his neck. "If I had young kids, I'd feel the same way. But guns aren't the answer."

Perkins stood up. He moved around the room, then returned to lean on the back of his chair, his fingers stroking across the leather back, his expression contemplative.

"I took a lot of psychology courses at Harvard," he said, "and I've been doing some reading on serial killers."

Hank groaned. Just what he needed. Psychobabble from an arrogant prick with a penchant for leather.

"I'm sure you know most of this, Hank," Dick generously conceded. "But once a serial killer has established a pattern, his actions take on a ritual quality with import given to each action, at least in his own mind. Then each killing becomes a ceremonial event, and it's almost impossible for him to make any changes."

Hank was reminded of one of the many reasons he disliked Dick Perkins. The man spoke as if he were getting paid by the syllable, wordiness overriding brevity in most exchanges.

"Bullshit," Hank said. "You can never count on anything when you're dealing with a murderer. Don't get lulled into feeling secure just because you see a pattern. Today it's blond girls, but tomorrow it could be redheaded boys."

"And you've got nothing?"

Hank could feel his eyes narrow at the condemnation in the man's voice. Civilians always wanted quick action. An arrest. Cops knew it was never that simple.

"I told you right after the election that this bastard wasn't going to be easy to catch. In a normal murder investigation we tie the murderer to the victim. In this case only the victims connect."

"Were they friends?"

"Not as far as we can determine. The girls all came from the Estates, but you know yourself the development is the size of a small town."

"What about the physical evidence? Once you have a suspect, you'll have enough to make a case, won't you?"

"When we get him, we'll have enough to bury him."

"It's rather ironic," Dick said. "Most of the people in the Estates moved out of Madison to get their kids away from the dangers of city life. They moved here because it was safer. Sometimes I wonder if they brought this evil with them."

•

"Damn politicians," Hank muttered as he made his way down the marble steps of City Hall.

The more time he spent with the mayor, the less he liked the man. Maybe it was Perkins's hair. Hank had never trusted men who wore mousse.

I'm probably jealous, Hank thought. He'd noticed his own hair was thinning, and he wondered how long he'd be able to wear the brush cut he'd sported since he'd been in the Marines.

The one good thing about the mayor was that he kept a well-stocked humidor. He pulled a cigar out of his pocket, ran it under his nose, and snipped the end off. Reaching into his pants pocket for one of the wooden matches he carried, he flicked the end with his thumbnail, cupping his hand to light the cigar. He puffed greedily until it was going nicely.

Damn, he loved a good cigar.

He was early for his meeting with Sheila Brady. Not wanting to waste the Indian summer day, he walked across Hodges Park and sat down on one of the benches.

Despite the fact that it was Saturday, the park was empty. It had rained earlier and the grass looked thick, the color deep and mossy. The white wrought-iron benches stood out against all that green. With City Hall on one side and stores fronting the other three sides, the park had always been a natural gathering place. Mothers used to sit and gossip while their kids played on the swings. The benches were vacant now, and the swings hung limp, mute reminders of the fear that gripped the town.

He wasn't surprised that the Parent Watch group had started talking about guns. Fear was a prod to violence. Ever since Lindy Pottinger's body was found, there'd been an increase in traffic accidents, domestic disturbances, and property damage. And not a week went by that there weren't at least two calls from hysterical parents who were convinced their children had been kidnapped.

When Hank finished his cigar, he crossed the street to the police station.

Upstairs in his office, he dropped down into the swivel chair, contrasting the worn patches on the arms to the flawless leather on the mayor's chairs. He read the lab reports on his desk and glanced out the glass wall of windows at the bullpen.

Since becoming chief, he'd impressed on his officers the need to keep order within the station house. No matter what crisis they had to deal with, he expected them to perform in a well-disciplined manner. He put rookies through a rigorous training period so that in an emergency they'd fall back on established routines.

Hank's eyes moved to Sheila Brady. She was at her desk in an alcove next to the coffee machine. Her hands busy on the keyboard of her computer, she was oblivious to his scrutiny.

Sheila had been one of three candidates for the vacant detective job. He'd rejected her application; the town council reversed his decision.

It was only later that he discovered Dick Perkins had pressured the council to hire her. Hank suspected that the mayor had a personal interest in Sheila Brady despite his much-publicized campaign plat-form of family values.

Hank had to admit that it would be easy to be interested in Lieu-tenant Brady. At thirty-two, she was about five foot six, slender with nicely proportioned breasts and hips. At first glimpse she looked frag-ile, but Hank knew she was well schooled in the art of self-defense. The muscles in her arms and legs were clearly delineated yet still re-tained a soft, feminine appearance.

It wasn't just her body that was a distraction. She had enormous blue eyes fringed by thick lashes, a long straight nose, and full lips. Her hair was blond, thick, and silky. She usually wore it in some kind of flat braided affair. He'd seen rookies get tongue-tied when they spoke to her.

For fifteen years he'd encouraged a tightly knit police depart-ment. He supposed he was a male chauvinist because he'd never been convinced that women could be equal to men on the police force. In-formal social networks were essential to a successful unit. And for the most part the locker room was where many of the decisions were made. Segregated facilities kept women out of the loop.

The clock on the wall gave a metallic click as the second hand jerked straight up, bringing Hank out of his reverie. As if she had heard the sound too, Sheila looked up. He beckoned to her and she rose without haste, walking across the room to his office.

He waved her to a seat across the desk. She'd been shaken when she called him the night before. Today she was back in control of her emotions.

"I've got the preliminary report back on your mystery package," he said.

"Any prints?"

"Only yours. Nowadays any idiot who watches television knows how to avoid leaving fingerprints." He picked up the lab report and scanned it again. "You were right. The blood was paint. They'll try to match the profile against company samples."

She nodded. "I talked to the manager at Wal-Mart and then stopped at Taylor's Toys. Maike Taylor said it's a series of six dolls. Goldilocks, Cinderella, Rapunzel, Sleeping Beauty, Little Red Riding Hood, and Snow White. Cinderella is the big seller. Neither place had sold any of the Goldilocks dolls in the last six months."

"What's your gut feeling here?" He placed the report on the cor-ner of his desk. "Do you think the package was from the murderer?"

Hank watched as Sheila considered the question. He liked the fact that she didn't leap to judgment but sorted through the available information until she came up with a logical conclusion.

She shook her head. "I don't think so. Whoever sent it either didn't know or didn't care about the details of the case. The killer takes pride in his work. The doll would have been naked, and instead of the blood there would have been flowers."

With the toe of his shoe, Hank pulled open the bottom drawer of his desk, then he leaned back in his chair and propped his feet on the open drawer.

"Any idea who might have sent it?"

"None. It doesn't seem like a kid's prank. I'll check the neighbors to see if they saw anyone." She touched the scar beside her eye, her mouth pinched in concentration. Sitting up straighter in her chair, she looked across at him. "I do have a hunch why it was sent."

"I hate hunches."

"Occasionally they pay off. In this case I think it's in response to a comment I made to a reporter. Did you catch the news out of Madison yesterday?"

"I did."

His tone was neutral, but it was obvious by his raised eyebrow that he had seen the interview with Melinda Lawson. Sheila shifted in her seat, and the color rose to her cheeks.

"A camera crew ambushed me in the parking lot on my way home last night. In Melinda's defense, I did agree to speak on camera."

"Melinda might be charming when you're talking to her off camera, but she's a pit bull when it comes to a story."

"That may be true, but it doesn't excuse the fact that I lost my temper when she referred to the murderer as the Goldilocks Killer."

Hank grimaced, knowing it was just the kind of remark that could be picked up by someone on the edge. The inability to prevent another murder had made the police easy targets for local anger.

"If your comment prompted this, it's probably someone in River Oaks. I don't know if a nutcase would drive out from Madison, or beyond, to drop a bloody doll on your doorstep," Hank said. "The segment aired at six and then a shorter version at ten. You got the package at ten-thirty. Sounds like someone local."

He didn't like the dark circles under her eyes. She'd probably been up late worrying about who in River Oaks hated her enough to send the doll.

"Considering the tone of Melinda's questions, you handled her very well. So you lost it at the end." He shrugged. "If it's any comfort to you, not everyone saw the news," he said. "I had a meeting with Dick Perkins this morning, and if he'd seen it you can be sure I'd have heard about it."

Sheila brushed a strand of blond hair off her forehead, her expression troubled.

"The fact that the box was delivered to my house instead of the police station makes me very uncomfortable. What if Meg had been home and had answered the door? I'm sure she would have opened the box without giving it a thought."

"You'll need to warn her, Lieutenant." Hank could sympathize with Sheila but could offer little comfort. Being a cop invited danger into the home. It was part of the life. "Don't overreact. My guess is that the package was delivered to your house because it was less risky than sending it to the station. Be warned, but don't put too much emphasis on it."

"I'll do a follow-up on the lab reports."

Hank shook his head. "No. Leave that to someone else. I'm putting Lois Coren on it. She's been working traffic, but I think she's got potential. She has an inquisitive mind, and her detail work is good. This will be a good chance to see what she can do."

"I'd really like to work it."

"Your time's too valuable for something this low priority." He grinned at her raised eyebrow. "No offense meant, but I'm convinced it's somebody's idea of a sick joke. Lois can handle it. I'm reassigning you."

"Reassigning me to do what?" Her eyes took on a deeper blue in her confusion. "And what about my caseload?"

"Talk to Vivian Mortensen. I told her I want you part time. She'll farm out some of your cases to the guys working local crime."

Before she could ask questions, he pushed his chair away from the desk, stood up, and walked across to the window.

"Did you know I turned down your application for the job?"

She was startled by the abrupt question. "Mayor Perkins was kind enough to let me know I owed my job to him. When I asked if there were strings attached to the employment, he backed off."

Hank chuckled. "A hint at sexual harassment. That must have cooled his jets. Lawyers always think they're going to be sued."

He could just picture Perkins's expression in the face of her challenge. Sheila's stock rose a notch. He let the humor of the situation fade before he continued.

"Yesterday I talked to Barbara Davis, the mother of the first victim. She agreed to look at those pictures you gave me."

He returned to his desk and set several pictures on the edge close to Sheila. The photos were closeups of Janette Davis, taken at the time her body had been discovered and then later in the morgue. Sheila had marked black circles on each of the pictures. Hank touched a fingertip to each of the circles.

"Mrs. Davis checked each picture with a magnifying glass," he said. "She confirmed the fact that a piece of Janette's hair had been cut off."

"I knew it," Sheila said. "The killer cut a piece of hair from each of his victims."

She let out her breath in a whistled stream. Hank touched his temple in a quick two-finger salute.

"That was a great piece of police work, Lieutenant. I didn't spot it. Neither did anyone else."

"Women are more conscious of hair," she said. "I'd seen Lindy Pottinger two days before she was killed. When I looked at the autopsy pictures, I noticed that a piece of her hair had been cut. I started checking the other victims. It was easy enough to miss. The killer didn't cut off much."

"Well, at least you caught it. And it gives us a positive link between Janette Davis and the other three victims."

He scooped up the pictures and put them back into the folder before sitting down again.

"Can we keep this out of the paper?" Sheila asked.

"We're going to try. Once I realized we had a serial killer, I talked to Wynn Foster, the *Weekly Sentinel*'s owner. She agreed to keep certain things quiet on the promise that her paper would have an exclusive on the story when it broke."

Hank sighed, knowing there had been leaks before and there probably would be again. After a moment he continued.

"Wynn's been pretty good about keeping the stories low key. She knows the news coverage feeds the killer's ego. Like most psychos, I'm sure this guy loves publicity."

Hank could see the flash of light in Sheila's eyes at the mention of the murderer. He wondered how he would feel if he had a young child. Frightened. Dedicated. Probably obsessed with finding the killer. That could work in their favor. Nothing short of obsession would crack the case.

"I'm reassigning you to work part of the time on the murders."
He liked the way she took the news: quiet elation, with only a slight
smile touching her mouth. "Every Monday we have a team meeting
to discuss new developments. You can ask any questions you've got at
this point."

"Owen James is the head of the investigation. Does he know
about this?" Sheila asked.

"Actually it was Owen's idea."

"He suggested it? I didn't think he even knew I was a cop."

Hank's mouth widened in a grin. "Owen's got seniority, so he's
allowed to ignore you. I think he's been waiting to see if you'd turn
tail and run."

Sheila looked directly at him. "Last night I considered it."

"We all have at one time or another." Hank looked straight at
her, his eyes hard. "For the moment, you'll be working on your own,
free to follow up any tangent. You'll need to go back to the first
killing and read through everything again in chronological order.
Hopefully you'll pick up something we've missed."

"Just because I caught the hair cutting doesn't mean I'll discover
anything more."

"Agreed. But it's worth a shot. So what's it to be? Will you take
the reassignment?"

"I will." Her words sounded like a blood oath.

"Time's running out." Hank eyed the calendar on his desk. "The
period between each of the deaths is shortening. The excitement
from the last killing is fading. When it does, he'll strike again."

Sheila took a deep breath. "I wish I didn't believe it."

"Believe it," Hank said.

He opened the center drawer of his desk, pulled out an unmarked
folder, and set it down on the blotter. Carefully he turned back the
cover, revealing a letter enclosed in a protective plastic sleeve that had
arrived in the morning's mail. He turned the letter around so Sheila
could see it.

Black letters cut out of newsprint were pasted on a single sheet of
white paper. The sentence was short, stark in its brevity.

THE TEACHER IS SELECTING A NEW PUPIL.

Chapter Three

The letter was a mistake.

The instant he had opened his gloved fingers to drop it in the mouth of the mailbox, he'd realized that Harker would take it as a personal challenge. He hadn't meant it that way and in his anger hadn't even considered that interpretation.

He knelt at the edge of the garden and ripped the weed out, crushing it in his hand. The skin whitened across his knuckles, and he could feel the pressure as it surged up his arm to his shoulder. The muscles in his jaw contracted. Anger was a physical thing, a tight ball in the pit of his stomach.

God, it was hot. Close to ninety. It was one of those freak return-to-summer days that occurred early in the fall. The humidity was high, a remnant of the predawn shower. Sweat sheened his forehead and pooled in trickles around his neck, mixing with the oils in his skin, buttery as it coated his flesh.

Saturday. He had spent the whole day outside. Weeding under the hot sun helped him to focus. He needed the discipline of physical labor to harness his rage; otherwise, it might lead to reckless actions.

He'd been furious with Harker when he sent the letter.

He suspected it had been the Chief of Police's idea for the *Weekly Sentinel* to print fewer articles on the children. The stories they did run were devoid of details and pictures. How dare Harker dictate the rules? The game was his.

It was time to quit.

He'd been working since sunup, stopping only once to eat a sandwich and drink some milk, icy cold from the refrigerator. He'd eaten on the porch steps. After lunch, he roasted some sunflower seeds and returned outside to eat them. All the while he chewed, his eyes inspected the individual gardens. Scanning back and forth across the rows, he examined the flowers and made mental notes on the plants that needed care.

He wiped his forehead with the back of his wrist, the dirt from his hands gritty against his skin. Sitting back on his heels, he turned his head to look along the front row of the main garden. The edge was one hundred feet long, an enormous blaze of shimmering gold.

Helianthus. The sunflower.

Although some of the smaller varieties flowered earlier, this was his favorite time of year, when the Giganteus was full-grown and the effect was breathtaking. The golden heads were heavy, a foot across, drooping and nodding above thick ten-foot stalks. He never grew the red or bronze strains; his beauties had golden petals, striking against the dark yellow or black-seeded centers.

Narrowing his eyes, the sunflowers blurred into an undulating ribbon. El Dorado. The city of gold. His golden paradise.

The breeze picked up. The wind whispered his name. He could hear his mother's voice in the rustling stalks as the drying leaves scraped against each other.

His mother had always hated the garden. Her world had been inside the house, filled with dark overstuffed furniture, fussy knick-knacks, and thin Oriental carpets. His total absorption in the garden was a source of annoyance to her. Her concerns meant little to him.

She was an ineffectual woman. Perhaps she had passions and desires, but he had never seen any evidence of them. Whoever was the strongest controlled her, and she took on whatever personality was required in order to survive. She had no persona of her own. She was clay; like the dirt in his garden, she waited to be molded.

He liked the tactile sensations as he buried his fingers in the dirt. The warm, moist soil against his skin excited him, and he frequently stopped to knead it between his fingers. He sighed and cupped his mud-caked fingers in front of his face. The loamy smell rose up, and he drew the pungency deep into his lungs.

He rose to his feet. Dampness had spread up and down his legs from the muddy patches at his knees, leaving the material of his pants dark and limp. He was looking forward to a hot bath. He'd make a drink and take it upstairs with him.

Pausing on the top step of the porch, he turned and looked back over the garden. Soon his golden beauties would be lost for another year.

Inside, he pushed up his sleeves as he stood in front of the kitchen sink. He turned on the water, fussing until the temperature was right. Not too hot. Just short of burning his skin. He squeezed the bottle of detergent into his hand and worked the soap into a thick lather.

His hands slipped back and forth, making soft sucking sounds. He closed his eyes and breathed in the fresh soap smell. A vision of Donna was projected on the inside of his lids. He could feel himself expanding, rising at the thought of her. He rubbed his hands together faster, the lather slick against his skin.

The image of Donna was fading. He pressed his lids together and her face came into sharp contrast. She was laughing.

His eyes flew open, and his hands came up to cover his face. Suds and water splattered him. Soap stung his eyes, and he plunged his head under the running faucet, gasping as the hot water sluiced across his face.

He jerked upright. Water cascaded down onto his shirt. Blindly he reached out for the towel beside the sink. He rubbed it across his face and blew out a breath in relief when his vision cleared. He shook his head, sending out a shower of droplets. He turned the water off with a violent twist of the handle.

Anger possessed him. Memories of Donna filtered through his mind. He gripped the edge of the sink, fighting for control. His desire for her was building again. Working in the garden helped to keep his need contained, but eventually nature would overwhelm his structured life and the cycle would begin again.

He'd learned to pace himself, to take pleasure in the planning stage and the selection process, thus heightening the sensations of the actual experiment. Only once had he acted on the spur of the moment, and that encounter had been rushed, less satisfying than when he'd spent hours organizing the event down to the final detail.

He turned to face the calendar on the wall. He reached out, his finger touching the glossy picture of the rusty bronze sunflower. Autumn Beauty. Delicate outer petals with a dark-centered bloom. Not one of his favorites. His gaze dropped to the wide column of numbers. A single date was circled with a heavy black line. The day had been chosen.

September twenty-first. Two weeks away.

Frustration struggled with discipline at this stage of the game. Plans needed to be completed. Details worked out. It was different this time. He'd always formulated his strategy while he searched for possible trainees. He remembered the excitement when he looked into the eyes of one of the candidates and knew deep in his soul she was the chosen one.

This time he'd made his choice first. Surprisingly, this decision increased his level of anticipation. Knowing her identity layered his preparations with provocative nuances. He could tailor the entire lesson plan to her needs and wants. Everything would be perfect for her. He shivered at the thought of his choice.

Sheila. Sheila Brady was his final selection.

•

"You can wait in here," the receptionist said.

Sheila smiled as she stepped inside the small consultation room of the River Oaks Animal Hospital. Meg gingerly set the cat carrier on the examining table.

"Dr. Santo will be with you shortly," the young woman said, closing the door as she left the room.

"Who's Dr. Santo?" Meg asked suspiciously.

Sheila shrugged. "Must be one of the other doctors."

"We always get Dr. Upton. He's cool for an old guy."

"Dr. Santo might be cool, too."

"I doubt it." Meg was staring at the wall of diplomas. "Look at this. A. Warren Santo. His first name must be really dorky."

Sheila walked over. "University of Illinois. Sounds reputable to me. And this certificate says he's from Chicago."

"Chicago. I knew it." Meg lowered her voice. "He could be a gangster. You know, like Al Capone."

"Al Capone? Where do you get such ideas?"

"We're doing a unit in school on crime in America. There's tons of stuff about Chicago and the gangsters. Lots of those guys used fake names." Sheila rolled her eyes and Meg continued in a stage whisper. "Then what do you think the A stands for?"

"Abraham? Andrew? Aloysius?" Sheila suggested. "He might be

Greek and then it could be Andropopolis. Or he could have had a job with the circus and it would be Acrobat."

"If he's old and his hair is gone, it could be Archibald." Meg was enjoying the game. "Wait. I've got the perfect one. Since he's a doctor, it could be Anatomical."

Sheila laughed and Meg covered her mouth to stifle her giggles. The door hinges squeaked, and they jerked to attention as the solid panel opened to reveal the white-coated veterinarian.

"Good afternoon. I'm Dr. Warren Santo," he said, shaking hands as Sheila introduced herself and Meg. "And by the way, the A is for Anthony."

A flush of color rose to Sheila's cheeks. "Sorry, Dr. Santo. We were being silly."

"I think my favorite was Anatomical." His eyes twinkled behind his wire-rimmed glasses. "Now let's have a look at the patient."

"It's a mourning dove," Meg said. "We think it has a broken leg."

She unlatched the door of the cat carrier, and Dr. Santo reached inside and removed the bird.

While Meg explained how they'd found it, Sheila had an opportunity to observe the doctor. He spoke in a quiet, no-nonsense manner, showing Meg how to hold the bird while he cut away the makeshift splint.

Dr. Santo certainly was different from Dr. Upton, who was at least seventy. Dr. Santo had a thick head of dark curly hair without any touch of gray. Sneaking a peek at the date on the diploma, Sheila estimated that he was in his late thirties.

He was also tall, at least six feet two or three. His arms were long and jutted out from the too-short sleeves of the white lab coat. His hands were large with long knobby fingers, but exceedingly gentle as he examined the bird's leg.

"Your daughter makes an excellent assistant, Lieutenant Brady," he said without raising his head.

"Agreed," Sheila said. "Meg put on the original splint."

"I am impressed," he said nodding across the examining table at the girl. "You were right. The leg was broken. This new splint is less bulky, so he'll be able to move around more easily. What have you been feeding him?"

"I dug up some worms and gave him lettuce and bread but I couldn't tell if he ate anything."

"A little something for every taste." Dr. Santo clipped the last piece of tape close to the bird's leg. "A mourning dove is part of the pigeon family. He might have eaten some insects if you'd tried that, but mainly he's a seed eater."

"Plain old birdseed?"

"Sure. You'll need three dishes. One for water. One for seed. The last one is for grit. That's just another name for fine gravel or little stones. Birds need that to help them digest their food."

"There's gravel next door in the Farringtons' driveway," Sheila said. "I'm sure they can spare a handful."

"Way cool," Meg said, then turned back to the doctor. "Will he be all right?"

"I honestly don't know. It depends a lot on whether he'll be able to fly."

"And if he can't fly?" Sheila asked.

"A friend of mine runs an animal shelter out on Old Missionary Road. Margaret Watson takes in all kinds of lost and injured animals, but her specialty is birds. The place used to be a country church so she calls it A Wing and A Prayer."

"Great name," Sheila said.

"It's a fun place to visit. Rather like a mini-zoo. You ought to drop by sometime." He raised his hand, palm toward Sheila. "Be forewarned. Don't wear good shoes. The animals have the run of the downstairs, so things can be a little," he paused, cocking his head to the side, "a little slipshod."

Sheila chuckled, liking his sense of humor. "I'll remember."

Dr. Santo placed the bird back inside the carrier, latched the door, then beckoned Meg to the sink to wash her hands. When he finished washing his own, he straightened up, removed his glasses, and turned to face Sheila. His glance wasn't offensive, but it was definitely thorough.

"Why don't you call me on Wednesday to give me a report?" he said. "Of course you can call before that if you have any questions. We've got an answering service. Twenty-four hours. Call anytime."

His words were staccato, almost stuttered.

"We'll call if there's a problem," she said, handing the carrier to Meg. She held out her hand. "Thanks for your help."

His handshake was firm. She smiled as he ushered them out of the examining room. Dr. Santo's boyish awkwardness was appealing.

In the parking lot, Sheila unlocked the car doors and set the cat carrier on the back seat along with the packet of birdseed Dr. Santo had provided. She waited while Meg buckled her seat belt, then started the car and pulled out of the parking lot.

"Whew," Meg said. "It's gross in there. All mediciney. Can't you still smell it on your clothes?"

"I didn't notice any odor," she said.

"Too busy checking out the doc?"

"Really, Meg."

"He has possibilities. A bit on the thin side, but a couple of your veal Parmesan dinners would fix him up."

Sheila was used to Meg's constant attempts to get her a date. "I suppose I ought to dust off the old wedding dress so if he proposes the next time we're at the animal hospital I'll be ready."

"You can laugh, Mom, but just remember. You're not getting any younger and Dr. Santo seemed pretty nice."

"The doc's probably married with six children," Sheila said, although she'd noticed he wasn't wearing a ring. "Wait until Nick hears you're willing to knock him out of the running in favor of a fancy white lab coat."

"I'm still pretty partial to Nick."

Sheila snorted in disgust. "Nick Biagi bribed his way into your heart with a kitten. Even after I told him how much I loathed cats."

"I've seen you sneaking pieces of chicken to Elmo when you think I'm not looking. 'Fess up, Mom. You're bonkers over the cat."

"Well, I have to admit Elmo's quite exceptional."

"I knew it," Meg said, crossing her arms over her chest in smug triumph. "Nick must have known you wouldn't be angry. You like him, don't you?"

Sheila heard the tentative note in Meg's voice. "Yes, I like Nick. He's interesting and I enjoy being with him."

"He's got a great job on the *Weekly Sentinel* and has his own photography business. I asked him once how much he got paid, and he said he made very good money, whatever that means."

"Good Lord, child. I appreciate your looking out for my best interests but you really shouldn't ask questions like that."

Meg was quiet while Sheila drove the car into the garage. Her face was thoughtful as she unbuckled her seat belt.

"Are you thinking of marrying Nick, Mom?"

Sheila was startled by the question. "We've only been seeing each other for a couple of months, little Miss Matchmaker, and I really don't know how serious I am about him. Maybe when I figure that out we could continue this conversation."

"OK," Meg said. "Just in case you're wondering, I don't have any hangups about your getting married again."

"I sort of figured that out, since you've tried to marry me off to everyone from the mailman to Chief Harker."

"Oh, Mom, not Chief Harker!"

"I thought you liked the chief. Every time you see him you both seem to have an enjoyable time." Sheila didn't mention to Meg that she envied her ease in talking and joking with Harker.

"I do like him. But it's bad enough having a mother on the police force. Just imagine having the Chief of Police for a dad."

"Trust me. It'll never happen." Chuckling at the thought, Sheila reached over and hugged Meg, kissing her all over her face until she squealed. "All right, you wretched child, let's get the patient into his cage. If you go around back, I'll go in and open the patio doors."

Sheila unlocked the front door and reached down to scratch Elmo, who was waiting in his usual spot on the hall rug. Meg was right. She was a sucker for the cat. With Elmo at her heels, she went through to the family room, opened the draperies, and unlocked the glass doors. Sliding back the door, she made sure the screen was closed so the cat couldn't get out.

"Need any help?"

Meg had already placed the bird in the aquarium and was settling the top in place. "Could you get me some bowls?"

Back in the kitchen, Sheila took out three plastic margarine cups. She filled one with water and returned to the family room. With her foot, she nudged Elmo out of the way as Meg reached in to take the cups. She put the water in the cage and filled a second cup with some of the birdseed.

"Would you keep an eye on him while I get the gravel?"

"I don't think he's going anywhere," Sheila said.

"Mommmm."

"Elmo and I will watch him like the proverbial hawk."

Margarine cup in hand, Meg ran next door. The cat rubbed against Sheila's leg as she stared out into the yard.

The day was drawing to a close. Sheila shivered. Ever since Harker had shown her the message cut out of newsprint, she'd been on edge. It was bad enough knowing that the murderer was on the loose, but the phrasing of the letter made his search for a new victim much more immediate. She hated the thought that another child was in danger.

The sun sank lower, the light taking on a reddish-yellow cast. Shadows crept across the flagstones, a tongue of darkness stretching toward the improvised birdcage. The dove cooed softly. The mournful cry hung in the air, the final note desolate in the gathering darkness.

●

Harker looked up from his desk at the tentative knock on his door. Lois Coren stood in the partially opened doorway.

"Do you have a minute, Chief Harker?"

"Sure, Lois. Come on in."

Lois was in her middle to late forties, short, and slightly overweight, with hair that had a mind of its own. When she had applied for the job of receptionist, she'd told Hank that when her husband took early retirement at fifty, he'd cleaned out their savings account, bought a Ford Bronco and a fifteen-foot fishing boat, and left town with a twenty-eight-year-old divorcee named Amber.

Knowing that Lois had two children to raise, Hank had hired her, a decision he'd never regretted. Her motherly attitude and unflagging cheerfulness were a real plus for the department. She treated most of them like overgrown children with little sense and even less ambition. She turned out to be such a good worker that he had encouraged her to take night classes so she could join the police force herself.

Lois cleared her throat, bringing Hank's attention back to the present.

"I've been working the follow-up on the box that was delivered to Sheila Brady's house," she said, "and I've turned up something that I think you ought to hear about. A couple of fingerprints."

"The lab report said there were no prints?"

"I assumed that was a preliminary report. I went to Madison to pick up the evidence and the reports. It was an old box, but the tape across the bottom was new. I figured that if the guy had taped the box himself, he might have left a print on the shiny side and it would be transferred to the sticky side of the overlapping tape. So I asked the lab to check for a reverse print, and they found a couple."

"Nicely done, Lois. Did you run them through AFIS?"

"Yes. The system kicked out a match."

"Isn't that good news?"

"Yes and no. It's a solid match. The trouble is, it's a cop."

Hank bolted upright. "River Oaks?"

"No." She set a series of papers on the desk. "The prints belong to a Madison police officer. Sergeant Doug Maloney."

"Why do I know that name? Maloney. Maloney." Hank repeated the name to jog his memory but nothing came. "I can't catch it."

"A friend of mine works personnel in Madison. I called her to get the scuttlebutt. Maloney's new. According to Gretchen, the guys on the force think he's a great addition to the department. Terrific story-teller, fun to be around, gets along with everyone. He's got a reputation for being a tough but reliable cop. On the other hand, the female officers think he's a creep. He comes off like God's gift to women and has a red-hot temper and a power-trip attitude."

"Quite a variation in opinions. Any paper on him?"

Lois flipped through several pages of her notebook. "During his first month in Madison, a female officer filed a grievance on him. Sexual harassment. He's been clean ever since. Gretchen says the word on him among the women is to stick to lighted areas and never turn your back."

"The guy may be a first-class jerk, but I don't see any connection between him and Sheila."

"Neither did I, so I did a little more checking," Lois said. "It turns out Maloney has only been in Madison for five months. He used to work in Milwaukee."

"I see," Hank said. "Did she and this Maloney work in the same department?"

"Yes." Lois leaned across the desk. With one finger extended, she tapped the sheet of paper closest to him. "Doug Maloney was her partner."

Chapter Four

"Don't get broccoli, Mom," Meg said. "We've had it every night for the past two weeks."

Sheila moved away from the broccoli and picked up a head of cauliflower. Meg rolled her eyes.

"Well, *you* think of something," Sheila said in exasperation. "Tomorrow we're having chicken."

"Corn." Meg pushed the grocery cart over to the pile of fresh ears. "It's perfect with chicken."

"Don't forget Beth's coming over for dinner on Tuesday. I was figuring to grill hamburgers and get some fresh corn then."

"I could eat corn every night." The girl's brown eyes pleaded.

"Occasionally you need other vegetables. How about corn for Tuesday and squash for tomorrow?"

"Ewww. I hate squash."

"So do I," a voice announced from the opposite side of the aisle.

Sheila peered across the bin of corn at the man with the glasses.

"You're no help, Dr. Santo. You're supposed to tell her it's nutritious."

"Lots of things are nutritious, but you don't have to eat all of them. Besides, squash is just plain yucky," he said, earning a giggle from Meg. "How is our patient coming along?"

"He's great," Meg said. "He ate a lot last night, and he likes popcorn so I'm using it to train him. Which reminds me, we need more birdseed, Mom. I'll get it."

Santo looked after Meg. "She's a charming child, Lieutenant Brady."

"Yes. I'm very proud of her, and she's been wonderful with the bird."

"Tending to a wounded animal teaches a lot to a child."

"I'll confess to you that my first instinct was to tell her to let it take its chances outside." At Santo's raised eyebrow, Sheila felt a flush of color rise to her cheeks. "I didn't think it would survive, and I didn't want Meg to get her hopes up and then watch it die."

"Sometimes it's easier for children to learn about death when a pet dies."

Sheila watched as her daughter returned. "The children of River Oaks already know too much about death."

"You should come over and see Cooper, Dr. Santo," Meg said, dumping a box of microwave popcorn and a plastic bag of birdseed into the bottom of the grocery cart. "You could come for dinner. Couldn't he, Mom?"

Santo avoided looking at Sheila, smiling down at Meg instead. "Thanks for the offer, but I don't usually make house calls."

"Please ignore my outrageous child," Sheila said, giving Meg a narrow-eyed glare. "She gets bored having dinner with me and loves having company, Dr. Santo."

"It's actually Warren. And I like having company for dinner too," he said. "I could stop over to see the bird if you'd both consider joining me for pizza afterwards."

"That'd be great," Meg said. "How about Wednesday?"

"Really, Dr. Santo . . ."

"Warren," he interrupted Sheila. "And Wednesday would be fine."

Sheila glanced across at him, half expecting him to be wearing a resigned expression. Instead, his eyes glittered behind his glasses, and he appeared shyly satisfied.

"Warren," she said, "even though you were railroaded into this, Meg and I would be pleased to join you for pizza."

She was surprised at her reaction to the veterinarian. She'd only met him yesterday, but something about him intrigued her. Even though she and Nick Biagi weren't in a totally committed relationship, she felt a twinge of guilt as she said, "Would six-thirty be all right?"

"I'll be there."

The corners of Warren's mouth turned up in a smile, which she couldn't help returning. She gave a little wave as he pushed his cart toward the checkout counter, then turned to Meg.

"I can't believe you did that. You put him in a very difficult position, you know."

"Sorry, Mom. But he kept sneaking peeks at you, and then I looked in his basket and I decided he couldn't be married 'cause it was just loaded with those loser TV dinners. No wonder he's so skinny."

"Much as you enjoy matchmaking, remember I can handle my own social life."

At Meg's grin, Sheila dropped the subject.

•

Hank leaned against the window of the second-floor conference room, waiting for everyone to get more coffee and doughnuts before the meeting resumed.

A set of double doors led into the main bullpen, and another door connected to his office. Most of the wall space was taken up with file cabinets, a blackboard, and floor-to-ceiling panels of fabricboard. Crime scene photos, a summary chart of the four murders, lists of evidence, witness interviews, aerial shots of River Oaks, and other assorted papers were pinned up on display.

Owen James, the senior member of the investigation team, sat across the table from Sheila. At first impression, big, lumbering, and rumpled came to mind. Owen, in his mid-fifties, was frequently underestimated, but Hank knew that he had a quick intelligence and a keen analytical mind. Best of all, he shared Hank's love of trout fishing, and over the years they had become good friends.

Next to Owen was Daniel M. Lundquist. At forty, Dan had a tall, slender body and wore clothes with an easy elegance. The men generally referred to him as Dandy Dan because he looked and acted more like a Southern gentleman than a police officer. He tended to be a dash pedantic when he spoke, but he had infinite patience for the minutiae of an investigation.

Lawrence Pazzarini sat beside Sheila. To compensate for his five-foot-eight height, he used a bark-and-growl form of communication. Heavily lashed brown eyes, dark curly hair, and a luxuriant mustache gave him a dangerous look. He had been Sheila's trainer during her first month in River Oaks. It surprised Hank that she never turned a hair at Paz's rough language or his macho attitude.

Part of the secret to her success as a police officer was that Sheila listened without judging. Hank got the impression that anything you told her was kept in confidence so it was easy to confide in her. It was troubling, though, that there was bad blood between her and her ex-partner.

When she was in Milwaukee, Sheila and her partner had been investigated by the Internal Affairs Division after a shooting. IAD had found no merit to the case, and they were cleared. Before he discussed the current situation with Sheila, Hank wanted to talk to Doug Maloney to see if he could discover the reason her ex-partner had sent her the bloody doll.

Sheila shifted her position in the leather armchair. The chairs were so large that if she sat all the way back she couldn't reach the table. Hank made a note to add a few smaller chairs to the conference room.

That's how it starts, he thought. Just like being married. First it's chairs, and the next thing you know everything begins to change.

He rubbed the thumb on his left hand. He'd cut the tip off when he was learning to cook after his wife left. Pam said she'd spent ten years with a man who was wedded to a whole town. She contended his job always came first and she was tired of coming in second. He hadn't bothered to explain that she didn't rank even that high; he understood her point and didn't want to alienate her. If he wanted a continued relationship with his son, he knew enough to try and placate her.

He'd made the divorce easy. Pam and Jeff moved to Oconomowoc, close enough for him to visit frequently. Over the years they'd worked out a relationship that was better than they'd had when they were married. She got a job as an office manager in a small accounting firm and eventually married the boss. Hank had given the bride away.

He checked his watch and walked back to the table. "All right. Let's get going."

Owen was slouched down in his chair, blotting a coffee stain on the front of his shirt. He struggled upright in his chair and tapped a copy of the composite sheets of photographs that Hank had passed around the room before the break.

"Before we start, Sheila," Owen said, "I'd like to compliment you on a great piece of police work in spotting the missing hair on each of the victims."

A rush of color flooded Sheila's cheeks as the others agreed with

Owen. Hank was surprised at the sense of pride he felt at her accomplishment. Despite his misgivings over her hiring, she was turning out to be an excellent addition to the department.

Paz flipped back and forth through the clipped set of photographs in his hands. The ends of his thick black mustache practically bristled with indignation.

"Wouldn't you think one of us would have noticed that the girls' hair had been cut?" he said. "Looking at the pictures now, all I can see are the missing chunks."

"If none of the parents spotted it, I don't see why any of us would," Hank said.

"What would the guy do with the hair?" Paz asked.

"Kristina Berg, the psychiatrist at River Oaks Hospital, said it varies a lot," Owen said. "The killer might put it in a drawer, like kids used to put treasured objects in a cigarbox. Others like to hold the token, using the memories it generates to stimulate sexual gratification."

"God, that's sick," Dandy Dan said.

Ignoring the comment, Owen took a bite of a doughnut. A shower of white powder fell on his shirt, and in annoyance he brushed it off.

"The purpose of today's meeting," Owen said, "is to bring Sheila up to speed. This is your big chance, Sheila; ask anything you want. You'll have more questions later, but this way you'll get some quick answers."

Sheila's cheeks turned red as all eyes focused on her. She looked down at her notebook and placed the point of her pencil beside the first question. "How have you generated a suspect list?"

"We set up a database of names for each of the murders," Dan said. "Then profile markers were established. A name will kick out of the system if it appears in connection with two or more of the murders or if it triggers enough profile markers. The name then goes on a high-priority list to be looked at more closely."

"Who set up the program?" she asked.

"Jen Puplava," Owen said. "She's our computer whiz. She made a fortune working for Microsoft but gave it all up to join the police force. After each new death, we requestioned anyone whose name appeared on the priority list. No one on the list knew all four girls. Or at least, no one has admitted to it."

"The FBI suggested the markers to use from their profile of the killer," Hank said. "They've been updating it after each murder, but nothing major has changed. According to them, he's got the characteristics of an organized serial killer. Unlike a spree killer, he's had a chance to cool off after each murder so that each killing is a new event, not a continuation."

"I'm still not clear on how the man can be so invisible," Sheila said. "Wouldn't you think a psychopath would be easy to spot?"

"You mean like the mark of Cain?" Paz grinned at Sheila. "I shouldn't laugh. I remember feeling the same way when they arrested John Wayne Gacy in Chicago. I couldn't believe he could commit that many murders in such a congested residential area without being noticed. The police and the media interviewed his friends and neighbors, and everyone said the same thing: 'He was such a nice man.'"

"Think Dr. Jekyll and Mr. Hyde," Hank said. "It's the perfect example of the split between the two personalities in a psychopath. One minute a dashing gentleman, the next a violent monster."

"Ted Bundy may be a more apt comparison when you look at the profile," Owen said. "Socially and sexually competent. He had controlled moods and was charming enough so that his victims weren't alarmed. In our case there's no evidence of injury on the girls' bodies that would indicate a struggle. They apparently went with him willingly."

Sheila shrugged her shoulders. "Sorry. It's just that I have this old-fashioned notion that crime scars the soul and should be obvious enough to warn others of danger. Instead, he's invisible."

"With the first murder, he may have just been lucky that no one saw him," Owen said. "The ritualistic presentation of the last three bodies indicates that he probably planned everything in detail so that he wouldn't be seen."

"People who molest and kill children are looking for power," Hank said. "The ultimate power comes from in-your-face crimes. The killer picked up each girl, held her someplace for a day and a half, then smothered and raped her. Afterwards, he took the body to Worley Woods. The details of the presentation of the body were arranged for maximum dramatic effect."

"Tiffany, the second victim, established the pattern. She was lying on a blanket, naked, lipstick on her mouth, arms crossed over her chest, and two red roses in her right hand. The next two were identical except for the number of flowers."

"You'll notice the presence of two roses in the second murder.

The murderer wanted credit for Janette's killing," Paz said. "He wanted us to know what he'd done."

Sheila looked up from her list of questions. "I assume we covered local sex offenders."

Paz used his thumb and first finger to smooth his mustache. "I was lucky enough to draw the Sex Crimes detail. The list we put together was made up of known offenders not only in River Oaks but in the four surrounding towns. After each of the murders, Kodjo Norton and I contacted each one of them personally."

"You two must have made a formidable impression," Sheila said.

"That was the point. The original list had sixteen names," Paz continued. "One of the perverts died. Two are in jail. And three of them moved after one or more of our visits. Ten still are in the area, but we've pretty much ruled out the lot. One or two items, like alibis or illness, knocked them off the suspect list. They're all low-grade felons."

Sheila ran the point of her pencil down the margin of her notes. "Is the cast of the shoeprint found at the third murder scene here or in Madison?"

"Madison," Owen said. He picked up his coffee mug, wiping up the wet spot on the table with the underside of his tie. "We think it might be the killer's, but we have no way at present to prove it."

"The shoe was identified as a man's size ten, Upland Hiker with a ridged rubberized sole," Paz said. "It's a popular shoe. Sold everywhere."

"I didn't see any DNA reports," Sheila said. "Did I miss them?"

"There's damn little physical evidence," Owen said. "The first murder was spur of the moment and should have offered us the greatest source for evidence. Unfortunately, there was a heavy rain that night, which obliterated any viable samples for testing."

"The autopsy showed traces of talc from latex gloves and evidence of condom use. A guy might carry a condom, but why rubber gloves?"

"We've considered the fact that he might be a health care worker or someone who would have a legitimate reason to carry gloves in his car," Paz said. "The rain would explain the scarcity of evidence in the first murder, but for the last three the killer made a determined effort to destroy any evidence. Not only did he use a condom and rubber gloves, he washed the bodies and wrapped them in the brown blankets before transportation to Worley Woods."

"The blankets were new?" Sheila asked.

"The state lab said all three blankets were identical and newly purchased. The original creases were still visible. Treadway Ltd. makes the blankets, and they're carried in discount stores throughout the state. Bob Feldhake, the guy from Hairs and Fibers, found some wood splinters embedded in each of the blankets. He says the splinters on all three blankets match. They appear to be from old pine flooring."

"So all we need is to find someone with a pine floor and then we've got our killer," Paz said, frustration etched in his voice.

He reached for the coffee carafe and poured himself another cup. Using the knuckle of his index finger, he brushed across his mustache, smoothing it before he took a sip.

"Does anyone have anything else?" Hank asked, looking around the room.

"I got a call from Seanne Patrick," Dan said. "She works in the FBI office out of Madison. Great with details and has the dogged persistence of a pit bull."

"Cut to the chase," Owen said.

"Brown synthetic fibers were found in the mouth, trachea, and lungs of the last three girls. As you know, they can't positively identify them, but Seanne has been working with all kinds of materials to see if she could come up with a match. She says they're consistent with the fibers used in stuffed animals."

"So the jerk pressed a stuffed animal over the nose and mouth of each victim, cutting off her breathing." The muscles in Paz's jaw rippled, reflecting the anger of the others.

"Time is running out," Hank said.

He pulled a folder from the pile in front of him and flipped back the cover. He didn't have to look at the cut-out newsprint. He knew the message by heart: THE TEACHER IS SELECTING A NEW PUPIL. He tossed the letter onto the table, the protective plastic cover making a snapping sound on the surface.

"You've seen the lab reports," he said. "Common paper stock, no prints, and the words cut out of the newspaper. When they removed the newsprint words, they could see both sides, and they traced the words to the last issue of the *Weekly Sentinel*. The letter was mailed from Madison, but the guy's probably local because he used the River Oaks paper."

"We tapped someone for content?" Owen asked.

"The hospital shrink thinks the campaign to cut down on the local coverage of the murders probably provoked him into sending the letter. He may see himself as the hometown hero not being appreciated."

Hank took a sip of coffee, then continued.

"The FBI profile indicates he's got a high IQ and he believes he's smarter than the cops. With no motive and no timetable, the only way we'll find this guy is if he thinks he's invincible and gets careless."

"Like sending the letter," Paz said.

"Exactly. Dr. Berg says he's a ticking bomb. He's on the prowl, and when he finds the right target, he'll make his move. As I look at the calendar, the most likely date is September twenty-first."

"The Sunflower Festival," Owen said.

"They should cancel the festival," Paz said.

"I suggested that, but the mayor vetoed it. He said it would totally demoralize everyone." Hank sighed. "Frankly I'd rather risk a little demoralization. On the bright side, he authorized additional funds for a solid police presence. And of course he's calling out his private army, Parent Watch. They're going to wear special armbands and circulate throughout the festivities."

"How do we know the killer isn't a member of the citizens patrol?" Dan had always been verbal about his dislike for the group.

Hank shrugged. "How do we know it's not a teacher or a banker or even, God forbid, a cop?"

"Is the festival that big a deal?" Sheila asked.

Paz snorted at her ignorance.

"The Sunflower Festival is to River Oaks what Mardi Gras is to New Orleans," he said.

"River Oaks was founded by a group of farmers who came here from Italy after the Second World War," Hank explained. "They grew sunflowers, which proved to be a very successful business for them."

Owen picked up the story. "The Sunflower Festival celebrates our heritage with a weekend of activities. A carnival sets up in the high school parking lot on Friday and runs through Sunday. Saturday is an all-day affair. It starts off with a morning parade. There's a craft show, 4-H exhibits, and various contests down in Hodges Park. At ten o'-clock on Saturday night there's a fireworks display."

Hank glanced around the table, seeing the same thought on each face. The Sunflower Festival was less than two weeks away. During the carnival or the fireworks display would be the perfect time to kidnap a child.

Chapter Five

"Do you want me to take a look at your math homework?" Sheila asked as she handed the corrected English report across the kitchen table.

Meg made a face as she stood up and gathered the pages of the computer printout. "Thanks for the thought, Mom, but the last time you helped me I got three wrong."

"It's depressing not to be able to do fifth-grade math."

"Don't worry. Beth's mom is even worse. Besides, she's no help in English or geography. All she does is yell at Beth that her grades should be better."

"See how lucky you are. I may suck at math, but I'm definitely aces in liberal arts. Am I good or what?" She raised both fists with thumbs extended.

"You're terrific." Meg leaned down and kissed Sheila on top of the head. "I'm going back to my room to put the changes into the computer. The report's not due until Friday, so if I run it off tomorrow, will you have time to look at it one more time? Or, after reading it so many times, are you bored with the subject?"

"How could I possibly be bored with the exciting life of Herman Melville? I'll go over your paper as long as I don't have to read *Moby-Dick*. Once was enough. I get seasick crossing the Wisconsin River."

Juggling her papers and books, Meg spoke over her shoulder as she headed toward her room. "Thanks for the help."

Sheila stood up and stretched. She washed off the countertops and put soap in the dishwasher and turned it on. Finished, she went out to the family room.

Even at five-thirty it was still warm enough to keep the windows and doors open. The police station had been muggy, and she'd changed into shorts after she got home. The slight breeze coming through the screen in the patio doors was refreshing.

"How's it going, Cooper?" she said as she stared down at the mourning dove nestled on the cedar shavings in the aquarium.

Meg had named the bird Cooper for his soft cooing sounds. Not only had the dove survived, but it was improving. A brush of fur against Sheila's bare leg made her jump.

"Damn it, Elmo! I hate it when you do that." She turned away from the patio doors. "You can't eat Cooper, so you might as well watch the news with me."

Sheila went to the kitchen for a can of beer and curled up on the couch. She turned on the news to check the weather, delighted to learn that the warm spell was going to last for a while.

Toward the end of the program there was an update on the murders.

The anchorman began rehashing the fourth murder. File footage showed the crowd gathered in the parking lot on the morning Lindy's body was found.

Sheila hated the condensed version of the crimes. Half the time, they misrepresented the facts, then insinuated the police were at fault for not finding the killer. She pressed the mute button as the camera panned across the group of gawkers.

Suddenly she sat upright, eyes intent on a man at the edge of the crowd.

The absence of sound filtered out other distractions, and the man stood out as if the lens were focused on him alone. He had not noticed the camera at first, but when he did, his head twisted in surprise and he turned his back.

The picture was on the screen for only a few seconds, but in that flash of time, Sheila noted the expression on the man's face. After eight years of police work, she had seen that expression often enough to recognize it.

Guilt. But guilty of what?

The news coverage continued, but Sheila's mind still held the picture of the man. She knew that one of the peculiarities of a serial killer was that he might revisit the scene of a crime or even go to the funeral of a victim. She was aware of the odds against her having spotted the murderer, but she had a sense of familiarity with the unknown man and a curiosity to find out his identity.

Reaching for the phone, she called the television station in Madison and asked them to send her a dubbed tape of the news footage. She disconnected and dialed Nick Biagi's number. It rang four times until the answering machine picked up. She waited until the message finished and was just opening her mouth to speak when Nick picked up the phone.

"It's Nick. Live from the darkroom," he said.

"Hi. It's Sheila. Want me to call back?"

"No. I've been thinking about you today. Let me just wash my hands."

In the background she could hear water running, and she snuggled into the corner of the couch to wait. She hadn't seen him over the weekend. Hearing the sound of his voice, she realized she'd missed talking to him.

She'd met Nick three months ago. He was taking pictures for the *Weekly Sentinel* at the scene of an accident. While she took notes, he followed her around, squatting beside her, face covered by the camera, alternately snapping pictures and asking her questions.

He called the next day to ask her for a date. She turned him down out of habit; she didn't date very often. For the next two weeks, he called every day she was at work—short, friendly conversations. He didn't ask her out, so she relaxed and began to look forward to the calls. She didn't know if she wanted to get involved with Nick, but she loved his voice. It was deep with rich mellow tones that sent shivers up her spine. That reaction finally convinced her to accept his next invitation.

Nick's voice boomed in her ear. "Sorry," he said. "I was just finishing the pictures from the Kitchie wedding over the weekend."

"How was it?"

"I felt really old. Joan and Neil are just the cutest couple you ever saw. From my standpoint, great subjects. Every picture will be a winner. But God, they're young. They have boundless energy."

"I've seen you on a shoot. You can out-bound them."

"Trust me. These two made my knees creak." He groaned for effect. "So what's up? You want to jump my bones?"

Sheila caught her breath at the stab of pleasure that tightened her abdomen. She hated to think that their relationship was based solely on sexual gratification.

"My whisker burn is just about healed, thank you very much. I've got to keep my eyes peeled for a clean-shaven man. Your beard is killing me." She ignored his chuckle. "I actually called on business. I want to look at some pictures in your files."

"Looking for something specific?"

"I saw some footage on TV about the murders and thought I recognized someone. I know you shot a lot of pictures at the crime scenes for the newspaper. What I'm looking for is basically crowd photos. You know, the people who show up and hang around any kind of disaster. Pictures from the funeral homes, too, if you took any there."

"A suspect?"

"No. It's just one of those things where you can't place the face but you have a feeling you know the person."

"Sure." Skepticism was in his voice. "I'm the enemy. The big bad media. You know, Brady, I can keep a secret."

"Don't go defensive on me, Nick. It's nothing more than I've told you. I'm curious about something. If it pans out, I might even tell you."

"Might?"

Sheila grinned at the tone of his voice. They'd had this argument before. Since their first date, she'd fought to keep her personal and professional lives separate. It was difficult in a small town, where she ran into him occasionally when she was working a case and he was taking pictures for the local paper.

"Give it a rest, Nick, and tell me what your schedule's like."

"How about tomorrow?"

"Meg invited her friend Beth for an early dinner, and then I'm taking them to the library for some kind of homework project. I could come to your studio after I drop the girls at the library. Would that work for you?"

"That's good," he said.

"Then I'll see you there some time around seven."

Sheila was still smiling as she hung up the phone. When talking to Nick, she found it easy to sink into the warmth of his voice and be reminded of the physical pleasure of being with him. However, when she got busy with her job or doing things with Meg, she didn't feel the same need for further commitment that he did.

Not that he'd asked her to marry him. He always spoke of taking their relationship to the next level, but he'd never spelled out what that meant. For all she knew, he might mean they should move in together.

And that was not even a possibility.

It was tough enough raising Meg alone. Sheila didn't think living with a man, even someone she loved, would be a good example.

She turned off the TV and debated sitting outside on the patio. It was a beautiful evening, and she knew that as fall progressed there wouldn't be many nights like this. She stood up and looked at the pile of folders waiting for her on the desk.

Duty sucked.

Giving one last glance outside, she pulled out the desk chair and sat down. She flipped open the top folder, locating the place where she'd left off.

She had just finished the autopsy report on Tiffany Chastain, the second victim, when something set off an alarm in her head. She closed her eyes trying to remember what she had read. No blood at the crime scene. Tiffany had been smothered somewhere else and brought to the woods. No clothes were found. No shoes.

"Damn! The shoes!"

Sheila hadn't called the state crime lab to arrange to pick up the cast of the shoeprint found at the scene of the third murder. Before she could forget again, she'd leave a message they'd get first thing in the morning. To her surprise, Joanne Burgess, one of her favorite clerk technicians, was still there even though the lab was closed. Sheila explained what she wanted, and Joanne went to check the inventory.

"Sorry this took so long," the older woman said, panting into the phone.

"I really appreciate this."

"Don't sweat the small stuff, honey. It's a slow night. I've been working on my resume. I heard of a great job opening. Coroner's assistant. How do these job specs sound? 'Recording the cutting up of cadavers, bottling organ and tissue samples, and labeling specimens of bodily fluids.'"

"It sounds perfectly disgusting," Sheila said. "Reconsider and join the steno pool."

"I can't type. Besides, I've got a lock on this job. Nobody else wants it."

"That's a surprise?"

"Hell, yes! The pay's outstanding! Wait, let me see if I have this form filled out right. Hold a sec."

All Sheila could hear was the sound of asthmatic breathing and the rustling of papers. Then Joanne was back.

"OK. I signed you up for the cast of the shoeprint. I'll bag it and it'll be at the front desk for you tomorrow."

●

Six-thirty. It was almost the end of his three-hour patrol shift, and Ray Florio was tired. It was beginning to get dark, and his eyes weren't the best in the dark.

When the Parent Watch honchos had asked him about his vision, he'd lied and said it was perfect. He was still p.o.'d that they hadn't wanted him to be a part of the patrol. Since retirement he'd been at loose ends. People treated you different when you weren't bringing home a paycheck. He was plenty fit for sixty-eight.

"Take a right on Ginkgo," he said as he squinted at the street signs in the early evening light. "We can drive down to the playground and then cut back through the alleys."

"Ginkgo?" Jim Kandinsky, Ray's patrol partner, slowed the Blazer and turned the corner. "What the hell kind of name is that?"

"It's a tree. All the streets in our patrol section have something to do with trees."

Ray'd been put off by Jim when he had first joined Parent Watch and they'd become partners. After several days on patrol, Ray realized that despite almost twenty-five years difference in their ages, they had a lot in common.

"How are your grandkids doing?" Jim asked.

"Good. Real good," Ray said. The mere mention of the kids made him grin, erasing the lines of worry on his forehead. "Jason is a real pistol. He's the image of his dad. Did real well in baseball this year. He's ten now and Lizzie is six."

"Tough about their mom," Jim said, slowing as they came to the end of the alley. "Nobody should die so young. The big C?"

"Yeah. Six months and she was gone. Nancy was a good mother. Raised those kids right, I can tell you. Bessie and I took care of them this summer. Now that school's started, Ray Jr. drops them in the morning and I pick them up afterwards. Don't like them walking."

Kids shouldn't have to be afraid to walk home from school. The thought of some maniac loose in River Oaks made Ray crazy.

They drove to the end of the street, then slowly cruised around the perimeter of the park. They always paid special attention to the open areas after school let out, when the swings and slides were crowded with kids.

Ray took a deep breath of the fresh air. It smelled of fall. There wouldn't be many more days this warm, he thought. Listening to the shouts of the children, he nodded his head. This was the way it should be. Kids playing outside, their laughter riding the wind.

"I bring the grandkids here whenever I can," he said. "Jean and Paul did the kids a good turn."

"Who?"

"The Wolframs. The park's named for them."

Jim shook his head, not recognizing the name.

"Old-time residents of River Oaks. They live over on Albion. You know. The big brick house across from the country club."

"Oh, yeah."

"Their son Dave was the building contractor for the homes here in the Estates. All the playground equipment was donated by the Wolframs." He sighed. "Wish they'd put in a few less swings and built a john instead. We always end up going home because one of the grandkids has to go to the bathroom."

"The kids or you?" Jim asked. "Admit it, Ray. You're the one with the short tank."

Ray snorted. "That's what happens when you get old."

Jim eased the car away from the curb and headed back to the residential streets.

"How's your little girl doing?" Ray asked.

"Honest to God, that kid will be the death of me. Sally'll have the cast on her arm for another three weeks. Get this. She was trying to walk around the deck on top of the railing when she slipped. The bone just snapped. Doesn't that beat all?" Suddenly Jim stiffened, his hands clenched on the top of the wheel. "Hey, what was that?"

Ray could feel a kick of adrenaline as his eyes scanned the area between the houses where Jim was pointing. For a moment he couldn't see anything, then a rabbit dashed out from under some bushes and bounded toward the back yard.

"A rabbit. Just a stupid rabbit," Jim muttered.

Ray relaxed against the back of the seat, covering his sigh of relief with a cough. He wondered if he'd have a heart attack if they came across any real danger. The car moved forward, and the rapid beating of his heart slowed.

Picking up the conversation where they'd left off, Jim said, "I'm too old to raise another kid. There's thirteen years between Sally and my next oldest."

"You musta started early."

"Married at twenty-one. Hell, my boys are twenty-two, nineteen, and eighteen." Pride was evident in his voice. "Sally was sort of a surprise."

"A little girl makes you feel young again," Ray said.

"I never been sorry we had Sally. The boys say she's spoiled rotten, but with three older brothers I think she's learned to stand up for herself. There's a kid that won't kiss ass."

Jim rolled through a stop sign and turned right, spinning the wheel at the mouth of the alley that cut behind the houses. He slowed the car on the gravel surface.

Ray hated the alleys. Compared with the openness of the street side, the alleys were filled with shadows. Plenty of places where weirdos could hide. He paid close attention to the fenced yards, looking for anything unusual or out of place.

The telephone rang. Ray jumped at the sound. He hated getting calls when they were on patrol. Usually it was just administrative crap, but when it rang he always expected it to be some kind of emergency.

Ripping open the Velcro cover of the bag phone, he pulled out the receiver. With stiff fingers, he searched for the button to receive the call.

"Hello, Central," he said. "Car four here."

"Acknowledged, car four. What is your position?"

Ray jerked his head sideways toward his partner.

"Just coming up on Sequoia and Willow," Jim said.

Ray repeated it, and Central barked a reply in his ear.

"We've been listening to the police scanner. There's trouble in your patrol sector. The police just got a call about a possible intruder."

Chapter Six

"Repeat, car four. Possible intruder. A woman called the police about a stranger entering the back yard at 83 Whitewood Way. Did you catch that number?"

"Yes, Central. 83 Whitewood."

"It's just six or seven blocks ahead," Jim said. He accelerated to the corner and swung the wheel, making the turn with a squeal of tires.

"We're on our way, Central," Ray said.

"You know the rules." The voice on the phone was dispassionate. "No bravado and don't get in the cops' way."

"Got it."

Ray disconnected. He gnawed his lip as he watched the houses slip by. Just remember your training, he thought, trying to concentrate on his breathing. Don't do anything stupid. Don't let anyone get hurt.

"It's the next street," Jim said, braking for the turn. "We'll go down Whitewood until we find the house, then we'll swing around through the alley."

"It's that brown split-level with the green shutters." Ray's voice was just above a whisper.

Ray narrowed his eyes to sharpen his vision, grateful that the setting sun was at their back. He caught a flash of motion between the brown house and the brick ranch on the other side.

"That one was no rabbit," Jim said. "Someone's definitely in the back yard."

He accelerated to the end of the block, turned the corner, and started back through the alley. An old blue Chevy Nova was parked halfway down. The rear hatchback was open, but no one was near the car. Jim eased forward until he was almost behind it.

"Get the license number."

Ray grabbed the pad and pen on the console between the seats. He stared through the windshield, jotting down the numbers on the license plate. Unbuckling his seat belt, he reached for the door handle and quickly stepped outside the car. He stood behind the open door as they'd been shown in their training classes.

"What do we do now?" he asked. "Wait for the police?"

"Dunno." Jim stepped up on the frame of the car, raising himself so that he could see over the fence into the back yard. He stiffened to attention. "Hey! Is that you, Bobby Jay? What the hell you doing in this neck of the woods?"

Ray heard a barked laugh on the other side of the fence. He sagged against the side of the car, the muscles in his legs jumping with the release of tension.

"Bobby Jay and I used to work for old man Kruesi when we were in high school," Jim said.

He grinned as a short, stocky man in dirty overalls and a white short-sleeved T-shirt pushed open the wooden gate. He grinned and extended a beefy hand.

"Howdy, Jim. Good to see you."

"Hope you're not up to anything, Bobby Jay, 'cause the cops just got a call about an intruder."

"No way!" In the distance, they could hear the wail of a siren. "You guys with the patrol?"

"You bet." Jim flicked a hand toward the yellow shield on the side of the car. "We stopped by to see what you was doing here."

"I'm raking leaves out of the gutters."

"I thought you worked for your dad doing carpet installations."

A frown of annoyance crossed Bobby Jay's face. "Not that it's any of your business, but I work as a handyman on the side."

Jim raised both hands, palm outwards. "Not prying, Bobby Jay. We're just doing our duty. You know how it is in town."

The other man nodded his head, his expression clearing. "You're right. I got a little girl myself."

Lights flashing and siren at full pitch, a squad car swung into the alley. The Parent Watch volunteers had been trained to back off once the police arrived. As the car approached, Ray gave the thumbs-up signal and got back into the Blazer.

"See you later, Bobby," Jim said.

With a wave of his hand, he eased the car down the alley and headed back to the street. Ray could feel his body tremble in the aftermath of excitement. He pressed his shaking fingers on the vinyl armrest against the door.

"Thank God it was a false alarm," Jim said. "I got to admit I was glad to see Bobby Jay's face instead of some stranger."

"Damn right. I never gave a lot of thought to what would happen if we ran into any trouble."

"Me neither. Up until now I figured we were offering some protection, but you know what I just realized, Ray? We'd be pretty useless in any kind of fight. At least the cops are armed."

Ray agreed. He'd felt naked back in the alley. Up until now he'd felt important riding around as part of Parent Watch, but the incident had shaken his faith in the patrol. What if they'd stumbled upon the killer instead of a friend of Jim's?

Thank God he and Bessie had raised Ray Jr. in less frightening times, although even then he had always kept a revolver handy in case of trouble.

No matter what Dick Perkins or Chief Harker said, he was considering carrying a gun on future patrols.

•

The dog's cold nose pressing against Hank's hot skin brought him out of the nightmare. He swung his legs over the side of the bed, and reached out to touch the black Lab's head. His mouth was dry and felt cottony, so he could only rasp out a few words.

"Thanks, Abby," he whispered, scratching the sensitive spot beneath the dog's ears. "It's OK, girl. It's OK."

He sat on the side of his bed, his body bathed in sweat and his heart beating with the speed of a woodpecker tapping on a tree. He didn't have to look at the clock to know it was close to four in the morning. He'd spent enough time in the woods to know another day was dawning; he could tell by the subtle change in the darkness of the night.

He hadn't had The Dream for a long time. He remembered the shrink in the VA hospital telling him to try to remember it, scene by scene, and then it would begin to lose its power. Refusing to admit that his mind couldn't control his thoughts even in sleep, Hank made a conscious effort to block any memory of it when he woke up. Eventually the nightmare came with less frequency, until it only occurred periodically when he was stressed.

With a final reassuring pat on the top of the dog's head, he padded off to the bathroom, turning on the water and letting it run until it was icy cold. He leaned over and splashed water on his face. The last vestiges of the night's terror disappeared in the sudden chill.

Cold water ran down his bare chest, sending a shiver through his body. He reached for a towel and wiped his chest, then buried his face in the soft terry cloth. He avoided the mirror. He couldn't confront the haggard face and haunted eyes. He'd seen them too often before.

His bare feet made little sound on the wooden floors as he crossed the bedroom and headed for the stairs. Abby watched him; then, with a disapproving snuffle, she lay down on the rag rug beside the bed. Downstairs he turned to the right, cutting through the living room to his office in the back of the house. He needed little light to navigate the familiar route.

He'd been told his grandmother had used the room for sewing because of the semicircle of windows that let in so much sunshine. His mother had turned the room into a garden room, and Hank never entered without smelling an imaginary bouquet of flowers.

Tonight he caught a trace of ammonia, a scent he always associated with the VA hospital where he'd recovered after the war. The air was always thick with the smell of antiseptic cleaners.

God, he'd been a wild kid when he joined the Marines! He'd left River Oaks after his eighteenth birthday party. His father had been tight-lipped with anger at such folly. It was his mother's tears, though, that had shaken Hank. He'd never seen her cry before, and for a moment he almost reconsidered his decision.

Once through basic, he'd gravitated toward the military police. Interested in law and order, he knew he'd found his niche. However, that had all changed on November 27, 1972.

With a shaking hand, Hank removed the stopper in the carved crystal decanter on the wet bar. The neck of the decanter chattered against the edge of the snifter as he poured several ounces of brandy. Swirling the liquor in the glass, he raised it to his nose. The first inhalation filled his head, and the tight muscles of his body relaxed.

He sat down in the desk chair. His body, naked except for boxer shorts, felt sticky against the cool leather. The high back supported his head, and he took a sip of the brandy, savoring the flavor as it blossomed on his tongue. After a second sip, he reached for a cigar, lit it, and stared across the back yard toward the still-darkened woods.

Memories crowded in, and he was blind to the serenity beyond the windows. He was back in Vietnam.

His second Christmas was coming up. He and his best friend, Josh Hannigan, a big Irish elf from Chicago, had finagled a week of R&R in Honolulu. With rumors of a cease-fire, excitement and antic- ipation combined to send the usual level of carousing into overdrive.

When Josh and Hank hit the Maui Sunset Bar, Air Force Sergeant Edward Boros was on his fifth zombie, a lethal concoction of rums. Eddie gestured loudly as he argued with one of the bar girls. Hank and Josh moved to a table at the back of the bar, where they drank beer and talked about their plans for after the war. Josh had just be- gun to get maudlin about going back to Chicago to propose to his high school sweetheart when they heard the scream.

Eddie Boros had his hands around the throat of the bar girl he'd been arguing with earlier. Two of his buddies were trying to pry him off the struggling girl. Fueled by alcohol and anger, Eddie tossed the men aside, grabbed the girl around the waist, and carried her down the hall and into one of the private dining rooms. He slammed the door.

The majority of patrons turned back to their drinks as if nothing had happened. Hank and Josh exchanged glances.

"Was he armed?" Josh asked.

"I don't know. He was in fatigues and he could have had some- thing in his pockets." Hank strained to hear any sounds of a struggle. "I think we better call the MPs."

"What are we? Chopped liver?"

"We're off duty. We're unarmed. And we're drunk."

Josh shook his head. "We're the Corps. We don't take crap from flyboys."

Hank placed his hand on his friend's arm. "We need to call for backup before we do anything stupid."

"Christ on a crutch! Don't be such a wuss!" With a crash, Josh shoved his chair back, pushed himself upright and leaned over with his fists on the table, his face only inches from Hank. His tone was taunting. "Even if you can't get it up, I'm going in."

It was the insult that had been Hank's undoing. After a night of drinking, what little sense he had left disappeared in a flash of rage. He jumped to his feet, facing Josh.

"Once we wipe the floor with this jerk, I'll teach you to show a little respect for your elders."

"You're only two months older than me, you blowhard."

Josh grinned, and his eyes were alight with the anticipation of battle. Hank slapped him on the back and they headed for the closed door. Several of the bar patrons noticed their movements and followed them down the hall. Hank turned and grabbed the front of the Hawaiian shirt of the man leading the pack.

"Go call the MPs," he said, shoving him back toward the bar.

Josh reached the closed door before Hank. "Right or left?" he asked.

"Right is right and wrong is no man's right." Hank slurred the words only slightly. "I'll take the right."

"And God be with you, me boy." The Irish lilt in Josh's voice was strongest when he drank. He grinned and raised a foot to kick down the door.

"On three," Hank whispered. "One. Two. Three."

Their booted feet hit the wood at the same time. The door crashed inward, and the momentum of their rush carried them into the room. They stumbled to a halt at the scene lit by the harsh overhead lights.

Eddie was standing in the center of the room, holding a grenade in his left hand and the pin in his right. Directly in front of Hank, the captive bar girl was frozen in the act of stripping, her naked body gleaming like alabaster. Her face was wet with tears as she stared dumbly at the two men who'd broken into the room.

Beside him, Hank could hear Josh begin another count. He cleared his mind of questions and waited.

"One. Two."

Eddie turned to face them as if finally aware of the danger.

"Three!"

Josh and Hank moved as a single unit. Hank hit the girl, knocking her to the floor. Doubling over, he pulled her into the circle of his body, shielding as much of her body as he could. Winded by the fall, she raised her head and gasped for breath just as the grenade exploded.

Deaf from the impact of the explosion, Hank never heard the

smack of metal against his back and legs. He felt no pain, only curiosity about what had happened. He was grateful that he'd managed to protect the girl. He eased her body away, recoiling as she flopped forward onto her stomach. Pushing himself up on his elbows, he stared at the splintered chair leg that was buried in the side of the girl's head.

In slow motion, he turned his head toward Josh, groaning at the sight of the bloody pulp that had once been his friend.

Twenty-four years later, nausea rose in Hank's throat, and he took a quick swallow of brandy to force it down. Not a day since that time had Josh's face been out of his mind. It had followed him through his recovery and even after he'd left the Marine Corps.

He'd been told that Josh reached for the hand holding the grenade, pulling it between himself and Eddie Boros as they crashed to the floor. Eddie released the grenade, and the blast tore their bodies apart. It was the explosion that had shot the wood splinter into the girl's head and injured Hank badly enough to have him medevaced to the states, ending his career in the Marines.

"If only we'd waited for help. Josh would be alive. The bar girl would be alive." Hank spoke his thoughts aloud. He raised the glass to his mouth, swallowing until the nightmare disappeared. "If only we'd waited."

•

"God! You look disgustingly fit." Chief of Police Norm Hallwestle reached across the desk, clasping Hank's hand in a bone-crushing grip. "About time you came up to Madison to see your old buddy."

"It's like a high school reunion," Hank snorted as he dropped into a chair. "I just ran into Hugh Wilson out front. Remember that time in freshman year when we took on Wilson and the Torrino brothers?"

"Remember? Christ Almighty, I never got a worse beating in my life. Two black eyes and a broken rib. Not to mention the whipping I got from my dad for fighting."

Hank chuckled. "My father made me copy out the whole Book of Psalms. My hand was so swollen from socking Louie Torrino in the mouth that to this day I hear a Bible verse and my hand aches."

Norm threw himself against the back of his swivel chair, rubbing his sausagelike fingers across his bald head. "That was one monumental fight. I see that prick Wilson with fair regularity. He's a hot-shot trial lawyer all cozy with the boys here in the capital. Treats me like a farm hand shoveling dung. Ran into him at a charity fundraiser last week. He introduced me to his wife as Hallwestle, but I knew he wanted to use the old nickname, Hallow Whistle."

"Next time you see him, ask how his trip to L.A. was." At Norm's raised eyebrow, Hank explained. "Wilson got picked up along with two prostitutes in a sting operation at a motel just off the strip. He gave his mother's maiden name and her address in River Oaks, so I got a call."

Norm's cheeks plumped up in a grin of pure pleasure. He was silent for a moment as if savoring the tidbit. "For that I owe you big time, Hank. But hey, what brings you here? You were pretty cryptic over the phone about why you wanted to interview one of my boys."

"It's no big deal. When Doug Maloney was in Milwaukee he was partnered with someone who's now in my department. They were investigated by IAD. She's new to our force, but she's up for a promotion, and I want to hear Maloney's take on the incident."

Nodding his head, Norm accepted the statement without question. In no time at all Hank was sipping coffee in a small interview room, listening to the brisk footsteps coming down the hall. He stood up as a uniformed officer strode into the room.

"Chief Harker? Doug Maloney. The boss said you wanted to see me," he said. He thrust out his hand, exerting slightly more pressure than necessary before releasing.

"Have a seat," Hank said, amused by the power play. He walked around the table to close the door, then returned to his chair. "This won't take long. I need to ask you some questions about Sheila Brady."

Hank was staring directly at Maloney and saw the slight shift in the man's gaze. It was the merest blink, but it convinced Hank that Maloney was the one who had sent the bloody doll to Sheila.

Despite the Irish name, Maloney had a Nordic look, complete with a full head of straight blond hair and bright blue eyes. He was six foot three or four, with wide shoulders and long legs so that he appeared even taller. His uniform looked painted on—a combination of good tailoring and a perfectly proportioned body. Hank suspected he owed his build to genetics rather than either diet or exercise.

"I assume you know Lieutenant Brady's working in River Oaks," Hank said.

"Yeah." Doug nodded his head several times. "She left Milwaukee before I moved out here to Madison. She was pretty excited to get out of the city. She liked the idea that her kid would be growing up in the country."

Maloney made it sound as if cows roamed free on the streets of River Oaks. Hank wondered how close the two partners had been. He'd guess it wasn't as intimate as Maloney's tone suggested.

"Sheila's up for a promotion, and I had some questions for you."

The tightening of the other man's mouth answered one of Hank's questions. He wondered if Maloney was angry about the promotion or about the questions.

"If there's anything I can tell you about Sheila, I'd be happy to."

Maloney stared across the table, his eyes wide and his expression open. All his sentence needs is an "aw shucks" at the end, Hank thought.

"I really appreciate that, Doug. All this is off the record, you understand." Hank waited for any objections but Maloney offered none.

"Sheila was a great partner. We worked real well together. Most of the guys called her the ice queen. She looks composed, almost shy, but she can be pretty aggressive. And in any kind of confrontation she doesn't back down."

Interesting way to put things. Hank made a few notes on the yellow-lined paper, then looked across at Maloney, whose chair was tilted back on two legs. He was a picture of ease except for the toe of his right shoe, which twitched back and forth in a nervous gesture.

"I read over the transcripts of the IAD investigation. Everything was in order, but I wanted to hear about the incident in a more informal setting. I understand you were injured. Are you fully recovered?"

"Yes. Passed all the medical red tape just before I took the job here in Madison."

"Bullet went through your leg but didn't tear it up bad enough to force disability?"

"Damn straight. Bastard nearly castrated me." The jiggling of his foot increased.

"Do you think the perp got what he deserved when Lieutenant Brady shot him?"

"Absolutely." His jaw tightened, and spots of color rose to his cheeks. His anger was still raw. "It should never have happened, though."

Hank tipped his head, eyebrows drawn down over his eyes. The comment was a mumbled throwaway, his to pick up if he chose.

"According to the report, everything was done according to procedures. Was there something that happened that didn't make it into the transcript that might be important for me to know? Something that you hesitate to mention because of loyalty to your partner?"

Maloney shifted his eyes to the wall beyond Hank's right shoulder. He pursed his lips as if weighing some decision.

"No. Oh sure, there are things you question after something like that. You know how something like that is. It nags at you and you wonder about it."

"I know what you're saying, Doug. But even if it's only an uncertainty, I'd like to hear about it." He waited for a moment, then offered further inducement. "Lieutenant Brady is being considered as one of the team leaders in our investigation of the murders in River Oaks."

Maloney rubbed the inside of his right thigh, eyebrows pulled together in a tight V. The front legs of his chair came down hard, and he leaned across the table, the muscles in his cheeks rippling with suppressed anger.

"Sheila Brady hasn't got the qualities it takes to be in command. It was her fault that everything went wrong that night. I wouldn't have been shot and the drug dealer wouldn't be dead if Sheila hadn't frozen under pressure."

Chapter Seven

"The only reason I got shot and the perp got whacked was because when the situation escalated, Sheila Brady froze."

Hank was surprised at the venom in Maloney's voice. It was obvious he blamed Sheila for his injuries. The question was whether his accusations were justified. Hank leaned forward, elbows on the desk.

"I'd like to hear how the event came down, Doug." He kept his tone nonconfrontational, his expression concerned. "It happened a year, year and a half ago?"

"Yeah. May the tenth. It was a Saturday night."

Maloney blew out his breath in an audible puff of air. His shoulders dropped, and some of the anger seeped out of his body. He leaned back in his chair, his eyes unfocused as he brought his mind back to the event. Absently he rubbed the inside of his thigh.

"We got a street tip on a major drug buy. Sheila and I rolled onto the scene, but our backup didn't show. I heard later that they got jammed behind some accident a couple blocks away." Maloney shook his head in disgust. "The timing was so screwed up that the instant we turned on our lights, the dealer split. We chased him for almost twenty blocks and finally cornered him near an empty warehouse. Then the guy abandoned his car and took off into the building."

"You called for reinforcements?" Hank asked.

"Not 'til we got there. The radio had been giving us trouble all week, and that night it just cut out completely while we were moving."

"So once he hit the warehouse, you went after him on foot?"

"Yeah."

"Alone?"

Maloney shrugged. "The radio crackled, and Sheila stayed to call in our position and get backup. I knew she'd be right behind me, so I went in. The warehouse was huge. One big room filled with windows and skylights and piles of abandoned junk. The moon was up and the place was lit like a stage."

Hank had several questions he wanted to ask, but he remained silent. Maloney was well into the narrative, and he knew any distraction would interrupt the flow of the story.

"I had my gun out, but I didn't shoot. I yelled at the guy to stop. He was running fast as hell. The wood floor was all beat up like, and he must have hit a weak spot. All of a sudden, his foot goes through the boards and he sprawls out full length. His gun goes skidding across the floor and disappears into a pile of crap."

Maloney stopped speaking, his eyes narrowed as if he were replaying the scene. He flexed the fingers of both hands to relieve the tension in his body, and then he leaned across the desk. His face was scrunched up as if he were in pain.

"Sheila comes in the door. The drug dealer pushes himself to his knees. As I approach the guy, she starts yelling and I hear her running up behind me. I turn to warn her about the floor. In that split second, the perp grabs my gun."

Maloney stared at a spot on the wall, his eyes narrowed, and his voice became a strained whisper as he described the situation. He licked his lips, then swallowed once before he continued the recital.

"She skids to a stop three feet from the guy. Her gun is out but she doesn't use it! Watches while the bastard shoots me."

Maloney's voice vibrated with outrage. He leaned against the back of his chair, his face shadowed. When he spoke again his voice was flat with only a trace of anger.

"The blast must have broken her trance because the next thing I know I hear this shot and the guy's writhing on the floor. Even though Sheila tried to do some first aid, I lost a lot of blood before the paramedics came."

"Was that the last time you were partnered?"

"Yeah. I was in the hospital for a couple days and then out on leave. I had to complete the IAD investigation and then take some physical therapy before they'd let me back out on the street. By the time I got back, she was on the job in River Oaks."

"Did you and Sheila have words about the incident before you made the IAD report?"

Maloney shook his head. His face took on an expression that was part worry, part shame.

"No. I overheard her telling the cops on the scene what happened and just went with her version. I figured it was over and it didn't really matter."

"You must have been bitter, though? If Lieutenant Brady hadn't applied for the job in River Oaks, would you have continued as her partner?"

"No way. How could I trust her after that?"

"Don't you think you should have told someone? You put her next partner at risk."

Maloney sat up straight, staring across the table, eyes wide in consternation. "Christ, I never really thought about that. Any cop could freeze under that kind of stressful situation. I guess if she had stayed in Milwaukee I mighta done something. When she took the job in River Oaks, I just figured she wouldn't run into such high-tension situations there, so it wouldn't happen again."

Hank had read the reports from IAD. Maloney's story was essentially the same except he had put a different verbal spin on it and implied that the shooting and his injury were the result of Sheila's hesitation.

Which version was true?

"I appreciate your candor, Doug," he said. "It's obvious I'm going to have to consider this very carefully before making any decisions. In the meantime I'm planning to keep real close tabs on her."

Although Maloney's expression didn't change, Hank knew the man had gotten the message. He might think he was safe for the moment, but he'd definitely weigh the risks before he delivered another package to Sheila.

Hank thanked Maloney for his cooperation and listened to the man's footsteps fade down the hall. He picked up his notebook and left the office. Once outside, he pulled out a cigar, lit up, and then got back in the car. He drove with the window open, the cigar smoke mingling with the fresh air, reminding him of raking and burning leaves as a kid.

He didn't take the expressway, but instead turned off on a two-lane highway going west out of Madison. Once the traffic thinned out, he tried to evaluate the interview.

On the plus side, Hank had the gut feeling that Maloney had nothing to do with the murders. Unless the man's name turned up again in another context linked to the murders, Hank could put him way down on the suspect list.

On the minus side, Hank was convinced that Maloney had sent the mystery box to Sheila. He obviously blamed her for the shooting incident. Considering that Maloney's comments were made off the record and would not be followed up officially, his accusations were suspect. Were his insinuations true, or was his vindictiveness prompted by other issues?

Perhaps it was time to ask Sheila about her relationship with her ex-partner prior to the IAD investigation.

Hank realized he disliked Maloney and considered whether this could cloud his judgment. He wished he'd talked to Sheila first. The unfortunate result of this interview was that Maloney's comments injected a measure of doubt in Hank's mind.

Aside from the unfavorable character traits attributed to Sheila by her ex-partner, it was the allegation of her freezing that troubled him most. He knew from experience that if an officer hesitated once, the odds of its happening again were extremely high. In a moment of crisis, people reacted automatically. If indeed she had a habit of choking, she'd put every officer on the force in danger.

•

"I hope that beer's cold and wet," Owen James said as he approached Hank in the back booth of the Duck Inn. "I've been thinking about the ribs all day, and I've built up a helluva thirst."

Hank poured Owen a tall glass from the frosted pitcher and pushed it across the table. Looking at him, Hank wondered if the man slept in his clothes. His wife had left him two years ago, and Owen's clothes, never a fashion statement, had slipped from disheveled to slovenly.

After a long pull on the beer, Owen wiped his mouth with the back of his hand. "How was your trip to Madison?"

"Interesting," Hank said.

Owen knew about the box with the bloody doll, so he told him about finding Maloney's fingerprints and his interview with Sheila's ex-partner in Madison. By the time he finished, Owen's eyes were narrowed and his forehead creased with worry.

"Do you think Sheila's at risk?"

"At a guess, I'd say no. I'd like to think he sent the doll in a moment of poor judgment." Hank shrugged and drank some of his beer. "On the other hand, I don't want Sheila or her daughter in any danger. If there's another incident, it might indicate he's stalking her."

Out of habit, Owen brushed at invisible crumbs on the front of his shirt. "Have you told Sheila about Maloney?"

"No. I want to talk to her about the IAD situation before she knows about Maloney's accusation."

"Do you think she froze?" Owen's expression was bland, eyes showing only a slight curiosity.

"How would I know?" Hank snapped.

Owen held up his hands. "Don't bite my head off. It's your problem, not mine. Back to Maloney for a moment. Could there be any connection between him and the murders?"

"Anything's possible."

"What say I put someone on him? Lee Wilder would be perfect. He's been on the force since before there were criminals. He knows everyone on the job in Wisconsin, and he's discreet. If there's dirt to find, Lee will ferret it out, and it won't get back to Maloney."

"That'd be great, Owen. You might mention that I'd like patrols on Sheila's street with more frequency. I've finally gotten used to having her around, and I'd like to make sure she's safe."

Hank avoided Owen's eyes as he poured each of them another glass of beer. There had been a speculative look on the older man's face that Hank refused to acknowledge. He changed the subject.

"Before we order, is there anything new?"

"I got a call from Maggie Ginthner over at the historical society. Maggie said the area of Worley Woods where the bodies have been found had an unsavory reputation in the past. The place used to be called Devil's Lick because of the salt deposits there."

Hank snorted. "The name makes me think of some kind of kinky sex."

"Might be. At any rate, forty or fifty years ago, the body of a young woman was found at Devil's Lick, and apparently the cause of death was stabbing. Since blood and salt are associated with witchcraft, it was rumored the dead woman was involved in some satanic ritual."

"Get out of here! Is she suggesting that these murders are somehow related to witchcraft?"

Owen grinned, his eyebrows raised over twinkling brown eyes. "I think she used the term 'witches' coven' several times."

"Is she nuts?"

"No. Actually, she came across as more sane than the usual tipster. She said that when she read about the ritual aspects of the murders, she felt she ought to call and tell us the history of Devil's Lick."

"God knows we've had crazier leads," Hank said. "Did you check for arrests on anything related to witchcraft?"

"Just ran down the info." Owen reached in his jacket pocket for a small spiral notebook, licked his thumb, and flipped through several pages. "Think back a couple years ago. A chicken was stolen from the O'Keefe farm and slaughtered near the picnic shelter in Duerkop Park. Aside from the dead chicken, we found melted candle wax and salt scattered around the area."

"Didn't it look like some sort of ceremony had taken place during the night?"

"Yeah, and since it was close to Halloween, rumors of witchcraft raced through the community."

Hank stared down into his beer and tried to bring back the details. "I wasn't here when it happened. I'd gone up north for some bowhunting. The excitement was over by the time I got back."

"Turned out it was a Halloween prank. Marc Schermerhorn and Dave Case were the first ones we thought of. Those two are so full of mischief, God alone knows how they've been able to stay out of jail. They admitted stealing the chicken and agreed to pay the O'Keefes double what the hen was worth."

"You got to admit, Owen, they're inventive boys. Never anything malicious or hurtful, just pranks and practical jokes." Hank chuckled, but Owen was less tolerant of young offenders. "Find anything else?"

"Rumor mostly." Owen raised the empty pitcher, and when the waitress came, he asked for a refill and two orders of ribs. "I told Lee Wilder about the witch thing. He said that about fifteen years ago, one of the teachers at the high school was accused of practicing satanism."

"Anything to it?"

"Not as far as the law was concerned. It never got into the system. The principal called Lee as a friend and gave him the rough outline of the situation and asked his advice on how to handle it. Eventually he called back to say the accusation was false. The boy who made the charge had gotten a failing grade in the man's class and had acted out of spite."

Hank was intrigued. "Satanism is an unusual allegation for a kid to make if he wants to get someone in trouble. Just out of curiosity, see if you can run down anything more on it."

"I'd be delighted to look into the Witches of River Oaks." Owen scratched his chin and tipped his head back to scratch his neck. He had a heavy beard, and it was easily visible late in the day. "The only new item I have is the lab report on the liquid residue on Lindy Pottinger's chest. The lab had a helluva time identifying it."

He riffled through several pages of his notebook. "It's a local brand of liquid fertilizer called Cychner's Everbloom, and it's used specifically for rose care. The roses found at the scene were probably soaking in this substance overnight."

Hank nodded. "I know the Cychners. They own the Rainbow Nursery out on Albion. Nice young couple. They've been running it for about four years. Did you talk to them?"

"Yes, and they were very cooperative. The only thing I picked up worth noting was that they co-sponsor a rose competition with the River Oaks Garden Club once a year at the VFW hall. This year it was on Sunday, June thirtieth—two days before Lindy Pottinger was kidnapped."

Hank felt a spurt of excitement. "Can we get names of people who attended? Anyone who worked the rose show?"

"I called the president of the garden club. She's putting together a list, and we'll run the names through our data files. She said it was a great success because the guest speaker was Babs Marti, a bowologist, whatever the hell that is."

Hank shook his head. "I haven't a clue. Maybe she meant biologist."

"No, I asked her to spell it. Woman was so patronizing I was damned if I'd admit my ignorance," Owen grumbled. "And that brings you up to date. New findings are sparse these days. Everything else leads to a dead end."

Hank sighed and ran his hand back and forth over the top of his head. The waitress returned with a new pitcher of beer and the ribs.

"This bastard's invisible as far as the rest of the community is concerned," Hank said. "He's got to be local. A stranger would be spotted in this paranoid climate. More troubling is the fact that the girls went with him willingly. He must be known to them and they trust him."

"We'll get him, Hank. He thinks he's invincible, but he'll get careless and make a mistake, or someone will eventually spot him. Unfortunately it may not be before he kills again."

•

After dropping Meg and Beth at the library, Sheila found a parking space on the street beside Nick's photography studio. Facing the park and City Hall, the studio was on the corner next to Paxton's ice cream parlor. The owner, Lynn Ellen, set lawn chairs in front of the store when the weather was comfortable. Tonight two mothers sat, eating ice cream and talking, while their children licked cones and stared at the photographs in Nick's picture window.

Despite his frequent muttering about the smudged fingerprints on the glass, she noticed that photographs of babies and animals dominated the front of the display.

Sheila smiled at the latest addition to the window. A little girl, less than a year old, was holding a baby chicken. The entire background was white, highlighting the perfect color match between the baby's buttercup-yellow dress and the fuzzy yellow chick. Although the girl was laughing, a single tear sparkled on the curve of her cheek, bringing an additional tenderness to the picture.

A bell hanging over the door rang as she entered the studio. Since she had never been in the studio before, she looked around.

The empty waiting room was a contrast in black and white. The chairs and tables were black; the walls, carpet, and lamps white. Despite the magazines, books, and toys piled in white wicker baskets, nothing detracted from the photographs around the room.

Her eyes were immediately drawn to the photograph on the far wall. She remembered Nick taking pictures when they went fishing but hadn't seen the finished products. Meg stood on the bank of the Wisconsin River holding a fishing rod as Sheila bent to scoop the fish on the end of the line into a net. Meg's face was radiant with excitement, a preview of the beauty that she would eventually grow into.

"Do you like it?"

Sheila didn't turn at the sound of Nick's deep voice but continued to examine the picture. "I never know what to say when you ask me that. Saying yes doesn't do my feelings justice."

He moved closer. "A couple of the other pictures I took were good, but this one was the best."

"You have a gift, you know. It's not just getting the subjects to cooperate. And it's not light or film speed or all those other technical things. You have a sense for seizing the perfect moment to snap the picture. You manage to capture the emotional highpoint. Freeze it in your lens."

"That may be one of the nicest things you've ever said to me," Nick said.

He touched her, resting the palms of his hands on her shoulders and drawing her against his chest. She let her head fall back, shifting her position until she was snuggled against his shoulder. They stood together, happy in each other's presence, until a movement beyond the picture window reminded Sheila that they were visible to the people outside.

With a sigh, she turned, smiling up at the tanned face with its carefully trimmed beard. "You have a knack for making me forget business."

"It's just part of my ongoing campaign to convince you what a fun-loving, dynamic, and unique person, not to mention all-around nice guy, I am."

"You know, Nick," she said with a laugh. "I'm almost beginning to believe it."

"Don't blame me if you suddenly come to your senses and it's too late."

"Other candidates are rising to the top of the list, are they?"

"Jeanne Anderson gave me the hot eye all the time I tried to take her picture yesterday. She kept fidgeting like she couldn't wait to get her hands on me." He shrugged his shoulders. "Of course, it could have been a reaction to the light in her eyes or to the fact she was tired of holding her great-grandson."

Nick ignored Sheila's hoot of laughter as he stooped to straighten the children's books scattered on the floor. The phone on one of the side tables rang, and he crossed the room to pick it up.

Sheila enjoyed watching him. He was a big man, a full head taller than she was, carrying a little more weight around his middle than he should. His hands were big, with short stubby fingers, and his feet always looked large enough to trip him. Yet, for all his size, he moved with a quiet grace unusual for a man. There was nothing effeminate about him, though; he was masculine without the machismo attitude.

He was in his mid-thirties, with reddish-brown hair that was thinning slightly at the crown of his head. The color of his sideburns was less red, and his beard was brown fading into gray. His lips, nestled in his beard, were full. His size and hairy appearance should have been intimidating, but his twinkling eyes gave him a huggable, teddy-bear quality.

"Sorry about that," he said, hanging up the phone. "Now that I have you as a captive audience, let me show you the rest of the place."

He led her into a short hall, opening the first door on the right.

At one end of the rectangular room were a sofa and two overstuffed chairs, upholstered in the same mauve and cream floral pattern. Straight ahead was a tiled bathroom, and at the other side of the room was an open space with three free-standing mirrors.

"I like the mirrors," Sheila said. "The cherry frames really add an elegant touch."

Nick snorted. "About ten years ago, a photographer was arrested for taking pictures of his female clientele undressing. It turned out the mirror in the dressing room was a two-way device like TV cops use in their interrogation rooms. Since these mirrors aren't set into the wall, they give a feeling of confidence to the clients."

"That's silly," Sheila said, looking around the room. "With the sophistication of technology these days, you could have any number of cameras in here."

"I know that and you know that, but for some reason my mirrors reassure people." He shut the light off and opened the door across the hall. "This is my conference room where I bring people to either look at photos or plan the shoot for an event like a wedding."

Thanks to the windows along the outside wall, the room looked larger than it was. There was a round table with four leather and metal arm chairs. A long credenza was on one wall beneath a pull-down video screen. The other end of the room was L-shaped with a small kitchenette and a wall unit containing a television, a VCR, and a CD player.

"I'm going to put you in here to look at pictures, but come on back and take a look at where the real work is done."

He opened a door at the end of the hall. The windowless studio, large enough to accommodate an entire wedding party or a multi-generational family group, appeared unbalanced. One side was starkly professional, crammed with cameras, lighting apparatus, video equipment, and various high-tech gadgetry.

The other side resembled a stage set, lavishly carpeted and furnished with elegant chairs, a table covered with a black velvet throw, and rolls of colorful fabric Nick used for backdrops. There was even a child's white wicker chair and a rattan basket of toys and stuffed animals. Without the bright lights to illuminate the sitting area, it had a tawdry, carnival look in daylight.

"My office is over here," Nick said, threading his way between the photographic paraphernalia.

He opened a door in the wall and switched on the light. Sheila was amused at the contrast between the other areas of the studio and

Nick's own space. Here chaos reigned. Negatives were fastened to lighted panels on the wall. Camera gear was scattered on the desk and dangled from the backs of chairs. Magazines were piled on top of the low file cabinets and in stacks on the floor.

And everywhere else there were photographs. Photographs spilling out of folders, stuffed in envelopes, overflowing cardboard trays, and attached to every conceivable surface.

"How do you find anything in here?" she asked.

He gave a quick glance around the room, then grinned. "I guess sometimes it does get out of hand, but believe it or not, I do know where most everything is."

A picture on top of one of the file cabinets caught Sheila's eye. "Is this a photo of someone's pet cow?"

Nick chuckled as she leaned over to get a better look. "Cow! You really are a city girl. That's Norma and Russ Gertsch's prize bull."

"Oh, so you took the picture for the paper."

"No. The Gertsches are advertising the bull for stud service. This way a prospective client gets a chance to see what the bull looks like without having to actually drive over and inspect it. Many buyers purchase cattle sight unseen. I take pictures for a lot of the local farmers. The photos are pooled together for convenience in sire directories. Sort of like a date book for cattle."

Sheila shook her head as she stared down at the huge animal. "I guess I assumed that each farm had bulls and cows."

"Well, some do, but you can't do too much inbreeding or you end up with poor stock. Some farmers like to breed in different qualities. It's all high-tech nowadays." He picked up several long open-topped manila envelopes. "These are the photos you'll want to look at. Let's take them back to the conference room and you can get started."

Almost at the door, he picked up the picture of the bull and handed it to her.

"A souvenir of your visit."

"I'll hang it in the living room over the fireplace." She followed him along the hall, holding her trophy with care.

"You don't have a fireplace."

"Well, I'm sure I can find someplace suitable."

"The bedroom would be good." He grinned over his shoulder. "A reminder of me."

He disappeared into the conference room before she could think of an appropriate comeback.

"These are the photos taken after the murders," he said. "They're jumbled together, but there are numbers on the back, corresponding to a list in the computer. Is there anything I can do to help?"

"For the moment there's nothing. I'm looking for a face in the crowd," Sheila said. "Quite literally that. I saw someone in a news broadcast, and I'm curious to find out who he is. The TV station sent over a dubbed tape of their news footage from last night, and I reviewed it before I came over so the face would be fresh in my mind. I'm hoping I'll find a better picture of him in your files."

He set the envelopes on the table, then reached in his pocket and handed her a magnifying glass. "You might need this."

"Thanks, Nick. I'll call you when I'm done."

Anxious to get started, Sheila pulled out a chair and sat down, giving him a smile as he headed for the door. She dumped the contents of the first envelope into the center of the table.

She worked methodically, scanning every picture where a face appeared. After a while her eyes felt fuzzy. She'd been stupid not to bring the TV station footage. After looking at so many pictures, she wondered if she'd remember the man well enough to pick him out of a crowd.

Twenty minutes later she found him.

Chapter Eight

He stood at the edge of the crowd in Sandrik's parking lot. Although his back was to the camera, and only the side of his head was visible, Sheila recognized him immediately as the man she had seen on the television the night before.

She set the picture on the chair beside her and returned to the pile of pictures. The process was slow, but she was determined to go through all the rest.

"How goes the hunt?" Nick said as he came into the room some time later.

Sheila flopped against the back of her chair, grateful for the interruption. "I just finished."

"And did you find the mystery man?"

"I think so, but there's not a clear shot of his face in any of them."

"Don't sound so depressed. I'd say you were lucky to find any." He came over to the table and massaged her shoulders. "Let's see what you've got."

Sheila spread the four photos she had culled on the surface of the table. Nick leaned over, staring down at the pictures. She pointed to the man in the first two pictures of the crowd in front of Sandrik's.

"This is definitely the man. That's a side view, and the second one shows him behind the grocery bag. The other two I think might be the guy, but I'm not totally convinced. I don't suppose by any chance you recognize him?"

Nick pulled out a magnifier and peered intently at the pictures. "As a matter of fact I do. It's Herb Reisler. He owns the Book Nook on the far side of the square."

"No wonder he looked familiar," Sheila said. "I went in there once with Meg to buy some books."

"I won't even ask if he's a suspect."

"Good," she said. "At the moment it's just curiosity on my part."

"Keep in mind that curiosity killed the cat," Nick said. "Come on back to my office and I'll get you the information on when and where these pictures were taken. Although, like the footage you saw on television, I'm pretty sure these were all taken at Sandrik's grocery store."

Once in his office, Nick flipped over the four pictures and entered the numbers from the labels into the computer. Since there was nowhere to sit down, Sheila wandered around looking at the odd assortment of objects scattered around the room. At the sound of the laser printer she returned to Nick's desk.

"Hot off the presses, my dear." He tucked a sheet of paper into an envelope with the pictures, then handed it to her. "On the printout is the time and place of each of the photos. The other notes are just for me, having to do with light, lenses, filters, and other things pertaining to that particular shot."

"I really appreciate this."

At her words, Nick wiggled his eyebrows and moved closer. Instinctively Sheila backed toward the door. He followed her, draping his arm over her shoulders as they walked toward the front of the studio. He leaned down, his mouth close to her ear.

"If you were really grateful you'd set a date to come to my place for dinner."

"If you're suggesting some kind of payback," she said, "I could arrest you for trying to extort favors from an officer of the law. Is that what I'm hearing?"

"Yep."

He tilted his head so that she could see the mischievous expression on his face. He licked his lips, and Sheila shivered at the sensual promise in his eyes.

"Definitely extortion." Sheila clucked her tongue. "What day?"

"Tomorrow? No, not tomorrow. I've got a meeting with Julie

Beard about her daughter's wedding. I might get out in time for a late dinner, but you never know."

Sheila was relieved that he was busy tomorrow, because that was when she and Meg were going out to dinner with Warren Santo. Even though it wasn't a date, she doubted if Nick would approve.

"How about Thursday?" she asked.

"This is a bad week. I've got a meeting that night. Would you want to do lunch?"

"That would be possible," she said, glancing at her watch. "I'd better get moving. It's a quarter to nine and I'm due to pick up the girls at the library in fifteen minutes."

"I'll give you a call Thursday morning."

He held the front door open, giving her cheek a chaste kiss as two older women were passing. Sheila waved as she walked around the corner to her car. It was dark and she was glad she'd parked underneath the street light.

She reached in her pocket for her car keys and stepped off the curb. Her shoes crunched on the rough surface. She looked down, and her eyebrows drew together at the small brown stones on the street beside her car.

Squatting down, she examined them. They weren't stones but birdseed, scattered on the ground in a loose strip along the length of her car. She reached out and scraped several seeds into her hand. Looking closer, she could see that it wasn't birdseed but sunflower seeds. The familiar hull was gone, leaving behind the small greenish brown kernels.

Sunflower kernels?

Raising her cupped hand to her nose, she sniffed and caught a faint nutty smell. She rubbed her finger over the kernels and then licked the tip of her finger, surprised to taste oil and salt. In the snack aisles of the grocery store, she had seen plastic bags of salted kernels but had never bought any. Rocking back on her heels, she stared at the kernels on the street. Had someone spilled a bag beside the car?

She stood up and walked around the car but could find no other kernels except the wide band beside her car door. It appeared as though someone had put them on the ground for her to find.

Why? Was it meant as some joking reference to Meg's bird? That didn't make sense. What did sunflowers have to do with the bird?

Sheila shivered. She didn't like mysteries. It reminded her of the box with the bloody doll. Turning her head, she scanned the area but could see no movement along the street. She felt vulnerable standing alone in the dark. Dropping the kernels back on the ground, she brushed her hands together to get rid of the feel of the oil and salt. Unlocking the car door, she got inside.

"Damn!" she said as she looked at the clock on the dash.

She was late. The library would close in one minute. She didn't want the girls outside in the dark. She started the car and drove as quickly as she could to the library, sighing when she spotted Meg and Beth sitting on the low brick wall in front.

"I'm so sorry, girls," she said as they piled into the car. "Something held me up."

"How come when I say that you always tell me I have to plan better?" Meg grinned, taking any real criticism out of her words.

"Moms are supposed to say that kind of stuff," Sheila said. "It's on page forty in 'The Mother's Little Handbook.' Buckle up, girls. Don't worry, Beth. I'll get you home before your mother has time to call in a missing person's report."

She relaxed as the girls chattered away, oblivious to her. After dropping Beth off and apologizing to Mrs. Lavorini for being late, she headed home. Elmo greeted them at the door, and Meg hurried off to feed the bird.

Sheila dumped her briefcase and the envelope of pictures in the family room, checked the answering machine, and then, feeling hungry, got out a plate of cookies and some milk. She and Meg had their snack and watched the end of the early news. By ten Meg was yawning, and Sheila sent her off to bed and cleaned up the dishes.

Back in the family room, she spotted the envelope Nick had given her. She picked it up and returned to the couch. She opened the flap, dumping the contents on the coffee table. Pushing the photographs to one side, she picked up the single sheet of paper that gave the times and dates when the pictures were taken.

She caught her breath as she read the dates printed on the white paper.

Thank God she hadn't read the notes in front of Nick. She could never have contained her reaction. All along she had assumed the pictures were shot at Sandrik's grocery store after Lindy Pottinger's murder.

The dates on two of the pictures were July fourth, the day Lindy's body was discovered. The date on the third picture was April thirtieth of the previous year, the day Tiffany Chastain was found in Worley Woods. In the last picture, Herb Reisler was holding a bag of groceries. Looking closer, she could see that he was wearing an over-coat. The date on the picture was January thirteenth—the morning Meredith Whitford's body was found in the woods.

Herb Reisler owned the Book Nook. The store specialized in children's literature and was a popular hangout. He probably knew all four of the murdered girls. So what was he doing in the crowd close to the scene of the last three crimes? And why did he look so guilty?

•

When Sheila arrived at the station in the morning, she went in search of Lois Coren.

The older woman was at her desk, talking on the telephone. She held up one finger and waved to the nearby chair. Sheila sat down, watching in amusement as Lois ran the fingers of one hand through her hair, which already looked as if she'd been trapped in a wind tunnel.

"Now don't forget to take some vitamin C for that sore throat. Four tablets every four hours should do it." Lois rolled her eyes at the obvious objections. "Honestly, Kodjo, one pill won't do the trick. Don't be such a baby. Just do what I tell you."

Listening to the conversation, Sheila found it difficult to hold back a grin. Kodjo was a six foot seven, African-American uniformed cop who looked meaner than a rabid dog. He was enormous, and most of the force, men and women, were in awe of him. Yet here was Lois treating him like an eight-year-old.

"Get a grip, Kodjo. It's only a cold, for God's sake. I've got to go. I'll bring you some chicken soup tomorrow," Lois said as she hung up the phone. "Now what can I do for you?"

"I stopped by to see if you know a Herb Reisler."

"Sure. He lives a couple blocks away from me. Why?"

"I'm doing a background check on him, and since you're a long-time resident of River Oaks I was hoping you could give me a bit of info on him."

Lois stared at Sheila, her mouth pursed in thought. "I really don't know Herb that well. I was a friend of his wife. Gloria and I were in the same church guild. A really nice woman. One of those who was a workhorse but didn't want any credit. She always said she did things that needed doing, just like anyone else would." She paused. "As if."

"I take it she's not around anymore."

"Kidney failure. Maybe fifteen years ago. She was only forty-five.

What a waste. They owned a bookstore, but Herb sold it when Gloria got sick so that he could stay home and take care of her."

Sheila narrowed her eyes, trying to keep the story straight. "Doesn't he own the Book Nook?"

Lois nodded her head. "Yes, but they had another store. Their first place was in that little strip mall across from the Piggly Wiggly. It had a cute name, but I can't remember what it was. The Write Stuff or The Write Way. You know, spelled with a 'W.'"

"So when did he buy the new store?"

"Maybe a year after Gloria died. He was really at loose ends. There were no children, and I think he needed something to do. He dotes on the kids that come into the store." Lois stared at Sheila, her face set in lines of concern. "Is he under investigation?"

"Do you know if he's ever been in trouble with the law?"

"I don't think he's ever been arrested, if that's what you mean. I could run him through the system."

"Thanks, but it's not important. Just a matter of curiosity."

"You know what they say about curiosity."

"Don't mention dead cats; it always freaks me out. I appreciate your help."

Sheila shivered as she rose from her chair. Lois was the second person recently to mention that curiosity killed the cat. Let's hope that's the only thing it killed, she thought.

●

Sheila groaned when she looked at her watch. It was almost five-thirty. Dr. Santo was coming in an hour, and she still had to talk to Hank Harker before she could leave the station. He'd been in meetings most of the day, but now he was back in his office. Before anyone else could get to him, she hurried across the room and knocked on the frame of his open door.

"Do you have a minute, Chief?"

"Sure. Come on in."

"I just wanted to tell you what I'm working on," she said, perching on the edge of a chair as she told him about seeing the man on television and her curiosity as to his identity.

"When I discovered that Herb Reisler owned a bookstore that catered to children, I decided he needed a closer look. I went back through the files and found his car was parked in the grocery store lot after the discovery of the first body in Worley Woods," Sheila said. "I found it on the list of license plates that were taken down that day."

"What about the last two murders?"

"His plates weren't picked up either in the parking lot or in the surrounding blocks. He was in the crowd outside Sandrik's, but his car wasn't. My guess is that he parked his car someplace in town and then walked over. I'm wondering why."

"Me, too," Hank said. "Do you want to follow up on it, or do you want to turn it over to someone else?"

"I'd like to work it. Tomorrow I'm going to drop by the Book Nook and talk to Reisler."

"Good," he said. "Keep me posted if anything comes of it."

"I will," she said.

Back at her desk she gathered her things; then she hurried to the locker room and then outside to the parking lot. She unlocked the door of her car and opened the door.

"Wait a minute, Sheila."

When Sheila heard Dick Perkins hail her, she debated driving off. She could always claim she hadn't heard him. Giving in to her better nature, she waited beside the open car door until he cut through the parking lot.

"Good evening, your honor," she said, holding the edge of the door as if it were a shield.

"Don't give me that 'your honor' crap. Call me Dick."

She tried to look coolly disapproving of his intimate tone of voice, but remembering the names her fellow officers called Perkins, she couldn't keep herself from smiling. He preened a bit, taking her reaction as positive evidence of his charm.

"Good to see you, but I'm afraid I can't talk long. My daughter's waiting at home for me, and I'm running late."

"Don't worry. I won't keep you. I wanted to run something by you." He moved closer, resting one hip against the side of the car and folding his arms across his chest. "I'm thinking of putting together a youth commission, and I was hoping you'd consider serving on it."

Perkins's back was to the sun, but despite his height, he didn't block the light, forcing Sheila to squint up at him. "What's the purpose of this group?"

"The young kids and teens haven't got a lot of outlets in this town. Aside from hanging around the mall and Hodges Park on the weekends and after school, they need places to go and activities to participate in."

"I agree," Sheila said. "Safe places. Right now the parents are so afraid that they've put massive restrictions on the kids. And the kids are beginning to rebel."

Perkins nodded. "The world is different than when we were growing up. We're heading for trouble if we don't consider providing some sort of youth center or at least some organized activities. And I'd really like you to be a part of the team."

Sheila tipped her head, eyes half closed in the late afternoon glare. Much as she approved of the idea, she didn't completely trust "Just-Call-Me Dick's" motives. She sensed that his interest in her was personal and suspected the invitation was based on his misguided assumption she might be interested in a closer relationship.

"The concept is intriguing. I'm aware that times have changed and we need to adapt to the teen situation. How soon will the commission be meeting?"

"I haven't chosen a starting date yet." He pulled on his earlobe. "I wanted to get some sense of who was available to work on it."

His evasive answer made Sheila even more suspicious of his intentions. "Well, you can consider me interested. Of course, I'll have to check with Chief Harker before I'll know what my availability is."

"Naturally," he said. "I realize Hank will have to OK your participation."

Perkins straightened up. His face was in shadow, and he loomed over her. She shivered as the sun went behind a cloud.

"Let me think about it, talk to the chief, and I'll get back to you. Right now I've got to get home."

Keeping her mouth fixed in a smile, she raised her hand in a dismissive wave and climbed into the car. Perkins watched her back out of the parking space, an intensity to his gaze that made her uncomfortable.

•

"Hi, Mother. How's everything in Florida?"

Hank leaned back in his chair and propped his feet up on the corner of his desk. He'd just talked to his mother two days ago. It was unusual for her to call more than once a week, and rarely around dinnertime, he thought, checking his watch.

"The weather's still pretty muggy, Hank, but at least it's not actively raining today."

Hank heard a man's voice in the background before his mother covered the mouthpiece with her hand. He rocked back and forth in his chair, waiting patiently until she returned to the phone.

"I was just reminded that I can't just chitchat or I'll use up my allotted time."

His eyebrows bunched together in confusion. "Where are you?"

"Now don't get cross, Hank, but I'm in jail."

"In jail?" His voice rose as he dropped his feet to the floor and leaned forward, pressing the receiver tightly to his ear. "What the hell did you do?"

"Well, I didn't murder anyone, if that's what you mean. Although I'd like to kill Rosemary Grant for forgetting to bring the key to the lock, since we had to stand for two hours in the hot sun while they figured out how to get us unchained."

"Jesus Jenny, Mother. What did you chain yourself to this time?"

"One of those steam shovel things. Although I'm not sure they use steam anymore."

Hank ground his teeth. "Get to the point, Mother."

"All right, dear. You see, Hank, a developer was planning to dig up an orange grove to build another set of condos. So Rosemary and I decided to delay the work and see if a little publicity would focus some negative attention on the project."

"That certainly makes sense." Hank sighed as he brushed his hand over the top of his head, rubbing the back of his neck. "Do you need bail or what?"

"I'm not exactly sure. I was listening to Rosemary sobbing that her children would slap her into a home if they found out she'd been arrested, so I missed some of the details. Then when they said I could make a call, I thought it would be nice to talk to you before I was hauled off to the slammer."

Despite his annoyance, Hank had to laugh.

"Is the arresting officer there?"

Once more the mouthpiece was covered, and he could hear muffled voices in the background. Then Della was back.

"Yes. He's right here. His name is Vernon Farrell, and he's been very nice to both Rosemary and myself. He wanted to call you, but I suggested that the news might be less worrisome if I spoke to you first. Do you want me to put him on the phone?"

"Yes, please. Now, Mother, if I get you out of this, you've got to promise not to chain yourself to anything for a whole month."

"A month is a very long time, Hank."

Before he could catch his breath enough to make a comment, she was gone. More sounds of voices, and then Della's decisive tones were replaced by a soft Southern drawl.

"Captain Vern Farrell here. Is this Chief Harker I'm talking to?"

"Unfortunately, yes. I gather the ladies are about to do some time."

"Oh no, sir," Farrell said. "Once your momma told me about you, I figured we ought to be able to find a way to keep her and her friend out of the system. I sent them off to one of the interrogation rooms, so we can talk more free like. I didn't tell them we weren't going to press charges, hoping that a bit of a scare might convince them not to get arrested again."

"I don't know Rosemary, but nothing short of the electric chair will scare my mother."

"She certainly is a feisty old gal." The voice on the other end of the phone sounded more amused than angry. "She wasn't in the station house more'n five minutes before she had some of the uniforms fetching cold drinks and helping her rearrange the furniture in the coffee room."

Hank snorted. "Just imagine what it was like growing up with that woman. My third-grade teacher retired midyear when Mother became convinced the reading list was long on fantasy and short on reality."

Farrell laughed. "Don't worry about your momma. After I give both ladies a lecture, I'll drive them home."

"I owe you one, Captain Farrell. If there's ever anything I can do for you or yours, let me know."

"Next time you're visiting down here, stop on by. In the meantime I'll mail you a fresh set of fingerprints as a souvenir."

Hank was still chuckling when he hung up. He couldn't wait to tell Jeff about his outrageous grandmother. Her stock would skyrocket in his eyes.

It wasn't quite so simple for Hank. Much as his mother amused him, he worried that her activism would get her in trouble. You'd think that at her age she'd be content to play bingo and hassle her bridge group. He could picture her at ninety, chained to the doors of some clinic, protesting the latest Medicare cuts.

He shook his head. She was probably paying him back for all the times he'd been in trouble. With another sigh, he returned to the stack of papers he'd been working through. It was after five, and he needed to finish up before he could go home for dinner. Picking up the letter on the top of the pile, he read it through briefly before signing it.

After working steadily for a half hour, he pushed back his chair and reached for his briefcase on the windowsill. He scooped up the items he'd set aside to be read at home, tossed them inside the briefcase, and closed the lid.

The phone on his desk rang. He glared at it, wanting to ignore it and go home. With a sigh of resignation, he reached out and picked up the receiver.

"It's Cienkus in Dispatch, Chief."

Hank pressed the phone to his ear as he caught the tension in John's voice."

"Trouble?"

"Big time, Chief. I've got a call on the line from one of our patrol cars. Someone just grabbed a girl."

Chapter Nine

"I don't know if it was a kidnapping, but it's turning into a hostage situation," the dispatcher said.

"Christ!" Hank jerked to his feet. His hand automatically touched the gun on his belt and then shot out to grab his uniform jacket.

"Richie Tyler, one of the new recruits, just called in for backup. I'm sending out two patrol cars. Thank God Pazzarini had that negotiation training. He's headed out to the scene. In the meantime I'm going to patch Richie into your phone so you can hear what's going on from him and give him additional instructions."

"Good job, Cienkus." The thought of a hostage situation brought a cold sweat to Hank's body.

"Chief Harker?" The rookie's voice was shrill and his breathing was ragged.

"I'm here, Richie. Take a deep breath, son, then tell me what's going on."

"Some guy grabbed a girl and is holed up in Schaffert's convenience store on Stewart and Delphia. Pat White got here first and he told me to call in for backup."

"Has he got a weapon?"

"Pat?" Richie sounded disoriented. "Oh, you mean the guy. I

don't know for sure, but the witness said she thought he did."

"All right, Richie, listen up. Pazzarini is on his way. He'll be in charge. I want you and Pat to cover the front and back doors. Neither one of you is to attempt entry to the store."

"Shouldn't we go in and talk to the guy?"

"Don't go near the place!" Hank shouted, then lowered his voice and spoke clearly and precisely. "If either of you disobeys my orders, I'll assign you to crossing guard detail at the high school. You got that?"

"Yes, sir!"

"You're doing just fine, Richie. Stay calm and wait until Paz arrives. Now go talk to Pat and I'll be there shortly."

Hank was half in his jacket as he hung up the phone. He reached in his pocket for his car keys and started out the door, stopping at Dispatch on the way.

"If he comes back on the radio, Cienkus, keep him calm. Stay on top of the situation and let me know if there's any progress."

Racing out to the parking lot, he cranked up the volume on the radio, turned on the siren, and headed for the convenience store which was ten blocks away. He tried to keep his own twenty-four-year-old memories from intruding on the present, but scenes from that day flickered behind his eyes like an old movie. Except for the blood, they played themselves out in black and white.

Approaching Schaffert's store, he spotted Pazzarini, who was holding a portable phone.

"What have we got?" Hank said as he got out of the car.

Paz shook his head, his dark eyes shadowed in the late afternoon light. "It's not what you're thinking, Chief. It's not another kidnapping. I called into the store and talked to the guy. He was trying to rob the place when a customer ran out and hailed the patrol car. He's in there with the clerk."

"All right, let's do this by the numbers," Hank said. "We want to get out of this with nobody hurt."

Paz stroked his mustache and raised the portable phone. "Amen to that."

•

"Sorry, but I gotta go," Meg said as she handed the bat to one of the neighborhood kids playing baseball in the street.

"Who's winning?" Sheila asked as she came out of the garage and gave Meg a kiss on the top of her head.

"Our side of the street. I got two hits."

"I'm sorry I'm late, but I ran into the mayor and talked to him for a while," Sheila said as she shifted her briefcase to unlock the front door.

"It's past six, Mom," Meg said. "Dr. Santo's coming in twenty minutes, and you still gotta get cleaned up."

"I didn't think I was that dirty," Sheila said, leaning down to pat the cat on the rug in the hall. She started toward the kitchen with Meg and Elmo tagging along behind her. "Don't worry, sweetheart. I'll wear something dazzling."

She carried her briefcase to the family room, stopping in the archway as she spotted the open patio doors.

"Did you leave the doors open and unlocked while you were outside?"

Meg covered her mouth with her hand. "I'm sorry, Mom. I unlocked them to feed Cooper, then when Bernie and Nelson rang the bell to see if I could play baseball, I just went out the front door."

"I've told you, Meg, you have to be super careful about the doors and windows. Someone could walk in and take something, or could be hiding in here when you come back inside."

"I know, Mom. I'll try to be more careful."

"See that you do." Meg looked so crestfallen that Sheila hugged her as she walked down the hall to her bedroom. The cat bounded ahead of them. "How was your day?"

"Great. All kinds of excitement." Meg threw herself on Sheila's bed. Elmo leaped up beside her, purring loudly as the girl began to pet him.

"You know he's not allowed on the bed." Sheila unclipped her beeper and put it on top of the dresser, then peeled off her blouse and slacks as she headed into the bathroom.

"Don't blame me, Mom. I saw you yesterday morning. Sound asleep with Elmo snuggled up at your back."

Knowing her daughter was right, Sheila turned on the faucet. The rush of water allowed her to avoid answering. She washed quickly and combed out her French braid, catching it in a barrette at the nape of her neck. She put on fresh lipstick, took a last look in the mirror, and dusted some blush across her cheeks.

"Now what's so exciting?" she asked, coming out of the bathroom and opening the door of the closet.

"Beth's having a birthday party even though the one last year was a total disaster."

"Why was it a disaster?"

Sheila pulled out a lemon-yellow knit dress, shaking her head as she remembered how the material clung to her like a second skin. This wasn't a date. They were just going out for a friendly pizza.

"The party was a big duhhh. Beth's mom totally embarrassed her."

"I can't believe that Mrs. Lavorini ever did anything the slightest bit embarrassing."

"Oh, then you'll love this." Meg pushed Elmo away and sat up cross-legged on the bed. "When we moved here, the kids at school were still talking about Beth's birthday. She got permission to have a boy-girl party. So everybody is all jazzed for it. The big night comes, and when the kids arrive, Mrs. Lavorini makes them all wear party hats!"

Eyes sparkling with enjoyment, Meg leaned forward, waiting for her mother's reaction.

"Hats?"

"Don't you get it?" Meg threw her head back and rolled her eyes. "Geeze, Mom. Kids in fourth grade are way too old for party hats. Beth said she almost died. Everyone was laughing."

Sheila had a sense that the generation gap had widened.

"I'm sure Mrs. Lavorini didn't mean to embarrass Beth. If it had been me, I might have done the same thing."

Something in Sheila's voice must have sounded slightly forlorn, because Meg scrambled off the bed and threw her arms around her mother.

"No, you'd never do anything that dorky. You're much cooler than Beth's mom."

The doorbell rang.

"Remember what I said about the door," she said, releasing Meg and staring into the closet. "Make sure it's Dr. Santo before you open it."

"Psycho-killers don't ring the doorbell," Meg said as she raced out of the bedroom.

"Sometimes they do," Sheila shouted back.

She reached into the closet for a white eyelet blouse and a soft A-line denim skirt. Not too dressy, but feminine enough not to be too casual. It was still warm outside, so she opted for a pair of leather sandals. She reached into her jewelry box for a pair of earrings, choosing a cascade of gold stars and silver crescent moons. A quick spray of perfume and she was ready.

Dr. Santo and Meg were outside, hunkered down next to the glass cage. Neither face was visible, but she could tell by the occasional nodding of Meg's dark braided head that she was listening carefully. Not wanting to interrupt, Sheila returned to the kitchen.

"If you can bring Cooper in next week, we'll take off the bandage and see how well he can move on that leg," Dr. Santo said as they came back inside. "I hope you're remembering to wash your hands after you touch him."

"Mom's big on cleanliness," Meg said as she closed the patio doors. "Come on, Elmo. Let's go find Mom."

"Welcome to our home, Dr. Santo," Sheila said as the threesome came through the archway.

"I thought we decided you would call me Warren."

"We did. I just forgot."

He gave her a quick smile, turned on the water in the sink, and scrubbed his hands. When he finished, Sheila handed him a towel, laying another on the counter for her daughter.

"How's the patient?" she asked.

"I'd say Meg has a real success on her hands. The bird is doing remarkably well."

Warren smiled over his shoulder at the pink-cheeked girl, then turned back to Sheila and gave her a very thorough inspection as he handed her the used towel. Before he glanced away, she caught the light of approval in his eyes and was curiously pleased.

"I'm starving," Meg announced in the sudden silence.

"Have you forgotten your manners?"

"Sorry, Dr. Santo," she said, then to Sheila, "My stomach's growling, Mom."

"Well then, let's go to dinner." Warren turned to Sheila. "Is Momma Dasse's all right with you?"

"Wonderful. My mouth's watering at the thought."

She reached up to the peg board on the wall for her house keys. After checking the lock on the kitchen door, she picked up her purse on the counter and made sure her flip phone was inside. She touched her waist, remembering she'd left her beeper on the top of the dresser.

"Sorry, Warren, I'll be right back." She started down the hall, calling over her shoulder. "Meg, would you make sure the patio doors are locked?"

Outside, Warren unlocked the doors of his Jeep Cherokee, helping Meg to scramble into the back and then seating Sheila in the front seat.

"As it turns out, Meg," he said as he climbed in and started the car, "I'm starving too. We'll eat our pizza, and then I'd like to show you both something at my house."

"What is it? Is it an animal? Did you bring something home from the animal hospital?"

"No hints. It's a bit of a surprise but one I think you'll like. You'll just have to control your curiosity until after dinner."

Arriving at the restaurant, they had a laughing argument over the best pizza toppings, eventually compromising on pepperoni, onions, and mushrooms.

The dinner went well. At times the conversation was stilted as Sheila tried to find common areas of interest to talk about. Meg was content to eat her pizza, ask Dr. Santo about his life, and tease her mother. Her eyes flickered back and forth between the two adults when the conversation lagged.

"Do you ski?" he asked as he licked pizza sauce off his lip.

"Mom doesn't, but I'm learning," Meg said. "Mom was a chaperone on one of our ski trips. We were only on the hill for four hours. You could hear Mom's teeth chattering all the way back home."

Sheila laughed. "You'd think being born in Wisconsin I'd love the snow and cold. I'm a warm weather gal, I'm afraid."

"That makes two of us," Warren said. "I worked with my uncle, who was a vet. He didn't have kids, and when he died he left me everything. For a while I debated moving to California. Twelve months of sunshine sounded pretty good, after freezing every winter in Chicago."

"Instead you chose River Oaks?"

"I had family here." He looked thoughtful for a moment. "I think Midwesterners have a difficult time moving away. The people here seem to have a lot of the old-fashioned virtues. Other places seem more superficial."

By the time they finished the pizza, Meg was even more curious about the surprise Dr. Santo had promised. Before she could ask any more questions, Sheila sent her off to wash her hands.

"Why don't we split the check?" Sheila suggested once Meg had left the table. "That way I won't feel guilty about your being railroaded into the house call and a dinner."

Santo removed his glasses and raised his eyes to Sheila's face. His cheeks reddened, but he had no hesitation speaking his mind.

"I'd like to pay the check," he said. "I wanted to ask you out, but I didn't have the faintest idea if you would think I was being too pushy."

"No. Not at all. I was glad to get the opportunity to know you better." She spotted Meg's return. "Brace yourself. She's going to bug you until she finds out the surprise."

Although the girl danced from foot to foot in anticipation, she waited until they were outside in the car before speaking. "Are you going to tell us before we get to your house, Dr. Santo?"

"I guess I could," he said, backing the car out of the parking space. "It's a garden."

"Oh." Meg's less than enthusiastic response made Sheila smile. "A plain old garden?"

"No. A very special garden. A bonsai garden."

"Bones eye?"

Warren made a snorting sound. "One wonders what children are learning in our schools today. Rather than giving you a long explanation, I'll just wait to see your reaction."

He drove to the old section of town and pulled into an asphalt driveway just a block from Nick's house. To the right was a small brick ranch house with an attached garage. On the left was a high wooden fence running from the garage to the corner of the side yard.

"The house isn't much," he said. "I bought it almost six years ago. I'd gotten into bonsai in a big way, and I needed more space."

He opened the car door, waiting until they had gotten out so he could lock the car. He escorted them to the entrance in the fence.

"Welcome to my garden," he said, holding the gate open to let them pass through. "It's still a little early, but I'll turn the lights on. When it's dark, they add to the overall impact of the layout."

Sheila led the way, her sandals crunching on the surface underfoot. In the gathering darkness the bushes and flowers were somewhat shadowy. She didn't know what she had expected, but when the lights came on she couldn't hold back a sigh of pleasure.

Pathways crisscrossed the garden, each section a combination of different levels of slatted wood staging and small pools of water. Ceramic lanterns lit the paths, lending a magical aura to the place.

Although some of the plants had been dug into the soil, the bonsai trees and flowering shrubs were showcased on top of the wooden platforms. Floral perfumes scented the air.

"These are really weird, Dr. Santo," Meg said. With one finger extended, she touched the nearest miniature tree. "They almost look real."

"In actual fact they are real. Trees, alive and growing."

"You mean baby trees?"

"No. In some cases the trees are very old, but they're supposed to look like miniatures of larger trees. They are called *bonsai*. *Bon* means 'tray' and and *sai* means 'tree.' In other words, a tree growing in a container, like a dish or even a rock."

"So what happens when it grows up? It's going to be too big for the tray thing." With hands on her bent knees, Meg leaned over to study the little plant. "Do you cut off the top?"

"If you did, you'd lose the shape of the tree. You have to keep pruning it and pinching off the new leaves so the next set of leaves is smaller. It takes a lot of patience and a lot of care."

Sheila set her purse on the gravel path and moved closer, content to listen as Warren explained to Meg about the cultivation of the plants. Somewhere in the fenced space she could hear the soft tinkle of bells. When she heard them again, she left and walked toward the back of the garden. A slight breeze touched her cheek, and she followed the shimmer of sound that accompanied it.

When the path turned, she faced a grotto and found the source of the bells. Blending naturally with the other granite rocks surrounding a small pond was a chunk of marble about eight inches wide. Above this base, a spray of slender brass wires fanned out in a cluster. A brass cuplike blossom was attached to the tip of each wire. The merest breath of wind set the flower stems moving and, as the cups struck each other, harmonic music filled the air.

Sheila stood transfixed. The tones had a mesmerizing effect, and she was loath to move away. She lost track of time, content to view the hot pink water lily with heart shaped leaves that floated in the center of the pond. She was so relaxed that she wasn't even startled when she heard Warren's voice behind her.

"I hope you like my bell flowers," he said.

He was so close she could feel the breath of his words on her neck. She turned, smiling up into his face.

"They're wonderful. A perfect addition to the atmosphere you've created. Everything seems so natural and balanced."

"You have no idea what a compliment that is. One of the fundamental precepts of bonsai is to show empathy with and a respect for the shapes found in nature. By pruning the trees and designing the overall garden, one indicates mastery over nature. A sense that man can control destiny."

Sheila wasn't exactly sure she understood his words, but the garden had cast a spell, and she was willing to accept anything within its fenced walls.

"I've rarely felt such a sense of well-being as I do now," she admitted.

"Then come with me and I'll show you one more thing that I know you'll like."

Warren took her hand, leading her along the pebbly path to another section of the garden. Here too there was a pond, but this one was larger than the others she'd seen.

He pointed to a bench set in front of a dwarf crab apple tree, and she sat down on the slatted wood. Leaning over, he opened a plastic container beside the bench and removed a wooden box of polished rosewood. The box was ten inches long and six or seven inches in height and depth. Small rectangular openings like windows were cut into the sides and covered with metal screens. Warren moved closer so that Sheila could examine it.

"Inside are three hand-cast bells," he said, "that have been tuned to the notes used in Buddhist temple prayer. When I turn the box over and then upright again, the hundreds of little beads inside will strike the bells, and you'll understand why they're called rain bells. Would you like to hear them while I check on Meg?"

"Oh yes, please."

Warren inverted the box, turned it back to its original position, and set it down on the edge of the pond. The air around Sheila was filled with the sound of falling rain. She was so enchanted by the experience that she wasn't even aware when Warren left her. She leaned against the back of the bench, closed her eyes, and let the soft chimes draw the tension from her body.

The muffled sound of a beeper cut through the hypnotic sensation.

Several seconds passed before Sheila realized it was her pager. One glance at the readout and she was on her feet, heading for the entrance to the garden—rain bells, flowers, and ponds forgotten in her haste to locate the telephone in the purse she'd abandoned on the path.

Sheila had just completed her phone call when Warren and Meg, drawn by the sound of her voice, arrived at her side.

"Trouble?" he asked.

"I'm sorry, Warren, but I'll have to cut this visit short."

"Ah, Mom, do you have to go in to work?"

"I'm afraid so." Sheila leaned over and kissed Meg on the forehead.

"I could drop you at the police station, and Meg could stay here with me until you're finished at work." He smiled down at the girl. "I've enjoyed introducing her to my hobby."

"Can I, Mom? I promise I wouldn't be any trouble."

"I know you wouldn't, honey, but I don't have any idea how long I'll be." Hardening her heart to the disappointment on her daughter's face, Sheila looked up at Warren. "I truly do appreciate your offer, but I've already called my neighbor. She's a widow who lives alone and loves to help out when I have to work at night. Besides, my house is on the way to the station, so I can pick up my car."

Without further argument, he leaned down and patted the girl on the shoulder. "We'll just have to plan for another visit, Meg. Now that you've seen the garden at night, I'd like you to see it during the day. Then you'll see how unique the bonsai trees are."

Sheila was grateful for his easy acceptance of the situation. As a police officer she found it difficult to develop relationships with men. Most were intimidated by the perceived power of her job or were unwilling to accept the fact that duty came first over her social life. She knew Nick was troubled by that aspect of her job.

As a veterinarian Warren dealt with emergencies; he understood the necessity for instant response to a summons. He seemed to sense that her mind was already occupied, because he kept Meg busy during the drive, asking questions about school until they arrived back at the house.

"Here comes Mrs. Krueger," Meg said, opening the car door. "Thanks for everything, Dr. Santo. You won't forget to invite us over again, will you?"

"I promise."

He raised his hand as if swearing an oath, and Meg dashed off to meet the sitter.

Sheila winced. "What an outrageous child! Please ignore her."

"She's a delight. Just like her mother."

In the overhead light, she could see the tips of his ears redden after his remark. "I'm sorry we had to leave so . . ."

He cut her off. "A call at this time of night means an emergency, so you better get going. I'll talk to you another time."

Sheila gave him a smiling salute as she got out of the car. She suspected he would call her soon and had to admit the thought pleased her. Before he had reached the end of the block, she forced her mind away from the charming vet and focused on the night ahead.

"Bless you, Agnes, for helping out," she said as she unlocked the front door.

"Don't give it a thought. You know I love taking care of Meg. She's never an ounce of trouble." The older woman reached down to Elmo, who was waiting in his usual spot on the hall rug. She scratched his head, and the cat arched his neck in pleasure.

Sheila opened her arms to give Meg a hard embrace. "I'm sorry about tonight, sweetheart."

"That's OK, Mom." The girl squeezed her tightly around the waist. "I think Dr. Santo liked you, so maybe he'll call again."

"Maybe? Thanks for the vote of confidence."

Meg giggled. Sheila gave her a quick kiss and opened the door into the garage, closing it before the cat could follow her. Thank God for Agnes, she thought as she started the car. Whenever her neighbor came over in the evening, she was prepared to stay the night if necessary.

Sheila gripped the wheel, conscious of her speed as she drove toward the station house. She flipped on the police radio, informed Dispatch of her estimated arrival, and then listened in stunned silence to the details of the hostage incident.

"The girl's unhurt?"

"Not a scratch. He was holding her with a toy gun. Some kind of water gun, but at first glimpse it looked real enough."

"Is he a nut case?"

"No. More like a druggie. He was high and came in to rob the store. One of the customers ran out and nabbed a passing cop. In his panic, he took the store clerk hostage. Pazzarini negotiated his ass off. The guy released the girl and came out without a fuss. He was arrested and brought in a couple hours ago. He's down in the lockup."

"Who sent me the emergency call?" Sheila asked, wondering why she'd been beeped so long after the fact.

"Chief Harker."

"I'm on my way," she said and disconnected.

The station house was ablaze with lights, and she could see the news vans parked in front as she pulled into the parking lot. She entered through the back door, taking notice of the charged atmosphere in the squad room as she headed for Harker's office. He saw her through the window and waved her in.

"Close the door and grab a seat, Lieutenant Brady," he said without preamble.

Totally mystified, she followed his instructions. "I hear you had some excitement tonight. The hostage-taker is in the house?"

"He's just been processed." A certain smugness showed in Harker's face. "Pazzarini did an outstanding job of talking the guy out. His name is Vincent Calero. He's twenty-two, five feet ten, medium build with shoulder-length, light brown hair. Any of this ring a bell?"

Sheila shook her head. "Not to me. Where does he live?"

"He was reluctant to give up his address at first. Eventually he admitted to living in a tent in Worley Woods."

"Near where the kids were found?"

"He said no. Said the tent was on the far south end of the woods. He gave Dandy Dan and Paz directions, and I sent them to get a search warrant and to toss the place. They just got back."

Sheila was aware that Harker was doling out the information. She didn't know if he was trying to prepare her for some nasty piece of information or had something else in mind. Never certain of his attitude toward her, she felt more off balance than usual.

"Did they find anything?" she asked, prompted by his silence.

"They found this," he said.

Harker opened the top drawer of his desk and pulled out a small plastic bag with a crime scene tag attached to the top. He set the bag down in the center of his blotter. Sheila leaned forward to examine the contents.

Inside was a shoelace.

She felt the blood drain away from her face. Lightheaded, she stared down at the plastic bag.

"You're a cop, Sheila. Don't even consider fainting," Harker barked.

Perhaps it was the shock of his using her name instead of her rank that snapped her out of the spell of dizziness. She leaned back in her chair and took a deep steadying breath. His remark about fainting made her angry. Swooning away like some Victorian heroine was not her style. She just needed a moment to deal with the sight of the single shoelace.

It was too late to block it out. She'd seen the words. A girl's name was printed in blue and repeated all along the flat pink lace. The name echoed over and over in Sheila's mind.

Lindy. Lindy. Lindy.

Chapter Ten

"Lindy Pottinger was wearing shoelaces just like this one on the day she disappeared," Sheila said, staring at the plastic bag on his desk.

"Are you sure?" Hank asked.

"Positive. A couple of weeks before she died, I took Lindy and my daughter to the mall. We bought the shoelaces at Richter's Shoe Shack. My Meg has a pair with her name on them." She took a shuddering breath and raised her head. "Did they find Lindy's shoes?"

"No. Just the single lace. Vincent Calero says he found it in the woods. He swears he can't remember where."

"Is it possible that he's the killer?"

"According to our boy Vinnie, he was in rehab for about six months. He was released July fifth. The day after Lindy Pottinger's body was found. Paz is running a check on his story, so we should know pretty soon if he's in or out as a suspect."

"What's he doing living in a tent around here? Is he from River Oaks?"

"No. He's got a sister in town. Francine Calero. She works at Heads First, the beauty shop in the mall. She came in a little while ago to answer some questions. Twenty-six, big hair, big eyes, short skirt. She's tough, but apparently has a soft spot for her brother."

"If everything's quiet now," Sheila said, "why did you beep me?"

"The press knows something's up, but I haven't released a state-ment yet. I wouldn't want Lindy's parents to hear about the shoelace on TV or read it in the paper." Hank sighed at the continued heartache for the families of the murdered girls. "I was planning to give the Pottingers a call, but I thought it would be easier for them to hear it from a friend. If you don't mind, you could stop over and tell them."

"I don't mind at all. Dorothy Pottinger and I were good friends before the murder."

He looked across at her. The soft curls caught at the nape of her neck, the glitter of jewelry at her ears, the lacy-looking blouse, and the short denim skirt all combined to give him a view of Sheila as an attractive and warm young woman. For the first time Hank saw be-neath the shell of competence and efficiency that she used to keep people, especially him, at a distance.

She shifted in her chair. "Is that all, Chief?"

He shifted his gaze, shrugging away any but professional feelings for the woman across from him.

"One more thing. I wanted to ask you a few questions about Doug Maloney."

"My ex-partner?" Sheila blinked in confusion. "He's on the job in Milwaukee."

"Not anymore. He quit and took a job on the Madison force."

"Did he really? We sort of lost contact when I moved out here."

So much for Maloney's suggestion that they were close friends, Hank thought. "I think there's something you need to know," he said.

His words triggered a withdrawal on Sheila's part as if she sus-pected that she wasn't going to like what he had to say. Watching her, he told her that Lois had found Doug's fingerprints on the box with the bloody doll. Surprisingly, her first reaction was relief.

"Thank God that mystery is solved." Some of the tightness around her mouth disappeared, and she sagged back in her chair. "I've been trying to decide what to do. I was afraid that the box might have been sent by the killer. I told you I didn't think so, but there was a part of my mind that wondered. Meg has practically been under house arrest ever since the box was delivered."

"How do you know that Maloney isn't the killer?" Hank asked out of curiosity.

She pursed her lips and shook her head. "Not Doug. His method is intimidation. Lots of bark and a machismo attitude. Sending that box would be just the kind of thing he'd do."

"For a joke?"

"Doug never jokes. It was probably meant to freak me out, and I'm sorry to say it worked."

"So why did he send it to you?"

Sheila changed positions in her chair, tugging her skirt over her knees and smoothing the lace edging on her blouse.

"I think in order to answer that I need to tell you about the shooting that IAD investigated. Doug thinks the reason he got shot was my fault. He said my yelling distracted him so the drug dealer was able to take his gun."

"Why were you yelling?"

"I wanted Doug to step away. It looked like he was trying to hit the perp with his gun. Once the drug dealer had the gun, Doug said I froze and just watched him shoot."

"Is this guesswork on your part, or did he verbalize this to you?"

"He told me." Sheila ducked her head to hide the embarrassed flush that rose to her cheeks. "All the time I was trying to stop the bleeding on his leg, he cursed me for my stupidity."

"And did you freeze?"

"I don't think so," she said, her voice reflective. "I have no proof, only a gut instinct that I reacted true to my training. That night, I was badly shaken up over killing the drug dealer. Doug was so convinced I had hesitated that I began to question my actions."

Hank ran both hands over the top of his brush cut, then locked them behind his head. "Why didn't any of this appear in the report?"

"When Doug heard the sirens outside, I think it snapped him out of his anger. He'd lost a lot of blood and was getting weaker. I think he hated most the fact he'd been shot with his own gun."

Sheila's eyes were unfocused as she retold the story.

"He grabbed my hand and said he'd been distracted when I came in yelling, and that enabled the perp to wrench the gun out of his hand. By killing the guy, I'd saved his, Doug's, life. When the paramedics and backup arrived, he was still conscious and gave them a statement before they put him in the ambulance."

Hank leaned forward. "He gave the first statement?"

"Yes. I was right there so I heard every word. When it was my turn I agreed with his story. Ever since then I've been bothered about that."

"Bothered that you hadn't been totally truthful?"

She shook her head. "No. The story we told was exactly the way that it happened. The only difference was that my professional conduct was never called into question. If I did hesitate or freeze, I was responsible for causing the death of another person. Admittedly the drug dealer wasn't much of a loss to society, but my actions endangered my partner. And in the future could endanger others."

Her final words came out in a rush. She sagged against the back of her chair, as if the confession had sapped her strength.

Maloney had lied. He'd said he hadn't talked to Sheila about the incident but had overheard her statement and had just gone along with her version. It sounded to Hank as though the man was trying to cover the fact that his attempt to beat the dealer was the reason his gun was taken. Doug Maloney was a first-class jerk.

Hank could understand what had been eating away at Sheila. Her concern was whether her actions or lack of them had caused an unnecessary death and put her partner at risk.

"It's up to you, Sheila, to make the judgment call on whether you hesitated or not. My opinion doesn't count. Think carefully, because whatever you decide will affect how you perform your job in the future."

Sheila accepted his words without comment.

"What was your working relationship with Maloney prior to the shooting?" he asked.

"Good. Our styles were totally different, but that seemed to work to our advantage. His reflexes were faster, so he usually drove. I was better watching the action on the street. He was big and intimidating, and I could go the softer route. You know how partners mesh."

Hank nodded. "Does he have an uncontrollable temper?"

"No. He used his anger when he knew it would work for us. Usually in some sort of face-to-face confrontation."

Hank caught the momentary hesitation before she responded and wondered if she were thinking of the night of the shooting. It wasn't uncommon for anger to follow in the wake of a tense situation, and even more common in the case of one that was life-threatening.

"What's his attitude toward women? Animosity? Disinterest?"

Sheila's eyebrow raised on the last word. "He's not gay if that's what you're asking. He's compulsively male. I think he feels obliged to hit on every woman for fear of disappointing her."

"Were you disappointed?"

"Very tactful, Chief." For the first time since the conversation began, Sheila smiled. "Of course he hit on me. He also was very annoyed when I turned him down. He sulked for a week, but eventually we got back to a solid professional relationship."

Hank could see that she believed the latter to be true. He'd be interested to hear what Maloney had to say about her rejection. During the interview he had referred to Sheila as the ice queen. It was easier for guys like Maloney to blame the turndown on the woman rather than admit to any shortcomings.

"The reason I'm asking so many questions about Maloney is I'm trying to decide if he's somehow tied in to the murders."

"I think you're on the wrong tangent, Chief. Knowing Doug, it's easy for me to believe he sent the bloody doll. It's in character. Murder isn't."

"Do you know him well enough to make that judgment?"

She cocked her head to the side and thought over his question. "Do we ever know anyone that well? What I do know is, if Doug committed a murder, he'd know enough to dispose of any physical evidence. He'd never leave that shoelace in a place where anyone could stumble on it."

"That could be," Hank said. "However, I'm not willing to take any chances. I'm cautioning you to be careful if you run into him. I don't like the fact he sent something to you relating to the murders. Until I'm certain he's not involved, I'm putting Doug Maloney on the suspect list."

•

By morning the station house was under siege by reporters, waiting for news on the robbery at the convenience store. Sheila elbowed her way through the crowd, dodging cameras and microphones as she made her way into the building. It was a relief to close the door behind the shouted questions. She was short on sleep and felt emotionally drained.

The previous evening she had gone directly from her talk with Chief Harker to the Pottinger house. Dorothy had known when she opened the door that Sheila had come about the murders. They had seen each other frequently since Lindy's death, but the friendship they once shared had disappeared. The Pottingers blamed the police for not catching the killer before he murdered their child, and as part of the force, Sheila shared in that blame. As gently as she could, Sheila told Dorothy about the shoelace. They cried together and then talked about Lindy. When Sheila left, she felt as though the discussion had brought some peace to both of them.

Seated at her desk this morning, Sheila could feel a headache coming on. She could hear the confusion outside, and it didn't improve her disposition. The phone on her desk rang. Annoyed, she snatched up the receiver.

"Bad day?" Nick's deep voice hummed through the phone lines, and she could feel the muscles of her back relax.

"As long as you ask, yes, I've had a rotten morning," Sheila said. "Meg misplaced her house keys. She was late getting up, so we didn't have time to search the house. This is the third time this month."

"Kids! They do the damnedest things."

Sheila chuckled at Nick's sarcasm. He had a way of putting small annoyances into perspective.

"Thanks. I needed that."

"My news won't improve your day. I can't make lunch today."

Sheila's eyes opened wide at his words. She'd completely forgotten about it. Guilt washed over her. She had remembered the dinner with Warren Santo but not the lunch with Nick.

"Don't worry, Nick. Let me grab my calendar and see if we can reschedule."

She took the day planner out of her briefcase and opened it to the right date. Today was Thursday, September twelfth. Nine more days until the twenty-first, she thought with a sinking feeling in her stomach.

"What's tomorrow look like?" she asked.

"Lunch?"

"If I can bring Meg. She only has a half day of school."

"That would be great. I have something for her."

"Not another cat, I hope?"

"Meg told me you were crazy about Elmo." He laughed, and the sound made Sheila forget her irritation for a moment. "It's not a cat, but it is animal-related: you forgot your cow picture. I think Meg will value it more than you do."

Now it was Sheila's turn to laugh. "Oh, she'll love it. She gets out of school at noon. Where do you want to meet?"

"How about Hogan's Place up by the library?"

"I've never been there, but I'm game."

"Then we *have* to go there. It's the best place to eat in River Oaks. Chuck makes a mean corned beef sandwich, and Jo's soup is unbeatable. I'll get there a little before noon to nail down a table. Come when you can."

"Terrific. Meg was muttering about you the other night. For some reason she misses you. She's going for an overnight at Beth's tomorrow, so it will be good for all three of us to be together."

"So you'll be alone." His voice deepened. "How about spending the weekend in Chicago with me? I'm going in to take some pictures of the city. It's only a four-hour drive. Just think, we could see a play and go to the art museum. Something a dash more highbrow than the historical society's show, 'River Oaks, the Pioneer Days.'"

"What could beat that?" Sheila sighed. "It's really a temptation, Nick, but I'll have to take a rain check. I'm swamped, and I'm using Meg's absence to catch up on some work."

"You ever hear the saying about all work and no play?" His voice held a hint of irritation. "I don't know how you expect our relationship to progress when you won't let me get closer. I share my work with you, but you totally shut me out."

"We've had this discussion before, Nick. You know I can't discuss current cases. I may never be able to share my work in the way you do."

"I won't bug you now, Sheila, but sometime we need to talk about what part of your life you *are* willing to share."

Knowing exactly what he meant didn't make it any easier to hear, and she had to make a concentrated effort to prevent their conversation from escalating into a real fight.

After she hung up, she sat for a moment trying to sort out her feelings. Nick wanted a more committed relationship, yet something held her back. She didn't know if her caution stemmed from her failed first marriage or from the realization that her attraction to Nick was mainly sexual. Much as she enjoyed being with him, she had never pictured walking hand in hand into the future with Nick Biagi.

To complicate things further, there was her undeniable interest in Dr. Warren Santo.

Shoving aside her personal problems, she quickly looked through the papers on her desk. There was nothing there that couldn't wait. She scribbled off several notes, then gathered her things, anxious to get out of the station house before she got another call.

This might be the perfect time to check out Herb Reisler, she decided, as she headed for the stairs to the back door. She ran the gauntlet of reporters and drove the two blocks into town.

The Book Nook was located in a section of small stores facing onto Hodges Park. Sheila drove around to the back and found Herb's teal-green Corolla parked next to the metal back door.

One barred window in back of the store looked out on the parking lot. Inside she could see boxes piled up, covering almost all of the glass. Driving around to the front, she parked the car and walked along the sidewalk to the bookstore.

As she opened the front door, Herb Reisler looked up from the customer he was helping.

He was tall and slightly stoop-shouldered. His face was weatherbeaten, deep grooves running from nose to mouth. With his full head of graying hair and faded blue eyes, he had a grandfatherly look.

Although she'd been in the store once before, Sheila looked around, taking in the details as she picked out some books that would be appropriate for Meg. The book showroom was painted canary yellow, and colorful posters of Disney characters, Star Trek figures, and movie stars were taped to the walls. It was a nice mix for all ages. Even a teenager wouldn't feel out of place in the cheerful atmosphere.

The bookcases varied in height, which made the room seem inviting rather than claustrophobic. To add to the casual atmosphere, brightly colored beanbag chairs dotted the serviceable carpeting.

"What can I do for you, Lieutenant Brady?"

Sheila jumped at the sound of Herb's voice. She'd been so engrossed in observing the details of the store that she hadn't even heard his approach. More surprising was his use of her name. She shifted the books she had gathered to her left arm and held out her hand.

The older man ducked his head shyly as he shook hands. His grip was limp and somewhat clammy; she controlled the urge to wipe the palm of her hand on her slacks.

"You must have a fantastic memory to recall all your customers' names."

A flush of red colored Herb's cheeks. "I saw you interviewed the other night on one of the Madison stations."

"That interview was not my finest moment."

"You did seem a bit flustered, but you handled yourself with grace and charm."

He had such a paternal expression on his face that when he reached for the stack of books in her arms, she handed them to him without question and followed him to the sales counter at the back of the showroom. She pulled out her credit card and set it on the countertop.

While he wrote up the transaction, she used the opportunity to examine the remainder of the store. Through an archway behind the counter, she could see a small office on one side of a short hall that led to a door marked STORAGE. Across from the office was a bathroom.

"All set, Lieutenant."

Sheila signed the credit card slip, and Herb pushed the bag of books across the counter.

"I'm working on the investigation into the murders of the four children," she said.

A flash of apprehension crossed his face, and his lips pulled together in a tight line. "It breaks my heart every time I think about those innocent young girls."

"Did you know them, Mr. Reisler?"

"Yes, of course. All four of them." He seemed surprised that she would ask. "You see, girls between nine and twelve are my best customers. At that age, they're a little afraid of growing up, and they hide from real life in a world of fantasy. Reading and movies are their sources of escape. Horses, fairy tales, and girlfriend stories sell amazingly well."

"Were these four girls friends?"

"Not that I'm aware of. I don't believe they ever came in together, although they could have been in the store at the same time. That I wouldn't notice. What I do remember was that each of the girls was an avid reader."

Sheila jotted several lines in her notebook. "Do you work here alone, Mr. Reisler?"

"For part of the day. I open the store at ten in the morning, and I'm alone here until two in the afternoon when my assistant, Josephine Iatesta, comes in."

"Could you give me her address and phone number?"

"Oh, she's here right now, working on purchase orders in the office. Would you like to talk to her?"

"If that's all right with you."

"Just a moment." He disappeared through the archway; after a moment of muffled discussion, he returned with a small, birdlike woman in her sixties. "Josephine, this is Lieutenant Brady. She has some questions for both of us about the murders."

Josephine's pale blue-eyed gaze sharpened as she glanced between Sheila and Herb. She folded her hands and pressed them against her flat chest. The ringless fingers shook slightly.

"There's no need to be nervous, Ms. Iatesta," Sheila said. "I wondered if anything unusual had happened on the days when the children disappeared."

"Mr. Reisler and I have talked about this so often." Her face scrunched up as if she were going to cry. "It's so hard to remember back that far, but as I recall, nothing out of the ordinary happened. I'm sure we would have talked about it if anything had."

"It's a long time since the first murder. Most people can't remember much about that day." Sheila hoped her offhand tone would lessen the older woman's agitation.

Josephine gave Sheila a tentative smile. "I know we both worked on the days the children disappeared. That was all anyone spoke about when they came into the store. The children . . ."

Her voice drifted into silence. Sheila noted the sheen of tears in her eyes before Josephine turned away.

"And prior to the last murder?"

"It was a Tuesday," Herb said. "The store was very busy. It was two days before the Fourth of July celebrations, and many people were buying books for vacation trips over the long weekend."

"Did you both work that day?"

Josephine nodded her tightly permed gray head. "Yes. Like always. I came in at two."

"I opened the store," Herb said. "I worked until five. I went home, ate dinner, and watched television."

"On the day Lindy disappeared, did you see Mr. Reisler when you came in, Ms. Iatesta?"

"Well, of course I did." She loosened her grip, and her fingers fluttered across the sales slips beside the cash register. "I always check in with Herb—eh—Mr. Reisler when I arrive."

"And when he leaves?" Sheila asked.

Herb interrupted. "When I'm ready to leave I just go out the back door. Usually Josephine has customers or is counting the register, so I don't bother her."

"I doubt if I'd remember if he said anything or not before he left. The days are fairly similar, so it's hard to single out any event unless it's quite unusual. To answer your question, I don't recall when he left on that day. All I know is that Mr. Reisler was not in his office when I locked the store. And that was five-thirty."

Sheila closed her notebook and smiled at the older woman. "Thank you so much, Ms. Iatesta. I appreciate your cooperation."

Before the sentence was completed, Josephine was already hurrying back to the office. Herb came out from behind the counter, picked up Sheila's bag of books, and walked her to the front of the store. With her hand on the door handle, Sheila turned to face him.

"Oh, by the way, Mr. Reisler," Sheila said, "I have one more question. After each of the last three murders, a crowd of people gathered in the parking lot of Sandrik's grocery store. I wonder if you could tell me why you were there on all three occasions."

Herb's face went ashen. Even the color in his lips faded. He would have dropped the bag of books if Sheila hadn't taken them out of his hands. His lips moved, but he didn't speak. Worried that he was having a heart attack, she led him over to the wooden chair beside the front door. He was oblivious to his surroundings. She pressed him down on the chair seat.

"Are you all right, Mr. Reisler?" she asked.

"I knew I shouldn't do it," he said, his voice so quiet she had to strain to catch the words. "The first time it was accidental."

At his words, Sheila set her books and purse on the floor and knelt down beside Herb's chair. His head was bowed, and he was hunched over as if he were exhausted.

"What was accidental, Mr. Reisler?"

He was motionless for a minute, and she wondered if he'd heard her question. Finally he sighed and raised his head, speaking directly to her.

"I was in the grocery store when Tiffany's body was found in the woods. By the time I came out, a crowd had formed. There were news trucks and cameras and lights. It was chaos, but it was also very exciting."

His eyes were questioning as he scanned her face. She nodded, understanding what he meant.

"The crowd was pressed close together, and people were talking to each other. Everyone had an opinion. The death of a child touches everyone. We all needed to talk. Maybe it was just a way to hold back the fear," Herb said.

He paused again but Sheila made no comment.

"No one has time to talk anymore," he said. "They hurry in and buy something and hurry out. It was nice to be included in that big crowd of people. Sharing our thoughts and even our fears. After it was over, I felt such a sense of community."

"So when the next body was discovered, you went back?"

Herb nodded. "It was the same. People talking. Reporters taping reports. All very exciting. Then when Lindy was killed I just couldn't stay away. It was like a guilty pleasure. I hoped no one knew I'd come there all three times. I was afraid people would think I was an old fool looking for excitement."

He sat up straight and leaned against the back of the chair. It was apparent that he felt tremendous relief having told her the story. She wondered if he had anything else to tell.

"Did you have anything to do with the disappearance of the girls?" she asked.

His eyes opened wide and he took a gasp of air. "Oh, my goodness, no!" he said. "Believe me, Lieutenant Brady, I had absolutely nothing to do with the murders. I'll admit I knew all four girls, but I would never have done anything to hurt them."

Sheila could see he was appalled by her question. His outrage appeared genuine, and she was inclined to believe him.

"I'm not suggesting you did, Mr. Reisler. Unfortunately I have to ask that question. I appreciate your telling me the reason you were in the parking lot. So unless there's something else you'd like to talk about, I'm finished."

Herb shook his head. Sheila picked up the books and her purse. She opened the door. Herb struggled to his feet.

"Thank you for coming, Lieutenant Brady," he said, once more the gracious store owner.

Back in the car, Sheila wrote up her notes and added them to the file she had begun on Herb Reisler. Seeing Herb on the television news, she had considered him a viable suspect. After talking to him, she wasn't so sure. It was more likely that Herb Reisler was a lonely old man, not the River Oaks Killer.

•

"Ray?" Bessie's voice floated up the stairwell. "What in heaven's name are you doing up in the attic?"

"Just looking for something," Ray Florio shouted, hoping she wouldn't make the trip up the stairs to check on him.

"Sakes, I've been calling all over the house looking for you. Jim, your patrol partner, called. There's been a change in the schedule. He wants you to call him."

"I'll call him later."

"All right, dear. Don't you go and make a mess of things up there. Lunch will be ready in ten minutes."

"I'll be down shortly," he said.

Ray listened until he heard her moving along the upper hallway to return to the first floor. He shifted the last of the storage boxes from in front of the old maple dresser.

The dresser had been his when he was a kid growing up on the farm with his two brothers. He'd been the oldest, the first to get married. He could still remember his parents' disapproval that he and Bessie were going to live in an apartment in town instead of remaining on the farm. Despite their feelings, his parents suggested he take his bedroom set. He and Bessie had been delighted because they couldn't afford to outfit a whole apartment with furniture.

Those had been wonderful hardscrabble years, he thought as he stared at the scarred surface of the dresser. Too bad his son and Nancy hadn't had more time together. Ray Jr. had traveled a lot before she got the cancer.

What's the saying? Life's hard and then you die.

He opened the narrow tie drawer, wondering if anyone kept a whole drawer full of ties nowadays. Everything was so casual. He could remember a time when men were required to wear jackets and ties for dinner at Tony McGuire's Lake House. Four years ago when the marina was built on Lake Lynn, the standards loosened up to lure in the boating crowd. Now only the old geezers wore ties.

Working his way through each of the drawers, Ray found the shoebox wedged in the back of the second drawer from the bottom. Carefully he pulled it out and set it down on the old coffee table beside the dresser. Wiping his dusty hands on the sides of his pants, he lifted the lid.

He removed the rolled-up dark green hand towel and set it down on the table. The terry cloth was old and stiff from disuse. Carefully he unwound the fabric.

In the center was a snub-nosed revolver and six bullets.

Chapter Eleven

Ray picked up the gun.

It was a .38-caliber Smith & Wesson. He liked the contrast between the dark metal of the gun and the deep brown of the checkered wood handgrip. He hefted it in his hand. It was a good weight. Nothing bulky.

The instant his hand closed on the grip, he stood taller, shoulders back, head held high. He could understand why young punks carried guns with them; physical limitations no longer mattered. Brute strength wasn't required to go up against an enemy. With a gun, you were invincible. Death was in the palm of your hand.

Growing up on a farm, Ray had learned to hunt, fish, and shoot. It was a natural progression in his journey to manhood. He'd tried to bring Ray Jr. up that way, but Bessie balked about the boy's learning to shoot.

She'd forgotten what a comfort the gun had been to her when he was traveling. He'd tried to explain that the world was much less safe than when they were first married, but she was adamant. After Nancy died and the grandkids had come to stay with them, Bessie told him to get rid of the gun. Instead, he'd hidden it in the attic, figuring that someday he'd need it.

The time had come.

Monday's intruder call while he and Jim were on patrol had really freaked him out. He'd never thought about what could happen if they came across real danger. As they raced to the area Ray considered his chances in a fight. He felt naked. Unarmed, he was useless.

They had been lucky that the intruder turned out to be a friend of Jim's. What if it had been a burglar or even the River Oaks Killer? Ray never wanted to be in a situation again where he felt so helpless.

From the beginning, some members of Parent Watch had mentioned carrying guns. Ray thought most of the talk was just that: a preening display of bravado by the young cocks on patrol. Now he understood.

He scooped up the bullets, wrapped them in his handkerchief, and shoved them in his pocket. He tucked the gun in his belt underneath the sweater vest. Before dinner he'd take it down to the basement.

Today was Thursday. Friday, Bessie had her garden club meeting, and the grandkids would be in school. He'd clean the gun and find a place in the garage to stash it until his next patrol shift.

Ray used the hand towel to dust away any evidence that he'd been going through the dresser. Bessie was as tenacious as a badger on a scent. She'd be up here tomorrow, poking around, trying to figure out what he'd been doing.

He grinned as he touched the slight bulge at his beltline. It had been a long time since he'd kept a secret from Bessie.

At the bottom of the attic stairs, he eyed the picture of his mother hanging on the wall. A shiver ran down his spine. He remembered how Mama used to cock her head and narrow her eyes whenever he tried to put something past her. She always said the same thing: "Take care, Raymond. Secrets can kill you."

•

Sheila looked up at the sky when she got out of the car at the River Oaks Mall. It was starting to cloud over. It looked as if the forecast had been right. Meg had grumbled, but taken a sweatshirt with her to school; now it was clear she'd need it. The wind whipped Sheila's skirt around her knees. The chill of fall was in the air. Pushing open the glass entry door, she looked at the directory to locate Richter's Shoe Shack.

The mall was a long rectangle with a six-screen movie theater at one end and Hartmann's department store at the other. The mall was only three years old and had proved to be a financial asset for the town as well as a social success for the community. One of the proposed additions was a teen center, but so far the plans had not been approved by the city council.

She sighed at the knee-length mink and leather jacket in the window of Porges Furrier. Winters in Wisconsin could be brutal. Too bad she couldn't afford such an extravagance. In the next window a soft blue wool dress caught her eye. It was a simple belted shirtwaist with pouch pockets on the front of the slightly flared skirt. Soft, cozy, and feminine, she thought.

"It would be perfect for a dinner and play in Madison."

Sheila jumped at the voice behind her. She caught Warren Santo's reflection in the store window. Without turning around, she smiled, and she could see the answering flash of white teeth in the glass.

"Is that an invitation?" she asked.

"Could be."

Pivoting, she faced him and said, "I was going to call you later. I'm sorry about last night."

He waved away her apology. Flipping open his jacket, he pointed to the pager clipped to his belt.

"Now I'm the one who's got a page."

"An emergency?"

His expression lightened at her question. A corner of his mouth lifted, and his eyes twinkled down at her.

"You know Alice McKann, don't you?"

"Yes. Her son is in Meg's class."

"You might not know she raises prize-winning Airedales. Tragedy has struck. A neighbor's mutt got loose, and," Warren's ears reddened, "as Alice watched in horror, Busterboy serviced Queen Mav of Dunworthy."

"Tragedy indeed." Sheila lost the struggle to keep a straight face. "The queen deflowered."

"Worse than that," he said, eyebrows lifted archly. "The line could be contaminated by peasant stock."

"I was just considering asking you to join me for a late lunch, but I can see you're needed to save the Dunworthy lineage."

"It seems I'm the one to cut our meeting short today. I'll take a rain check though." He was clearly pleased by the invitation. "And if you get the dress, I'll invite you for dinner in Madison."

Sheila watched as he waved and walked toward the exit, wondering what it was about the man that intrigued her. He was good-looking, but so were a lot of other men who'd asked her out. He wasn't much of a talker, but she sensed a mutual attraction, and she liked the fact he wasn't aggressive in his approach.

She cocked her head, considering the blue dress again. Perhaps she'd try it on after she'd finished her business in the mall. She hadn't bought anything in a while, and it looked like a warm and practical dress for the fall.

"Who are you kidding, Brady?" she said under her breath, turning away from the temptation.

In the center of the mall was an exhibit of the latest bow-hunting equipment and accessories, along with several racks of camouflage clothing. A wide cloth banner hung above the display. The black letters were six inches tall, stark against the iridescent red fabric. Sheila laughed when she read the words.

"Buy Now. Be Prepared for the Fall Rutting Season."

•

"Don't worry so much. The place is empty."

Recognizing the mayor's voice, Hank hunched over his beer, hoping that he, and whoever he was with, wouldn't come into the bar. Besides, this was Monroeville, fifty miles from River Oaks. Hank had been playing golf, but what was Dick Perkins doing there, so far from home?

"We'll have to make it a quick lunch. It's a long drive back."

The female voice made Hank immediately aware of a potentially uncomfortable situation. The woman who had spoken was not Carolyn Perkins, Dick's wife.

"It's too dark in the bar. Let's sit over by the windows," Perkins said.

Hank sighed with relief as their voices faded into the other room. He probably shouldn't jump to conclusions. Perhaps the mayor was taking his secretary, Bianca, out to lunch. The older woman was gaunt and looked as if she could use a good meal. A soft tinkling laugh that came from the dining room, however, convinced him that it was not Bianca Cozzi.

Hank tossed a couple of bills on the bar beside his empty beer glass. The mayor's lunch might be perfectly innocent, but there was no point risking possible embarrassment. He'd get out while he could.

He had to admit to a certain curiosity about the identity of the woman, though. Her voice had sounded familiar. As he exited the bar, Hank risked a glance at the woman seated across the table from Dick Perkins.

He recognized her immediately. Only a week ago he had visited her home and talked to her. The woman lunching with Perkins was Barbara Davis, the mother of the first murdered girl.

Outside, he pulled out a cigar, biting the end off and spitting the piece on the ground. He lit it, taking several puffs before his anger began to dissipate.

Driving back to River Oaks, Hank paid little attention to the fall colors. His mind was busy going over the details of the investigation into Janette Davis's murder. By the time he reached the police parking lot, he thought he had the answer to one of the questions that had nagged him during the original investigation.

Back in his office, he turned on his computer, pulled up his files on the first murder and went through his observations on the case. He jotted down notations, cross-checked them against the summary of the first murder, and then made a quick scan through some of the original reports.

For some time before the murder, Barbara Davis had held a secretarial position with Judge Paula Craig. Hank had interviewed the judge, who told him Barbara was good at her job and, as far as she could tell, didn't have any particular friends, male or female, at City Hall.

At the time of the murder of the Davis girl, Dick Perkins wasn't yet mayor, but rather a lawyer in private practice. He would have been in and out of City Hall on a daily, or at least weekly, basis. It was more than likely that he and Barbara Davis had known each other.

Even considering the little Hank had seen of Barbara and Dick at the restaurant, he'd sensed an easygoing relationship of long standing. Checking back on Barbara's list of who she knew in town or had any connection with, he found that Dick Perkins's name never had been mentioned.

Hank's mouth hardened with irritation as he remembered all the briefings he'd given Perkins after the election. The mayor might not be guilty of murder, but at the very least he had been guilty of deception in hiding the fact he was acquainted with Barbara Davis and her daughter.

He stood angrily and turned to stare out the window, blind to the scene outside. It was lucky that Perkins was still away, off having lunch with Barbara Davis, or he'd go over and confront him about obstructing the investigation.

"Stupid jerk!"

"Sorry." Sheila Brady stood in the partially opened doorway, her eyes wide with apprehension. Backing out of the room, she said, "I'll come back later."

"Get in here," Hank barked. "And close the door."

She hesitated just long enough to bring him back to his senses. "I'm sorry. I was just venting. It has nothing to do with you."

When he jerked his head toward a chair, she let go of the doorknob and crossed the room. She sat on the edge of the seat, hands folded on the notebook in her lap, feet crossed beneath her chair. Her schoolgirl demeanor amused him, lightening his mood.

He circled around behind his desk but didn't sit down. He had to get to the bottom of this new development as soon as possible, and Sheila could help him. He might have personal reservations about her abilities under pressure, but he knew she had a quick, intuitive mind and was an excellent interviewer.

"You wanted to see me?" he asked.

The abrupt question made her jump. "Nothing that can't wait."

"I don't want to wait. Tell me what's up, and then I want to give you another assignment."

The offer of another assignment seemed to convince her that his anger wasn't directed at her. She sat back in the chair and told him about her interview with Herb Reisler.

"What's your feeling about Herb? Do you think he's a good suspect?"

Sheila grimaced, her blue eyes troubled. "I'll admit he looks like a good suspect. He knew the girls. They probably would have gone with him if he offered them a ride. He was at Sandrik's grocery store after the last three bodies were discovered. Even with all that, I don't like the feel of it. Reisler strikes me as a kind and lonely man. He doesn't seem bent."

"I've known Herb for years, and I have the same general feeling." Hank pulled out his chair and dropped down into the seat. "For the time being we'll keep him on the suspect list. Over the years, I've learned that even seemingly nice people can do very bad things. Anything else?"

"Yes. One more thing. I dropped by the Shoe Shack. I remember Gayle Richter told me she bought the business from Ebenezer Jimson, who had a store over by the hospital."

"Old Ebenezer was a real character," Hank said, wondering where she was going with this.

"My grandfather owned a shoe store," she said. "He knew all his customers by name. He liked to say he had fitted shoes for four generations. In the back room he had rows of ledgers where he'd entered all the purchases made in each family over the years. He could look back and tell you what your shoe size was when you were twelve. On a whim, I asked her if Ebenezer Jimson had ledgers like that."

"Did he?"

Sheila looked up at him, triumph clearly written in the sparkle of her eyes. "I just checked them into the file room."

"Nice going, Sheila." In his enthusiasm, he smacked the arm of the chair with his open palm. "Are they like your grandfather's?"

"More or less. Not as accurate as Ebenezer got older. The writing's shaky and hard to read in some places."

"Don't worry. I'll put Lois Coren on it. She'll decipher them."

"While I was at it, I looked up Herb Reisler's shoe size. Unless his foot has grown or changed in the last ten years, he wears a size ten shoe."

"The same size as the Upland Hiker print at the scene of the third murder."

"Exactly." She grinned and closed her notebook.

Her eyes are her weakness, Hank thought, as he stared across the desk. She could control her facial expression, but he could read the emotion in her eyes. He wondered what her life was like and why she'd become a cop in the first place. He'd seen the vulnerability beneath the surface control and was curious.

"You have another assignment for me?" she asked.

Hank dropped his gaze and shuffled through his notes until he could organize his thoughts. Clearing his throat, he glanced at her, his attitude all business.

"I'd like you to interview Barbara Davis, the mother of the first victim."

"Any particular angle you want me to pursue?" Sheila asked.

He brushed his hand over the bristly top of his head. "I checked my notes on her. She said she'd initially moved from Green Bay to River Oaks because she got a great job offer. Rumor had it that she was having an affair with someone who lived here, although no one in Green Bay or in River Oaks could confirm the existence of a boyfriend."

He told her about seeing Davis and Perkins at the restaurant and his suspicions about a prior relationship.

"Any idea whether Dick used to spend time in Green Bay?" she asked.

"Yes. His brother lives there." Hank could feel the muscles in his jaw tightening with a new surge of anger.

"So you're putting Perkins on the suspect list because you think he's having an affair with the mother of the first victim?"

"No. I'm putting him on the list because I think it's highly suspicious that he never told me he knew Barbara Davis and her daughter."

A frown pulled at Sheila's mouth. "Maybe it's the mother in me, but I can't believe Mrs. Davis would keep his name out of the investigation."

"She either trusted him completely or believed he couldn't have committed the murder."

Silence filled the office. Sheila shifted in her chair.

"And am I correct that Mrs. Davis lives near Chicago now?"

"After Janette died, Barbara moved to Bushnell, one of the far north suburbs of Chicago, just over the border in Illinois. Can't be two hours away. She manages the Sand Ridge Country Club in Bushnell."

"Private golf course?" Sheila asked.

Hank caught her meaning, pleased with the quickness of her mind.

"Definitely private and very exclusive. I'll check this afternoon to see if Perkins has a membership." He made a note on his calendar, then flipped back a page or two. "I've got Barbara's home address here too. 2818 Corydon, Bushnell."

Sheila wrote down the address, then looked across the desk at Hank, her head tilted, eyes thoughtful.

"Mrs. Davis was a single parent. After Janette's body was found, did she stay in the house alone? Did she have any family in town?"

Hank shook his head. "No family here. As I recall, an older woman, an aunt, came to stay with her. I can't remember her name."

He sat forward, typing some words into the computer until he found the file he needed. He searched for a moment, then nodded as the information came into view.

"Carol Shoup; Barbara's aunt from Illinois. She came to stay with her. A tall, gaunt woman. Tight-lipped as a nun. The two women hadn't been close."

"If I don't get anywhere with Mrs. Davis, I'll try to talk to the aunt."

He printed out the aunt's address and phone number and handed it across the desk to Sheila. She nodded, made a few more notations, and then closed her notebook.

"How did the bond hearing for Vincent Calero go?" she asked.

"Not bad, considering. Judge Craig took into account that Calero didn't use a real gun, no one was hurt, and he had no priors. He's a low risk for fleeing, but as a condition of the bond, he has to live with his sister until his court date."

"I assume the media were present in full force."

"It was a zoo. Despite my statement yesterday, they were convinced we had the killer. Vinnie's story checked out, though. He was in rehab twice. The first time was during April and May of last year, giving him a total alibi for Tiffany Chastain's murder. And he was released from Chippewa Falls the day after Lindy's body was found."

"No passes for good behavior?" she asked.

"Not a chance. The security is tighter there than in most prisons."

"How did he account for the shoelace in his tent?"

"He just says he found it." Hank threw his hands in the air. "He didn't lawyer up, so Owen and I interviewed him twice. Unfortunately, his memory's a bit fuzzy. He says he's been clean since his release except for some pot. He swears he found the shoelace in the woods. Trouble is, he can't remember where."

"Is he lying?"

"I don't know. I told him I was pretty sure the court would cut him some slack if he could remember, but I'm not holding my breath on that. He's totally uninvolved in anything other than his own destruction." Hank shook his head in disgust. "He was on heroin when he went in to rehab. When he got out he thought it would be OK to smoke a little pot."

"You know what they call that? Changing seats on the *Titanic*." Sheila shrugged. "I'm amazed that there hasn't been a leak about the shoelace."

"We've been lucky, but it won't last. Too many people know, and it's too juicy a tidbit. Unfortunately, once people know about the shoelace, they're going to think Vinnie knows something about the murders."

"The press would kill to find out what he knows," Sheila said.

"And so would the murderer."

•

It was getting late, only an hour to midnight. He stood in the deep shadows under the tree at the back of the yard.

The lights were on in the family room, and it was just like watching a play. The dark-haired child must be in bed. He was glad because now he could concentrate on Donna.

She was alone except for the cat. It stared out the patio doors; its thick, furry tail flicked back and forth restlessly.

She had grown up to be a beautiful woman. She was everything he could have imagined, and yet she was different. Her hair curled softly at the back of her neck, and the lights shimmered on its surface as she bent over the papers in her lap. It was the warm gold of sunshine.

He stood in the dark, watching Donna inside the lighted room just as he had done so many years ago. His eyes caressed the curves and angles of her body. She moved with a natural grace that made him ache to hold her.

He debated moving closer to the house, but he couldn't risk it. One scare for the night was enough.

It had happened when he first arrived. So intent on watching the activity inside the house, he hadn't heard the man two houses away come outside with the dog. The first inkling that he was not alone was a low growl.

A German Shepherd was standing about ten feet away on the other side of the bushes at the back of the yard. The hackles on its back rose, and the guttural sound coming from the dog's throat was enough to freeze him in place.

"Lacey. Come here, girl."

The dog ignored the voice. Head jutted forward, body low to the ground, the dog inched forward.

He didn't know if the dog would attack. He'd come prepared for every contingency. Moving slowly, he thrust his hand into the pocket of his slacks for a handful of doggie treats. One dropped on his shoe, making a rustling sound as it disappeared beneath the ground cover. The dog's ears pricked up, eyes searching for the source. Carefully he picked another one out of his hand and threw it at the dog's feet.

The dog didn't move. It either hadn't seen the treat or wasn't hungry. The animal took another step forward and growled. In the moonlight, he could see the bared teeth. He tossed another treat.

This time the dog reacted. Its head moved, eyes following the thrown object. The treat smacked the ground a foot in front of the dog; it sniffed the air, then moved closer, finding the treat and wolfing it into its mouth.

Wanting to get the dog away from his position under the tree, he threw another cookie to the side of the dog. Again the animal sniffed and turned to the right until its nose picked up the scent.

The dog owner's voice rose in anger. "Lacey, where the hell are you? Lacey, come!"

He removed the knife from his pocket and extended the blade. He couldn't take any chances on being found. If the dog or the owner came any closer, he'd kill them. The dog pricked its ears and trotted away.

"Goddammit, Lacey!" The man's voice was slightly muffled as he leaned over to grab the dog's collar. "What the hell are you eating? No wonder you're getting fat. Let's get your business done and get back to the house."

The dog gave a single bark before its owner jerked the collar for silence. The footsteps faded, and he was able to catch his breath. His luck was holding.

He'd been lucky that no one had seen him any of the four times. On the last three, it didn't surprise him because he'd planned everything and had run through several rehearsals to make sure the timing was right. A good strategy was the framework for a good session.

His eyes returned to the patio doors of the family room. He could feel his body responding to the excitement of Donna's closeness. Her gold earrings glittered in the lamplight. He wasn't close enough to see the scar beside her eye, but he knew it was there. He could feel his own power expand at the look of her. He couldn't wait to tell her about all of his adventures. She would understand his need to practice before he could show her all that he had learned.

He tensed as she looked up from the papers she was reading and stared into the back yard. He could see her eyes; the fear was there. It was the look he remembered. It was as if she had already sensed his presence. He stepped forward, then reminded himself it was not time yet. But soon. Very soon.

●

"Stop being so nervous." Sheila spoke aloud, wanting to hear a voice in the silent house. "You have just a few more pages to go."

She looked up from the couch where she was sprawled, wading through a folder full of reports. All she'd done lately was read. Keeping the four cases separate wasn't easy, but she felt she had a handle on each one.

Why was she so edgy?

All evening she'd been restless, unable to settle down. She had a sense that she was missing something. She had hoped that by immersing herself in the summaries of all four cases she would settle her thoughts, but something continued to nag at her.

What was it?

She knew from experience that the harder she tried to bring back the memory, the less chance she had of grasping it. She pulled her gaze away from the darkness outside and glanced around the room for reassurance.

Everything was normal. Meg was in bed. Elmo was watching the bird outside on the patio. She riffled the pages on her lap and sighed with relief. She was almost at the end of her self-imposed reading assignment.

Shrugging away her sense of alarm, she flipped back to where she'd left off. She slouched against the arm cushions, rubbed her eyes, and continued reading. Fifteen minutes later, she finished the last page in the file folder. She didn't have to look at the clock to know that it was late. Her body was tired.

Closing the cover of the file, she dropped it into the briefcase beside the couch. It was eleven-thirty. Time for bed. She stood up and stretched, flexing her back muscles to ease the stiffness.

"Come on, Elmo. Leave the bird alone."

She had been conscious of the cat standing in front of the patio doors. Used to his bird-watching stance, Sheila had ignored him. Only now was she aware of his absolute stillness and the fact that he was ignoring the bird as he stared unblinking out at the darkness beyond the glass doors. The intensity of his gaze unnerved her.

Heart pounding, she walked over to the cat and leaned down to pet him. The hair on his back was raised. His concentration made her uneasy, communicating a sense of fear. The mourning dove cooed. Her gaze lifted to the darkness of the night, and she was suddenly afraid.

Chapter Twelve

Was someone outside? Sheila's body stiffened at the thought that someone might be watching her.

Elmo meowed. The sound brought her back to reality. Thank God the cat hadn't brushed against her. In her present state, she would have screamed at the touch of his fur. She reached down and scratched him behind his ears. The purring vibrations against her hand brought her some equilibrium.

"Thanks, Elmo, I needed that."

Outside she could hear the barking of Lacey, the Glowens' German Shepherd.

She listened, reassured when the dog didn't continue to bark. If anyone was outside, Lacey would announce it. She didn't welcome strangers to the neighborhood.

Shooing the cat away, Sheila made sure the patio doors were locked and the safety bar in place. The bird was nestled in a dark corner of the aquarium, only his tail feathers visible in the light from the family room. Everything was quiet.

She drew the draperies. In the lamplight, the soft red and gold plaid material added to the warm comfort of the family room. Her apprehension faded.

Putting the rest of the folders back in her briefcase, she closed it and set it on the floor beside the kitchen door. Elmo was lying on the floor, one paw scrabbling under the edge of the stove.

"So you jammed one of your toys under there, did you?" Sheila said.

She watched as he worked at it for a moment, then got down on her hands and knees to see what he was trying to get at. A glint of metal caught her eye, and she reached under the edge of the stove and pulled out Meg's lost keys.

"Now how did these get here? Elmo, did you knock them off the counter?"

She'd never known the cat to pay the slightest bit of attention to the keys. As if to prove her point, he returned to reaching beneath the stove. Leaning over until her head was touching the floor, Sheila peered under the edge, discovering two cat toys and a cat treat. She scooped them out.

Elmo sniffed them suspiciously. He finally selected the cat treat and sat down on the floor to eat it.

Sheila stared at the keys in her hand. She'd yelled at Meg for misplacing the keys, but now it seemed more than likely that the cat had played a part as well. If Meg had left the keys lying about, it was conceivable that the cat might have played with them. A more likely scenario was that Meg had dropped the keys and without realizing it had kicked them under the stove.

Getting to her feet, she rehung the keys on the peg board.

She glanced around the kitchen. Meg had made a snack before she went to bed and had left a trail across the countertop. A loaf of bread, a milk glass, a plate, and a knife covered with peanut butter and jelly were scattered across the surface.

Sheila sighed. She twisted the end of the bread bag and located a fastener before putting it back in the refrigerator. Filling the tea kettle, she dumped the dirty dishes in the sink and added hot water and detergent. The dishes were washed and put away by the time the water was boiling. She reached up for a mug and filled it with water, then dropped in a tea bag.

A blob of jelly and some seeds from the bread were scattered on the countertop. She moved her teacup and reached for the sponge, wiping the counter clean. That new wheat bread was good, but the damn seeds are a nuisance, she thought as she picked up her cup of tea.

Seeds!

Sheila's mind latched on to the memory that had eluded her all evening. Something about seeds. Knowing she'd never sleep without checking, she swung her briefcase up on the kitchen table, opened it, and searched through until she found the folder summarizing the third murder.

A cast had been made of the footprint found at the scene of the crime. It was the photograph of the print that she was looking for. If she remembered correctly, there was a seed in the picture.

Aha! There it was. The photo showed a seed pressed into the dirt beneath the shoeprint. It was a sunflower seed.

She shook her head. Something else she'd read along with this reference to the sunflower seed had triggered an alarm.

Trying not to force the memory, she dropped the folder on the table and reached for her mug. She rocked from foot to foot as she sipped, her eyes unfocused. The tea tasted good. She liked the pungent lemony aroma. She smiled as she remembered that Nick had introduced her to the brand. He'd recommended it the first time they went out.

The first time. The first victim.

Pictures in her mind shifted. In the reports she'd read tonight on the death of Janette Davis, there was a reference to sunflowers.

Janette's body had been discovered, partially buried, in a strip of woods running along Hill Farm Road about two miles from town. A rock bearing traces of blood and hair had been found in the brush nearby.

Sheila dug into her briefcase again. Finding the right folder, she pulled out a chair with the toe of her shoe and sat down on the edge of the seat. She scanned the pages. Finding nothing, she started over. This time she read slowly and was rewarded when she spotted the item on page nine.

"The strip of woods runs between Hill Farm Road and an abandoned field of sunflowers."

Seeds. Sunflowers.

The first child had been killed in an old sunflower field. There had been a sunflower seed at the scene of the third murder. Sunflowers were everywhere. Sunflowers and River Oaks went together.

Sheila took a slow sip of tea, letting her mind float as she worked through her thoughts. Harker and the other local police officers were so used to sunflowers that the presence of a seed at the scene of the murder would elicit little comment. The focus of the plaster mold had been on the identification of the shoe.

There were no sunflowers growing near the spot where Meredith

Whitford's body was found. Granted, the seed could have been carried there by an animal, or even blown by the wind.

But—what if the seed had been brought into the woods by the murderer?

She leaned back, wondering if discovering the seed was a molehill or a mountain. Was she grabbing at any straw for lack of more substantial leads?

Harker had told her to investigate anything she thought might hold any possibilities. So far the only things that had piqued her interest were Herb Reisler and now the sunflower angle.

Staring down at the seed in the photograph, she remembered one other incident. The sunflower kernels beside her car.

Did the kernels have some connection to the murders?

She shivered at the possibility. She really didn't know if the seeds had been purposely placed beside her car. If they had been, it reminded her more of the delivery of the bloody doll rather than the murders. Was it her old partner Doug, up to more dirty tricks?

She dumped the folder back in her briefcase and closed the lid. Enough for tonight. She'd mention the sunflowers to Harker and see what he thought. In the morning she'd stop by the forestry department at City Hall to get the name of a resident expert in sunflowers.

•

Sheila slept poorly and had to hurry next morning to get Meg to school on time. She did think to remind her that she'd pick her up at noon for lunch with Nick. She stopped at City Hall and found Jane Lederer, the city forester, reading the newspaper over her morning coffee. They chatted for a while, and then Sheila asked about a sunflower expert.

Jane suggested Dominic Ferraro. Not only did he have a wonderful garden in the old part of town, but he maintained a greenhouse, where he experimented with new strains of sunflowers. Jane called and he agreed to see Sheila. Ten minutes later she pulled up in front of the ivy-covered brick house on the wide corner lot and moments later rang the doorbell.

"Come in, Lieutenant Brady." Dominic Ferraro opened the door and led Sheila into the house.

He was a short, rounded man with a benevolent expression. His sparkling blue eyes and darting, spritelike movements added to his air of cheerfulness. His skin was tan and leathery, making it difficult to tell his age. At a guess, Sheila thought he was between sixty and sixty-five.

"Since it's such a lovely day," he said, "I thought we might as well sit in the garden."

She followed him through an elegantly furnished living room to a set of French doors that led outside to a large brick patio across the back of the house. It was a square enclosure with gardens on two sides and a greenhouse on the third side at right angles to the house. Black wrought-iron chairs and a glass-topped table, shaded by a bright yellow umbrella, were in the center of the patio. At the angle where the two gardens met, there was a small stone pond filled with goldfish and waterlilies.

"What a perfect retreat, Mr. Ferraro," Sheila said, looking around.

"Please," he said. "No formalities. I gave all that up when I retired from teaching. My friends call me Dominic."

"And I'm Sheila."

His round face crinkled in a smile, and he gave a half bow. Sheila warmed to him immediately.

"Jane mentioned that you needed information on sunflowers. Would you like a tour, or would you prefer getting down to business?"

"I'd love a short tour," she said. "I've passed your house often and I've been curious to see the gardens. A friend of mine, Nick Biagi, is one of your neighbors."

"Dear Nickie. What a talented man. He takes photos of all my experiments. Who else? Italians have an eye for beauty," he said, leaning forward and patting her arm.

Sheila found herself blushing under his beaming attention.

"This isn't the best time to see the gardens. You'll have to come again at the beginning of the season to see some of my favorites."

"Do you only grow sunflowers?" she asked as he led her toward the neat brick pathway between rows of sunflowers.

"You sound just like my wife, Maisie. She says it's boring." He chuckled. "One year she planted two climbing roses against the house, but as a concession to marital harmony she chose yellow."

Sheila smiled. "I gather River Oaks had a lot of farmers raising sunflowers."

"I don't usually wax poetic," Dominic said, "but the center of this country was a sea of golden flowers, running from North Dakota as far south as Texas. This whole section of Wisconsin used to be field after field of sunflowers. It was the main source of revenue for River Oaks and many of the surrounding towns."

"I've seen the sunflower motif all around town but assumed it was strictly decorative." Sheila brushed a strand of hair off her forehead. "Is there still money in sunflowers?"

"It's one of the world's leading oilseed crops. Soybeans is the only one bigger. The area that used to be the Soviet Union has the largest number of acres of sunflowers under cultivation, followed by Argentina. As a paying crop, it's dead here in River Oaks." Dominic shrugged his shoulders. "Nowadays most of the townspeople grow sunflowers for fun, not profit."

As they walked, Dominic pointed out the differences between the various plants. Sheila had never realized there were so many varieties. She listened in fascination as he gave her the history of the sunflowers and took her through the greenhouse, where he was experimenting with new strains. By the end of the tour, she was thoroughly impressed with Ferraro's knowledge.

"How lovely," she said, touching the buttery yellow petals of a flower with a black center at the edge of the patio.

"They're called Valentine." He cupped one of the flowers in his hand. "The head isn't so overwhelming on this plant, and they hold well when you cut them and bring them indoors. Maisie favors these for the kitchen table."

"Is it true that they always face the sun?"

"Yes. The French word for sunflower is *tournesol*, which means 'turn with the sun.' Many cultures worshipped the sunflowers, you know. You see the motif in decorative arts from the Aztecs of Peru to our own American Indians."

"And of course everywhere in River Oaks."

"Yes. I always like to say River Oaks grew from sunflower seeds." Dominic pulled out a chair for Sheila but didn't sit down. "My wife sends her apologies. She had to leave for her garden club meeting, but she wanted you to sample her sunflower seed bread. I thought a glass of iced tea might go well with that. So if you'll be patient for a moment, I'll be right back."

Sheila had just completed jotting down some notes when he returned with a tray.

"My grandfather had a large sunflower business and four sons. All of them stayed on the farm except my father, who went into banking." He broke off a small piece of the bread and dipped it in his tea. "Since I never had to labor over the sunflowers, I found them exotic when I visited the farm as a child. Later as a teacher I wanted the children to learn the heritage of River Oaks, so we raised them as a project in the classroom."

"I'm sure the children enjoyed that."

"There was a great deal of rivalry as to who could grow the tallest." Dominic beamed in remembrance, then he sighed. "Some days I actually miss teaching."

"I wonder if you can identify a seed for me."

She reached in her purse for the photograph of the seed found at the scene of the third murder. He pulled reading glasses out of his shirt pocket and propped them on his nose as he took the photo.

"It has various names. Giant Greystripe. Mammoth Russian. It grows ten feet tall and produces one enormous flower. Quite an ordinary seed," he said. "Everyone in town grows them. It's the seed we use for the contest."

"What contest?"

"Don't tell me, young lady, you have never heard of the River Oaks Sunflower Festival." Dominic glowered at her.

Sheila laughed, holding up her hands in defense. "I just moved here in January."

"Well, in that case you're excused for your ignorance."

He handed back the picture, then linked his fingers and folded his hands on his chest in a lecturing pose.

"Four years ago the city council wanted to revive interest in the sunflower heritage of River Oaks. The Chamber of Commerce sponsored a contest for the children to see who could raise the largest sunflower. It was such a success that they've had it every year."

"The entrants are children?" she asked.

"Yes. Only children under sixteen."

"How does it work?"

Sheila carefully set her glass down on the table, giving Dominic her full attention. A contest for children. She felt a tingling sensation. This might be another link to the four girls that could be investigated. And each connection meant the possibility of additional suspects.

"The kids sign up at Gill's hardware store and get a packet of sunflower seeds. They're hardy and don't need a lot of care. The seeds, not the children."

He beamed at his joke, and Sheila smiled absently, anxious for him to continue.

"If the kids get them in the ground, they'll grow. It's a summer project. The week before school starts the flowers are measured and judged. Lots of prizes, in lots of categories. The winners will be announced on September twenty-first during the Sunflower Festival."

Sheila's stomach lurched. Chief Harker had said the festival would be the perfect place for the killer to strike. If there was a connection between the murderer and sunflowers, it added credibility to his theory.

Forcing her mind back to Ferraro, she asked, "Who's in charge of the contest?"

"Why, I am." Dominic grinned proudly. "I've been running it for four years."

"Do you have a list of the judges and the names of the children who entered?"

"No." He frowned. "But I could get it for you."

"Could you, Dominic?" she said, trying to hold back her urgency. "I'd really appreciate it."

"Not at all. I take it it's important." For a long moment he said nothing, his cherubic face serious. "Does it have something to do with the murders?"

Sheila hesitated but decided she needed to be honest to ensure his cooperation. "Yes. At least I think it might."

"I'll get you the list this afternoon." He stood up as she prepared to leave. "I had wondered why you needed the information on sunflowers. I won't ask you to break your professional silence, but someday I'd like to hear about it."

Sheila nodded, too deep in her own thoughts to say more.

They walked silently through the house, and as he stood in the open doorway, Sheila thanked him for his hospitality. In the morning sunlight he looked older. He held her hand gently, then released it.

"There's an old Tewa Nation song," he said, "that says sunflowers are watered by the tears of Navajo girls."

•

"Gosh, you smell good," Nick said, nuzzling Sheila's neck as she sat down. He grinned across the table at Meg and handed her a rolled-up tube secured by a rubber band. "Honestly, kid, your mother has no respect for my talents. She forgot to give you this."

Eying him suspiciously, Meg removed the elastic and unrolled the photograph of the bull. "Cool. Dumb but cool. It'll be perfect on my wall."

"Didn't I tell you she'd love it?"

"I stand ashamed and apologetic for leaving it behind," Sheila said.

"How'd you get her to stand still?" Meg asked.

Nick groaned, covering his bearded face with one hand. "Him. It's a bull. Don't they teach you anything at school?"

"We don't get into sex education until next year." Meg grinned at the startled look on Nick's face. "Beth and I snuck a peak at the workbook and it's really a bore. No photos of Brad Pitt."

Before the conversation could get more outrageous, Sheila suggested they order lunch. While they waited, Nick explained more about cow picturing.

"It takes a couple hours to get a decent photograph because there's so much prep work."

Nick unrolled the picture of the bull, anchoring it on the table with the salt and pepper shakers.

"This is Black Gordon. He was easy. All we had to do was wash him down, brush him up a bit, and cut out any snags in the tail. A touch of Vaseline to accentuate the muscular structure."

"I never thought of cow makeup," Meg said.

"You'd be surprised." Nick was pleased by her interest. "If the white hair has a yellowish cast, we cover it with baby powder or white paint."

"Isn't that cheating?"

"Not really. In life, appearances count. Even with cows. The dairy farmers are mostly interested in buying a good milk producer. It's a strong selling point, however, if the cow looks clean and healthy."

"Who's posing the cow—eh—bull?" Meg asked, pointing to the forearm holding the head of the animal.

Nick squinted down at the picture. "I think that's Warren Santo. He's one of the vets I work with."

"We know Dr. Santo," Meg said.

"Oh really?" Nick shot a glance at Sheila.

"We take Elmo over to Dr. Upton at the animal hospital," she said. "We got Dr. Santo instead."

"I didn't know Elmo was sick."

"Not Elmo," Meg said. "Cooper. The bird I found."

"Aha. Now I have the picture. No pun intended. And did the good doctor perform a miracle and cure the injured bird?"

Sheila heard the touch of acid in Nick's tone but chose to ignore it. Meg giggled.

"No. Dr. Santo says the leg is healing great," she said. "He said the next time he makes a house call, he'll take off the bandage and see if Cooper can walk or fly."

Their lunch arrived, and they were quiet as the waitress set the sandwiches and drinks on the table. After she left, Nick gave Sheila a level look.

"I'd like to hear more about Dr. Santo at another time," he said, then turned to Meg. "How are you going to spend your half day of freedom from school?"

Meg took a bite of her sandwich and glanced back and forth between Sheila and Nick, sensing the tension beneath the surface. Although her lips felt tight, Sheila smiled, and the girl launched into speech.

"I'm going to the movies with Mrs. Lavorini, Beth, and her two brothers."

"The dreaded Brian and Brad." Nick grimaced. "Quite a handful, those boys. The Lavorinis were in last month for a family portrait. I considered selling the business before we were done."

"I told you, Mom. They're gross." Meg rolled her eyes. "Beth said we wouldn't go if we had to sit with the boys."

"And do you?"

"For once Mrs. L. mellowed out. She said we could sit by ourselves, but only if we were close enough so she could keep an eye on us. It's not like we're babies," Meg grumbled, pulling on her long braid of dark hair.

Since Sheila was grateful for Mrs. Lavorini's vigilance, she didn't comment. "Have you figured out what you're going to get Beth for her birthday? Maybe Nick could do another bull picture for you."

Nick wiggled his eyebrows, and Meg laughed. "Thanks but no thanks. I've got to come up with something ultra, ultra special."

"When is this great social event?" Nick asked as he took a bite of his sandwich.

"A week from Saturday. It's going to be totally wonderful. Kind of an all-day thing."

"Last I heard," Sheila said with a frown, "it was going to be a sleepover."

"It is, but first we're going to meet for the parade and the contest judging and then . . ."

"Wait a second," Sheila said, holding up both hands, palms outward, for silence. The muscles in her throat were tight, and she swallowed the knot of anxiety that rose in her chest. "What's all this about?"

"Ah, Mom, don't you remember? I told you ages ago."

It was clear Meg was annoyed. Sheila'd been less attentive, practically absentminded since she'd been working on the investigation.

"I'm sorry, honey," she said. "Tell me about Beth's party again, and this time I'll listen to every word."

"Her birthday is September twenty-first, the same day as the Sunflower Festival." Meg spoke slowly and clearly as if her mother were hard of hearing. "We're going to meet at Beth's house after lunch and walk over to Hodges Park. There's a flea market and a 4-H exhibit and contests. It's going to be way cool."

Meg stared across the table, seeking reassurance. Sheila smiled but remained silent.

"Then we're going back to Beth's and have dinner. Mr. Lavorini's going to grill on the patio." Meg's brown eyes were fixed on Sheila's face as if she sensed her mother's rising concern. "After dinner we're going to walk over to the high school to see the carnival and the fireworks display."

Sheila knew before Meg said the words what was coming and did all she could to keep her face expressionless. Single parenting sucked. She would end up playing the heavy in this situation, but it couldn't be helped.

Meg was not going to the Sunflower Festival.

•

Sheila pulled into the parking lot at the station, her mind trying to deal with her worry over Meg. She'd have to talk to Mrs. Lavorini about the party. Her daughter would be angry, but it couldn't be helped. Safety came first.

She was so preoccupied that when she opened the door and found Doug Maloney standing beside the car, she let out a small shriek.

"Sorry, Doug," she apologized. "I didn't see you."

He leaned over the open car door. Still seated inside, she felt oppressed by his closeness. She tried not to think about the fact that he'd sent her the bloody doll.

"You look terrific," he said.

Ignoring the compliment, she said, "What are you doing in River Oaks?"

"What? No 'Hello, Doug, it's great to see you' chitchat?" He heaved a dramatic sigh. "Did you know I'm with the Madison police now?"

"So I heard," she said. "I met your chief at a seminar right after I moved here. Seemed like a good guy."

"He is. Great working conditions and outstanding pay and benefits."

"I'm glad for you." She reached for her briefcase on the seat and thrust it at him. "Here, Doug. Hang on to this while I get out. I'm getting a crick in my neck."

Having no choice, he accepted the case and stepped back. She shifted in the seat, attempting to rise with some degree of grace, grinding her teeth as her skirt hiked up to reveal her legs.

"Thanks," she said, reaching for the briefcase.

He held it away from her, teeth flashing in a grin. "It'll cost you a drink."

"Much too early for me, Doug." She started for the side door of the station house. "Come on up and have a cup of coffee."

She pulled out her ID and stood poised beside the security door, waiting for him to join her. She could see the anger just below the surface as he stared at her. He'd always hated it when she treated him with indifference, but she'd never seemed to be able to handle his familiarity any other way.

"I don't have time," he said. "I've got to get back to Madison."

He set her briefcase down on the asphalt surface. Sheila shaded her eyes in the late afternoon sun.

"You look good and fit, Doug. I remember how I always envied your tan."

He laughed, pleased by the compliment. "I played a lot of golf this summer."

"What do you shoot now?"

"Low eighties."

"Damn. The best game I ever shot was a hundred five, and I'm not sure that wasn't just a fluke."

"If you'd ever go to the driving range and work on your game, you'd get down into the nineties."

"I hate the driving range."

Her poor golf swing had been a standing joke between them when they were partners. The banter reminded her that they had worked well together up until the shooting. She wished she knew how to defuse his anger. She walked back across the blacktop until she was standing beside him.

"I regret that I was already gone when you returned to work," she said. "It never sat right with me, Doug. Up until then we'd been good partners."

He stood over her, his face in shadow. She didn't shrink under his scrutiny. She let him see that what she had said was true. He gave a short nod of his head.

"We were good partners," he agreed.

"You never did tell me what you're doing in town. Business or social?"

"Both. The governor set up a drug action committee that supplies schools with drug prevention programs. My chief tapped a few of us to go around the state explaining to the school boards what's available and what kind of financial help they can expect. I drew River Oaks."

"What's the social part?" she asked. "Are you dating someone in town?"

"I'm always hopeful. Now that we're not partners anymore, I thought you might have dinner with me."

Her dismay must have been evident. He gave her a long look, his gaze hardening.

"I can't. I'm working late." She leaned over and picked up her briefcase. "In fact, I'm going to have to run. I've got a meeting with Chief Harker. It was good to see you, Doug."

Without waiting for a reply, she walked across to the door and ran her ID through the security slot. She could feel his eyes on her back as she waited for the door release. Opening the door, she turned and gave a wave as she entered the building. He didn't return the gesture.

Upstairs she put her things away and dumped her briefcase on the top of her desk. She listened to her voice mail, jotting down the names on a scrap of paper. Nick Biagi, Warren Santo, and Dick Perkins had called. After having practically no men in her life, now she had too many.

She scratched off Nick's name. She had no time for a fight. The point of her pencil touched Warren's name. Was he going to ask her out on a real date? He seemed interested. Was she? She didn't know.

Putting a question mark beside his name, she moved down the list. Why had the mayor called her? She'd left a message yesterday that Harker had vetoed her taking on extra committee work while she was working on the investigation. She'd hoped that would be enough to let him know she wasn't interested. Obviously not.

She glanced at her watch. She was due in Harker's office five minutes ago. Grabbing her notebook, she crossed the room to his office.

"Sorry I'm late, Chief," she said.

"Come in and close the door."

He barked the words, and Sheila noted the tight muscles in his jaw and the frosty glint in his brown eyes. She didn't know whether he was angry at her or was just in a bad mood. She'd never known how to take Harker.

Because of her gender, she'd been on the defensive since she'd joined the police force. With every supervisor, she was made aware of her femininity to some degree. Harker, on the other hand, kept her off balance because he reacted as if she had no gender. She didn't know if that annoyed her on a personal or a professional level.

"So who are you mad at today?" she asked.

Harker frowned at her as if her question were impertinent. To Sheila's surprise, he answered her. "Perkins again."

"Yesterday I turned down a spot on the youth commission he's putting together," she said. "I told him you'd reassigned me and I was already overloaded."

"I know. He was just on the phone to see if I'd reconsider. I told him to back off. I don't like his interest in you. Until we get a few things resolved, don't have anything to do with him. Understood?"

At her nod, Hank waved a hand, indicating that the discussion was over. He noted that the tightness around Sheila's mouth had smoothed out. Her reaction confirmed his suspicion that Perkins's attentions were unwelcome. Which was all the more reason to worry about the mayor's preoccupation with Sheila.

"Have you scheduled an interview with Barbara Davis?" he asked.

"Yes. She couldn't see me until tomorrow."

He opened his mouth, then closed it as he looked across at Sheila. If she mishandled the interview with Barbara Davis, Perkins would come down hard on the department, and Sheila would be a logical target.

"Aside from you, Owen is the only one I've told about the Perkins complication," he said.

"I'll handle Barbara Davis with kid gloves, Chief."

It surprised him that she had read his mind. He thought he had been subtle. He spotted the amusement in her eyes and opted to move on.

"A couple months after the first child was killed here, we got a call from Townsend, Minnesota. An eleven-year-old girl had been strangled, and the Chief of Police, Bob Emerick, was checking on similar cases. It happened in October, almost two years ago."

"Was she raped?"

"No. The only real similarities were the youth of the victim and the fact her underpants were missing."

"Like Janette."

Hank nodded. "I talked to Emerick when the second child was killed. We were contacting other cities to see if they had anything with the same bizarre characteristics. He said they'd arrested a boy in the neighborhood for this strangulation case. I forgot about it until I got a call last week. Emerick said he'd come across his notes from when we'd talked originally. His case had mistakenly been listed as closed, but in actual fact, the kid they arrested had a total alibi for the time of the murder."

"So he's back to trying to tie it in to our murders?"

"Maybe. They've exhausted all leads and are searching for miracles. Just like us."

"Any possibility it might be our guy?"

"I honestly don't know. A different method of killing and the lack of ritual characteristics doesn't automatically rule him out."

"Janette was killed in July, and this murder was in October. If it's our guy, he may not have decided on the ritual aspects he would use later."

Hank nodded. "I told Emerick we were still open to any possibilities. He faxed over the details, and I gave the info to Owen."

"If the killer is from River Oaks, what are the chances he committed a murder in Minnesota?"

"He could have gone there for business or a vacation. It's not that far away. On a hunch I called a friend of mine, Chuck Pickard, who works for the state of Minnesota tourist board. Townsend's a suburb of St. Paul. I asked Chuck if he could find a list showing the scheduled events in the Minneapolis–St. Paul area two years ago in October. He called about an hour ago and said he didn't have a complete list, but he'd send over a preliminary one."

Lifting a fax from the top of his desk, he handed it across to her. He waited while she read down the list. Close to the bottom of the page, she stopped and looked up, her eyes questioning.

"Midwest Republican Lawyers Conference?"

"Yes," Hank said. "I did some checking. One of the speakers was Dick Perkins."

Chapter Thirteen

"Are you suggesting that Dick Perkins might have killed this girl?"

Sheila looked shocked. She gave a quick look over her shoulder to make sure the door was closed.

"I'm not suggesting anything at this point," he said. "However, until we find the murderer, everyone is a suspect."

Harker's anger returned when he remembered the family portrait on the mayor's desk. How could the man risk losing Carolyn Perkins and the two children sitting on her lap? Hank looked up and found Sheila staring at him across the desk. From the sympathy in her eyes, he knew she had read his mind again.

"Just because he's capable of cheating on his wife," she said, "doesn't mean he's capable of murder."

Her words were so logical that for the first time that afternoon Hank was able to view Perkins with some objectivity.

"Thanks, Sheila," he said, giving her a long look. "In actual fact, I don't know if Dick Perkins is guilty of anything."

"Let me see what Barbara Davis has to say. She may put all your suspicions to rest." She tapped the cover of the notebook in her lap. "Besides, I've got a new angle for my interview."

Hank listened as she ran down the facts she had learned from Ferraro about the sunflowers; he agreed that the sunflower contest could be the link between the girls and the killer.

"Owen predicted this might happen if we put you on the investigation." He grinned when she narrowed her eyes. "He said it's like putting the cat among the pigeons. It stirs things up. You've done a great job following this through, Sheila."

Her pleasure showed in her face. He meant what he said. She'd been instrumental in breathing new life into a stagnant investigation.

"Dominic Ferraro sent over the list of judges for the last four years. He included the names of the children who entered the contest this year. He's checking, but he doesn't know if anyone kept the names from previous years." She held up her hand as he started to speak. "And no, Lindy Pottinger's name wasn't on the list."

"Damn and blast."

Hank didn't know whether his words were due to Sheila's ability to anticipate what he was going to ask or because there were no easy answers in this case. He brushed a hand over the bristles on the top of his head.

She closed her notebook with a satisfactory smack. She started to rise, hesitated, then looked across at Hank, a question in her eyes.

"What's up?" he asked.

"I just ran into Doug Maloney in the parking lot."

"No kidding. What did he have to say for himself?"

"He acted like it was a reunion. We talked for a minute or two, and then he asked if I'd have dinner with him. I turned him down. Knowing that he sent me the doll package made the whole encounter creepy, especially since for the last few days I've had the feeling that someone's watching me."

"You mean at home?"

"Yes, and once or twice when I've been around town. Last night I had the sensation that someone was behind my house looking through the windows."

"Did you check it out?"

"This morning I discovered the ground cover was trampled as if someone had been standing or walking behind my house. There were no real footprints, though. The pachysandra is pretty thick back there. I found a dog biscuit, so it's possible it was my neighbor with his German Shepherd."

"Do you feel threatened?" he asked.

"Not particularly. At first I was afraid this sense of unease might have to do with Meg, but I've felt it strongest when she's not around."

"No hang-up calls? No anonymous letters?"

A question flashed across her face. "The kernels."

"What kernels?"

"Beside my car. It was Tuesday night. I found a pile of sunflower kernels beside my car. They were the salted kind they sell in the snack section of the grocery store."

"Did you see anyone around?"

"No. Actually I thought it was a joke. Something to do with the bird Meg found. I was rushing to pick up Meg at the library, and by the time I got home, I'd forgotten all about it."

Hank frowned; he didn't like what he was hearing. Sheila didn't strike him as a flighty person, prone to imagining things. If he found out it was Maloney he'd nail the bastard for stalking. Meanwhile he'd beef up the patrols around her house. A murderer was on the loose, and Sheila was now working on the investigation. If the killer saw her as a threat, she could be in danger.

The phone on Hank's desk rang. Annoyed at the interruption, he snatched up the receiver. "Harker."

"No need to bark at your mother, Hank. They told me you had someone with you, but I told them to put me through anyway."

Hank sat up straighter, knowing that daytime calls from his mother usually spelled trouble.

"Is this an emergency?" he asked.

"I'm at the airport, dear, but my flight doesn't leave for a few minutes."

A tight ball formed in the pit of Hank's stomach at the word *airport*. He had the ominous feeling he knew why she was calling. He looked across the desk at Sheila, who stood up, preparing to leave.

"Hold on a second, Mother." Then he said, "Sheila, If Doug contacts you again, I want you to let me know immediately. In the meantime I want you to be careful. Have a talk with your daughter, and in general stay alert. Do you follow me?"

He saw the flicker in her eyes at the mention of Meg. Reminding her of her daughter's safety would keep Sheila on her guard. His eyes followed her as she left the room, then he returned to the phone.

"OK, Mother. What's up?"

"Who's Sheila?"

"One of my police officers," he said. "Never mind that. Am I correct in assuming that you're coming home for Teresa Battaglia's funeral?"

"Why, how clever of you, Hank. No wonder you're the Chief of Police. Yes, that's why I'm coming. I felt tied to her in many ways. Teresa and I were in college together. She married Earl the same year I married your father. You remember their farm out on Crooked Creek Road. Earl fell into the combine the year you came back from Vietnam."

He shuddered at the grisly memory. "A godawful way to die. Are you flying into Madison?"

"That's why I called, dear. Laurie Brown's going to pick me up at the airport. We're meeting friends for dinner. Sort of a memorial to Teresa. I just wanted to warn you that I'd be coming and would need a place to sleep for a few days. The wake is tomorrow, but we'll have lots of time to visit."

Every time his mother came to visit, she turned the house upside down. He liked his bachelor existence.

"How long were you planning to stay?"

"You always ask that, Hank. Sometimes I wonder if you'd rather I went to a motel." He could hear the amusement in her voice. "I have to run, dear. They're calling my flight. See you later."

He hung up the phone, trying to remember in what shape he'd left the house. Someone came in once a week to "do" for him, as his mother loved to say. That was two days ago, and he'd barely been home since, so the place should be fine.

A quick glance at his watch. If he left at five, he'd have enough time to get to the grocery store and still take Abby out for a long walk before dinner. The Labrador would be thrilled to have Della in the house. His mother spoiled the dog, and Abby reciprocated by lavishing the woman with unconditional dog love. She never treated Hank with the same degree of devotion, he muttered. But then again, neither did his mother.

•

"Did you buy the blue dress?"

Sheila smiled at Warren Santo's question, relaxing her grip on the receiver. "Don't you even say hello?"

"Part of police training must be to answer a question with a question."

"Didn't you learn that in veterinary training?"

"No. Our patients never ask questions."

Sheila laughed. "I forgot. How's the Dunworthy lineage?"

"Safe from contamination from the peasant population of River

Oaks. That's why I called. I figured you'd want an update."

"I have to admit," Sheila said, leaning back in her desk chair, "I've been worrying about Queen Mav."

"She got a shot of estrogen. That'll keep her from having a litter of mutts. Now all we have to do is pray she doesn't have complications."

"Does that happen?"

"More times than not. A minor one would be a false pregnancy, but there's a possibility of aplastic anemia or uterine infections. Queen Mav could end up useless as a breeding animal."

"I had no idea," Sheila said. "I thought dogs had a much simpler life than humans."

"Simpler, maybe. But they're prone to many of the same diseases humans get," Warren sighed. "Usually their owners aren't willing to pay for the more complicated health problems. Animals need comprehensive health insurance like their owners."

"I suppose so," Sheila said.

She felt a twinge of guilt. If the bird Meg found had needed expensive care, she didn't know if she would have been willing to pay.

"Sorry. That's my own personal hobby horse," Warren said. "Would you be interested—eh—would you have time for a drink after you get off work tonight?"

"I'd like that, Warren, but I can't. Meg's at a friend's house and I'm working tonight."

"Oh, that's all right. I know it's late to ask. I just thought . . ."

His awkwardness made her regret her instant refusal. "I have a counteroffer. Would you like to accompany three females on an outing on Sunday?"

"I have a bad feeling that two of the three might be less than five feet in height."

"Nice guess. Unfortunately you're right. I promised Meg and Beth I'd take them to the show in the afternoon. How do you feel about Benji movies?"

There was a brief silence on Warren's end, followed by a sigh. "I see dogs all day. I suppose one more mangy hound won't kill me."

"Just for that kind of selfless sacrifice, I'll let you off the hook. We're going to see the new Spielberg movie at the mall." Warren laughed, and she caught the relief in his voice. "I'm doing some interviews the early part of the day, and then I'll pick up Meg and Beth in time for the four o'clock show. Probably the easiest thing would be to meet the three of us in front of the box office. It's my treat this time."

"Only if you let me buy something to eat afterwards."

"Agreed." She could see Lois Coren heading for her desk, a manila folder tucked under her arm. "I've got to run now, but we'll see you at the mall on Sunday. And incidentally, I did buy the blue dress."

Not bad for a hang-up line, Sheila thought as she replaced the receiver. She was still smiling when Lois plopped down in the chair beside Sheila's desk.

"Who is he?" Lois asked.

"Who is who?"

Lois rolled her eyes. "Believe me, kiddo, the only time a woman wears a grin like that a man is lurking somewhere in the bushes."

Sheila could feel the heat rise to her cheeks. "I was talking to the vet about an injured bird."

"That would be Dr. Santo. He's single."

"Do you know everyone in town, Lois?"

"I make it my business to know." The older woman looked pensive. "When I was first married, a friend of mine got cancer. She was a real private person. Never told any of her friends, and I was too busy to notice the physical changes in her. By the time I knew, it was too late to do her much good. I always felt bad that she'd gone through it without a friend to talk to. So now I make it my business to learn as much as I can about the people in town."

"It is awful how much we miss when we're busy. I regret not being around more when Meg was a baby," Sheila said. "I was determined to get through my training so I'd have a job and be able to raise her. My mom was the one who saw her take her first step and say her first words."

"Who was it that said women could have it all? Horse pucky. You gotta give up something." The older woman snorted. "Well, listen to me running off at the mouth. Lois, the philosopher cop."

"You always make good sense."

"Yeah, sure." Lois grinned, then her face turned serious. "The chief said to give you this list. I waded through those old ledger books of Ebenezer Jimson and made a list of everyone in town with a size ten shoe."

"Is it a lot?"

"Let me say this. Either it's a very common shoe size or it's the only size Jimson carried. It bothers me that it's not a validated source, but I suppose these days any clue is better than none. And I've got a little bonus for you. I had to run over to the dentist at lunch."

Lois touched her jaw and Sheila could see the slight swelling.

"Are you all right?" she asked.

"Dr. Zage put in another crown. He's got three kids to put through college, and I'm his favorite patient. Hell! I've got enough crowns to be considered royalty."

Sheila laughed and waited for Lois to get to the point.

"At any rate, it's right next door to Farm and Field Outfitters. The store's owned by Jack Yates, the son of a friend of mine. Haydie told me that when he bought the store he put in all these fancy computers. Said he'd be able to purchase inventory with more precision once he knew the buying habits of the customers."

Guessing where this was leading, Sheila looked with interest at the folder in Lois's lap.

"So you're ahead of me, kiddo. Jack carries work boots as well as hiking and hunting shoes. Unfortunately he's a tight-assed SOB. Big on invasion of privacy issues." Lois stood up and handed Sheila the folder. "I had to call his mother before he'd give me the list."

Cackling at her own joke, Lois left. Sheila could hear her all the way down the stairs. Thank God for tenacity like that, Sheila thought as she opened the folder and leafed through both shoe lists, identifying the names of men in River Oaks.

It was interesting how many people she knew. She'd felt the same way when she looked over the judge list that Dominic Ferraro had sent her. Nick, Dick Perkins, Warren Santo, Paz, Owen James, and even Chief Harker had judged the sunflower contest at one time or another. The list read like a who's who in River Oaks.

Gathering the two shoe lists and the list of sunflower contest judges, she headed to the computer room. The database would be run against these new lists, another set of markers to narrow down the possible suspects. Enough cross-matching surely would help her to zero in on the killer.

•

"You look like hell, Hank," Della said, staring at Hank over the top of her highball glass. "Aren't you getting any sleep?"

"Not much."

On the other hand, Hank thought his mother looked terrific. The

Florida tan went well with her curly white hair and silvery blue eyes. Stylishly simple clothing, a profusion of gold jewelry, and an air of bustling energy camouflaged her plain face and short stocky build.

"It's these murders, isn't it?" she said. "That's all anyone could talk about at dinner tonight. Once we'd toasted Teresa and discussed the messes our children were making of their lives, the subject reverted to the murders."

With the toe of one shoe, she pried off the other, then reversed the process. Her sigh of relief was more of a groan.

"You're going to break your neck in those shoes," Hank said. "You should consider buying some nice sturdy ground-grippers."

Della sniffed loudly as she pulled her legs up on the living room couch, trying not to disturb the black Lab, who lay with her head in Della's lap.

"Don't try to get me off the subject, Hank. I want to talk about the murders. I gather you had an editorial in the *Weekly Sentinel* about the Sunflower Festival."

"Yes. And there will be another one this week."

Hank took a long pull of his Scotch. Dick Perkins had been opposed to the article, but Hank had been adamant. Denying that the killer existed was foolhardy. Being prepared wasn't.

"I know you mentioned on the phone that you wanted to cancel the festival."

"No one knows what kind of timetable this psycho is working on. The fair atmosphere and the carnival at the high school will attract a lot of children. We're doing as much as we can to be prepared. The force on alert. The Parent Watch volunteers. My article was to remind all the parents to be on their guard."

"From what I hear, they will be," Della said. She touched the glass to her chin, her eyes hidden beneath half-lowered lids. "People are frightened, Hank. When they're in a panic they say things that could be taken in the wrong way."

Hank caught a hesitant note in his mother's voice. He propped his feet up on the corner of the coffee table and settled back in the deep leather chair. He took another swallow of his Scotch and waited for her to continue.

"Is it true that you arrested and released a man who had one of Lindy Pottinger's shoelaces in his possession?"

Hopefully he'd never find out who had leaked the information to the newspapers. He'd be tempted to strangle the bastard.

"We didn't release the man. He's out on bond. As far as we can verify, he had absolutely nothing to do with the murders. He says he found the shoelace in the woods."

"Is Herb Reisler a suspect?"

Her question, coming out of the blue, threw him. "You know I can't answer that, Mother."

He was surprised by the troubled look on her face. She rarely showed anything but a cheerful expression to the world, which included her son. It had taken him a long time to realize that beneath the didactic manner and humorous comments, his mother was sensitive and easily wounded.

"Josephine Iatesta was at the dinner tonight. She works part time at the Book Nook. She took me aside and said that a policewoman . . ."

"Police officer," Hank corrected automatically.

"Officer, then," Della said, "came in and asked all kinds of questions. Josephine asked me why you would be bothering Herb like that."

"Really, Mother, why on earth would she ask you?"

"I think she felt since I was your mother I would know. So I told her you were investigating shoplifting in the stores on the square."

Hank stared across at Della, who was busy patting Abby's head, much to the pleasure of the dog.

"Why did you tell her that?" he asked, more out of curiosity than annoyance.

"You know how I feel about gossip, Hank. It has the power to distort reality. Innocent situations get blown out of proportion, and suddenly the truth is buried in an outpouring of half-truths."

"Is there gossip about Herb?"

"No. At least I hope not. It's just that something unfortunate happened years ago, and the gossip after the event nearly ruined someone's life."

"Herb's?" When Della remained silent, he asked, "Are you going to tell me about it, or do I have to get out the rubber hose?"

She shot him a look of censure. Taking a sip of her drink, she set it down on the table beside the couch.

"It was some twenty years ago. You were out of the marines but still in college. Four of us were in the middle of a bridge game in the living room here when Ruth Kohlmetz broke down in tears. Well, the upshot of it was that she was very upset because it was her fault that Herb Reisler had almost been arrested for behaving inappropriately toward a child."

Hank bolted upright. "Are you sure?"

"Despite what some people think, Hank, I'm not an idiot. Of course, I'm sure." Her mouth was pursed in disapproval. "That's exactly why I wanted you to hear this story from me. You see, dear, it wasn't true."

"Sorry, Mother. Before I put my foot in it again, why don't you tell me the whole story?"

"Ruth said she'd been in Herb's bookstore and he'd come out of the washroom with the Donatelli girl. Lisa? No, she was the older girl. Maria, I think it was. Whatever," she said, waving her hand. "The child was only ten or eleven at the time. Maria was crying and her clothes were all in disarray, and Herb was trying to straighten them. He told her to stop crying, that he hadn't meant to hurt her."

"How did he explain himself to your friend?"

"That's the trouble. Ruth had come into the store while he was in the bathroom. He didn't see her when he came out. He took the girl into the back office, and Ruth was so frightened she ran outside and went straight to the police station and told Chief Malina."

"I see," Hank said. "So based on what she'd seen, your friend accused Herb Reisler of molesting Maria Donatelli?"

"Yes. She was terribly worried about leaving the girl, as she put it, in Herb's clutches." Della shrugged. "So Malina marched over to the bookstore and confronted Herb."

"And?"

"It was all a terrible misunderstanding. Herb had been helping Maria get a book from one of the upper shelves. It slipped from his hand and smacked the child on the nose. Her nose started to bleed."

Della's eyes were frosty as she stared across at Hank. He could see she was still furious over the whole affair. He didn't comment, only nodded for her to continue.

"Gloria took the child into the bathroom while Herb went to get some ice from the delicatessen next door. They got the bleeding to stop, and Gloria washed the spots of blood off Maria's clothes. When Ruth came into the bookstore, all she saw was Herb coming out of the bathroom with Maria. She didn't realize that the girl's mother had been in the bookstore the whole time and was still there, helping Gloria clean up the mess in the bathroom."

"Thank God the mother was there. Without her, it could have been worse. Herb might have been arrested."

Della shook her head. "Even so, it did get worse. Ruth told a few friends about the incident. Pretty soon it was all over town. And like the children's game of telephone, the story became garbled until it sounded as if Herb was really guilty."

"So that's the gossip you were referring to."

"Exactly." Della's mouth tightened. "As you can imagine, Herb and Gloria were horrified that anyone could think such a thing."

"What did they do?"

"Gloria, God rest her soul, was a very smart woman. She spoke to Father Beaumont at St. Theresa's. He told the story at Mass. Maria and her mother were at the service and confirmed everything."

"I don't suppose that scotched all the rumors, though."

Della snorted. "Not by a long shot. For a while it looked as if the Reislers' business would go under. Gloria involved herself in every committee in town and was so visible that people felt obligated to support the bookstore. Like all scandals, eventually it became old news. There was nothing concrete to keep it alive. It might not have been talked about, but, human nature being what it is, I doubt if everyone has forgotten."

At the conclusion of the story, Della looked as if she could use another drink. Sensing her agitation, Abby picked up her head. The dog pressed her muzzle against Della's arm. She stroked the soft head and ears and seemed to find comfort in the rhythmic actions.

Hank could understand why Della was worried. If it were known around town that Herb was a suspect in the child murders, someone was bound to remember the old gossip.

"I'm glad you told me about this, Mother. If I'd heard the rumor first, I might have jumped to the wrong conclusion."

"Herb's a good man, Hank. He's had a rough time since Gloria died, and I wouldn't want to see the talk start up again."

After Della went to bed, Hank finished his drink and took Abby out for a walk while he smoked a last cigar. The night air helped to clear his mind as he went over his mother's story.

Truth was a funny thing. Everyone had their own truth based on who they were and what they believed. Della was a righteous and moral person. Pedophilia was beyond her comprehension. She knew Herb and was convinced that nothing improper had happened that day at the bookstore. Hank was more suspicious.

Over the years, he had found that many times a fragment of truth was at the core of a piece of gossip

Hank didn't know yet what he would do with this information.

He didn't know if he'd talk to Reisler, but it might be interesting to talk to the child Della had mentioned. Maybe Maria Donatelli still lived in River Oaks.

Giving Reisler the benefit of the doubt, Hank would try to keep the investigation quiet. He understood the damage that would be done if the rumors started up again. On the other hand, the primary objective was the safety of the children.

So for the moment Herb Reisler would join Dick Perkins and Doug Maloney on the prime suspect list. His background would be scrutinized like the others until he could be positively eliminated.

Time was running out. It was September thirteenth. Hank was convinced the killer was targeting September twenty-first, the day of the Sunflower Festival.

Only eight days left.

He couldn't let the time pressure push him so much that he missed a vital point in the investigation. He needed to focus. The best way to find the killer was to follow every lead and find an answer to every question.

Hank dropped the cigar butt, grinding it out with the toe of his shoe as he considered the latest question. Was there any truth to the rumor that Herb Reisler might have molested a child?

•

He sat on the front stairs waiting for full darkness. His head occasionally moved as he followed the progress of the cars driving by on the road. He could feel the restlessness eating away at his control. Now that he'd found Donna, he was afraid he'd lose her again.

Like sunflowers drawing bees, Donna drew men.

It wasn't her fault. He'd told her how it bothered him. She had danced around him, flicking the hem of her skirt so that he could see her panties. She said the other boys meant nothing.

He'd believed her. She had taught him the touching game when they were children. A shared secret that made them soulmates. She was his alone. He tried to tell her that the last time he saw her.

He had waited for her behind the school. He had told her that he had a present for her. She had gone with him to the garden. He had given her some of the enormous sunflowers.

She laughed at his prize flowers and threw them on the ground. She wanted the roses. He picked one but held it behind his back until she came to him and pressed her body against his.

With his other hand, he touched her skin. Silky soft and heated satin. He told her he wanted to play the new game again, and she laughed. She told him she had found others who played better than he did. She described what they did to her and how clever they were. He wasn't clever, she said. He was stupid. He covered his ears, but he could still hear the singsong voice chanting the names of the other boys.

She saw his anger. The laughter caught in her throat, and she turned to run away. He caught her at the edge of the garden. He hit her.

Her hands came up to clutch at his shirt, and her eyes widened with fear. He could see himself reflected in the blue of her eyes. He was big and powerful. He hit her again, and she fell with a thud against the tree. He turned her over and saw a cut on her head and a trickle of blood beside her bruised mouth. Her eyes were open, and she waited for him in silent anticipation. With shaking hands, he undressed her.

Donna's clean soap smell rose to mingle with the earthy odors of the woods. His hand stroked her skin, and when she did not pull away he knew she was ready for the touching game. Beneath the canopy of leaves he searched out the secrets of her body. He was the teacher. She was not laughing when he finished.

Sitting on the stairs, he stared up at the night sky. It was fate that he had found Donna again. He would be patient. Once he had her in his possession, he would no longer fear the dark thoughts and powerful urges that threatened to tear him apart. Once more she'd belong to him, and he would be complete.

He couldn't risk discovery so close to the time of fulfillment.

He stood up. It was going to rain. Humidity, like thin layers of fabric, brushed against him as he walked toward the sunflowers.

The night sounds surrounded him. He liked to be out in the night. In the summertime he used to climb out his window onto the roof. He'd strip off his clothes and lie naked on the shingles, warmed by the heat that they'd absorbed during the day.

His stepfather had caught him coming back inside and had beaten him. He hadn't turned on the lights in the room because he was ashamed of his stepson's nakedness.

The moon had been up, and he had seen the flash of light in his stepfather's eyes as he raised the belt over his head and brought it down with all the force of a whip. The man gained power from violence. His mother had cried in the background, but eventually she had crept from the room, leaving him with no hope for a reprieve.

God, how he had hated his stepfather.

His heart was racing by the time he came to the circle. It was his special place, and he was furious that someone might have violated his property. He had to know.

In the center of the circle, he pulled away the grass covering until he found the newly dug surface. He used a clawed garden hoe to pull back the dirt. It wasn't buried very deep. There'd never been a need before.

Enough light filtered into the circle to let him see a corner of the black plastic trash bag. He used his fingers to dig away the dirt from the top of the bag. Brushing the last of the dirt off the knotted top, he untied it and reached inside.

The sneakers were there. He could feel the cold rubber soles against his hand. He should have known that no one could find this place. His secret was safe. Wanting to touch them, he withdrew the shoes, setting them on the ground in the center of the circle.

The laces on the right shoe were still tied in a bow. Even in the semidarkness, he could see the letters spelling out Lindy's name. His gaze shifted to the left shoe, his eyes widening in disbelief at the empty eyelets.

The shoelace was missing.

How had Vincent Calero found his treasures? It was obvious he had invaded the circle and stolen the shoelace.

Grabbing the tennis shoes, he crammed them back into the plastic bag. Why hadn't Calero told the police where he'd found the lace? He would have to find out what game the man was playing. No one was going to screw up his plans.

The day and the time had been selected. One week to go. One week until his date with Donna.

Chapter Fourteen

Vinnie Calero heard the sharp scrabble of the squirrels as they chased up the trees that hung like a canopy above his tent in the woods. He kept his eyes closed, breathing in the musty smell of fallen leaves and clean autumn air.

The phone rang, cutting into his dream.

Memory crowded in, and he squeezed his eyes tighter and wished himself gone from this place. He wasn't in the woods. He was lying on the daybed in the storage room off the kitchen in Francie's apartment. Opening his eyes a slit, he closed them quickly as the bright light seared a trail of pain from his eyeballs to his temples.

He'd had way too much to drink last night. He coughed to clear his throat. The sudden movement made his head feel as if it might explode. He could taste acid in his throat and swallowed convulsively.

He rolled over and faced the wall, breathing in the fresh air from the window above his head. Thank God he'd left it open. He was so used to sleeping outdoors that the air in the apartment was claustrophobic.

The apartment complex wasn't that big. It was an old four-story brick building, located past the stores running along the side of Hodges Park facing City Hall. Francie's apartment was at the end of the hall with a view of the parking lot behind the old movie theater.

The bathroom wall butted up against the theater so that when they ran an adventure flick, the explosions rattled the ceramic toothbrush holder on the countertop.

The storeroom smelled of cat urine and old cardboard. He needed to get out of the apartment. He'd tried yesterday, but a local television crew had been camped outside the front door.

Much as Francie had sworn at him for his stupidity after bailing him out, he could tell she was enjoying the notoriety. Before she went to work yesterday she'd spent hours on her makeup and worn a tight leather microskirt and a knit top.

"You up, Vinnie?"

He didn't answer, hoping she'd leave him alone. Footsteps approached the door. She knocked once tentatively and, when he didn't respond, knocked again, this time louder. The thumping sound vibrated inside his head, setting off pulsing beats of pain behind his eyes.

"Come on, Vinnie. It's already past one o'clock."

"How come you're not at work?"

"I got the day off. A couple reporters followed me to the beauty shop yesterday. Ronnie didn't think it was good for business."

Her voice was an irritating whine. The phone rang, and Francie hurried away to answer it. Keeping his eyes shut, Vinnie struggled to sit up. He bit back a groan. His stomach turned at the sour smell of his body.

He'd get up and take a shower. As long as he was stuck in this place until his court date, he might as well take advantage. After a couple of months in the woods, having a bathroom was a real bonus.

With Francie still on the phone, it was safe to make a run for the bathroom. He rummaged in his duffel bag, then remembered she'd washed all his clothes. Opening the door, he spotted a laundry basket on one of the kitchen chairs. He tiptoed across the floor. Grabbing underwear, a T-shirt, and a pair of jeans, he hurried down the hall, waving at Francie, who looked up from the living room sofa where she was still talking.

He stood under the water, letting the spray hit the top of his head and run down his body. At first his headache intensified, but as the warmth and the humidity invaded his body the pain began to ease off. By the time he had recovered enough to wash his body and shampoo his hair, the room was filled with steam.

"Coffee's ready," Francie called outside the door.

After his shower, Vinnie padded barefoot down the hall to the kitchen, rubbing a towel through his shoulder-length hair. Francie was sitting at the kitchen table. He could tell she was irritated because she didn't look up at his approach.

Anger didn't become her. Her full lips were pulled in a tight line, and her nose was knife-sharp, giving her thin face a pinched, haughty expression. With her curly black hair, pouty red lips, and flashing brown eyes, Francie looked her best when she was laughing.

"Don't be mad at me, Francie. I know I screwed up bad this time and I'm sorry." He leaned over to kiss the top of his sister's head. "And thanks for taking me in."

He smiled down at her, and he could see her soften. Over the years his charm had saved him time and again. He'd used it to get out of jams and felt some guilt, but not enough to keep from trying to get his way.

"Do you want breakfast?" she asked.

"Just toast."

He poured himself a cup of coffee. Holding it between his palms, he raised it and inhaled. The strong nutty aroma combined with a trace of vanilla filled his head, and he let out a sigh of pure pleasure. He took several small sips, letting the warmth flow through his body.

Francie got up and pulled out a chair for him, then opened the refrigerator to get the bread. He watched her, trying to predict her mood as she puttered around making the toast and getting out butter and the orange marmalade she saved for his visits. She was good to him. She deserved better.

"The Chief of Police called," she said, setting the toast in front of him.

Vinnie slathered jam on the toast and took a bite, licking the corners of his mouth to get the last of the jam. "How is Chief Harker this bright morning?"

"He wants you to call him later. He's hoping your memory is better today."

The phone rang.

"It's probably another reporter," Francie said. She started to get up, then sank back down at the table. "The answering machine can take it this time. The phone's been ringing off the hook. I thought for sure it would wake you."

"Maybe Hollywood's calling," Vinnie said. "I read about a guy who found a key piece of evidence in a murder case. He sold the story to the movies and went out to California to write the screenplay."

"Yeah, right. I can see that happening."

The phone continued to ring, and Vinnie offered daydreams to distract her.

"Wouldn't that be fine, Francie? *The Vinnie Calero Story.*"

He raised his arm, waving his hand from left to right as if reading a theater marquee. Despite the continued ringing of the phone, he could see the hint of a smile in Francie's eyes. It was hard for his sister to resist him when he teased her.

"The Vinnie Calero Story," she said, her voice wistful. "It sounds nice, doesn't it?"

The answering machine finally clicked on, and the phone stopped ringing. Vinnie could see reality creeping back and hurried to keep his sister from thinking too hard.

"Who knows, Francie? Stranger things have happened. Maybe that shoelace will turn out to be good luck after all. Although the damn thing almost got me arrested for murder. How'd I know it belonged to a dead kid?"

"You gotta tell the police where you got it. Chief Harker said if you could remember where you found the shoelace the robbery charges might be dropped."

She leaned across the table, squeezing his arm in her eagerness. He shook it off.

"Harker just wants to nail me. Cops will say anything to get you to cooperate." He threw both hands in the air in a gesture of contempt. "When have they ever done anything but hassle me? Every time I'm on the street they bust my chops."

"I've told you before," Francie said. "Long hair and grunge clothes don't go well in River Oaks."

Everywhere he went it was the same, Vinnie thought. The cops always stopped him and asked for ID, and if he didn't pull it out fast enough they roughed him up a little. Not so he could do anything about it. They knew how to do it. No marks. No lawsuit.

Even if he could remember where he found the shoelace, he wasn't about to tell the cops. Clearly they wanted the info bad. He could see it in Harker's eyes. Cold, cold brown eyes. Ice eyes.

"If Harker wants to know so badly where I found the shoelace, then the info has to be worth something," Vinnie said. "If that's true, I ought to be able to parlay that into a ticket out of River Oaks. At the very least, maybe one of the papers will offer money for an interview. If reporters are calling, I must be pretty hot stuff."

"Oh, Vinnie, do you really think they'd pay you?"

Her face glowed with an innocent excitement that made him angry. "Don't get your hopes up, Francie. It's not going to happen."

"Why not?"

"Because I can't remember where I found the stupid shoelace."

"Really? I thought you were just holding out on the cops."

Her eyes started to fill up again, and Vinnie got to his feet. He padded back to the storeroom and closed the door, flopping face down on the daybed.

He had to get away from River Oaks.

Francie wouldn't give him any dough, and he was broke. That was the only reason he'd tried that stickup. He'd found the plastic gun in the woods. He'd been smoking, and it seemed like a great idea. He should have known he'd screw it up.

If only he could remember where he'd found the shoelace.

•

"No. Janette didn't sign up for the sunflower contest," Barbara Davis said. "I moved to River Oaks in May, but Janette stayed in Green Bay with my sister to finish the last weeks of school. By the time she arrived, it was past the sign-up date."

"Was Janette happy with the move?" Sheila asked.

"No. I knew once school started she'd be all right, but in the beginning she was lonely."

Sheila could see the heartache on the woman's face as she tried to answer the questions. Even after two years, the pain was raw. Losing a child was every parent's nightmare. The agony might ease, but it would never go away.

She hadn't expected to like Barbara Davis.

Since the mayor's wife, Carolyn, was a tall, elegant blond, Sheila had been expecting someone very sophisticated, worldly-wise, and much younger. Barbara was in her mid-thirties, a little overweight with big hands and feet. She appeared matronly rather than sexy.

"Did Janette have any friends in town who might have grown sunflowers for the contest?"

"She really didn't know too many people. She had only been in River Oaks a little over six weeks before she was killed. We weren't living in the Estates at first. I was renting a house in the old part of town. There weren't any kids Janette's age in the area, so she was pretty much alone. I bought her a puppy, to keep her company, but somebody poisoned it."

"Somebody poisoned Janette's dog?" Sheila was taken aback by the statement. "Did you call the police?"

Barbara shook her head. "No. I couldn't be sure. It just seemed strange the way it died. I found some meat scraps that someone apparently had given him, and I tried to keep him from eating them. I must have been too late, though; the next morning the puppy was dead."

"How awful for Janette."

"Right after that the realtor called with a rental over in the Estates. I jumped at the chance to move. The place was full of kids, and I thought it would be easier for Janette to make friends."

"It must have been very hard for you, knowing how miserable she was," Sheila said. "My daughter and I moved to River Oaks this past December, right at the start of Christmas break. Meg cried almost every day. I felt like the worst mother in the world because I'd taken the job."

Barbara smiled for the first time since the interview had started. "That's just the way I felt. I'd really wanted to get away from my ex-husband. He drank, and I didn't think it was good for Janette to be around him, and when I heard about the job of secretary to Judge Craig, it seemed the perfect opportunity."

"How'd you hear about the job?" Sheila asked.

"A friend of mine called me."

"Dick Perkins?"

Sheila knew she was taking a chance and, if she was wrong, would regret the question. Barbara was motionless, her eyes wide and unblinking as if she were stunned.

"You know about . . ."

She cut off the words too late. She sagged in her chair, her whole body deflating in reaction to the admission.

"I'm sorry, Mrs. Davis," Sheila said. "I needed to know."

"Don't be sorry." Barbara sighed. "I kept telling Dick that eventually word of the affair would come out and there would be hell to pay. Men never listen. Is that why you came to see me?"

"Yes. That and the sunflowers. I thought it might be easier for you to talk to me."

Sheila sat on the end of the couch, her face expressionless as Barbara gave her an apprehensive look. It was a moment before she spoke, and then it was as if a dam had broken when the story tumbled out.

"I've always wondered if Janette's death wasn't a punishment for my sins. I told the police that I was shopping at the mall. It had started to rain, just like it is now, and when I came out to the parking lot I discovered I had a flat tire. I flagged down the courtesy patrol and they changed it, but I was too late to pick up Janette."

"That wasn't true?"

"Not everything. My car was in the mall parking lot. I wasn't shopping, though. The reason I was running late was that I'd lost track of time. I was in a motel room with Dick Perkins."

•

Driving back to River Oaks, Sheila tried to fit the new information into some semblance of order. The reason Barbara was willing to keep Perkins's name out of the investigation was that she had been with him when Janette was kidnapped.

The question in Sheila's mind was whether that was true.

No one knew exactly what time Janette met the killer. The girl had gone up to Hodges Park to look at the stores. She was supposed to meet her mother at two-thirty in front of Charlotta's Place, a Swedish boutique on the square. When her mother didn't arrive and it started to rain, she tried to call from the store. When she couldn't reach her, she left. That was three. Janette never arrived home.

The assumption had always been that she had been walking home when someone stopped and offered her a ride. It would take fifteen minutes for Janette to walk to her house, so the time of the kidnapping was set at three-fifteen.

Barbara said that Dick had dropped her in the parking lot to retrieve her car at three-fifteen. He had driven away before she noticed that her tire was flat. She didn't get to Charlotta's Place until four, and by that time Janette was gone.

It was raining hard when Sheila got to Madison, and she had to concentrate as the traffic thickened. Once she was on the bypass, she let her mind return to the first murder.

What if Janette hadn't gone directly home?

It was conceivable that Dick could have spotted the girl as she was walking in the rain. He knew her, and it would be natural for him to stop. She would have gotten into the car willingly.

Barbara's blind spot was her belief in Perkins's innocence. Sheila had a clearer vision. If the kidnapping had taken place later than three-fifteen, Dick Perkins could have done it.

Sheila followed the signs for the turnoff to River Oaks. She'd have to stop at the store to pick up something for dinner. Agnes Krueger had invited Meg to come next door to make cookies. When Sheila returned, the three of them would have dinner and sample the goodies. What a godsend it was to have Agnes as a neighbor.

It was always a problem working on the weekends or on days when Meg wasn't in school. She was really too old for a sitter, but ever since the arrival of the bloody doll, Sheila had been afraid to leave her daughter home alone.

Damn Doug! She hated him for making her so paranoid.

Maybe she should have tried to talk to him right after the shooting incident. If they'd discussed it, then maybe they could have ironed out their feelings. He might not be so bitter, blaming her as he did for his injury. She might be able to put to rest her own doubts when he accused her of hesitating.

Robbie had accused her of the same thing when their marriage was falling apart. He had said she'd lost the spontaneity she'd had when they were first married. Every time he wanted to do anything, she had to stop and think about it.

When Sheila tried to explain that she had to consider the baby, Robbie became angry. He didn't want to hear about Meg. He hated the fact that he had responsibilities.

One night Meg was fretful and Sheila came to bed late. She had an early class in the morning. When Robbie wanted to make love, she was not as welcoming as he'd expected. Meg started to cry, and when Sheila tried to go to her, he became angry.

She touched the scar beside her eye. Robbie said he'd never meant to hurt her, but he had.

A week later he left.

The first year they were separated, they'd talked from time to time. He was in California, running with a fast crowd that made quick deals and big profits. He sent her money for Meg's care and admitted that he wanted his freedom. Once she signed the divorce papers, he didn't call very often. After six months, he stopped sending money.

The last time she talked to him, she told him she was going to the Police Academy. He laughed. He told her she wasn't the heroine type; she was a victim.

A victim? Robbie blamed her for letting him abuse her!

He told her that since she hadn't been strong enough to protect herself, how did she think she could protect the citizens of Milwaukee from real criminals?

Sheila thumped the steering wheel of the car with the heel of her hand. She could hear his words as clearly as she had every day of her police training. It was her mantra for survival. She drew strength from Robbie's criticism.

She would never be a victim again. The training would give her back control, and no one would abuse either Meg or her again. It was only after the shooting of the drug dealer that the other things he said came back to haunt her.

He had told her she was too soft to be a police officer. She didn't have enough guts to kill a bug. What the hell would she do if she came face to face with a killer? She ought to give it up before she caused someone's death.

Sheila stared through the rain-covered windshield of the car, seeking answers to the question that had plagued her ever since the shooting incident. Had Robbie's prediction come true? Had she hesitated, causing her partner's injury and the other man's death?

•

Vinnie stood with his hand on the receiver, unwilling to break the contact. He could hear the sound of his heartbeat in his ears. What a rush.

He stared down at the notes he'd scrawled on the back of an envelope he'd found in the trash can. He folded the envelope and put it in his wallet. It was one valuable piece of paper. It was his ticket out of River Oaks.

Ma used to tell him he'd been born under a lucky star. No matter how much he messed up, he'd always manage to squeak through somehow. Usually it was Francie who bailed him out. This time, though, he'd done it on his own.

This time he'd hit the jackpot.

A TV interview. And not some stupid local station either. This was network. This was big time. Who would have figured that something as simple as finding a shoelace would be the miracle that he needed to start over?

He was smart enough to realize he'd only have one shot at making the most of this opportunity. Once he told his story, he'd be old news. He'd played hardball with the guy on the phone, who kept talking about ratings and timing.

"Just give me the bottom line," he'd said.

He could tell how badly the guy wanted the interview. He tried to cover it, but Vinnie'd heard the desperation in his voice. The scoop of a lifetime, he'd said.

The guy was no match for Vinnie Calero. A thousand bucks for one interview, and an even bigger payday if Vinnie could remember where he'd found the shoelace. Not that he'd said he couldn't remember. As the TV guy had told him, they'd work out the details in Madison.

Vinnie checked his watch. Four o'clock. Francie had said she was going to her girlfriend's for dinner. He wanted another beer, but he knew he needed a clear head for the night ahead. He'd lie down for a while and see if he could sleep. Vinnie went back to the storeroom and threw himself down on the daybed. He wasn't tired, but his head ached.

He'd leave the apartment plenty early so he'd have enough time to hitchhike to Madison. He'd use the fire escape outside the kitchen window, just like he had last night.

He'd climbed up to the roof for some fresh air, but then had discovered he could cross the roof of the movie theater and go down the metal ladder on the other side. That way the news people stationed outside the apartment never saw him leave or return.

It had been worth it to get out, even if he had to face Francie's screaming and crying when he got back.

He hated the way she bossed him around and tried to tell him how to run his life. Just because she was older didn't make her right. The worst part was that every time he tried to prove he knew what was best, it turned out all wrong.

Maybe this time it would be different. What could be better than getting paid for a television interview? Especially a thousand bucks! Too bad he couldn't remember where he'd found the shoelace.

He'd thought back on it time and again. It had been a day or two after he got out of rehab. Francie'd sent him money to buy a bus ticket from Chippewa Falls to Madison, but instead he'd hitched rides until he ended up somewhere north of River Oaks. Then he started walking.

The bus money had been spent buying some weed off one of the kids who'd given him a ride. That night he'd smoked a joint and then he fell asleep.

A noise woke him.

He was still groggy, but he knew he was lying on his back in a garden. Giant sunflowers hovered menacingly over him, but when he looked up the moon was so bright that it practically blinded him. He listened for the noise. When nothing happened, his eyes drifted closed.

Then he heard the sound again, and this time he knew what it was. Someone was digging. He tried to muster the energy to turn his head in the direction of the noise, but instead he must have dozed off, because the next thing he remembered it was just after dawn and a thin mist was falling on his face. He staggered upright, wobbling on his feet until he found his balance.

He remembered that his throat was dry and he was hungry, so he cut through the garden in search of water. Moving deeper into the rows of sunflowers, he stumbled and fell to his knees.

The sunflowers pressed together overhead. He was disoriented. Still on his hands and knees, he thrashed around, and suddenly he fell through an opening.

Vinnie bolted upright on the daybed.

He remembered now! He had stumbled into a circle of sunflowers. He saw the freshly turned ground and recalled the sound of digging during the night. Someone had buried something.

The dirt was loose, and he used his fingers to dig until he unearthed a plastic garbage bag. He opened the bag and discovered it was full of clothes. Kid's stuff. Nothing he could use except the shoelace in case he scored some heroin and needed to tie off a vein.

A smile pulled at the corners of Vinnie's mouth as he looked around the storeroom. He licked his lips in anticipation. He vaguely remembered where he'd been that night and ought to be able to pinpoint the circle of sunflowers again.

This could be worth a lot of money. If he played his cards right, he could name his price.

Chapter Fifteen

He stood in the doorway of the bedroom. He hoped she'd like it. Once she saw the room she'd appreciate the trouble he had gone to, and she'd realize how much he loved her.

He'd gotten the idea when he saw the pink gingham bedspread just like the one on Donna's bed. He couldn't resist touching the soft pillows and cool sheets; it reminded him of all those years ago when he'd watched her from his darkened bedroom window.

Later Donna had told him that she'd seen him when he came too close to the window. After that she left her shade up and turned on all the lights.

Now the excitement was building. It was Saturday night. In one week Donna would come to stay with him.

He hated the waiting, but he had to keep his emotions under control. His own safety was paramount at this point. He had one more detail to take care of before everything would be ready for Donna.

Turning off the lights, he went downstairs. It was dark outside, but it was too early yet to leave. He needed to relax before he went out. He was all keyed up, and when that happened, it was easy to make a mistake.

He sat down in the overstuffed chair in the living room and

rested his head against the back of the chair. He was tired from hanging the last of the wallpaper. He could feel little pops under his skin as the tension eased in the muscles of his arms and legs. Physical activity had always helped curb his urges.

It was when he was rested that they returned, more insistent than ever. The restless periods were hard to get through. Memories helped, but as time wore on they became less effective. Then he needed a new experiment.

He opened the fresh bag of sunflower kernels he'd left on the table beside his chair. The kernels made tinkling sounds as he poured them into the cobalt blue glass bowl. When he was little, Mother had never let him touch the bowl. She said it was too fragile for his big clumsy hands. Lovingly, he rubbed his thumb along the thin fluted edge.

He had been craving sunflower kernels all week. He never ate them anywhere else except in the living room or on the front porch. So far he'd been able to fight the temptation to eat them when he was out in the world. It was all a matter of learning control.

He picked up a handful of kernels and put a few on his tongue, rolling them around in his mouth as he sucked off the salt. Even though he wanted to chew them, he forced himself to wait. Part of his power lay in controlling his desires in order to heighten the pleasure while lessening the risk of discovery.

A frown etched his forehead as he reached for more kernels. Donna had come back into his life just in time. It was getting too dangerous finding good subjects for his experiments in River Oaks. Even tonight's business was risky.

He wouldn't need to experiment once Donna came to stay. Just the thought made him groan.

He could picture her fresh from the shower, coming into the bedroom. She'd wear a silky nightgown that outlined the curves of her body. She'd sit at the vanity and let him comb out her hair, stroking it as it fell down her back in a shimmer of gold. The sunflower earrings would swing back and forth with every move of her head.

He leaned back and closed his eyes, playing out the daydream in his mind.

It was raining outside. An occasional gust of wind threw the drops at the window beside him, and the tapping sound made him smile. If it hadn't rained that first time, would things have been any different?

He'd already driven past Janette when he recognized her. He

stopped, backed up, and offered to take her home. She'd been walking for a while, and she was wet. Inside the car, the air conditioning chilled her. He wanted to dry her face with his handkerchief, but he'd given it to her instead, afraid to touch her because she looked so much like Donna with her blond hair and blue eyes.

Although it was only four o'clock, it was dark because of the storm. Thunder boomed overhead, and Janette let out a tiny shriek. To keep her calm, he began to talk. He wasn't even aware that he'd told her about Donna until she'd asked him where it had happened.

The wiper blades scraped back and forth across the windshield, the hypnotic rhythm accompanying the beating of his heart. His sweating palms slipped on the steering wheel as he pulled off the road at the place. They sat in the car and he told her about the sunflowers, the misting rain creating a cozy veil around them.

Janette wanted to see where the gardens had been.

The rain had stopped. They left the car and walked to the edge of the field. He knew he should take her home, but he wanted to prolong the time she stayed with him. Besides, she was eager to learn. He could see by the shine of her eyes how much she wanted to know and to understand.

Then the sun came out suddenly, and in the beam of light her skin glowed like golden satin. It was as if Donna had come back to him. He touched her.

When she started to cry, he panicked. He hadn't even known he had the rock in his hand. He hadn't meant to kill her. He had only wanted to teach her the touching game. It was only afterward when she lay so still that he felt the power. He understood then that for him, it was the only way he could teach them.

Donna had been the one to show him the touching games. Then one day she changed the rules. She took his hand and pulled him into the shed behind his house. She told him what she wanted him to do, but he didn't understand. She was so tiny and he was afraid he would hurt her, but she cried in his ear and begged him to hurry. When he couldn't do it, she laughed at him and ran away. He covered his ears in shame, but he could still hear her laughter inside his head.

A flash of lightning brought him back from the past, and he blinked to rid his mind of Donna's image. Anger coursed through his body at the rumble of thunder overhead. In the sound he could hear the echo of her laughter. She shouldn't have told him about the other boys.

He reached for more kernels. His fingers encountered nothing but the cold glass surface. He picked up the empty bowl. He turned it in his hands, admiring the gleaming color. The blue bowl was the color of Donna's eyes when she taunted him for failing.

With a flick of his wrist, he threw the bowl against the wall, watching impassively as it shattered in a shower of blue glass.

•

"After Meredith died, we bought a dog," Ellen Whitford said, glancing out the picture window at the three boys playing soccer while a Great Dane bounded after them. "Even with Sergeant on guard I'm never totally at ease."

"I can't even imagine how you cope," Sheila said.

Mrs. Whitford's eyes filled up, and she dabbed at them with a handkerchief. Sheila waited, giving the woman a chance to regain her composure. No need to hurry. She had already talked to the families of the other victims.

She'd driven to Madison early in the morning to interview Tiffany Chastain's parents about the sunflower contest. Tiffany had signed up to grow sunflowers both summers before her death.

By noon, Sheila was back in River Oaks and had stopped at the Pottingers. Hugh was helping out at a church outing, but Dorothy was home. She said Lindy had grown sunflowers for the contest only once, and it had not been this past summer but the year before.

"Please excuse me for getting off the subject, Lieutenant Brady," Mrs. Whitford said. "I'm always a little distracted when my husband's out of town. The boys can be a real handful. Now where were we?"

"We were talking about the sunflower contest. I wondered if Meredith had signed up?"

"Oh, yes. She loved the contest. She raised sunflowers for two summers. The second year we had two in the contest. Meredith and Robert." Mrs. Whitford pointed to the tallest of the three boys and smiled in remembrance. "He was furious that her flowers were so much taller."

Except for Janette, the other murdered girls had participated in the contest. Sheila was pleased that she'd confirmed another link between the girls.

"Do you recall the names of any of the people who came to judge the flowers?"

Mrs. Whitford shook her head. "I can't remember anyone specifically, although I do remember that one of the judges last year was Chief Harker."

Sheila was about to comment when her pager vibrated. She unclipped it from her belt and read the display. The call was from Dorothy Pottinger, Lindy's mother.

"I'm sorry, Mrs. Whitford, but I need to make a call," Sheila said, reaching for the phone in her purse.

"Go right ahead. I'll just run and check on the boys."

Mrs. Whitford left the room, leaving Sheila to speak privately. She dialed the number, and it was picked up on the second ring.

"Hi, Dorothy. It's Sheila."

"I didn't know whether I should call you or not. It's something I forgot about."

"Go ahead and tell me. As I said before, anything is better than nothing."

"After you left, I was telling Hugh about your interest in the sunflower contest, and he reminded me of something that happened about a week before Lindy died."

"Something to do with the contest?"

"No, not with the contest. Someone left sunflowers on our doorstep."

Sheila gripped the phone tightly as she pressed it to her ear. "A bouquet?"

"No. It was nothing that formal. Just three or four loose flowers. Hugh said it was like someone dropped them there, almost accidentally."

"No note?"

"No. Just the sunflowers."

"Can either you or Hugh remember when the flowers were left?"

"No. Hugh says he thinks it was during the week before Lindy died, but he can't remember the exact day. Frankly, neither one of us gave it a thought until you mentioned sunflowers. I'm sorry we can't be more specific."

"That's fine, Dorothy. I appreciate your calling me. If you think of anything else, let me know."

Sheila put the phone back in her purse just as Mrs. Whitford returned to the living room.

"I'm sorry for the interruption," Sheila said as the woman sat down again. "I only have a few more questions."

"Take all the time you want, Lieutenant. If there's anything I can tell you that might help to move this investigation forward, I'm glad to do it."

"Can you recall anything unusual that happened in the weeks prior to Meredith's death? Something or someone that seemed out of place?"

"Truly, Lieutenant, I've gone over that time so often and I haven't been able to discover anything. There wasn't any hint that Meredith was in danger. None of us saw any lurking strangers or loitering cars. Nothing. It was a very cold January. People hurried from house to car, so anyone hanging around the area would have been easily seen."

Her expression was bleak.

"Did you receive flowers of any kind in that week?" Sheila asked.

"You mean a delivery?"

"Yes. Or flowers left at the door?"

"No. They would have frozen outside."

Mrs. Whitford pursed her lips and shook her head. Suddenly she stopped, her head cocked to the side and her eyebrows drawn together in a frown of concentration.

"There was something," she said. "Not flowers. Something else."

Sheila kept perfectly still, waiting. Mrs. Whitford blinked several times, and then her expression cleared.

"Ah. Now I remember. It was just something silly. I opened the front door to get the newspaper, and they were on the top step. It wasn't flowers, though. It was seeds. Sunflower seeds."

●

"So you're saying the seeds and the sunflowers are a sign left by the killer?" Paz asked, tugging on one end of his mustache.

"Yes," Sheila said. She glanced at the other faces around the conference table. "I think that once the murderer has selected his victim, he leaves either the seeds or the flowers as a physical manifestation to indicate she's the chosen one."

"Sounds biblical. I hope you're not implying that we've got some kind of religious nut on our hands?" Dandy Dan frowned, clearly put off by the prospect.

Sheila shook her head. "No. We've had no indication that religion plays a part in the guy's fantasies. But he is ritualizing the killings, and the seeds or flowers may be part of the whole package. Don't you think that marking the territory of the victim would fit in with the psychological profile?"

"Possible." The single word was spoken grudgingly. Dan looked across the conference table at Sheila. "He'd get off big time on this. Not only because of the symbolism, but because of the risk of being discovered leaving the flowers and seeds."

Owen James reached for a doughnut on the plate in the center of the table. He bit into it, and a glob of cherry jelly oozed out of the side and dropped onto the front of his shirt. Sighing, he reached for a napkin.

"Why not choose either the sunflowers or the seeds?" he asked as he scrubbed at the stain.

"My guess is that he used what was available," Sheila said. "Ellen Whitford said she found sunflower seeds outside the front door a few days before Meredith was killed. It was January, and sunflowers wouldn't be in bloom."

"Coulda got 'em at a florist," Paz said.

"Before you guys got here, I had Lois Coren do a little checking," Hank said. "She spoke to the florists in town that are open on Sunday. The others she called at home. None of the River Oaks florists handle sunflowers during the winter."

"They're probably sick to death of the flowers by the time summer's over. God knows I am," Paz said. "How 'bout Madison?"

"The florists Lois talked to in Madison said sunflowers would be a special order, and I don't think he would have gone that way. Our boy is too smart to risk a paper trail. The seeds would be easier." Hank's phone rang and he went into his office, talking over his shoulder through the open door. "Keep going. I'm expecting a call from the mayor."

"OK, so the Whitford girl got seeds and Lindy Pottinger got the real flowers," Dan said. "How many? Four?"

"I asked the Pottingers," Sheila said, "but they didn't remember. I don't think it was four. When Lindy was found with four roses in her hand, chances are the Pottingers would have remarked on the similarity and mentioned it during the investigation." Sheila sighed. "The trouble is that in River Oaks, sunflowers are everywhere. Nobody even notices them."

"Agreed," Dan said. "How about the Chastain girl? She was killed in April. You'd have to ask your expert Ferraro if any sunflowers bloom that early. I doubt it, though."

"I talked to Tiffany's parents, and they can't remember either seeds or sunflowers." Sheila shrugged. "They might come up with something after they think about it."

"And if they don't? What happens to your theory then?" Dan asked, a hint of sarcasm in his tone.

"It still holds." Sheila's voice was firm. "According to what the FBI profiler told us, a killer works out the ritualistic aspects of the crime according to some inner criteria. Tiffany was the first one to appear naked in the woods. At that point the killer might not have established the marking of the victim as a part of the whole pattern."

Hank heard the last bit of byplay as he returned to his seat. He was pleased that Sheila had met Dan's skepticism without defensiveness. She'd come a long way since her first meeting, showing no hesitation in her presentation. She was confident of her answers.

"If this theory is correct, and I'm not saying it isn't," Dan temporized, "do you think he made the original contact with the victims through the sunflower contest?"

"Yes," Sheila said. "Possibly as a judge."

Hank glanced around the table as the men considered Sheila's comments. He could see they were coming to believe, just as he had, that her hypothesis was a solid one.

Sheila rubbed the scar beside her eye, the only visible sign of her anxiety over their reaction. Hank caught her eye and nodded his approval.

Breaking the silence in the room, he asked, "Well, gentlemen? Have we a consensus?"

Owen was as good at reading the mood of the room as Hank. "I believe we do. I suggest we make the sunflower angle our prime focus and see if we can't nail this jerk."

Hank reached for the thermos of coffee and poured a mug full. He raised it and took a swallow. "After I talked to Sheila this morning I had a meeting with Dick Perkins. Apparently Barbara Davis called him after Sheila's interview. He admitted to the relationship. He wanted to run for mayor and knew that gossip about his affair would hurt his chances."

"I can understand fearing the scandal before the mayoral election," Owen said, "but why didn't he tell you about it after?"

Hank ran one hand across the top of his head. "He said, and I quote, he did it to protect his wife and Barbara Davis from any publicity."

Paz snorted. "By God! The man's a saint."

"He asked if it had to be public knowledge. I said that unless we found it was pertinent to the murder investigation, we'd keep the information between the five of us in this room."

"Did you tell him he was on the suspect list?" Dan asked.

"We discussed it. He was a judge for the sunflower contest, so he'll be investigated right along with the rest." Hank drank some coffee, waiting until all eyes were on him before continuing. "We talked about the sunflower connection, and I warned him of the real possibility of a child being kidnapped during the festival. It took some convincing, but he agreed to call a special meeting of the town council."

"For today?" Owen looked at his watch. "Three o'clock on a Sunday? I doubt if the city fathers," he nodded to include Sheila, "and mothers, have ever met on the weekend."

"Today they did. That was the mayor on the phone. The council just voted. The Sunflower Festival has been canceled."

"You're kidding!" Paz's words reverberated in the stunned silence.

"Can they do that?" Dan asked.

"Apparently so. It'll cost us. The town will have to pay a penalty to cancel the carnival, but Perkins apparently explained that the expense would be a lot cheaper than a lawsuit against the town—and the members of the town council—if anything happened."

The relief at the cancellation registered on all of the faces around the table. Hank smiled grimly.

"We don't know for sure if the killer was planning to make a move this weekend, but if he was we've bought ourselves a little time. Not much, mind you, but some. We've got to make good use of this week."

Hank could feel his muscles tensing as he thought of the limited time they had. He knew the killer was primed and ready.

"If the murderer had planned something for this weekend, he's going to be furious," he said. "We know he's highly organized, and this will throw everything out of kilter. He'll take the cancellation of the festival as a personal insult. Anger may push him into the very act we're trying to prevent."

•

"Is Nick mad at me, Mom?" Meg asked as Sheila closed the garage door and walked around to the front door.

"No, sweetheart. He's annoyed with me." She stood on the doorstep with her keys in her hand, thinking back to the disastrous ending to the movie outing.

"Because of Dr. Santo?"

"Yes. It was a little awkward when we ran into Nick and his neighbor's son at the ice cream parlor."

"Shouldn't I have asked them to sit with us?"

Sheila laughed and hugged Meg. "I'm glad you did. It seemed to be the only sensible answer. Now that I think of it, you and Beth and Jeff were the only ones who behaved sensibly. I didn't even realize Jeff was in your class. I know his mother."

"Don't you remember, Mom, I told you Beth has had a crush on this boy for just forever. It was Jeff."

"I guess I forgot. No wonder the three of you were giggling so much." Meg stared down at the sidewalk, and Sheila sighed. "I suppose the three of you were amused by the adults."

Meg raised her head. Her expression was contrite, but there was a definite twinkle in her brown eyes. Sheila tried to look severe, shaking her head in mock despair.

"Wretched child," she said. "Laughing at your mother."

Meg giggled. "Sorry, Mom, but it was kind of funny. Dr. Santo and Nick sort of glowering at each other, and you looking all red-faced."

"Perhaps we better drop the subject," Sheila suggested. "It's an episode in my social life that I'd just as soon forget about. I tell you what. I'll feed Elmo while you take care of Cooper."

She unlocked the front door and then stopped. The throw rug in the front hall was empty. Holding her arm out to the side, she prevented Meg from entering.

"Where's Elmo? Stay right here, Meg. I want to make sure everything is all right before you come inside."

Meg was wide-eyed as she stood in the doorway. With her left hand, Sheila pressed the girl's shoulder for reassurance. With her right hand she opened her jacket, unsnapped the holster, and reached for her gun. Suddenly Elmo appeared at the end of the hall, sauntering toward them with his usual arrogant swagger.

"Elmo!" Meg yelled. She bolted around Sheila and knelt down in front of the cat. "Where have you been? We missed you."

Sheila holstered her gun before Meg could see it and become frightened. Her heart beat raggedly as she glared at the cat, who seemed to be behaving normally. Still, she sensed that something was wrong, although she wondered fleetingly if the fact she had started carrying her gun made her more susceptible to paranoia. Harker had suggested it. In the past she had always kept her gun in her locker at the station, but he'd insisted, and she'd finally agreed to carry it all the time.

She walked out to the kitchen with Meg and Elmo, unlocked the security bar, and opened the patio door. Crisp fall air swirled around her, restoring some sense of normality.

"Dinnertime, Cooper," Meg said as she stepped outside.

She removed the top of the aquarium and reached inside to stroke the feathers of the mourning dove. She checked to make sure the bird still had gravel, then picked up the other two dishes.

"Go to the kitchen door. Elmo will keep an eye on Cooper," Sheila said, smiling down at the cat on watch behind the screen.

Meg skipped away. Sheila walked back to the kitchen, but before she could reach it, the door opened. She came to a stop, staring at Meg in dismay.

"Did you unlock the door?" Sheila asked.

"No. I just pushed on it and it opened."

While Meg was busy getting birdseed and water for the bird, Sheila tried to remember when she had last used the door. She had taken out the recycling bin in the morning. Was it possible that she hadn't closed the door tightly enough for the lock to catch?

She held the door for Meg as she took out the dishes for the bird, closing and locking the door behind her. She tested it to be sure it was closed all the way. The sensation that something wasn't quite right returned.

Going along the hallway, she checked the bathroom and Meg's bedroom. Her daughter's room was in its usual state of disarray, with clothes overflowing the dresser drawers and piled on the chair in the corner. Shaking her head, Sheila wondered how she would even know if the place had been ransacked.

Standing in the doorway of her bedroom, Sheila felt a chill.

She checked the closet, but her clothes appeared in perfect order. Nothing appeared out of place on either her dresser or her bedside table. The windows were locked, and the dust on the windowsills was undisturbed.

But when she went into the bathroom, fear shot through her like an electric jolt. Someone had been in there. A can of talcum powder was lying on the braid rug, and a white dusting of powder was scattered over the sink fixtures and the top of the counter.

Careful not to disturb anything, she stepped closer and discovered the source of the trouble. In the white powder beside the sink were several very definite paw prints. Behind her she heard the cat meow, and she braced herself for the touch of fur against her leg.

"No wonder you weren't on the rug when we came in, Elmo. You were in here playing," she muttered. "I don't know why I put up with you, you mangy beast."

She leaned over and rubbed the cat under his chin, letting the rhythmic purring soothe her. She had been surprised at the depth of her alarm about Elmo when he hadn't been in his usual spot. Much as she grumbled, the cat had found a place in her heart.

Just as she straightened up, she caught a flash of metal. She reached under the edge of the sink cabinet and found an earring. She held it up, the gold sunflower dangling at the end of a short chain.

"So that's what you were playing with. Damn it, Elmo. You've got to leave my things alone."

She rinsed the earring off under hot water and dried it. Her jewelry box was open on the far end of the counter. As she searched for the matching earring, she made a mental note to start closing the lid.

"What did you do with the other one, Elmo?"

Unable to find it, she dropped the sunflower earring in one of the partitions and closed the lid. She picked up the bottle of talcum powder and washed off the residue on the countertop. Folding the throw rug so she wouldn't trail the spilled powder through the house, she turned out the light. With her foot, she nudged the cat toward the door.

"Come on, Elmo. I'll get you some dinner and you can pretend it's Cooper." She spoke over her shoulder to the cat, who followed after her as she walked toward the kitchen. "I don't know why you can't follow the bird's example. He never gives me any trouble."

•

"Jesus Jenny!" Hank threw his napkin on the table as he rose to answer the phone. "I'd like to get through one meal without that damn phone ringing."

Della looked slightly anxious as she stared at Owen James sitting next to her at the dining room table. He ignored the interruption, finishing the last bite of cake and wiping his mouth before leaning back with a contented sigh.

"That was a damn fine dinner, Della," he said as he brushed the chocolate cake crumbs off his chest. "I can see why Hank gains weight when you're in town."

Della laughed. "I think it's more likely it's because I drive him crazy and he drinks more when I'm here. I'm glad you could join us. A pork roast is too much for just two people, and it's good for Hank to have a real sit-down meal in the presence of company rather than eat on the run, as I suspect he does most days."

"The last couple weeks have been busier than usual."

"I gather. I know he's concerned that there will be another attack on a young girl. Every time the phone rings I cringe that something awful has happened."

"Canceling the Sunflower Festival may have bought us some time."

Della raised the coffee pot and Owen nodded. She filled his cup, then her own. Just the thought of the murders chilled her, and she put her hands around the china cup, letting the warmth comfort her. She tried to think of something more pleasant to talk about, and a question flashed in her mind.

"Who's Sheila?"

Owen was startled by the sudden question. "Do you mean Sheila Brady?"

"I don't know. I was talking to Hank and he had someone in his office. I was curious because his voice was more concerned than usual."

"Hmmm," Owen said, one eyebrow raised in interest. "Then it probably was Sheila. She's one of the detectives working on the murders."

Della waited, but when he made no further comment, she picked up the serving knife and pointed to the chocolate cake. "More, Owen?"

"Goodness, Della, is that something in the way of a pressure tactic?"

"Of course not. You've been eying it ever since Hank left."

He handed her his dessert plate. She cut a thick slice of the cake and placed it in the center of his plate.

"I was in interrogations during 'Nam," he said, "but we never considered using chocolate to get information out of people."

"No wonder we didn't win the war."

Della leaned back in her chair and waited. Owen gazed hungrily at his cake, then set his fork down and turned to her.

"Sheila Brady's been on the force about eight or nine months. She's a single mother with an eleven-year-old daughter. She's blond, has a knockout figure, and is a damn fine officer with good instincts and a creative mind." Owen took a deep breath. "Anything else you'd like to know?"

"Hank repeated several times that he wanted her to be careful. The tone of his voice suggested she might be in danger," she said.

"It's possible." Owen traced the pattern on the silver fork with his thumb. "Her ex-partner did a nasty bit of harassing, and she has a feeling she's being watched. Having a child the same age as the victims doesn't help either."

"No wonder Hank's worried." Della took a sip of coffee. "He's never been keen on women in his police force. Much as he tries to be liberated, he's old-fashioned enough to want to protect a woman in danger. Must shake him up a bit that he can't."

Owen grinned. "It shakes him quite a lot. Don't get the idea that Sheila's the swooning heroine type. She's well trained. She'll be careful."

"I hope so," Della said.

"Don't we all?"

Picking up his fork, he took a large bite of cake. She was glad that she'd made the effort to bake. Hank was indifferent to food, but Owen relished every bite. She caught his eye and he nodded.

"While we're trading information," he said, "maybe you can help me. About fifteen years ago a kid accused one of the high school teachers of practicing satanism. The principal's dead, and the teachers I've talked to knew nothing about it. Apparently it was kept hush-hush for fear of ruining the man's reputation."

"Satanism?" Della shook her head. "I never heard anything."

Owen took another bite of cake before he spoke. "Damn. Another dead end. For some reason this is bugging me."

"You should go out to see Gerry Butler at Park Ridge Estates. Before her retirement, she was the high school librarian," Della said. "In fact, if you want, I could drop by and see her."

"That would be swell if it wouldn't be too much of a bother."

"To be perfectly honest, I love talking to Gerry. She's the kindest person I know, and nothing ever gets by her. She always has the best gossip."

Owen chuckled and returned his attention to the cake. He'd just finished the last bite when Hank's footsteps sounded from across the hall.

"Sorry, Mother," he said, "but we have to go back to work."

"At this hour?"

"We've got trouble."

At Hank's words, Owen stood up and grabbed the jacket on the back of his chair. Della caught her breath in fear.

"Don't tell me a child is missing." She placed one hand flat on her bosom as she felt her chest tighten.

"No. Thank God." Hank shook his head. "I just got a call from Norm Hallwestle in Madison. A body was found in a Dumpster in the university area around six o'clock tonight."

"Someone from River Oaks?"

"I'm afraid so, Mother," Hank said, squeezing her shoulder for reassurance. "It's Vinnie Calero, the man who discovered Lindy's shoelace in the woods."

"I thought he was safe and sound in his sister's apartment," Owen said as he put on his jacket.

"So did I," Hank said. "Somehow he got to Madison and someone killed him. He was strangled; tied around his neck was Lindy Pottinger's other shoelace."

Chapter Sixteen

"Vinnie was strangled with the shoelace?" Paz shook his head in denial. "No way. You'd never get enough leverage with a kid's shoelace."

"Good conclusion," Hank said, "and you're right. The M.E. says the shoelace was tied around Vinnie's neck after he was dead. The ligature marks suggest rope."

"So the killer wants credit," Paz said. "The arrogance fits the profile, all right."

Hank rubbed one hand across his forehead and up over the top of his head. He was tired. Once they had confirmed the body was that of Vinnie Calero, Dan was routed out of bed and joined Owen in Madison. Hank had notified Sheila and Paz of Vinnie's death, telling them to report for the morning meeting at seven.

At times like that, Hank wished he worked in a big city. His department was overworked already, and Vinnie's murder only made the situation worse.

After interviewing Vinnie's sister, he had called Dick Perkins. The mayor, already at odds with Hank over the Barbara Davis affair and the cancellation of the festival, had been furious at the turn of events. Perkins had been on the phone twice this morning, and it was only eight o'clock. This was a hell of a way to start the week.

"Why didn't the sister report Vinnie's disappearance?" Dan asked, adjusting the material of his trousers over his knee to prevent it from pulling.

"She didn't discover he was gone until around one on Sunday afternoon," Owen said. "She wasn't worried at first. Apparently he'd also gone out on Friday night, and she thought he'd done the same thing. When he wasn't back by dinnertime, she was afraid to let anyone know. She didn't want them to revoke bail."

"So what's her take on this?" Paz asked.

"Francine said when she got home from her girlfriend's house on Saturday, Vinnie was edgy. 'Keyed up' was how she put it." Hank took a sip of his coffee, wincing at the bitterness. He liked it strong, but this stuff could raise the dead. "At first she thought he was on something. He calmed down while they watched a movie on the tube, but during the news there was a report on the murders, and they showed his picture. She said he started talking real crazy, saying things about being famous and giving interviews."

"Ye gods. Don't tell me we have that to look forward to!" Dan said. "A big scoop on CNN. Vinnie telling about finding the shoelace! With him dead it'll be twice the hype."

"Maybe he did get an offer of an interview. Maybe that's why he went out," Owen said. "Can we get the phone company to give us a call log for the apartment?"

"Great idea, Owen. I'll get someone on that," Hank said.

The list of things to do was getting longer, he thought, as he jotted down a notation. Despite the anger over Vinnie's murder, the tension in the room had more to do with excitement than anxiety. For the first time in many days there was movement on the case.

Paz leaned back in his chair, one hand stroking his mustache. "When did she see him last?"

"Saturday night." Hank checked his notes. "At midnight, Vinnie said he was tired. Francine cleaned up the kitchen and then she went to bed. Her bedroom is toward the front of the apartment. Vinnie's is off the kitchen at the far end. She said she never heard him leave."

"They're setting the time of death at about two o'clock A.M. Sunday, so we're looking for someone who might have been out and about in Madison sometime between midnight and say three in the morning," Owen said.

"For the record, Dick Perkins has no alibi for that time period," Hank said. "Carolyn and the kids were visiting her sister in Minneapolis. Dick didn't go. Saturday he worked at home on a speech for the Rotarians, watched TV, and went to bed about eleven."

"What a loser!" Paz threw up his hands in disgust. "The one time his philandering could have saved him, and he slept alone."

Hank let the amusement die down before he continued. "I want Herb Reisler and Doug Maloney checked, as well as anyone else who's on the secondary list. See if we can eliminate anyone with a solid alibi."

"I have another name to add to the suspect list," Owen said. "Dominic Ferraro."

"My sunflower expert?" Sheila asked in surprise.

"The very same. I've been trying to track down a rumor of a kid at the high school who accused one of the teachers of satanism," Owen said. He grinned at Hank. "Actually it was Della who got me the information."

Hank frowned. "I should have known. You two looked entirely too chummy at dinner last night. What did she find out?"

"Dominic Ferraro was the teacher the boy charged with satanism. The kid, Greg Edwards, failed biology, and the principal believed the boy made the allegation out of spite. He recanted, and the investigation went no further."

"It's pretty thin," Paz said.

"I did a quick check on the kid, then I talked to his mother this morning. Greg Edwards died three months after his accusation. It was called an accident, but the mother never believed it. She always thought someone had killed him."

"Did she mention Ferraro?"

"Actually, no. She seems to think that some kids had beaten him up and he died. She used the word hooligans. She said Greg went trout fishing on a little pasture stream over in Micheff County only eight or ten miles from their home. He was found by a couple of school kids, his body half in the stream and half on the bank."

"I vaguely remember," Hank said. "The county sheriff reported that the boy slipped on a rock, fell into the water, and drowned. The autopsy report, however, showed that while there was water in the lungs, he'd actually died of head injuries. His head and face were all bruised, like he'd been in a fight."

"If he hit his head on a rock when he fell in, that would account for the bruises, wouldn't it?" Sheila asked.

"That was the opinion at the time," Owen said. "I think Mrs.

Edwards preferred foul play to a simple accident. He was her only son, and she was terribly upset."

"So you're suggesting that Ferraro might have offed him?" Paz leaned across the table, staring at Owen.

"Stranger things have happened. I think he's worth investigating."

"I agree," Hank said. "At this stage of the game we look at anyone who even sneezes funny. Now, let's get back to Vinnie."

"The two questions I'd like to get answered," Dan said, making a large check mark in his notebook, "are whether the killer lured Vinnie out of the apartment or whether he just got lucky? And why did he kill Vinnie?"

"I don't know the answer to the first, or the second." Hank shrugged his shoulders. "It would seem, though, that Vinnie must have known more than he admitted."

"He couldn't have seen the murder committed, because he was still in rehab when Lindy was killed. So it has to be the shoelace," Dan said. "I thought Vinnie said he couldn't remember where he found it."

"That's what he told us." The muscles in Hank's neck tightened as he glanced around the room. "My guess is that the murderer believed that Vinnie knew where the shoelace was found and killed him to prevent him from telling anyone."

•

"Are you dating Warren Santo?"

Nick's quiet question came through the phone loud and clear. Sheila sighed. She had known that once the ordinary chitchat was completed he'd ask about Warren.

"Not really. I invited him to go to the movie with the girls, and then he asked if we'd like to get ice cream at Paxton's."

"So I gathered."

"Don't make a big deal of it, Nick." She hated having to explain herself. "Warren's been taking care of the mourning dove Meg found. He's easy to talk to. I don't know if there's any more to it than that."

"It sounds like you want to pursue it."

Sheila closed her eyes and took a slow steady breath. She could hardly be angry at him for questioning her. She'd never defined their relationship and had never discouraged the conclusions he had drawn. Perhaps she should have. In truth she didn't know if she wanted a fully committed relationship with Nick. She liked him, enjoyed his company and his lovemaking.

Did she love him?

"I don't know, Nick." Sheila wondered if she was answering her own question or his. "All I know is that I don't want to fight with you or hurt your feelings."

"Why don't we get together for dinner?"

"I can't. We've got an emergency here, and Harker has the lot of us working overtime. Meg's coming here after her Girl Scout meeting, and we're going to grab a bite before we go home."

"Putting me off for someone in uniform?"

She heard anger beneath the lightly spoken words. Resting her elbows on her desk, she cupped the phone close to her mouth to create some semblance of privacy.

"No. I'm not stalling, Nick. I know you want to get things resolved, but it's just not possible tonight. We might be getting a break in the murders, so I can't take time away from here for anything other than Meg. This week, the investigation takes precedence over my social life."

"In other words, standard operating procedures. Right, Brady?"

Sheila winced. "That's not fair, Nick."

"Maybe not, but it is pretty close to the truth," he said. "I'll admit your job has never been easy for me to handle. Just the fact that you wear a pager annoys me. I half expect you'll get beeped in the middle of lovemaking. When we're together I want your mind solely focused on what we're doing. Maybe I'm selfish, but that's the way I feel."

Sheila shook her head. "You're not selfish. Maybe I just needed to hear your complaints to understand. I'm not insensitive, Nick."

"I know you're not. I'm probably not putting any of this well. I'm jealous of your commitment to your job, and besides that I worry about you. Working on the investigations could be risky. If you come too close to the murderer, you could be in danger."

"Danger is part of the job."

"Maybe so, but I don't have to like it. You need to be careful, Sheila."

"I will. Don't think I don't appreciate your concern. I really do." She swallowed a lump in her throat. "Our relationship is important to me, and it's going to take more than a five-minute conversation to iron out the complications. Let me get through this week, and then we'll get together and talk things out. Can you wait until then?"

Sheila pressed the phone close to her ear, but all she could hear was the sound of Nick breathing. Finally he broke the silence.

"Yes. I can do that," he said. "I understand your job and Meg take precedence over your social life, but I worry that misunderstandings will get in the way. I don't want to lose you, Sheila."

"I don't want to lose you either," she said. "I didn't handle the situation at the ice cream parlor very well. I know we were all uncomfortable. I'm sorry."

"Don't remind me. I behaved like a first-class ass." Nick sounded more chagrined than angry. "Look, Brady, let's call a truce. We'll get together when we can. Until then, we're friends. Right?"

"Agreed. Will I see you at Career Night at the high school?"

"That's tomorrow? Yes. I'll be in the photo lab with an exhibit that I worked on with the advanced photography class. Are you going to flash your badge and show your uniform?"

Sheila laughed. "No. At church they were looking for help to serve refreshments in the gym. Meg volunteered the two of us."

"She's a great kid. I'll try to get loose and see you both. If not, give her a hug for me."

"I will. Look for me behind the punch bowl."

After she hung up, Sheila sat staring at the far wall, her vision unfocused as she thought about Nick. It always came back to the central question: Did she love Nick enough to marry him?

She didn't know the answer. Her job would always be a problem. He hated being cut out of a whole portion of her life. She could understand that but didn't know if the situation could ever be corrected. No wonder so many cops were divorced.

Now that she'd talked to Nick, she supposed she ought to call Warren Santo. That would be even more awkward. As she reached for the phone, it rang.

"Sheila?"

"Good heavens, Warren. You must have extrasensory powers. I was just reaching for the phone to call you," she said, then laughed. "I know that's usually a line, but in this case it's true."

"Are you sure you have time to talk? You sound harassed."

"No more than usual. I could use a visit to your bonsai garden about now. When I'm really stressed, I close my eyes and pretend I'm beside the pond listening to the little brass bells."

"I feel honored that you'd include my garden in your meditations."

"Even if it was cut short, it was a charming evening."

"I hope some time soon you'll be able to spend more time look-ing around and getting the full sense of internal balance and peace. Meg too, of course," he added hastily. "Sunday didn't seem to be the proper occasion for a return visit."

"Which reminds me, I owe you another apology. Meg didn't re-alize . . ."

He cut her off. "There's nothing to apologize for. I knew you had to be dating someone, and besides, I like Nick."

"Nick's been a good friend. We've been going out for a couple of months. We're not engaged or anything."

"Oh."

Sheila could feel a blush rising to her cheeks as she realized her last answer implied she was available. She started to speak but Warren interrupted again.

"I wondered if . . . I mean I was hoping you weren't totally com-mitted, because even if I haven't said anything, I do enjoy being with you and talking to you."

"Please, Warren, this is getting awkward. I have an idea," she said. "Let's give it some time. Hopefully in a few days, I will have fig-ured out whether I want a new relationship or just a friend."

"That sounds like a good solution," he said. "Yesterday Meg told me you're both serving punch and cookies at Career Night at the high school, so maybe I'll see you there. Tell Meg to drop by the bi-ology lab. I'm bringing the cocker spaniel puppies I told her about for show and tell."

Thankfully, both men currently in her life were fond of Meg, she thought as she hung up the phone. Much as her daughter kidded about Sheila remarrying, it would be a difficult adjustment. For both of them.

If I get busy enough, Sheila thought, I might be able to forget the whole subject of men and dating. It was all so different than it was when she was in college. Dating and her social life took up a ma-jor part of her time then. Now it was only an occasional blip on the screen, surrounded by a sea of responsibility.

•

He sat on the top step, looking out over the gardens. Fall was taking hold. A cool breeze brushed across the sunflowers, and the heads nodded in a silent rhythm. The drying stalks rubbed together in a sharp rasping sound.

The cuts itched. He glared down at the long sleeve that covered the bandage on his arm.

Damn cat! It had jumped up on the counter, knocking over the talcum powder. He swore. No time for a cleanup. He grabbed the cat and pressed its paws in the white film until he had several visible prints. It hissed, digging its back claws into his arm. In anger he threw it out the bathroom door, smiling grimly as it hit the floor with a dull thud.

The cuts had bled. He could see the red spots forming as it soaked into the shirt material. He hurried through the house and out the kitchen door, pushing the door closed behind him.

It was only when he got home that he realized he'd dropped one of the sunflower earrings.

He stood up and walked down into the garden. He stepped into the rows of Paul Bunyan hybrid. His choice had turned out to be a winner. The sunflower stalks were twelve feet tall, and he'd planted them close together to create a forest effect.

Once inside the rows, he felt as if he were in a whole different world, isolated and protected. He counted the stalks, cutting to his left when he reached the fourteenth. He pushed aside the plants as he moved diagonally across the plot until he reached the heart of the field and the opening in the center.

The unplanted circle was surrounded by a wall of stalks, and at noon the sun beat down, making the air thick with heat. His senses filled with the heavy scent of the mulch. He'd brought in layers of long grass to create a soft bed, where he could lie and stare up at the circle of sky above the nodding heads of the giant sunflowers. The size of the plants and the seed heads dwarfed him, and he felt that he was a child once again.

He pulled the bauble from his pocket. He rubbed it between his fingers until the metal was warm, then he extended his arm above his head. The earring spun freely, sparkling in the sunlight as if it had a life of its own. The gold sunflower blazed, and he squinted at the intensity of the glow.

He felt her presence as a painful memory and a much-desired future event. It was almost as if she were with him in the cocoon of flowers. He would bring her here. At last she would understand his world. Everything he'd done was only in preparation for that moment when he would see in her eyes a reflection of her pride in his achievements.

It was almost time. He would have her all to himself, and he would help her to understand. This time he would be the teacher.

●

Hazel Florence sighed as she looked out the upstairs window at the pile of leaves forming at the corner where the fence met the garage. Winter was coming. With each passing day the warmth from the sunlight grew weaker. All too soon, she'd be staring out at snow-covered streets. Now that her body was so stiffened by arthritis that she couldn't get out much, winter seemed endless.

Her daughter Kathryn had tried to make the room cheerful with bright chintz curtains and a floral wallpaper. Hazel never minded it in the summer because she was able to get outside and sit in the yard. It was only in winter that the room became her prison. She had come to live with Kathryn and Paul three years earlier. She'd still been somewhat mobile then and enjoyed walking the streets in the Estates, looking at all the new houses. Then the arthritis got worse and for a while she couldn't even close her hands. It was dreadful to have to rely on others for the intimate details of your life.

The bedroom faced west, so she caught the last rays of the setting sun. Hazel didn't mind that the room was always warm. The warmth burrowed beneath her skin, melting the oils and lubricating her stiffened joints.

The sunlight receded from her lap and inched across the carpet. The days were getting shorter. It wasn't seven yet, and already the light was fading. Each time the sun went down, the shadows leached the heat from her body and she wondered if she would wake up the next day frozen in position.

She used to be so active. A social butterfly, her husband Albert used to call her. She'd loved going in to Madison for concerts and lectures at the university. Once they'd gone to Chicago for a week and had seen three plays. My, how she'd enjoyed that.

It was a long time ago, Hazel thought, her eyes misting as she stared blindly out the window. Albert had been gone for twenty years, and his old butterfly had clipped wings. Now the back yards along the alley were her theater, and she, the unseen audience.

"Land sakes, I'm getting to be a regular watering pot lately," Hazel muttered, wiping her eyes.

Despite her infirmities, she had much to be thankful for. At seventy-eight she had all her vision, most of her hearing, and a brain sharp as a butcher's knife. She still did the Sunday *Chicago Tribune* crossword puzzle, although now it took her most of the day. Her grandson Peter faxed it to her right from his home.

Kathryn and Paul had gone to the movies. How blessed she was to have such a generous and loving family. Kathryn was so good to her. Their roles were reversed now. She was the child, dependent on Kathryn to carry her from the bed to the chair.

Out of the corner of her eye, Hazel caught a movement in the alley. The shadows had deepened, and she squinted to sharpen her vision. A man was in the alley, standing at the fence behind the house. He was just on the edge of her vision, and she wished she could move to get a better look at him.

She could see his shoulder and his arm as he reached over the fence to open the latch on the gate. He opened the gate slowly and peered inside the yard, then pulled the gate closed and moved along the alley to the next fence.

"How strange," she said, her eyes following him.

She didn't recognize the man. It was troubling because she knew everyone on the block by sight. It made her uneasy having a stranger roaming the neighborhood. She had read the papers and knew all about the maniac who was killing children.

The man moved down the alley. Hazel was frightened. From her upstairs vantage point, she could see a group of children playing in the Raffertys' yard just four fences away.

Her lips trembled with indecision. She hated to be a busybody.

"Nonsense," she snapped, drawing herself as straight as she could. "Better a meddler than a fool."

She reached for the telephone. Her hands were so stiff that she had to use both of them to move the portable phone to her lap. She raised it to dial, but in her awkwardness she hit the receiver against the arm of the chair. It dropped back to her lap, slid across the blanket covering her legs, and fell to the floor.

Looking out the window, Hazel saw the man approaching the fence three away from the Raffertys' yard.

The phone lay on the floor just beyond her feet. She extended her arm, but her fingers were at least two feet away from the wretched thing.

In her frustration, she started to cry. A sob caught in her throat as she chided herself for being such a ninny. She had to think of some way to reach the phone. She might be able to get out of the chair, but she'd never be able to bend over without falling.

"You don't have to get up out of the chair, you silly goose. You need to get down."

She placed her cupped hands at the ends of the chair arms and pushed. Her body inched forward. She used the heels of her slippers to pull as she pressed backwards with her hands and arms. By the time she was perched on the edge of the seat, her body was bathed in sweat.

The drop to the floor wasn't far, but her bones were brittle, and she gave a moment's thought to the possibility of breaking something. Trying to keep her body loose, she pushed away from the chair.

Her bottom hit the carpet with a jarring motion. Other than being a little short of breath from the exertion, she wasn't hurt.

Leaning sideways, she used her hand to rake the phone close enough to reach. This time she gripped it firmly. She had always thought it was lazy to use telephones with memory buttons so you wouldn't have to look up the number. Now she blessed the technology that enabled her to push one button to reach the Raffertys' house.

She hesitated. Perhaps the man had gone away. By stretching her neck she could see over the windowsill down into the alley. The stranger was approaching the Raffertys' fence.

Pushing the button, she raised the phone. The dull buzz of the busy signal sounded in her ear. A small cry escaped her, and she bit her lip in frustration. She wanted to smash the phone against the wall. Instead she pushed the button for 911.

•

"Car four here, Central." As Ray Florio spoke into the car phone, he reached for the laminated map of their patrol sector.

"The police just got a call about a stranger in the alley that runs between Ash and Teak. The five hundred block."

"It's just a couple blocks away," Jim said, peering through the windshield at the numbers on the houses.

"We're on our way, Central."

Ray's hand shook only slightly as he replaced the phone. He and Jim had been changed to a later shift because someone on the patrol had canceled. His head ached from straining to see clearly in the gathering darkness.

Jim switched on the car lights, the beams picking out the details along the street. Ray felt his heart beating steadily as they sped along the streets. He touched the pocket of his windbreaker for reassurance.

The tires squealed as the car swung into the alley.

Caught in the lights from the car, two figures froze in a frightening tableau. A man was holding the hand of a little girl and appeared to be dragging her down the alley.

The Chevy Blazer skidded in the slippery gravel, and Ray elbowed the door open before the car was completely stopped. He fumbled in the pocket of his coat as he shouted at the man holding the girl. The man released the child's hand, picked her up in his arms, and headed down the alley.

"Stop or I'll shoot," Ray shouted as he scrambled out of the car.

The man turned around to look over his shoulder, but he kept on going, racing toward the open mouth of the alley. Ray pulled the gun out of his pocket and steadied his hands on top of the car door.

Taking aim, he squeezed the trigger.

Chapter Seventeen

"Honest to God, Chief Harker, how could I know it was his kid? I thought the guy was trying to kidnap her."

Hank ground his teeth as he stood behind his desk, leaning on the back of his chair. He tried to ignore the distraught expression on the older man's face.

"What in the name of all that's holy did you think you were doing, Ray? The only thing that keeps me from throwing you in jail is the fact that the bullet hit that telephone pole. But even then, a wild shot might have ricocheted and killed both the man and his daughter."

Ray's face, already pale, looked almost translucent in the overhead lights.

"As it is," Hank continued, "you terrified that poor kid. And not only her. What about the other kids in the yard?"

Nodding his head, Ray opened his mouth. He licked his dry lips before he could speak.

"I can't tell you how sorry I am, Chief. I've got grandkids of my own. Just like everyone else, I'm scared to death that this killer will take one of them." His face was screwed up in a grimace. "I can't get the thought out of my mind that I mighta killed someone."

Hank sighed. Adrenaline from the shooting had drained away, and Ray looked pathetically frail. He seemed to have aged visibly since his arrival at the police station. Some of Hank's anger faded. He looked up at the knock on the door. He walked around the desk and stepped outside his office, pulling the door closed behind him.

"What have you got, Paz?"

"I just got off the phone with Dennis Conroy's wife. His story checks out. He was supposed to pick up his daughter at the Raffertys' but forgot the address. He thought he was in the right block, so he just started peeking in each of the yards until he found her."

"Too bad the shot missed him. If it had nicked him a little, he might have learned it's not smart to sneak around the alleys in a town that's paranoid about strangers."

"Agreed," Paz said. "Since Conroy's story checks out, do you want me to release him?"

Hank rubbed his face with both hands. If he hadn't been so tired, he might have been less angry at the man's stupidity.

"Yes, go ahead and release him. After you remind him that he might have had his head shot off or his daughter killed with this escapade."

"I'm going to enjoy this. He's been a pompous ass since we brought him in." Paz stroked his mustache and chuckled. "It's payback time."

Opening the door of his office, Hank stared at Ray Florio's slumped figure. Charging him with disorderly conduct and getting him to resign from the citizen's patrol ought to be sufficient punishment. Even though he didn't approve, Hank could understand the thought processes that led up to tonight's fiasco. In fact, he was surprised that it hadn't happened sooner.

Fear had a stranglehold on the town. The cancellation of the Sunflower Festival had demoralized everyone. They saw it as an indication of how little control the police department had when they couldn't guarantee the safety of the children at the annual event.

Hank looked at Ray with compassion, knowing that if he had been in his place, and had the murderer in his sights, he wouldn't hesitate to pull the trigger.

•

"Can Beth and I go down to the biology lab to see Dr. Santo's puppies?" Meg asked.

"Sure, but don't be gone too long," Sheila said. "It's nine o'clock. Try to be back in a half hour to help clean up. Do you know where it is?"

"We'll find it."

The girls waved breezily and hurried out from behind the buffet table, cutting through the crowd in the cafeteria. Sheila's feet hurt. It had been a mistake to wear heels, although since she didn't get dressed up all that often, she was glad to have a chance to wear something more feminine than either her uniform or her sweats. Still, despite the fact that the floral print dress had short sleeves and a full skirt, she was warm in the close air.

The number of people who had turned out for the high school Career Night surprised her, especially since it was a Tuesday night. The woman from church who'd recruited them said that the town really supported the event. Even so, Sheila hadn't expected such a crush.

The event would be over in an hour, but it seemed to Sheila that the crowd had increased rather than thinned out. She poured a cup of punch and sipped slowly as she looked around the room.

His face serious, Dick Perkins stood in the center of the room, talking to a circle of people. Although Sheila had overheard talk about the murder of Vincent Calero, she suspected that the mayor was being asked about the Sunflower Festival. Most people seemed to understand the reasons behind the cancellation of the eagerly awaited event, but they still weren't especially happy over the decision.

She had acknowledged Perkins's greeting with a forced smile when he came to get his wife some punch. She had never particularly cared for him, and she liked him even less now that she knew about his affair with Barbara Davis. Hoping her face revealed none of her antipathy, Sheila had poured the punch and given him a paper plate with some cookies.

Out of the corner of her eye, she spotted Chief Harker shepherding an older woman, whom she assumed was his mother, around the room. They stopped often. Mrs. Harker was obviously well liked, because her arrival was met with smiles and hugs.

It was interesting to observe Harker in a social situation. He moved confidently, and although he wasn't a hugger, there was something warm about his smile and his handshake.

It must be the eyes, Sheila thought, realizing that before tonight she'd never seen them as anything but hard brown.

Just then, Harker looked up, saw her, and nodded a greeting. She smiled, surprised by her pleasure at his acknowledgment. It was the first time she was aware that she had actually begun to like Hank Harker.

All in all it had been a good evening, she thought. Career Night was the first big event that she'd attended since she and Meg had moved to River Oaks. She was pleased by the number of people she knew and by the number who stopped by to say hello. She had been so busy since her arrival eight months ago that she hadn't realized the town already felt more like home than Milwaukee had in eight years. She suspected it was having her own home that had given her a sense of investiture in the community.

Now if only she could get her social life under control.

Earlier, both Nick and Warren had come to the cafeteria, although thankfully not at the same time. With each man the awkwardness disappeared after a moment or two, and she was able to chat casually with both of them.

"You seem very far away, Lieutenant Brady."

Sheila had been so deep into her own thoughts that she jumped at Dominic Ferraro's comment. She could feel a blush of embarrassment rise to her cheeks as she recalled he was now on the suspect list.

"I'm so sorry," she said, setting her empty paper cup on the table. "I almost didn't recognize you without your sunflowers around you. Would you like some more punch?"

"Very much so."

He held out his paper cup, and she filled it.

"I was actually thinking about River Oaks," she said. "I just realized how much the town means to me even though I've only been here a short time. It's as if I've found a real home."

Dominic beamed at her as if she were a particularly bright child. "You know the saying. Home is where the heart is."

"I don't usually pour out my thoughts like this, but . . ."

"No need to apologize. I find it very charming and feel honored that you would share your thoughts with me. Besides, with your dress you look as if you belong in my garden, although I suspect my wife wouldn't approve."

Only a little later, just after Dominic left, Sheila felt as if someone were staring at her. Several times during the evening she'd experienced the same uneasiness, but she had never been able to pinpoint the source. This time, as she glanced around she was jolted to see Doug Maloney leaning against the wall. When he caught her eye, he walked toward her.

"What are you doing here?" she asked. His eyes narrowed, and she regretted blurting out the words.

"I was tapped to give a presentation on the governor's new drug program."

"I hope it went well," Sheila said. "We've run out of cookies, but there's a little more punch left if you'd like some."

He grimaced. "No thanks. I just wanted to come over and say hello. You look really good. I don't think I ever saw you out of uniform."

Sheila ignored the compliment and the leer that accompanied it. The muscles of her body tensed, and she was grateful for the table between them. "Unfortunately I'm too warm and my feet hurt."

"It would be fun to get together to talk about our old Milwaukee days. I'm going to the Duck Inn for a beer before I head back to Madison. Want to join me after this shindig is over?"

"Sorry, Doug, but I can't. I have to clean up here, and then I've got to get Meg home to bed."

"No problem. Maybe another time."

The smile stayed firmly in place, but it didn't spread to his eyes. Doug rarely got turned down, so he'd never learned to laugh it off. Mindful of the bloody doll, she searched for a comment to defuse the situation. Relief came in the form of Chief Harker and his mother.

After the introductions, Doug excused himself on the grounds that he had to drive back to Madison. Harker's eyes were flinty as he watched Maloney leave.

"What was he doing here?" Harker asked.

Mrs. Harker looked puzzled by her son's gruff words.

"The man was my partner when I worked in Milwaukee," Sheila said to Della by way of explanation. Then, to Harker, "He said he was giving one of the governor's drug presentations. He stopped here on his way back to Madison."

"What did he talk to you about?"

"I'd say that's an impertinent question, Hank," Della said, clearly shocked.

"Sheila works for me. My questions have to do with an ongoing investigation."

"We're back, Mom."

Sheila turned at the sound of Meg's voice. The girls were pink-cheeked and out of breath from running across the gym. She quickly introduced them to Mrs. Harker and asked how the puppies were.

"Oh, Mom, they were so cute. There were three of them. Two girls and a boy. And still so tiny." Meg held her hands apart to indicate their length. "Beth and I wanted to take them home."

Della laughed. "I have to admit, girls, that I felt exactly the same way when Hank and I stopped by to see them. The male was my favorite. All tummy and paws."

"Did Dr. Santo let you hold one, Chief Harker?" Meg asked.

"No. He said they shouldn't be handled just yet."

"That's what he told us. I just thought with you being Chief of Police and all you might get special privileges."

Harker's eyes narrowed as he stared down at Meg. Her eyes sparkled and her mouth widened in a grin.

"We've been working on a special unit in school on abuse of power in the government," Meg said. "We talked about graft and fraud today."

Sheila held her breath, waiting for Harker's reaction. He was motionless for a moment and then gave a great snort of laughter. Della and Sheila joined in.

"You are going to cause a great deal of trouble when you grow up, young lady," he reached down and pulled on the end of Meg's braid. "It will be your mother's punishment for teaching you to be so outspoken."

"And you both are going to break some hearts," Della said, including Beth in her comment. "I can see the makings of two lovely young ladies."

Uncomfortable with the compliment, the girls covered their mouths and giggled. Sheila suggested they start cleaning up and they escaped, heads together in conversation.

"You should be congratulated, my dear," Della said to Sheila. "Your daughter is a real charmer."

"Thank you. I'm very proud of her," Sheila said.

Someone called Harker, and he moved away from the buffet table.

"How long will you be staying in River Oaks, Mrs. Harker?" Sheila asked.

"Mrs. Harker was my mother-in-law," the older woman said. "A perfectly dreadful woman, so I'd be pleased if you called me by my first name. It's Della. And, to answer your question, I'm not sure how long I'll stay. Long enough that Hank will be delighted to see the back side of me."

Without being asked, Della began helping Sheila with the cleanup. Her white curly head bobbed as she gave a running commentary on the people who remained in the gym. She was full of questions, and before long Sheila was telling her all about growing up in Milwaukee and moving with Meg to River Oaks.

By the time Harker returned, they were finished and walked out to the parking lot together. Della gave Meg and Beth a hug. She didn't hug Sheila but squeezed her hand as she said good night. Harker waited until Sheila had bundled the girls in her car before he started his own, following her out into the street.

The girls chattered all the way to Beth's house, leaving Sheila to think about what a nice time she'd had at the high school. She especially liked Harker's mother. She had never thought of Hank as a child. She pictured him as a rigid little boy, breaking up fights between his friends and lecturing classroom cheaters.

Waving to Mrs. Lavorini, who was waiting for Beth, she backed out of the driveway and headed for home.

"Have you done all your homework?" she asked as she parked the car in the garage.

Meg yawned. "I just have to read five more pages in my world cultures book."

"OK. Get it done and then get washed up for bed. It's later than I thought," Sheila said.

"Look, Mom," Meg said, skipping ahead. "Somebody left us flowers."

"Don't touch them!"

Sheila's shout brought Meg to a halt beside the stoop. Her head jerked around, and her eyes looked enormous in the porch light. Sheila hurried to her, gripping her shoulder in a convulsive spasm of fear.

Lying on the stoop were five sunflowers.

•

"I think you should stay in Milwaukee with Meg," Harker said.

Sheila shook her head. "Once Meg is safe, I'll be back. I'm not being stubborn, Chief. The only way to end this reign of terror is to catch the killer. If the flowers were a warning, then the investigation is getting hot."

"And if the sunflowers indicate that he's selected his new victim?"

Her mouth was dry and she had difficulty swallowing. "Then he's made a mistake. I'm positive the flowers were intended for me. I'm not a defenseless child. I'm armed and well trained."

First she needed to get Meg to safety. She had called her mother in Milwaukee. Explaining that she had an emergency, she asked if Meg could come for a visit and felt instant relief when her mother told her to bring her that night even though it was late. For the last twenty minutes, Harker had been trying to convince Sheila to remain at her mother's as well.

From the moment she had paged him, her safety and Meg's had been top priority. He had insisted she remain outside until his arrival, then had gone into the house to make sure no one was inside.

"I could order you to stay in Milwaukee," he snapped. Harker was unused to defiance, especially from a woman.

"But you won't. You want to catch this guy, don't you?"

"I'm tough, Lieutenant, but I'd never consider using you as bait."

"Why not?" Sheila kept her voice low. Meg was down the hall, packing her suitcase. "If the killer is warning me about the investigation, he's feeling off balance. He's changing his pattern. First he sent the letter, then he killed Vincent Calero, and now this. He's getting careless. Each mistake or change in pattern increases our chances of catching the guy."

Harker stopped pacing and turned to face her. His face had taken on the look of granite, the muscles of his jaw popping with tension. Sheila raised her chin. She met his stare with one that she hoped reflected her determination rather than the ball of fear knotted in her stomach.

"I don't like the fact he's focusing on you," he said.

"Better that than one of the children. At least I'm prepared."

No hint of the softness she'd seen earlier in the evening remained in the hard brown eyes. His mouth was pulled tight as if he'd eaten something bitter. Perhaps he had. Harker wasn't used to not getting his way.

"All right," he said, his words clipped. "When you return in the morning, come directly to the station. Don't come back to the house until you've talked to me. Got that?"

"Yes, sir." She gave him a salute, more cocky than she felt.

Once Meg finished packing, Sheila locked up the house and tucked her daughter into the car. Harker drove behind them until they reached the expressway to make sure they weren't followed. She blinked her lights in thanks for his concern.

Sheila rubbed her eyes. God, she was tired. The pounding in her temples increased as the lights from approaching cars spread across the windshield. She flexed her fingers to ease the cramping from her tight grip on the steering wheel.

She turned her head to look at Meg. The girl was slumped against the car door, her head pillowed on a rolled-up sweater and her arm tucked around the seat belt to hold it away from her face. She had fallen asleep before they got to the expressway, worn out from crying when Sheila told her she was taking her to Milwaukee.

Meg had been frightened by her mother's explanation that some-one had been prowling around the house. She didn't like the idea that Sheila would be all alone, and she had been upset about leaving Cooper and Elmo. It was the possibility of missing Beth's party on Saturday that finally had triggered the tears.

At least there wasn't much traffic, Sheila thought. It would be close to one in the morning by the time they reached her mother's house on the north side of Milwaukee. She didn't relish trying to ex-plain the situation to her. Her mother had never understood Sheila's desire to join the police force in the first place. Now she would have to downplay the danger.

She sighed at the thought of the grilling she would get, but there was no way to avoid it if she wanted her mother's help. The only con-solation was that her mother adored Meg and would keep the child safe.

As the drive continued, Sheila remembered that Nick had asked her to call him when she got home. She debated telephoning from the car but was much too tired to give explanations. He would be an-gry when she failed to call, and in all likelihood it would worsen the situation between them.

She wished they were just starting to date again. That period had been so much fun. They had picnicked and fished and swum their way through the summer. He had dragged her along for hikes in the woods and picture-taking expeditions. Meg had been included in most of their outings, but there were also the special times when she and Nick were alone.

One night he'd built a roaring fire despite the fact that outside the temperature was close to ninety. He'd made love to her on the rug in front of the fireplace with the air conditioning going full blast to counteract the heat. Later, they'd drunk wine and curled up on the couch.

That night he was truly romantic. He'd given her a rose and read poems to her by the light of the fire. Remembering how happy she'd been, tears filmed her eyes, and she blinked to clear her vision.

She yawned. The music on the radio made her sleepy. She began to recite speeches from Shakespeare that she'd learned in high school. When she ran out, she started on poetry. She could recall only a few of the poems that Nick had read to her that night. "The True Lover" by A. E. Housman was her favorite. The only Housman she remembered was a shorter poem she'd had to memorize for an English Lit class.

"*With rue my heart is laden, for golden friends I had.*" She spoke the words out loud, letting the sound of her own voice fill the car. "*For many a rose-lipt maiden and many a lightfoot lad.*"

She paused as light filled the inside of the car. A truck pulled around her, and she held the wheel tightly as it passed. Once the roaring sound had faded, she went back to her recital.

"*By brooks too broad for leaping the lightfoot boys are laid. The rose-lipt girls are sleeping in fields where roses fade.*"

She grinned at the conclusion, proud that even in her exhaustion she could remember all the words. She repeated the last line.

"*The rose-lipt girls are sleeping in fields where roses fade.*"

Sheila's hands jerked on the steering wheel. Rose-lipt. Lipsticked. Oh, dear God! Was that the significance of the lipstick? Was the murderer echoing the Housman poem when he painted each mouth with lipstick and put roses in their hands?

Not Nick! Please God, don't let it be Nick!

The words came out of nowhere. They repeated themselves in her head, and she felt sick at heart that she could even consider the possibility that Nick might be guilty of such a crime.

Nick was kind and good and a generous lover. He couldn't be a cold-blooded killer.

A sob tore through Sheila's throat. She put her foot on the brake and slowed enough to pull off the road onto the shoulder. Appalled and frightened by her own thoughts, she began to cry. Meg stirred in her sleep, and Sheila covered her mouth with her hands to muffle the sound.

Finally her sobbing tapered off, and she dried her eyes and blew her nose. She wound down her window and took a deep shuddering breath of the cool fall air. Her tears had released the fear and the anger she'd felt when she found the sunflowers—fear for Meg, and a fury that the killer had invaded her personal life.

Someone had put the sunflowers on the front stoop. It didn't necessarily have to be Nick. The flowers had not been there when she and Meg went to pick up Beth and go over to the high school. Anyone who was at Career Night would have known the house was empty and they could leave the flowers in safety.

She began mentally to check off the people she had seen in the gymnasium: Maloney, Perkins, Ferraro. Even though she hadn't seen Reisler, she suspected he had been there. She had no reason at all to suspect Nick of being the killer.

He'd been sweet and loving on the phone the day before. She remembered the sad tone of his voice when he said he didn't want to lose her. He had shown only concern for her, even when he warned her that she needed to be careful.

Was it a warning or a threat?

She struggled to bring back his words. He had said something about its being risky working on the investigation. If she came too close to the murderer, she could be in danger.

Repeating the conversation, she realized she could put a whole other spin on the meaning of the sunflowers. Instead of marking her house with the sunflowers, maybe the murderer felt threatened by her and was warning her to back off. She'd talk to Harker about that in the morning. For now she had other things to occupy her thoughts.

Could Nick be the killer? She didn't think so, but she'd have to consider it.

She pulled the car back on the road. As she continued the drive to Milwaukee she began to review all the things she knew about Nick. She brushed aside a sense of betrayal. She was a cop first, a woman second.

•

His shadow blended with the trunk of the tree. He stared at the house with cold eyes. The wind had picked up, and the branches overhead creaked and groaned as they brushed against each other. He slammed his fist into the trunk and felt the latex glove tear.

She was gone. He could tell by the pattern of lights that the house was empty.

He'd given up on trying to keep his desires under control, so he had come for her early. He couldn't wait until Saturday as he'd originally planned.

How dare they cancel the Sunflower Festival! It would have been

perfect. It had begun with sunflowers and it would end with sunflowers.

The first time he had seen her naked was in the summer when the
sunflowers beneath her window were in full bloom. He was outside,
and he stared up through the waving stalks and nodding flower heads
to the vision in the house next door.

He swore under his breath and struck the tree again.

Her shades were drawn, just like they always were now. She had
changed. When they were children, she would let him watch her. She
never pulled the shades then. She knew he was there inside his bedroom, watching. Their windows faced each other, and she was aware
of his presence. She would smile as he huddled in the darkness, and as
she smiled she would touch herself.

Everything was ready, and now Donna was gone. Maybe she was
meeting someone else. God, how he hated that! He had told her long
ago that she belonged to him. She had shaken her head and danced
around him, brushing her fingertips against him as he tried to catch her.

He would see her at school and she would tell him to meet her in
the woods. He'd go to their special place and wait, but she'd never meet
him. The next time he would talk to her she would tell him that she had
gone home with one of the boys in her class and had forgotten.

Just like tonight, he thought. He hated it when she didn't meet
him. She needed to be punished for her thoughtlessness. She would
be sorry for making him wait.

Chapter Eighteen

"So you think that Nick Biagi is the murderer because of this poem?" Harker asked, one eyebrow arched as he stared down at the sheet of paper with the lines of poetry written on it. "Have you got anything else?"

"He wears a size ten shoe, he was a judge every year in the sunflower contest, and he knows the schoolgirls because he takes the class pictures," Sheila said. "And no, I don't think Nick is the murderer. I just think he has to be considered because of the coincidence of the poem and the lipstick on the girls."

"Agreed," Harker said.

She turned her neck trying to get the kinks out of it from sleeping the night before in her old bed at her mother's house. The mattress had been worn out before she was twenty, and time hadn't improved it. She suspected she looked as if she hadn't slept.

"One more thing." Harker picked up a pencil and turned it in his hands, looking across his desk at a spot somewhere over her right shoulder. "My mother is worried about you. She doesn't think you should stay in the house alone. Is there someone who could stay with you?"

Sheila might have been offended by the question except that she could see he was uncomfortable asking.

"If that's an easy way to find out if I'm sleeping with someone, forget it." She kept her tone breezy so he'd realize it was a joke. "Thank Della for her concern, but I'll be fine. The house is very secure."

"Excellent," he said, obviously glad to drop the subject. "Oh, by the way, there was a piece of paper torn from an envelope in Vinnie Calero's wallet. The hunch about the murderer luring him with the offer of an interview was on the mark."

"No kidding. Anything we can use?"

"Lots of dollar signs. The letters NBC. The name Don Faxon. And the name of a bar in Madison that's about a block from the alley where Vinnie's body was found in the dumpster."

"Is there such a person as Don Faxon?"

"Not as far as we can find out. Lois called all three networks, the local stations, and a batch of cable newsmagazine shows. No one ever heard of the guy. Probably a phony name."

Sheila shook her head. "Why didn't Vinnie check to make sure the offer was legit?"

"He wanted to believe it." Hank shrugged. "You might be interested to know that none of our prime suspects has an alibi for the time of Vinnie's death. They were all tucked in bed. So that's it for now. When you're ready to leave today, stop by my office."

Sheila returned to her desk and began to sift through the paperwork that had arrived overnight. She checked her phone messages. On the personal side, Warren Santo had called before she got back from Milwaukee, but there was no message from Nick.

She didn't feel comfortable calling Nick now that he was on the suspect list. She bit her lip. Did she really think he could be guilty? He had been around Meg so much that surely she would have noticed if his behavior was inappropriate. God, what a mess!

She dug into the pile of paperwork and was amazed when she looked up and discovered it was five o'clock. Remembering that her mother ate early, she called, eager to talk to Meg. Now that her daughter was rested, she was far more cheerful.

"Gramma helped me make chocolate chip cookies," she said. "They're awesome."

"I'm drooling just thinking about them. Save me one or two."

"There's tons. We made a double batch so I can bring some home." Meg paused for a moment then asked, "How soon can I come home? Beth's party is on Saturday. Will I be home in time for that?"

"I don't know, sweetheart. The Sunflower Festival has been canceled, so you don't have to worry about missing that. Give me a couple days to straighten things out."

"Did you stop by the house to feed Cooper?"

"Not yet. I'm going shortly," Sheila said, praying the bird wouldn't starve to death now that he was in her care.

"Make sure you give Elmo a special hug. I miss him."

"What about me?"

Meg giggled. "Well maybe a little. Did you call Beth's mom?"

"She was out, but I left a message. I told her you were in Milwaukee visiting your grandmother. I asked her to call me."

"Good. I didn't want Beth to worry because I didn't show up for school today. It's a bummer because I was supposed to be her partner for our science project. Now she'll be stuck with some dork."

"Maybe she'll end up with her true love, Jeff."

"As if." Meg sounded sad but then immediately perked up. "Gramma said I could call Beth every night."

"Don't forget it's long distance."

"I won't, Mom." She sighed at the motherly reminder. "Tomorrow we're going to go to a museum, and Thursday we're going to the mall for some shopping and a movie."

"Sounds like a packed program for the two of you. Enjoy it while you can. I called the school this morning and told them you'd be out for a few days, and your teacher said I could stop by and pick up your assignments."

"Oh joy."

"I better get going. Try not to drive Gramma crazy. Remember to brush your teeth, and don't forget how much I love you."

Sheila felt rejuvenated after talking to Meg. Just knowing the girl was safe eased her mind. Harker was right. If Meg had stayed in River Oaks, she'd be too worried about her daughter to keep her mind on work.

She had finished straightening up her desk and was ready to leave when the phone rang. It was Warren Santo.

"It was good to see you last night," he said. "I liked that flowery dress you were wearing."

"Thanks. It was my last hurrah for summer."

He took a deep breath and then said, "I thought over what you said the other day. I don't want to rush you, but I would like to see you. I think I could convince you that I'm just the kind of man you'd like in your life. Either as a friend or something more."

Sheila caught the husky note in the last sentence and smiled. Apparently Warren found it much easier to talk on the phone than in person.

"Having said that, how about a late dinner tonight? The animal hospital's open until seven, so I'd be free around eight. Oh, wait. I forgot. You've got Meg to worry about."

"Actually I don't. She's gone for a few days. And a late dinner sounds just right. I've got to do a few things when I get home, and it will give me time to feed the animals and run some laundry."

"Which reminds me," Warren said. "I should take a look at the bird. I'd like to see whether he can walk on that leg."

"Meg's counting on it. By the way, where do you want to eat?"

"How about Nonno Pino's, the new Italian place in the mall?"

"Perfect. I've wanted to try it."

"I'll pick you up a little after eight."

Sheila hung up. Too bad she couldn't tell Warren about finding the sunflowers and why Meg was in Milwaukee. He was a good listener. Despite what she'd told Harker, she was a little nervous about being in the house alone.

Checking the time, she straightened her jacket, picked up her purse, and headed for Harker's office. She knocked, then peeked around the partially open door.

"I'm going to head home," she said.

He finished signing a letter before he looked up. "Excellent timing. I'm ready to leave. I'll follow you in my car."

"You're coming home with me?"

"I want to check the place out." He held up his hand as she opened her mouth to argue. "You'll be doing me a favor. My mother will demand a report when I get home."

Sheila muttered all the way down to the car. She knew that if she'd been a male officer, Harker wouldn't have dared suggest such a thing. She didn't know whether to call him on it or let it go. The closer she got to home, however, the more her anger was replaced by apprehension at what she would find at the house.

She pulled into the garage, and by the time she was out of the car, Harker was waiting for her. She made no comment as they walked to the front door. At least there were no flowers on the stoop, she thought as she opened the front door.

In the center of the hall throw rug was a handful of sunflower kernels.

Heart pounding against her ribs, she touched Harker's arm and pointed. She unbuttoned her jacket and reached for her gun. Harker's was already in his hand.

"Elmo. Elmo?" she called.

She waited, but the cat didn't appear as he had before, and she heard no meow to indicate his presence. The thought of what she might find sickened her. Please, God, she prayed, but couldn't put into words what she wanted to say.

Covering each other, she and Harker went through the house room by room. They moved without words as if they had been partners for years, one opening the door and the other entering the room with drawn gun, then reversing the order.

Sheila breathed through her mouth, the sound loud in her ears. The muscles of her shoulders ached with tension as they entered each room or opened a closet door, expecting to find Elmo's body.

The kitchen and family room were in order. The patio doors were locked, and Cooper was asleep in the corner of the aquarium. Meg's room was in the usual disorder, although the hall bathroom was neat. The house was silent. No sign of Elmo. No sign of a disturbance in any of the rooms, until they reached the last one, Sheila's bedroom.

The blue and green plaid comforter and the top sheet had been turned back as if waiting for her to go to bed. Lying on the white pillow case was a single sunflower, the head almost large enough to cover the entire pillow.

"Stay here," Harker said.

Sheila was barely conscious of his words. She couldn't take her eyes off the flower. The killer had been in her room and touched her things, and he wanted her to know it. She started to tremble.

"The bathroom's clear," Harker said, but his words came from a great distance. "Sheila, look at me."

His sharp tone demanded her attention. She turned to face him, blinking her eyes several times as she tried to bring him into focus. He placed his hand on the top of her shoulder. Her body shuddered and then her gaze sharpened.

"Sorry, Chief," she said.

She caught her bottom lip between her teeth to keep it from trembling. Looking into his eyes, she saw a flash of compassion but knew that any offer of comfort from him would be her undoing. She took a deep breath, and his hand fell away.

"Look around, Sheila," he said, "and see if anything is missing. Don't touch. Just look."

The whole situation was so bizarre that she desperately wanted to touch something just to ground herself in reality. To keep from making a mistake, she wrapped her arms across her chest. Without opening drawers, she could see nothing out of place in the bedroom. The hook on the back of the bathroom door was empty. She returned to the bedroom and had to swallow before she could get the words out beyond the lump of fear in her throat.

"A yellow cotton nightgown was hanging in the bathroom. It's gone."

"Did you take it to Milwaukee?" Harker asked.

"No. I forgot it. I had to borrow one from my mother."

Harker beckoned to her, bending over to stare at the sunflower on the pillow. She moved closer and looked down. Beside the flower head was a cluster of blood droplets. Stark red against the white of the pillow case. She counted.

Five drops of blood. The fifth victim.

"Do you think he killed the cat?"

Her voice broke on the last word, and she pressed her lips tightly together to keep from crying. Dear God, how could she ever tell Meg?

"We'll get the techs out here to check it," Harker said, his words clipped with anger. "Is there a phone in the kitchen? I don't want to touch anything in here."

Unable to speak, she nodded and walked out the door. She moved on automatic pilot, her emotions in turmoil. She was almost past Meg's door when she heard it.

"Elmo?" she called.

She glanced at Harker's face and thought she saw confirmation of the small cry she'd heard. She retraced her steps to the doorway of Meg's room. Listening, she heard nothing and called again.

"Elmo."

After a moment of total silence, she heard a frail cry. Her heart was beating so loudly that she couldn't pinpoint the sound. Harker moved around her and crossed the room to Meg's dresser. He dropped to his knees, leaning over to peer under it.

"So there you are," he said.

Sheila charged across the room, getting down on her hands and knees beside Harker. She swallowed the lump in her throat as she spotted the cat wedged into the far corner under the dresser.

"I can't believe he was able to get under there," Harker said as he eyed the opening. "Is he stuck?"

Head pressed to the carpet, Sheila clucked her tongue. "Come on, Elmo. It's OK now."

The cat meowed but didn't move.

"He might be hurt. Let me try to lift one end, and then you should be able to reach him."

He stood up, and as Sheila waited, he raised one end of the dresser until she was able to get her arm and shoulder underneath. Her fingers touched fur, and with a scooping motion she swept the cat forward until she could reach him with both hands.

"Got him," she said as she pulled the cat against her chest and hugged him.

Elmo's slight body trembled, and the silent shaking touched Sheila with fear. She set him in her lap and, as Harker watched, checked to see if he was injured. She wasn't even aware that she was crying until a tear splashed on the back of her hand.

"Sorry to be such a baby," she said, wiping away her tears with the sleeve of her blouse. "I'm very fond of this hairy beast."

"He's OK?"

"Seems to be."

She set him down on the carpet. Harker stepped closer and Elmo hissed, arching his back. With no sign of any injury, the cat raced from the room.

"The way he's acting makes me wonder if this is the first time someone's been in the house," Sheila said.

Walking out to the kitchen, she told him about Sunday's excitement when Elmo had failed to appear. She had accused the cat of knocking over the talcum powder, but now she wasn't so sure.

"I didn't see any signs of forced entry," Harker said. "Who has keys to the house?"

"Meg and I. No one else."

"How about a spare key?"

"It's right here." Sheila reached up to the peg board on the kitchen wall. Her fingers sorted through the keys hanging on the hook. "It's gone. Someone took it."

"Any idea who?"

"No. I don't even know when I saw it last. So anyone who's been in the house in the last several months could have taken it." Her stomach dropped at the sudden remembrance. "Meg left the patio doors open last week. She was playing out front, so anyone could have come in through the screen door and taken the key."

"Once the technicians finish here, you'll need to have the locks changed."

While Harker called the police station to report the break-in, Elmo stayed close to Sheila. He rubbed against her, purring loudly. Finally she picked up his dishes and put fresh food and water in them.

The ordinariness of the action revived her spirit. Anger began to push away the emotional paralysis she had felt since entering the house. She was a professional. Only by keeping her emotions detached could she help find the killer and make sure he never hurt anyone again.

She set Elmo's dishes down in the corner on his mat. Remembering Cooper, she got out two small plastic bowls, and filled one with water and one with birdseed. She carried the dishes into the family room, set them on a table, and removed the security bar so she could open the patio doors. Picking up the bowls, she stepped outside.

It was only when she leaned over to remove the empty dishes that she saw the blood on the cedar shavings. The feathered body of the mourning dove was tilted sideways against the corner of the aquarium. The bird was dead. A bloody mass of tissue was all that was left of his legs and feet.

•

"Get down, Abby," Hank said as the black Lab placed her head on Sheila's knee and stared up at her with soulful eyes.

"She doesn't bother me. I like dogs," she said.

Her hand stroked the top of Abby's head, and he could see some of the tension of the past few hours seep away. She was sitting in a corner of the couch beside the fireplace. He'd suggested that she take off her shoes and curl up, but he wasn't sure if she'd even heard him.

He touched the cigar in his pocket. He wanted a smoke but didn't want to leave Sheila alone. Her face still had a pinched look that he didn't like. He could hear Della moving around the kitchen and was impatient for her return.

"The smoke won't bother me, you know."

Sheila's words startled him.

"You don't read minds, do you?" he asked.

"It didn't take psychic powers to call that one. You've been twitching ever since you finished lighting the fire," she said. "It's a nice fire, by the way."

"Boy Scout training." He grinned as he pulled out the cigar. He raised an eyebrow in question. "Are you sure you don't mind?"

"I don't mind. Besides, it's your house; you can do what you want in it."

He lit up before she could change her mind, then puffed contentedly, aware of her eyes on him. Thank God she wasn't a chatterer, he thought. She seemed content to sit quietly and renew her energy.

She picked up the glass of Scotch at her elbow and swallowed the last of it. He hadn't given her much. In her shocked state it was more of a restorative. She'd handled herself remarkably well until they arrived at his house. Once safely inside, she had reacted emotionally to Della's genuine sympathy.

"Good heavens, Hank, you're not smoking that smelly old thing in the house?" Della asked as she came into the living room with a large tray.

Hank winked at Sheila as he got up, saying, "Really, Mother. I was just reminded that it was my house."

"Nonsense, dear. It's a disgusting, nasty habit. Especially now that we're ready to eat."

He took the tray from her hands and set it down on the coffee table. He was surprised at the array of food she'd managed to rustle up. She must have gone shopping, he thought, as he eyed the ham and cheese sandwiches and sniffed the thick pea soup.

"I thought we could just eat here by the fire," she said as she bustled around distributing napkins and silverware. "No, don't get up, Sheila. Hank can fetch what we need. Would you like some milk?"

"Actually I would," Sheila said.

"I'll get it," Hank muttered, taking his cigar with him as he headed out to the kitchen.

Whistling for Abby, he let her out into the yard while he stood on the porch and smoked. He was grateful for the returning sparkle he had seen in Sheila's eyes when he left the room. No doubt she was amused by the way Della bossed him around. If it chased away the shadows, he was happy to be the butt of a joke.

He'd seen the look of horror on her face as she stared down at the mutilated bird. Just the thought of it sent a jolt of anger through his body, and he could feel the muscles in his jaw tighten.

He wondered if the fact that Sheila was blond and blue-eyed had drawn the murderer to her. There was a childlike quality to her. Her beauty, a fresh, well-scrubbed look of innocence, was beguiling.

She'd mentioned using herself as bait, and he'd dismissed the idea. Now he was furious that he hadn't ordered her to remain in Milwaukee. But would she be any safer there?

"Don't dawdle, Hank," Della called. "The soup's getting cold."

He shouted for Abby, who dashed past him, heading back to the living room. Taking a final puff, he tossed the cigar away and returned to the house. He poured a glass of milk for Sheila and one for Della. He grabbed a beer and carried all three into the living room.

Della had done her work. Abby was curled up on the rug in front of the fireplace. Sheila's shoes were beside the couch, and she was tucked in the corner with a light blanket over her lap, a mug of soup cupped in her hands. He set the milk down on the end table between the couch and Della's chair.

"I forgot to thank you for taking Elmo over to the vet," Sheila said.

"No problem. Warren takes care of Abby, too."

"Did you tell him about the b-bird?" She stumbled a little over the word.

"Yes. When I got there, he was working on a beagle who'd been hit by a car. Dr. Upton checked out Elmo and said he couldn't see any injuries, but he'd keep an eye on him."

"I feel a hundred percent better." She looked over the rim of her soup mug, her eyes apologetic. "I couldn't leave him alone in the house."

"Of course you couldn't," Della said, glaring at Hank.

"What did I do?" he said at his mother's implied criticism. "I said she could bring the cat over here. It was her idea to board it with the vet."

Hank snorted when Della turned to Sheila for confirmation.

"So much for trusting your only son," he said, pleased when Sheila chuckled. "At any rate, I waited until Warren was done with the beagle and then told him what happened at the house. I didn't give him any specifics other than the fact the bird was dead. He said to tell Meg how sorry he was and for you to call him when you could. Oh, and he said he'd take a rain check on the dinner."

"He's a nice man," she said. "Meg will be glad that Elmo is safe with Warren."

"It occurred to me that you might want to give Meg a call. You probably don't want to tell her anything about tonight, but I bet it would do you good to talk to her."

Seeing the smile of happiness on Sheila's face, he was glad that he'd thought to mention it.

"Only after you finish your dinner," Della said, earning a smile from both Hank and Sheila.

"There's a phone in the den," he said, pointing to the French doors that led off the living room.

"Would it be all right if I give my mother your phone number, in case she needs me?"

"Of course," he said. "It's just nine o'clock. It's been a long time since my son was that age. Will Meg still be up?"

"Yes," she said, "if they're home. My mother loves having Meg all to herself and plans activities to keep her amused. Mom took care of Meg when I first joined the force. They get along like two old friends."

"How lucky you are to have such support," Della said. "It's difficult enough being a single mom. Family and friends are a godsend in a crisis."

"Agreed," Sheila said, nodding to both Della and Hank in thanks for their hospitality.

The fire crackled, adding a cozy touch to the evening. The conversation was light and general as they finished their meal. Afterwards, Hank helped Della carry the dishes to the kitchen while Sheila went into the den to call her daughter.

"I'm glad you brought her home, Hank. She looks exhausted," Della said, once they were out of hearing. "Was there any sign of forced entry?"

Hank leaned one hip against the corner of the counter, watching as his mother cleaned up the kitchen. They had agreed the first time she came to visit that she would cook and do the cleaning so she would feel comfortable staying with him.

"No, and the spare key is missing. We found fresh traces of a graphite product in the kitchen door. Sheila said she didn't put it there. The doorknobs on that door had been wiped clean."

"Dear Lord in Heaven," Della said, placing her hand over her heart as if to keep it from bursting with the shock. "That settles it. She can't go back until the locks are changed. She needs protection from this madman."

"Will new locks protect her?" Hank could hear the harshness in his tone even before his mother turned, eyebrows raised in surprise at his vehemence. "I can't watch her twenty-four hours a day, and she'll never agree to a bodyguard."

"Well, Hank, somehow you've got to keep her safe."

"I'll do my best, Mother," Hank said. "The trouble is if this man is as obsessed with Sheila as he was with the other victims, he'll stop at nothing. So far every time he's taken a child, no one has seen him do it. It's like he's invisible."

"How soon do you think he'll try something again?"

"Soon." Hank shook his head. "I'm still convinced that his target date is Saturday."

"Today's Wednesday. Three more days," Della said.

She pressed her lips together, and he could read the fear in her eyes.

"Oh, Hank, it's dreadful. It's like having a date with death."

•

He turned back the bed, smoothing the freshly laundered sheet and fluffing the pillow. He shook out the creases in the yellow cotton nightgown. It would have been better if he could have washed the nightgown so it would be clean for her, but now he was glad he hadn't. He could smell the scent of her in the moving air. Spreading it on the bed, he stepped back to get the full effect of the room.

Everything was ready. It was exactly the way the room had looked the only time he'd ever been in it. It was the summer he turned sixteen.

It was hot that summer. His stepfather had gotten him a job working on one of the dairy farms. He lived in the farmhouse during the week, coming home only on the weekends. The chores started before dawn and ran until dinner time. It was backbreaking work that left him little energy to do anything more than sleep.

He missed Donna every night as he stared up at the ceiling boards from his cot in the unfinished attic. He couldn't always see her on the weekends. His stepfather kept close tabs on him, but he managed to sneak away a few times to be with her. She'd let him touch her, but it was so rushed he found little pleasure in it.

She was excited about his birthday and asked him what he wanted her to give him. Her eyes flashed with mischief as she waited for the expected answer. He told her he wanted to lie with her on her bed. She was excited by the risk involved. He could see it in her eyes.

They planned it for several days, and he couldn't wait for the appointed time. It was a Sunday. She hadn't gone to church with her parents. She'd pretended she was sick. He had done the same.

His mother came to check on him just before leaving. She'd felt his forehead just as though he were a baby. When she left, he dressed and raced downstairs, watching as Donna's parents left for church. He counted to a hundred and then ran over to her house.

She met him downstairs, took his hand, and led him up to her room. At the doorway she made him close his eyes, then she opened the door and pulled him inside. When he opened his eyes, he was overwhelmed with the soft feminine touches that made the room uniquely Donna's.

He lay down on the bed and took her in his arms, cradling her head against his chest. If he had died at that moment he would have gone without a murmur.

She became restless, moving against him, getting him excited. He tightened his grip on her until she stopped struggling. She started to cry and he released her. He sat in the middle of the bed, trying to explain that he only wanted to hold her. Nothing more.

Her tears turned to anger. She bunched her hands into fists and punched him in the chest repeatedly. He was so surprised by the attack that he did nothing to defend himself. His lack of reaction angered her further, and she jumped off the bed, running out of the room.

By the time he followed her down the stairs, she was nowhere in sight. From then on, whenever he dreamed about her, he was in her room and she was lying on the bed waiting for him.

He turned off the lights and walked into the front bedroom to get everything ready. Taking out a pair of latex gloves, he held one under his nose and breathed in the sweet smell of talcum powder. He pulled the gloves on, molding the membrane to each finger. The plastic wrapper rustled as he took out the brown blanket.

Downstairs, he reached into the cabinet under the sink for the bottle of chloroform. He set it on the counter beside a small, heavy-duty plastic bag. Inside was a white linen handkerchief folded into a perfect square. He got out a new pair of latex gloves and stripped off the ones he was wearing.

Everything was ready for morning. Donna would never hide from him again. Tomorrow he would have the power to make her obey his every wish.

Chapter Nineteen

Sheila yawned.

The bed at Harker's had been comfortable, but she had slept fit-fully. Her dreams had been troubled and she was grateful that she couldn't remember any of them clearly. She was aware they involved someone chasing her, but she hadn't seen a face she recognized.

Hank must not have slept well either. At the breakfast table, he spoke in monosyllables while his mother chattered away as she served scrambled eggs and toast. Periodically he peered over his newspaper to glower at the two of them.

Della was a delightful woman, and having an unexpected house-guest didn't seem to have bothered her in the least. She had given Sheila just the right amount of sympathy and coddling to make her feel safe and welcome. This morning Della had been adamant that Sheila not return to her own house. Before Sheila left with Hank, Della had convinced her to stay one more night.

Eventually she'd have to go home. The thought of it frightened her. Despite the break-in, she wasn't afraid for herself. It was Meg's welfare that worried her. Even after she concluded the house was safe, she didn't know whether she should bring Meg back to River Oaks.

At noon she was meeting the locksmith at the house. No doubt her shadow, in the form of Chief Harker, would try to come with her. He'd made her promise she wouldn't go anywhere unless she told him where she was going.

This would be a good time to call Warren and check on the cat. She reached for the phone and saw Paz at the coffee machine. He nodded to her, jerking his head in the direction of Hank's office.

"He's ready for us," he said as he poured a mug of coffee. "We all heard about the break-in at your house. How are you holding up?"

"A little short of sleep, but otherwise fine," she said.

"I looked at the report." His expression was grim. "You're not staying there, are you?"

"No. And Meg's in Milwaukee, so I don't have to worry about her."

She wasn't comfortable announcing that she was staying at Harker's house. They hadn't driven to the police station together. Hank had dropped her at the house, waited until she got her car out of the garage, and then followed her to work.

Jotting down a reminder to call Warren after the meeting, Sheila walked with Paz to Hank's office, arriving just as Owen wandered out of the bathroom and turned in their direction. Dandy Dan was already seated in the conference room. Hank came in from his office and sat down at the head of the table.

"By now you've seen the preliminary reports on the break-in at Sheila's. No prints. Not even on the bird's glass cage. Many surfaces had been wiped down. The point of entry was the kitchen door. The knobs on both sides of the door were clean of prints."

Owen passed a set of clipped computer printouts to each of them.

"We have six prime suspects. I've given each of you a printout of everything we know about them that pertains to the case. The list includes Nick Biagi, the photographer; Doug Maloney, Sheila's ex-partner; Herb Reisler, owner of the Book Nook; Elliot Jenkins, the CPA—."

Dan interrupted. "Elliot's my accountant. When the hell did he get on the list?"

"Yesterday while you were out," Hank said. "It turns out that he's also the accountant for the families of the last three victims. He lives in the Estates and his office is in City Hall, where he would have run into Barbara Davis and maybe even her daughter. His name came up in that Internet sting operation the State Police were running to catch pedophiles."

"Good God!" Dan looked stunned. "We've had the man to dinner at our house."

"I don't think it's catching," Paz said.

"If it's any consolation," Hank said, "Jenkins said he had downloaded the wrong files. He had no intention of subscribing to any of 'those' kinds of services."

Owen continued speaking: "The last two on the list are Dominic Ferraro, the sunflower expert, and Dick Perkins, our beloved mayor."

"Isn't Ferraro a little long in the tooth?" Paz asked.

"He's sixty-two," Owen said. "That's well within the age range for pedophiles, although beyond the age suggested by the profiler."

"Part of the reason the guy is invisible is that he appears normal, fitting into the daily activities of the community without drawing attention to himself," Hank said. "Don't dismiss anyone. It doesn't take brute strength to do what he's done. It could be anyone in the whole town."

"A couple new things have surfaced." Owen waved a piece of paper. "We've been looking into that two-year-old murder in Townsend, Minnesota."

"Is that the one their chief is trying to tie in to our murders?" Paz asked.

"Yes. We had asked the tourist board for a list of all the events in the Minneapolis–St. Paul area for the weekend of the murder. Yesterday we got a finalized list," Owen said.

He nodded to Dan, who picked up the story.

"We know Perkins was there for a conference at that time, but two more of our suspects were also there. On Sunday of that weekend, the Horticultural Society had a special exhibition of sunflowers. Dominic Ferraro was one of the exhibitors."

"We still don't have any real proof that this murder ties in with ours," Paz said.

"On the other hand, we don't have any proof it doesn't." Owen shrugged. "We've got to begin to make assumptions. We know we're getting close. We need to rule in or rule out some of these suspects."

"If you're done haggling, I'll continue," Dan said. "The second event was a juried photography show held on Saturday of that weekend. A picture called 'Life in Death' won second place for Nick Biagi."

No one looked at Sheila, but they couldn't have missed her sharp intake of breath.

"That picture is hanging in his living room," she said. "It shows an old dead tree which has fallen over, and in the hollow trunk is a nest, or whatever you call it, of raccoons. When I commented on it, he told me he'd been aced out of first place by an amateur. It appeared to be a real sore point with him."

"He's still mad after two years?" Paz leaned forward, obviously intrigued by the thought. "So picture this. He's just been screwed by some amateur photographer. He's furious, but he hasn't got any way to release the tension. He drives around, picks up this girl, and kills her. Early days in a serial killer's program, a killing is usually triggered by some stressful event."

In deference to Sheila, no one commented on Paz's scenario. She was sad at the realization that her relationship with Nick was over. She would never be able to see Nick again without thinking of her total lack of trust and her suspicion that he might have committed murder.

Each of the suspects was discussed in detail. By the time the meeting was over, depression had settled over the room. They still had failed to reach a firm conclusion.

"I know it's frustrating," Hank said as he looked around the table, "but we're getting close. We have lots of pieces to this puzzle, and by following every lead we're going to find the missing link. This is a dangerous time. The killer is off balance and starting to act out of character. First by killing Vinnie and then by breaking into Sheila's house. We have to look sharp, watch for more mistakes, and above all else be careful."

As everyone filed out, Sheila glanced at her watch. Eleven-forty. Plenty of time to get to the house. She'd have to call Warren later to check on the cat. The last to leave, she stopped in the doorway to Hank's office.

"I've got to duck out, Chief. The evidence techs are done with the house, so I called a locksmith. He's meeting me at the house around noon to change the locks."

"Give me two minutes and I'll drive over with you."

Sheila stepped all the way inside the office and closed the door. She walked across to his desk and stood directly in front of it. He looked up, a wary expression on his face.

"You can't do that," she said.

"Do what?"

"You can't follow me around. I'm not just a woman. I'm a police officer. You've got to treat me like one. If Owen were being stalked, you wouldn't have him check in with you every time he went to the bathroom."

Hank held up his hands in surrender.

"You're right. I may not like it, but you're right," he said. "I think it's a throwback to my Neanderthal days in the Marines. There were only two kinds of women. Ladies and those who weren't."

"Face it, Chief, it's the nineties. No matter which of those categories I fit into, I'm a trained police officer, well schooled in self-defense."

"I know that."

"Offering your protection might be a charming, gentlemanly gesture, but it weakens me, knowing that you don't trust me to take care of myself."

"Wait a second," Hank said. "The fact that I'm concerned about you has nothing to do with your qualifications. I do trust you, Sheila. I've watched you since your arrival, and if there were any flaw in your training I would have seen it. And for what it's worth, I believe your story about how things went down when you shot the drug dealer. You didn't hesitate."

Sheila closed her eyes to hide the emotional impact of Hank's words. His vote of confidence required a real leap of faith, and because of that it was all the more meaningful.

"Thank you," she said. The words were simple, but she could see in his expression that he understood. "I had already decided that Maloney was wrong, but I would have no way to prove it. It means a great deal to me to hear you say that you believe in me."

"Once I heard your story I understood why he had insinuated that you were unprofessional. You turned him down. It's just that simple."

She shook her head. "It can't be that. He told me he'd forgotten it ever happened."

"He was lying. Trust me, Sheila," he said. "Men like Maloney hold grudges when they get blown off, and to make matters worse, you saved his life and shot the bad guy."

"You mean he accused me deliberately?"

"I think so." Hank looked totally disgusted. "The reason he wanted you to back up his story was so that no one would realize how he'd lost his gun. He was trying to bash in the dealer's head with the gun, and the perp wrestled the gun out of Maloney's hand. When he accused you of hesitation, he knew you'd be so worried about your own actions that you wouldn't think about his."

His tone was slightly patronizing, but Sheila decided to let it slide. He was probably right, she thought. How stupid was she that she hadn't seen it? She could have saved herself many sleepless nights questioning her conduct.

"Men make life very complicated," she said.

A slow smile spread across Hank's face. "I personally might have phrased it differently. Life is simple. Women complicate it."

"Truce," Sheila said. "I'm in no shape to play word games. Besides, I've got to run. And I'll be fine."

Hank frowned. "Remember. Don't go into the house until the locksmith gets there."

"How do you know he's not the killer?"

"I'll take that chance. Just make sure *you* don't take any chances." As she started for the door he held out a piece of paper. "To show you I'm a changed man, you can take care of this. Ray Florio called in to say that someone killed his grandkids' dog. I'd go, but I'm not ready to see that jerk yet. You can talk to him."

"No problem," she said, "and thanks."

She was glad she'd be the one to talk to Ray. The shooting in the alley had been the topic of conversation on Tuesday, and she had overheard several comments during Career Night at the high school. Most people thought Ray Florio was a foolish old man.

Part of Sheila's introduction to River Oaks had been to attend a meeting of Parent Watch. She remembered meeting Ray because he was so much older than the other men and women on the citizen patrol. When she had talked to him, his dedication to the safety of the children was obvious. Hank had been breathing fire over the gun incident, but even he admitted that Ray was devastated over the whole affair.

The locksmith was already at the house when she arrived. She let him in, explained what she wanted, and was pleased with the estimate. While he changed the locks she looked over the house.

She couldn't believe the mess the evidence techs had left. She tried to remove the oily residue they had left behind after dusting for fingerprints. The stuff was resistant to the cleaners she had in the house. She'd have to ask the techs what they used.

Thankfully, Cooper's glass cage had been taken to the lab along with the dead bird. She gathered clean clothes for the morning and then called Warren. He was out. She asked him to call her at Hank's to give her a report on the cat.

The locksmith finished by two o'clock. Sheila tested the keys in each lock and tried the new deadbolt on the kitchen door. Satisfied, she wrote him a check and left when he did. She sat in the car, transferring the new keys to her keyring and removing the old ones. Just knowing that no one had keys to the house anymore made Sheila feel that the house was safe again. She pulled out of the driveway and headed for Ray Florio's house.

Ray lived three houses from Nick in the old section of town. The two-story house was nicely landscaped and very well cared for. She pulled up in front and rang the doorbell. A short, older woman answered the door.

"Mrs. Florio? I'm Lieutenant Brady. I came about the dog."

"Oh yes. Please come in." She opened the door to let Sheila enter and then closed it behind her. "Ray's outside. It was such a terrible thing to have happen. The children were so upset."

Sheila walked behind the twittering woman, taking in the furnishings of each room. She liked the homey feel of the house. Everything was well used, and the decorative pieces were kept for sentiment rather than show.

"I'm still pretty shaken up about the puppy, so I'll let you talk to Ray. He can tell you all about it. Ray," Mrs. Florio called as she opened the door from the kitchen into the screened-in porch. "A policewoman is here to see you."

"Lieutenant Brady," Sheila said, extending her hand to the older man rising from a wicker chair. "We met at a Parent Watch meeting when I first moved to River Oaks."

"Of course I remember." Ray wiped his palm on the side of his trousers before taking her hand. "You've come about the dog?"

"Yes. I don't have any details. You said someone killed your dog. Are you sure it wasn't an accident?"

"An accident? I wouldn't be so damn mad if it had been. The dog was fed some ground meat with pieces of glass in it."

"Glass?" Sheila was shocked. "Maybe you'd better start at the beginning."

She was worried about the red-faced older man. Hopefully, he didn't have a heart problem, because she could see his blood pressure shoot up at the mention of the dog.

"It was my grandkids' dog. Only a pup really. A mutt, but a cute little bugger."

"Was the dog here when it died?"

"Yes. I pick up the kids after school, and we stop at their house so they can change clothes. Since they got the pup they've been bringing him over here. Then after work their dad picks up all three of them."

"It was OK when you picked it up today?"

"Right as rain. Bouncing all around and peeing on every blade of grass. A little while later, Jason lets out a shriek. Bessie and I go tearing outside. The dog's throwing up. There's blood in the vomit."

"Did you take it to the vet?"

"No. I knew by the amount of blood that there wasn't any point. Bessie took the kids into the house and I stayed beside the pup, but there wasn't anything I could do." Ray looked ready to burst into tears. "I just sorta patted his head until it was all over."

"I'm so sorry," Sheila said. "I have a cat, and I know how I'd feel if the cat was hurt."

Ray nodded, accepting her condolences as if the puppy were a member of the family. That's how pets are, Sheila thought.

"I started to clean things up. When I looked real close at what he'd thrown up, I could see little pieces of glass. That's when I called the police."

"Did you leave everything as it was?"

"Once I saw the glass, I did. I covered the pup with a towel for fear the kids would see it. Then I took a look around the yard. Over in that corner," he said, pointing to a small wooded area about five or six feet across, "I found a piece of newspaper with a meat stain in the center. The glass was mixed with the hamburger and left there for the puppy to find."

"I know puppies can bark a lot. Did you have any complaints about the dog or have any idea who would do such a thing?"

Hot color flooded Ray's face, and Sheila could see the veins in his temples. "I know exactly who did it. All because the pup got loose last week and got into his precious sunflowers. The bastard who killed the dog is my neighbor, Dominic Ferraro."

•

"I take it Ray has no proof that Ferraro killed the dog?"

Hank rocked back in his chair, his hands linked behind his head. Sheila shook her head.

"None. He said that when the puppy got loose, he'd heard Ferraro swearing and yelling at the dog. I gave the newspaper the meat was sitting on to the lab so they can test it. If nothing comes up, it's just Ray's word against Ferraro's."

"Let's hope they find some usable prints. Poisoning's bad

enough, but broken glass is just plain savage." Hank slapped the arm of his chair with his open palm. "I'll never understand anyone who deliberately hurts a child or an animal."

Sheila was silent, and when he looked up he could see that her mind was far away.

"Poisoned," she said. "Janette Davis, the first victim, had a puppy and somebody poisoned it. Do you suppose there's any connection?"

Hank brought his chair upright. "Both the shrink and the profiler said that the guy probably started out killing or maiming small animals. Do you have any details on the Davis puppy's poisoning?"

"No. It was just a comment Barbara made when we were talking about how hard the move to River Oaks had been for Janette. I'll give her a call and see what I can get."

Without waiting for his reply, Sheila rose from her chair and hurried out of the office. Hank watched her through his office window as she sat down at her desk, picked up the phone, and dialed.

Despite her air of efficiency, she looked tired. Dark circles like bruises beneath her eyes attested to the fact that she hadn't slept well. She had agreed to stay one more night at the house, but Hank doubted he could convince her to stay longer.

How could he keep her safe?

He hadn't been able to stop the killer from taking the children, so how could he hope to keep him away from Sheila? He wished once more she'd never applied for the job in River Oaks. Coming here had put her in danger. Her blond hair and blue eyes had drawn the killer's attention.

He didn't want anything to happen to her, but his hands were tied over the amount of protection she would accept. No matter what she said, he intended to put a guard on her when she returned to her house.

So what if she was irritated. She was part of his department, and it was his job to watch out for her welfare. He was annoyed that for some reason he felt defensive about his actions. As Chief of Police he was responsible for her safety. That was all there was to that.

He took his eyes away from the shiny blond hair pulled neatly into a braid behind her head. No matter what his mother said, it wouldn't be a good idea for her to stay too long at the house.

He sighed. Della had invited Sheila to come back in time for dinner tonight. It was already a quarter to six. He reached for the phone. He'd better let his mother know they'd be running late. He was just hanging up when Sheila returned.

"When Janette Davis's puppy was poisoned, she wasn't living in the Estates," Sheila said without preamble. "Barbara said they rented a house in the old part of town. The house they rented was two doors away from Dominic Ferraro."

"Jesus Jenny! This could be the break we've been waiting for. If Ferraro is capable of killing puppies, it's conceivable that he might be capable of killing small children," Hank said, just as the phone on his desk rang. "I think we better bring Dominic Ferraro in for a chat."

He reached over and picked up the phone. It was for Sheila. Handing the phone to her, he reached for his uniform jacket. When he heard the small cry, he looked up to see Sheila, mouth open and eyes wide with fear.

"Sheila?" he said, hurrying around the desk to her side.

He reached her just as her knees gave way. He grabbed her around the waist and eased her down onto a chair. Her face was paper-white and her breathing labored.

"It's the Milwaukee police," she said. "Meg is missing."

Chapter Twenty

"Meg is missing," Sheila cried. "Oh, God, Hank, what am I going to do?"

Hank squeezed her shoulder for reassurance, picked up the receiver she'd dropped in her lap, and leaned over to press a button on the phone before hanging up.

"You're on speaker phone now. This is Chief Harker," he said. "Who am I talking to?"

"Hey, Hank. It's Cal Williams."

"Good to hear your voice, Cal. What have you got?"

"At around five o'clock a smoke bomb went off in the movie theater at the Lakeview Mall. The movie had started, and the only light in the theater was from the screen. When the place filled with smoke, the audience panicked. There was mass confusion with people screaming and shoving to get outside. Lieutenant Brady's mother was holding Meg's hand when suddenly it was jerked out of her grasp. When Mrs. Landis got outside she searched for Meg but couldn't find her. By that time security had arrived, and when she told them her granddaughter was missing they called the police."

Hank looked at his watch. Six o'clock. Meg had been missing for almost an hour.

"Is my mother all right?" Sheila asked. Her voice shook only slightly, and some of her color had returned.

"She's desperately worried, but she's not injured. She's here in the mall security office, and I'll put her on when we're done."

"How about security cameras?" Hank asked.

"I've got a crew working on the tapes right now. So far we don't have anything on that. I need to ask a few questions."

When Sheila only nodded, Hank said, "Shoot."

"Is Meg the kind of child who might wander away once she got out of the theater?"

"Absolutely not. She'd stay there until she was sure her grandmother was all right. She's a very responsible child."

"Your mother said you've been divorced for ten years, Lieutenant. Any chance the girl's father would have taken her?"

"Robbie?" She was stunned at the thought. "I haven't had any contact with Robbie for five years. The last thing he'd do would be to kidnap Meg. He left me because he didn't want the responsibility of a child."

"The reason I'm asking is that your mother heard someone say, 'Don't worry, Meg, I'll get you out.'"

"Did she see who it was?"

"No. The smoke was thick and it made her eyes water so she couldn't see him. He must have set off the smoke bomb as a diversion. We found it under a seat, not far from where Mrs. Landis and Meg were sitting. The weird thing is there was a circle of sunflower seeds around the bomb."

"Oh God, Hank. It *is* him."

She reached out, and Hank took her hand and gripped it tightly to give her some sense that she wasn't alone.

"It's who?" Cal said. "Do you know who we're looking for?"

"This is the situation," Hank said. "You know the serial killer who's been preying on kids in River Oaks?"

He could hear the other man's sharp intake of breath. "You think that's who took her?"

"It sounds like it. He broke into Lieutenant Brady's house sometime in the last two days. And his trademark is sunflower seeds. Time is real short, Cal. See what you can do to speed up the surveillance tapes."

"We'll put everything we can behind this."

Hank listened to how they planned to handle it. "Looks like you got your end in line. I'll work from this end and get back to you. Give me your pager number."

They exchanged numbers, and then Hank picked up the receiver and handed it to Sheila. He avoided looking at her eyes, knowing he would see a hopelessness that he was already feeling.

"Oh God, Sheila, it's all my fault." Mrs. Landis's voice, thick with tears, came through the speaker. "I can't bear the thought that Meg is missing."

Hank switched the phone off the speaker so Sheila could have some privacy while she talked to her mother. He patted her shoulder and hurried out of the room.

Downstairs in the communications room, he made a conference call to Paz, Dan, and Owen. When he told them about Meg, their response was immediate. They would return to the station. He located Lois Coren, Pat White and Richie Tyler and briefed them about the situation.

After a couple more calls, he headed back upstairs, arriving just as she hung up the phone. The face she turned to him was pale but composed. He could see she'd been crying, but her emotions were under control again.

He crossed the office to stand beside her. He wanted to offer comfort but suspected she'd fall apart if he did.

"Do you want to go to Milwaukee?" he asked.

She shook her head. "No. This is where he'll bring her."

"All right. I've got people calling and making contact with everyone on the suspect list and everyone who was on the sunflower judge list. We'll see if we can't eliminate some of them. If they're home, they can't be our guy. It's six. He can't be back from Milwaukee yet. The earliest will be sometime between seven and seven-thirty."

Sheila's teeth started to chatter, and he took her hands in his and rubbed them to warm them up. He knew she wasn't really cold. The chill she felt was fear.

"You do think he'll bring her back to River Oaks, don't you?" she asked.

"Yes. He lives here."

"How can you be sure?"

"Your mother heard the man speak to Meg. Called her by name. He said, 'Don't worry, Meg, I'll get you out.' His words indicated that he knew her and that his presence would reassure her."

Sheila's eyes opened wide and she shook her head as if to rid herself of her thoughts. "Nick? Oh God! You think it's Nick."

"I called and got his answering machine, so I sent Pat White over to the studio and his house. He's not at either place."

"It can't be Nick. He'd never hurt Meg."

"Nick is the person Meg would be most comfortable with. She wouldn't be alarmed by his presence. She would go with him willingly if he assured her that your mother was all right."

"That's probably true."

"I called Cal back, and Lois is faxing a picture of Meg and one of Nick to him. We've also put Nick's license number and a description of his car out on the air."

"What if it's not Nick? Oh, God! This is so hopeless. If you haven't been able to find this monster in two years, what makes you think we'll find him now?"

Sheila pulled away from him, folding her arms around her waist and hugging herself. Just then Lois Coren entered with a tray holding several mugs and two carafes.

"I brought both coffee and tea. I thought you could use something."

"Bring it in here," Hank said, opening the door to the conference room.

Lois set the tray on the table, pouring out a mug of tea and carrying it over to Sheila, who stood beside the table as if she didn't know where she was.

"Drink this. I made it real strong," Lois said.

She pulled a chair away from the table and nudged Sheila toward it. She sat down and Lois pressed the mug into her hands, standing over her until she took a sip.

"It'll be all right, honey," the older woman said.

"Will it?" Sheila asked, her face a mask of anguish.

Hank returned to his office, leaving the two women together. He'd never felt so utterly helpless. Anger roiled through his body with such force that he wanted to smash something with his fists. Breathing deeply, he let some of the tension ease away. Then he picked up the phone and called his house.

"It's Hank," he said when his mother answered. "I don't know when we'll get home. I know how much you like Sheila so I'll tell you this, but you'll have to keep it to yourself. Her daughter is missing."

"Not Meg. Oh, that sweet child!" Della cried. "Dear God, Hank, I thought she was safe in Milwaukee."

"She was. She disappeared from a movie theater where she'd gone with her grandmother."

Hank gave her the few details that he knew.

"Poor Sheila. She must be frantic. Do you want to bring her here?"

"I'm sure she won't leave at this point, Mother. As soon as we know a little more, I'll bring her home for something to eat. She's going to need all her strength," Hank finished grimly.

"Is there anything at all I can do?" she asked.

"Pray, Mother. Just pray. And for God's sake don't tell anyone!"

By seven-fifteen, most of the suspect contacts had been made, and everyone crowded into the conference room to offer Sheila encouragement and hear the results.

"All right, folks, listen up." Hank rapped on the table for attention. "We'll deal with the suspect list first. I don't know who made the calls, so speak up when I call the name. Elliot Jenkins."

Lois Coren raised her hand. "Jenkins is the CPA named in the Internet sting. I reached him at home. His wife confirmed that he'd been there since a little after five."

"One down," Paz said, drawing a line through the names on his note pad.

"Herb Reisler?" Hank said, looking around the room. "Reisler?"

Richie Tyler, the rookie, leaped to his feet.

"Sorry, Chief. It's me. When I couldn't locate Reisler at his home, I called his assistant and she said he was having dinner and then playing bridge at the senior center. I drove over and he was there."

"Nice job," Hank said as the red-faced Tyler sat down. He knew his mother would be grateful that Reisler had been cleared.

"Dick Perkins," Hank said.

Owen raised his hand. "According to his wife, Perkins was in Chicago for a dinner last night and a breakfast speech today. He called her this morning when he checked out and said he was going to play golf and wouldn't be home until late."

"Did she know where he was playing?"

"No. She didn't know if the game was in the Chicago area or if he was coming back to play in Madison. I tried his car phone, but there was no answer. I called all the courses in Madison and Sand Ridge Country Club where he's a member. His name wasn't listed in any of the pro shops, but that doesn't mean he's not there. His wife said she'd try to locate him and have him call you."

"Good," Hank said. "Who's got Maloney?"

"Yo," Paz said. "Doug is off duty today. I tried his apartment, but he wasn't there. I called a friend of mine in Madison, and he's going to stay on the apartment until Maloney turns up. I also had Dominic Ferraro. His wife said he'd gone out around two. He didn't tell her where he was going, just said he'd be back late."

Hank nodded, then turned to Pat White. "Did you have any luck on Nick Biagi?"

"No. His photography studio was locked up. No lights. No car. I drove over to his house and he didn't answer the doorbell, and when I looked in the garage window, his car was gone. I checked the neighbors, and one guy said he saw Nick around two o'clock throwing a duffel bag of stuff in the car."

Sheila shifted in her chair. "Generally he carries his camera equipment in duffel bags when he's going on a shoot."

Hank made no comment. "Good job, everyone," he said. "Dan, you had the list of sunflower judges."

"The contest ran for four years." Dan stood up and started passing out some papers. "Twenty judges were needed every year. Some guys judged all four years, so we ended up with a list of forty-five names. I put all the names down and lined out any that we managed to locate. We couldn't find twenty-six."

"Owen will split up the list to make sure we have everyone covered by one of us," Hank said. "I suggest half of you get something to eat now and the other half later. We're going to stay on this until we locate everyone on the judges' list."

He stood up and walked around to talk to Owen. He noticed that most of the people in the room stopped beside Sheila to say a few words or just to give her an encouraging touch. Paz was the last to leave and dropped to one knee and put his arms around her, whispering into her ear as he held her.

Sheila's tears and the lost expression on her face ripped at Hank's guts, and he turned away. Owen had been watching her too and refused to meet his glance.

"How much time have we got?" Owen asked.

"Maybe twenty-four hours. Maybe less." Hank spoke softly so that Sheila wouldn't hear.

"Christ, Hank, where will he take her?"

"I don't think he'll take her to his own house. He has to have another place."

"When I give out the assignments, I'll have them ask if any of the suspects has a summer cottage or access to another house."

"Thanks, Owen," Hank said. "I'm going to take Sheila home and get her to eat something. I'd like to convince her to stay with my mother, but I don't think she'll do it."

Hank heard Paz leave and walked back to Sheila with Owen. She brushed away her tears and blew her nose, giving them a watery smile as she stood up.

"We made a lot of progress in a short time," she said. "Put my name down to make calls, Owen."

"I will, kid." Owen put his arm around her shoulders and walked with her back to Hank's office. "We'll find her, Sheila. Everyone's working on it. This time we've got a head start. Hank set up a couple of check points on roads leading from Madison to River Oaks. We'll get Meg back."

Hank knew exactly what Sheila was thinking. If they didn't find her soon, it would be too late. When they got her back, she'd be dead.

•

"Try to get a bit more soup down," Della said.

Sheila stared across at the older woman, wondering if she could swallow without gagging. At first she'd still felt cold, and the hot chicken soup had warmed her. But now a numbness was setting in, and she was grateful for it. If she thought about Meg, she was afraid she would go out of her mind.

"How about a roll?" Hank said, putting one on her plate. "I think I read once that starches were good when you had a long night ahead."

Sheila appreciated his solicitude but found it trying. He looked totally out of his depth. She could see that he wanted to offer comfort but was unsure if it was appropriate.

Besides, she thought, he's not convinced I won't have a breakdown. I can't. I have to pretend it's someone else's child or I won't be able to think. I'll go crazy.

She took a bite of the roll, but her mouth was so dry she couldn't swallow it. Picking up her glass of milk, she washed it down. She broke off a chunk of the roll and fed it to the dog, who was sitting beside her chair, her head on her knee. When she looked up, Hank was watching her.

"Abby will be your friend for life," he said.

"I hope you don't mind." Sheila leaned over to scratch the dog's head. Abby responded with a wagging tail that slapped against the legs of the chair.

"Neither Abby nor I mind. She only gets spoiled when my mother comes to town, so this is an extra treat."

His eyes glittered in a flash of a smile. He got up to pour a cup of coffee, lacing it with a shot of brandy.

"That's sacrilegious," Della said.

"Otto Malina said brandy in coffee was the best way to sharpen the mind and stay sober doing it. Otto Malina," Hank explained to Sheila, "was the Chief of Police I trained under and eventually re-placed. I learned a helluva lot from the man. He was a tough law-and-order cop."

He opened the back door, letting fresh air in through the screen before he pulled out a cigar and lit it.

"That's a disgusting, nasty habit, Hank," Della said.

"You always say the same thing, Mother." He leaned against the frame of the door, blowing out a long stream of smoke.

"Did Otto Malina grow up in River Oaks, too?" Sheila asked, changing back to a safe topic of conversation.

"No," Hank said. "I think he moved here from Madison after he was married."

Della picked up the story. "He and his first wife bought a big farm on the outskirts of town but only worked a portion of the land. Otto wasn't much interested in farming, and when he became chief of police he didn't have the time for it."

It was easier for Sheila to eat now that Hank's and Della's atten-tions weren't centered on her. She forced herself to lift her spoon and swallow the soup. She knew she would need all her strength for the night ahead.

"Was he a good police chief?" she asked.

"I thought so," Hank said. When Della looked skeptical, he added, "You have to admit, Mother, he was good for the town."

"Yes. I'll give him that, but he was a hard man. The only softness I ever saw in him was his devotion to his second wife."

"Did he divorce his first wife?" Sheila asked.

"No. His first wife died when he was about forty-five. He remar-ried in less than a year to a woman who was divorced and had a young son." Della frowned in disapproval.

"Her name was Angelina Delasandro," Hank said, opening the door to flick ashes outside. "I saw her from time to time. She was beautiful, with striking blue eyes and long hair, black as the night sky. She was much younger than Otto. He was crazy about her, but he had a lot of trouble with the son."

"I think Nino was a disappointment to him. He wasn't the strong, athletic sort. He was awkward and somewhat wimpy. He had a slyness about him that I never liked," Della said. "Otto was tough on him. Word was that he beat him regularly. Eventually Nino ran off. Before he left, he stole the money Otto was paid for the sale of part of the farm."

"It's funny," Hank said, taking a sip of coffee before he continued. "Otto always said that parcel of land was jinxed. He'd broken his leg once just walking through the brush. He was in a cast for two months."

"Worse than that," Della said, her eyes troubled, "he built a house for his sister and her husband right next door. Their child was killed, and her body was found on that jinxed piece of land. It was a terrible shock. This was twenty years ago when there wasn't so much violent crime. Strangely enough, it's the same place where Janette Davis, the first victim, was found."

"No, it wasn't," Hank said. "The case was still open when I joined the force. I remember talking to Otto about it. His niece's body was found on his farm, but Janette Davis was found on the Ravenhurst place."

"That was the bad-luck piece of property that Otto Malina sold off," Della said. "After his niece was killed, he didn't want any part of the land. And the money from the sale was the money his stepson took when he ran away."

"Jesus Jenny!" Hank said.

He stared across the room at Sheila, and she could see his mind was whirling with the same idea that had struck her.

"What happened to the stepson, Della?" she asked.

Della's eyes widened and she glanced from Sheila to Hank, biting her lip at what she read in their expressions.

"I don't know. As far as I know, he never came back to River Oaks."

Clenching the end of the cigar between his teeth, Hank grabbed the receiver of the wall phone and dialed. "It's Harker. Put me through to Owen."

Sheila reached out for Della's hand, her eyes intent on Hank as he took his cigar out and tossed back the last of his coffee. She could hear her heart pounding and swallowed the lump of fear in her throat.

"It's Hank, Owen. I need you to get a file out of storage. You remember the case of Malina's niece? She was killed on the same piece of land where the first victim's body was found." He listened and shook his head. "No. The Ravenhurst place was originally part of Malina's farm. Call me back the instant you have it."

Hanging up the phone, he tossed his cigar out the door and came back to the table. He didn't look at either Sheila or Della but stared down at the oak surface as if he were sorting things out in his own mind. Sheila waited, nails biting into the palms of her hands to keep from speaking.

"I always thought Malina's stepson killed the girl." Hank spoke slowly, obviously working out the story as he went along. "The boy ran away about six months after the niece died. If Malina suspected the kid and did nothing about it, he wouldn't have been able to live with the knowledge. He was already drinking pretty heavy when I joined the force. After that it got worse and worse. He literally drank himself to death."

"What if the stepson has come back to River Oaks?" Sheila's words came out in a raspy whisper. "Maybe he's the one who is killing the children. What did Malina's niece look like?"

Della gasped. Her hand jerked and she knocked over Sheila's empty glass.

"Oh, God, Hank. It was so long ago, I never thought about it. She was blond. She was very young when she died. Maybe eleven or twelve, but she looked older."

"How old was the boy?" Sheila asked.

"In his teens," Hank said. "I think maybe fifteen or sixteen."

The phone rang and he leaped to his feet, snatching up the receiver before it could ring a second time.

"What have you got, Owen?" He listened, his eyebrows drawn together in a frown as he made notes on a piece of paper. "I don't know if there's a connection. I'll let you know shortly."

He hung up once again. When he turned around, Sheila could see the flash of excitement in his eyes, and for the first time since she'd heard that Meg was missing, she felt a spurt of hope. Please God, she prayed. Keep her safe.

"The girl's name was Donna Rosetti. She was twelve. She died from a blow to the head when she was thrown or fell against a tree. She was partially clothed when she was found."

"Was she raped?" Sheila asked.

"I don't know. The autopsy report is missing. It looks like Malina gutted the file." He paused, then spoke directly to Sheila. "Owen said he'd forgotten, until he read over the reports that were left, that Donna's body was found beside a field where Malina's stepson raised sunflowers and roses."

"It's got to be him. It's just got to be him." Hank said nothing, but Sheila could read the confirmation in his eyes. "He could have changed his name and moved back here. How old would he be now?"

"Owen said the murder happened twenty-one years ago. The boy was sixteen, so he'd be thirty-seven. Doug Maloney is thirty-three. I suppose he could be lying about his age. How old is Nick?"

Sheila bit her lip as she tried to remember. "I think he's thirty-five. He told me once that he's only been living in River Oaks since he was twenty-three. Has he always had that beard?"

"Yes. He told me he grew it because he had such a baby face. If he's Nino Malina, he could have grown it so no one would recognize him." Hank's face was expressionless and his voice neutral. "Dick Perkins is thirty-nine. He's definitely not Malina's stepson. He grew up in River Oaks, and his parents are still alive and living in Arizona. Still, we can't count him out, until we know this theory holds together."

"Ferraro is too old, so we could leave him out," Sheila said, then shook her head. "Wait. You said Mrs. Malina was divorced. What if Ferraro is the boy's real father?"

"I suppose he's the right age. Is Mrs. Malina still alive, Mother? Or the girl's parents?"

"I don't know. Donna's parents moved out west a year after the girl was killed. Mrs. Malina moved after Otto died. The house has changed hands three or four times since then, so I doubt if the present owners would know her. As I recall, she bought a place north of here. Now what was the name of that town?"

Della squeezed her eyes shut, trying to force the memory into her brain. Suddenly her eyes popped open.

"Malvin."

"It's about an hour north of here," Hank said to Sheila. "I've got a friend who lives there. He's a real estate agent, so he should be able to find out where she lives. I've got his number in the den."

After Hank left the room, Sheila looked across the table at Della. "Do you think it's possible that it could be the Malina boy?"

"I only saw Nino a few times. He wasn't a particularly personable child. Withdrawn and somewhat sullen. He was suspended from school once when he dissolved aspirins in the class guinea pig's water bottle. He said he wanted to see if it would kill him."

"Did it?"

"Yes. The school suspended him and his stepfather beat him." Della's voice was thoughtful. "I never approved of the way Malina handled him. Any time I saw the two of them together, Otto was either glowering at the boy or yelling at him. It was no surprise to anyone when Nino ran away."

"Would you recognize him?"

"I doubt it. He had stringy hair that was well below shoulder length. It was a real point of contention with his stepfather. Twenty years ago, long hair around here was considered a sign of drug addiction and rebellion, not a fashion statement."

Della stood up and began clearing the dishes from the table. Sheila joined her, grateful for anything that kept her from thinking. The waiting was agony. She was afraid to count too much on the Malina boy being identified as the killer for fear of disappointment.

Hang on, Meg. We're getting closer. Sheila wanted to promise God a boon if He'd keep her child safe, but she couldn't think of anything important enough to tempt the Deity.

Abby scrambled to her feet and hurried over to the sink. Her tail wagging, she pressed her body against Della's leg until the woman responded by getting out the dog's dish.

Sheila took over the task of feeding the dog. After she filled the water dish, she reached for a mug on the countertop. She was pouring coffee when she heard Hank's footsteps in the hall. Her hands began to shake. She set the mug down as Hank came into the kitchen.

"Mrs. Malina is dead."

His words struck Sheila like a blow. She wanted to cry out at her disappointment.

"Sheila!"

A wave of hopelessness washed over her, and she was only vaguely aware of Hank when his fingers dug into her shoulders. She tried to focus on what he was saying.

"God, Sheila, I'm sorry. I shouldn't have told you like that. It doesn't matter about Mrs. Malina. I know where her son lives."

It took a second or two for Sheila to understand the meaning of the words, and when she did, her knees buckled. Hank took her whole weight, letting her rest against his chest. She closed her eyes. A moment of oblivion was all she could allow herself and a quick prayer of thanks. Taking a deep shuddering breath, she pushed away from the comfort of Hank's arms.

"I'm all right," she said, reaching for her mug and taking a quick sip of the strong black coffee.

"Come and sit down, dear," Della said. Her face was pale and her eyes concerned.

"I think I better stand for a bit," Sheila said. "Just to get my bearings. Go ahead, Hank. What did you find out?"

"Mrs. Malina changed her name back to Delasandro when she moved to Malvin. She died in the last week of June, a little over two years ago. The first victim, Janette Davis, was killed a week later."

"Do you think his mother's death could have triggered Janette's killing?" Sheila asked. "A grieving son, unbalanced from a previous murder, is so filled with grief and rage that he kills someone else?"

"Yes." Hank bit off the single syllable. "According to Fritz, Mrs. Delasandro's son was devastated when his mother died."

"Where does the son live?" Della whispered the words as if afraid they might be overhead.

"The man travels a lot. He's on the road through the week and lives in Mrs. Delasandro's house in Malvin most weekends." Hank paused and Sheila's muscles tightened as he turned to face her. "And every summer he grows masses of sunflowers."

Sheila's heart was pounding so hard that she had trouble catching her breath.

"I asked Fritz if he'd seen him in the last couple of days. He said the last time he saw A. W. was about three months ago."

"A. W.? I thought his name was Nino Delasandro," Sheila said.

"It is. Nino is just a nickname. His initials are A. W. The A is for Anthony."

Sheila's fingers went numb and the mug slipped from her hands, smashing on the floor and splashing her legs and feet with the last of her coffee.

"A is for Anthony," she said. "That's what Warren said the first time I met him. Meg and I were joking about his first initial. He said, 'The A is for Anthony.'"

Hank and Della were staring at her as if she'd lost her mind. It was so clear to Sheila. Why hadn't she seen it before?

"Anthony Warren Delasandro. Dr. A. Warren Santo."

Chapter Twenty-One

"Warren Santo has been positively identified as Anthony Warren Delasandro," Hank said, coming back into the conference room. "I faxed Santo's picture to my friend in Malvin. Fritz recognized him immediately."

Paz gave Sheila a hug. Hank smiled reassuringly at her as he sat down.

"I have another piece of evidence," Owen said. "I called Barbara Davis. She said that Dr. Santo is the one who gave shots to Janette's puppy."

"What a piece of scum," Paz said. "Children trust veterinarians. Janette would have accepted a ride from him. And so would all the other girls."

"Janette's puppy was poisoned when Mrs. Davis was renting next door to Dominic Ferraro," Sheila said. "Ray Florio is convinced that Ferraro gave the meat with the glass in it to his grandkids' dog, but Santo lives only three blocks away. It's more likely that Santo's the one who killed both puppies."

Paz smoothed his mustache. "I checked the data files. He wears a size ten shoe, and he was a judge for the sunflower contest twice."

"Did he have access to your keys, Sheila?"

"Yes. He came to the house to check on Meg's bird and we went out for pizza afterwards. He could have taken either the spare key or Meg's keys, which were lost for several days."

"All right. Now all we have to decide is where Santo will take Meg," Hank said. "It's one of two places. His house in River Oaks or the Delasandro house in Malvin. Any thoughts?"

"The logical spot would be the farmhouse in Malvin," Owen said. "It sounds isolated. His house in River Oaks is in a residential area. The chance of discovery would be far greater here."

"I agree," Paz said.

"Sheila?" Hank asked.

"I don't know. What if we choose the wrong one?"

"No matter which house we decide on, Owen and Paz will stake out the other one. If we've got the wrong place, we're only an hour away."

Sheila drew in a slow steady breath. "I think he'll take her to the house in Malvin."

Hank nodded. "Then it's unanimous. Fritz is going to meet us at the real estate office in Malvin. He said he'd have a floor plan of the house ready for us."

"Did you tell him why we wanted it?" she asked.

"Yes. He can be trusted. He's an old Marine buddy. Any second thoughts?" he asked.

Sheila squared her shoulders and raised her chin. "No second thoughts."

"It's not too late. One call and we could have police, FBI, state troopers here, all armed to the teeth."

"We've been over this before, Hank. Santo's not rational. If he knows we're on to him, he'll use Meg as a hostage, if he doesn't kill her in blind fury first. We've got to find her and get her out of there before we call in the cavalry."

Hank could understand Sheila's fears, but his own experiences haunted him. If anything went wrong, it would mean Meg's death and probably his and Sheila's too.

"I realize none of you approve of breaking into the house without backup to rescue Meg," Sheila said, glancing at each face around the table. "So I appreciate the fact you're willing to go along with the plan. God keep us all safe."

"Amen to that," Owen said.

•

"God keep us all safe." Hank repeated the words over and over as he drove north to Malvin.

He glanced sideways at Sheila. In the lights from an oncoming car he could see that her head was against the headrest and her eyes were closed as if she were conserving her energy. Now all he could do was pray they got to Meg in time and that somehow they could rescue her before Santo could hurt her.

"How much longer?"

Sheila's soft voice came out of the darkness. Hank turned his wrist to check the time.

"It's nine o'clock. We'll be in Malvin in five or so minutes." He knew the time must be passing very slowly for her. "I didn't ask before, but how did your call to your mother go?"

"Rough. She's devastated. She's convinced it was all her fault, and she's terrified for Meg's safety. I couldn't tell her our plans, so I just tried to reassure her." Sheila sighed. "How do you know Fritz?"

"We were both in the Marines and ended up in the VA hospital together. He lost his leg, but he's handled it well. He refers to his prosthesis as his peg leg."

"It's none of my business, but what were you in the hospital for?"

"A grenade exploded. I was hit in the upper back and the back of my legs. According to the doctors, it was questionable whether I'd walk again. Their question. Not mine," Hank said. "It took six months, but I walked out of the hospital."

"That must have amazed the doctors."

"It did until I got outside and collapsed beside the car."

"Did you really?"

He chuckled. "I'm afraid I did. Mother screeched and told me I was a damn fool. My father just pulled me up and helped me into the car."

"I suppose you ordered your body to heal and it did," Sheila said.

"That's about right. Like they always say. The first step is the hardest. In my case it was the first movement. Each day I pushed my body a little harder until I could walk across the room. Once I got out of the hospital, I enrolled at the University of Wisconsin, figuring I might as well get an education while I was recovering. At the end of four years I could walk without any sign of an injury."

"You must have a high pain tolerance."

"Pain is just one more obstacle to be overcome. It's like everything else in life. You've got to get through it." Hank slowed down as they entered the outskirts of Malvin. "The real estate office is up ahead on the right."

They parked in front and went inside.

Fritz Duncan came out of his office as they entered. He took Hank's hand in a grip of iron. Ten years older than Hank, Fritz looked at least five years younger. He was a bluff, bearlike man with a thick head of brown hair. Baby blue eyes twinkled in an unlined, almost cherubic, face.

"And you must be Sheila," Fritz said.

He took her hand and held it as they eyed each other. Hank could see the muscles in Sheila's body relax as she took the measure of the man. There was an honesty and warmth about Fritz that engendered trust.

"I just made a fresh pot of coffee. The wind's picked up and it's a bit chilly out."

Moving with only a slight hitch in his walk, Fritz led them into the conference room. The smell of coffee was welcome after the long drive. Fritz wasted no time getting down to business.

"The Delasandro house is on County M. I drove past it on the way into town." At Hank's look of alarm, Fritz rolled his eyes. "Don't get your knickers in a twist. I'm no amateur. There's always traffic on that road. I didn't stop or slow down. Just kept moving."

Hank put his hand on Sheila's shoulder and asked, "Is he there?"

"Yes. The lights were on. Both upstairs and down."

A shudder ran through Sheila's body. Hank pulled out a chair and Sheila dropped down on the seat. Fritz poured her a cup of coffee, a questioning look on his face.

"The missing child is Sheila's daughter," Hank explained.

"Oh, my dear, I'm so sorry," Fritz said. "You must be frantic. Catch your breath and drink some of this while I show you the layout of the house."

He poured two more cups of coffee and handed one to Hank, then opened a yellow folder on the corner of the table. He pulled out several papers and motioned Hank closer.

"When you leave here, drive through the traffic light and turn left on County M. This is a layout of the Delasandro property. Here's County M running along the south edge of the farm."

"Any other houses nearby?"

"Nothing until about a mile after you pass the Delasandro house.

It's set well back from the road. I checked the mileage as I drove past. It's eight-tenths of a mile along M to the gravel entry."

"Gravel drive?" Hank frowned. "Why couldn't it be dirt?"

"If it's dirt you're looking for, I've got just the spot. The property next to his is undeveloped. Couple acres of woods. Belongs to the city. They did some logging in there this year, and there's a dirt road that runs parallel to the Delasandro lot line."

"How far is it from the driveway?"

"A hundred yards once you reach the trees." Fritz straightened up, glancing back and forth between Hank and Sheila. "You're figuring to go in alone, aren't you?"

"Yes."

Fritz knew the story of the disastrous hostage rescue. In the hospital, Hank had waked him up with his nightmares.

"It's good to face down the ghosts," Fritz said. "I don't suppose you'd let an old peg leg join the attack?"

"I thought about it earlier, but I decided that the smaller the group, the better the chance of success." Hank was grateful that his friend asked no further questions. "You can best help by telling us about the house."

Fritz nodded in understanding. "It's pretty simple. No basement. First and second floors only. Wide porch across the front of the house. The oak door leads into a small foyer. A wood-framed glass door opens into the living room. Beyond that is a small dining area and the kitchen at the back."

He pointed to each of the rooms as he spoke. His voice was calm and his words clearly enunciated, a commander outlining battle plans.

"There's a small hallway off the kitchen where the stairs leading to the second floor are located."

"Back door?"

"Yes. The door opens into the little hall, and the stairs are straight ahead. Upstairs the main bedroom is on the left. On the right is a smaller room and a bath next to that. Straight ahead, over the living room is another small bedroom."

"Are the stairs and the second-floor hall carpeted?" Sheila asked.

"No. Hardwood floors. No runner on the stairs."

"Do you know if he has a security system?" Hank asked.

"He did some extensive rehabbing after his mother died. All new windows and doors and an alarm system. It's hooked in to the telephone line. You can disable it from the garage, but that means the phone will be dead."

"We'll just have to pray that he doesn't try to make a call."

"Any other questions?" When Hank shook his head, Fritz set his coffee on the table and said, "I've got some other things for you. I'll be right back."

Hank met Sheila's eyes, and he could see the tight control she had over her emotions. If she showed any signs of falling apart, he'd use it as an excuse to leave her behind. Even with that understanding, he had to fight his instinctive desire to protect her.

"Will you be able to remember the layout? It's dark out, so there's not much point in taking this stuff."

Sheila's eyes were intent on the drawings. "I'll remember."

"I brought some blankets and a thermos of coffee," Fritz said, as he returned carrying several plaid blankets and a black canvas backpack. "There's also a hunting knife and a couple of small MAGlites. Big shine and no bulk. An emergency kit's in the bottom along with a flare gun."

"Good Lord, Fritz. It wouldn't surprise me if you had a tank parked outside."

"I've got something better than that," Fritz said with a wide mischievous grin. He shoved a hand in the pocket of his pants and pulled out two sets of keys. "Keys to the Delasandro house."

"You're kidding!" A jolt of excitement shook Hank. "How the hell did you get them?"

"I sold the house to Mrs. Delasandro, and I dealt with A. W. after she died. Remember I said he got new doors and windows? Well, I was the one who oversaw the work. He gave me a set of keys in case there were deliveries while he was gone or if there was some kind of emergency at the house." Fritz handed one of the keyrings to Hank. "I always make duplicates as insurance in case I misplace the first set. The gold key fits both the front and back doors. The silver key is for the side door of the garage."

Sheila stood up. "I don't know how to thank you," she said.

"Give your girl a hug for me," Fritz said, handing her the other set.

"I'll let you give her one in person." She closed her fingers around the keys and stood on tiptoe to kiss his cheek.

"We'll try to get in and out without alerting him," Hank said. "I don't know how long it will take to locate Meg and get her out. Once we've got her, we'll call for back up."

"You need a contingency plan. From my office window I have a clear view north and west. If anything goes wrong, send up a flare. I'll be able to see it and I'll send help fast," Fritz said. "Otherwise, if I haven't heard from you after an hour, I'm calling the police."

Hank knew his friend was right, but he didn't want the police arriving too soon and running the risk that Santo might hurt Meg. "It's nine-fifteen. Say fifteen minutes to get there. If you haven't heard from us by eleven o'clock, send in the troops."

His handshake was firm as he tried to communicate his appreciation for Fritz's help. He picked up the canvas backpack and the blankets. Sheila's eyes were bright with tears as she accepted the thermos. Hank took her arm and led her outside. By the time he had the car started, he could see she again had her emotions under control.

Fritz stood in the doorway, his face expressionless as they pulled away from the curb.

Eyes intent on the road, neither of them spoke. Sheila's vision was sharper than Hank's. She spotted the sign for County M before he saw it. He turned left, marking the mileage on the odometer, and drove slowly so that he wouldn't have to brake when he located the house.

On the right, the road ran along a harvested field of corn, then came to a stand of trees, then another open area. The ground was covered with dark circular mounds and larger rectangular plots. As they drew closer, he could see that these were gardens filled with row after row of sunflowers. Most of the plants were tall with huge heads, nodding in the wind.

"There it is," Sheila whispered, rolling down the window for a clearer view.

The white frame house was set back against the dark woods, too far away to let them note any details. Light gleamed from the first-floor windows, illuminating the welcoming front porch. The second floor was dark.

"Watch for the dirt road," Hank said.

His hands cramped with tension as he gripped the wheel. He didn't want to use the brake while they were still out in the open. He took his foot off the gas as they approached the trees. The instant they were out of sight of the house, he braked slightly, then let the car coast forward.

"A little farther," Sheila said, pointing ahead to the logging road.

Hank turned into the opening. The moon was out, and the area was lit well enough to allow him to turn off the car lights. It was difficult to really call this a road, he thought. Just two dirt tracks with grass growing in the middle.

He drove slowly, unable to see the ditches and soft spots until the wheels dropped into them. With a hand on the dashboard and the other on the armrest, Sheila was braced against the worst of the jolting.

Hank cursed under his breath until they reached the end of the track and the woods opened into a clearing. He inched around in a circle, pointing the car back along the logging road, then shut off the engine.

Sheila sat still as her eyes adjusted to the darkness. She tried to swallow, but her mouth was too dry.

"Are you OK?" Hank said, turning toward her.

His voice sounded loud as the silence of the night enveloped them. Too nervous to speak, she nodded her head.

"Watch your door as you get out."

She jumped when the overhead light went on and scrambled out of the car. Easing the door closed, she pressed against it until she heard it latch and the dome light went out. She shivered in the chill air, grateful for her gabardine slacks and long-sleeved uniform shirt.

Now that the time for action had come, she was calm. She needed to detach her thoughts from Meg and concentrate on her training.

"I can't see the house lights, so I don't think he could have seen ours," Hank whispered from the back of the car.

He opened the trunk and took out the canvas bag. Sheila moved close to him, aware of how far voices carried in the woods.

"Have you ever used a flare gun?" he asked.

"No."

He reached into the backpack and pulled out the gun. The bright orange handgrip was a sharp contrast to the short white barrel. He handed it to her and she was surprised that all the weight was in the handgrip. She assumed that once it was loaded the balance would improve.

"Push the orange button on the side to open the gun, and drop a flare inside." He handed her one. "Close the gun. If you want to shoot, just point it to the sky and pull the trigger. Got it?"

Sheila nodded and handed the gun back.

"I'll take the backpack with the emergency kit, the flare gun, and extra flares," Hank said. "Here's a flashlight and a hunting knife."

Sheila took the thin black flashlight and shoved it into the pocket of her uniform pants. The knife was about eight inches long. The blade was encased in a leather sheath with only the bone handle showing. She reached around to jam the sheath into the top of her pants at the small of her back. When it was secure, she touched her holster, making sure it was firmly attached to her belt.

"I'm going to leave the keys here," he said.

He bent over to place the keyring on the ground behind the rear wheel on the driver's side. "Our first objective is to get Meg out of the house. If we manage it without alerting Santo, you bring her back here and call for reinforcements. I'll stay behind to make sure Santo doesn't get away. Any questions?"

"No," Sheila said.

"We'll cut across the woods until we reach the edge of the clearing. Once we get our bearings, we'll work out a plan. We have an hour and a half before Fritz calls the police."

Slipping his arms through the straps of the backpack, he closed the trunk and headed across the clearing to the woods. Sheila followed.

With the moonlight, they didn't need the flashlights. It was difficult walking through the heavy brush, and several times Sheila got tangled up in the branches. The trees began to thin out. Her face and hands were scratched, and she could taste blood from a cut on her lip. She wiped her mouth with the back of her hand and hunkered down beside Hank at the edge of the woods.

The cleared areas between the trees and the house were dotted with flower beds of various sizes and small areas of sunflowers, planted in tight rows. The first-floor lights were still on.

Hank put his mouth to her ear. "If we walk inside the rows, it will bring us out at the corner of the house close to the garage."

Sheila nodded. He stood up and stepped out of the cover of trees. He crossed the opening to the sunflower field and disappeared inside.

The instant she stepped into the space between the rows, her body tensed. The sunflowers were planted close together. They rose over her head, blocking out the moonlight. The wind brushed across the tops of the nodding flower heads, and the brittle leaves smacked against each other.

By the time she reached the opening at the end of the sunflowers, she felt as if she were suffocating. She took several deep breaths as she waited for Hank's instructions.

"Garage."

She nodded at the single word, following him as he walked along the edge of a small sunflower garden. Here the plants were short, only five feet. Less formidable than the taller ones. They reached the end of the flower bed. The garage was straight ahead with the house on the right. They hurried across the open area, circling behind the garage until they reached the side door.

Hank had the garage key in his hand. She heard the scrape of metal against metal, and then the door opened into the dark interior. He stepped inside, reaching back to take her hand and guide her inside. When he closed the door, they were plunged into darkness.

A faint light illuminated Hank's hand. With his palm cupped over the end of the flashlight, there was just enough light to let them recognize Warren Santo's Jeep Cherokee. Moving to the side of the car, Hank lit up the interior. The car was empty. On the passenger side of the front seat was a bouquet of flowers.

Five roses for the fifth victim.

If there had been any question in either of their minds, the roses were the final confirmation. The physical evidence of Santo's crimes filled Sheila with anger and loathing. She didn't dwell on Meg's immediate danger, only the need to rescue her and rid the world of a monster.

She put her hand on Hank's arm, and when he bent his head, she whispered, "Let's go get Meg."

"First the alarm," he said.

He pulled up his trouser leg to reveal a knife strapped to his leg. In an instant it was in his hand, and he moved around the car, stabbing the blade into the tires. The air whistled as the tires flattened. It was a minute or two before he returned. Shielding the light, he led her back to the door.

"I cut the phone and the alarm system," Hank said, close to her ear. "My guess is he'll want to see the ten o'clock news. Let's see if we can locate Meg before it starts."

They crept across the open ground to a side window partially covered by a hedge of arborvitae. By squirming between branches they could get close enough to see into the house. The window was in the dining room, but Sheila could see into both the living room and a section of the kitchen.

Warren Santo, his back to the window, sat in an overstuffed chair in front of the television set. On the table beside him was a brown ceramic lamp with a beige silk shade, a can of beer, his eyeglasses, and a bowl of sunflower seeds. The television was on, the sound loud but muffled by the closed window.

Sheila could see all of the dining room and most of the living room. There was no sign of Meg. The scene had such an air of normalcy that for a moment she wondered if they could be wrong; then she remembered the flowers in the Jeep and had no further doubts. She tore her eyes away from the window, afraid that her hatred would somehow communicate itself to Santo. Hank touched her arm and they pushed through the hedge.

They skirted around to the back of the house, locating the back door and moving close enough to peek into the kitchen.

The room was unlit, but there was enough light coming from the living room to show them that it was empty. Sheila could see the small hallway where the second-floor stairs were located. Neither the back door nor the hallway was visible from the living room.

Once again Hank touched her arm, and she followed him away from the house. They had just reached one of the small gardens when the lights in the kitchen flashed on. Dropping to the ground, Sheila lay with her head facing the house. The light poured out the kitchen windows, but she was so far away that it didn't reach her.

Her heart began to race as she saw Santo come into the kitchen. Oh, God! Was he going upstairs? She prayed silently, words stumbling over each other as she begged for Meg's safety. She went numb with relief when Santo opened the refrigerator and took out a can of beer.

She closed her eyes as he faced the window, opening them only when she heard Hank move. The lights were off in the empty kitchen, and she could see straight through the house to the living room. Santo was back in front of the TV.

"It's almost ten," Hank said, his voice just above a whisper. "We need to make our move now."

"I'm ready."

"If Meg is in the house, she's upstairs."

"Agreed—and I'm the one who has to go in the back and find her." Hank opened his mouth but Sheila cut him off. "Meg will be terrified, and if she's groggy she might not recognize you and either put up a struggle or cry out."

Hank was silent. She was close enough to him to feel the resistance in his body. He was a pragmatic person, and she knew once he considered it, he would know she was right.

"You win."

He bit off the words as if they were distasteful. And they probably were, she thought. Hank hated yielding on anything.

"I'll go around to the front and keep an eye on Santo," he said. "I promise you I won't let him come anywhere near you or Meg. If it looks like the game is up, I'll come in the front door blasting. We have to move fast, though. I don't know if he'll watch all of the news, so figure you have ten minutes to find Meg. Is that enough time?"

"It'll have to be," Sheila said. Her stomach lurched in a sickening free-fall sensation.

"Good."

"What if I don't find her?" Sheila voiced her fear in a rasping whisper. "What if he's already killed her and left her in Worley Woods?"

"Santo held the other girls for forty-eight hours. He's a creature of habit. Trust his pattern."

He didn't give her time to form any pictures in her mind. Pulling her to her feet, he followed her over to the back door and leaned close.

"The TV's on loud enough so it should cover any noise from your entry. Go up the side of the stairs. Place your feet as close to the wall as you can to keep the wood from creaking."

She nodded her understanding.

"Give me three minutes to get in place before you go in. Once you get Meg out, head directly for the car." He placed his hand on her shoulder, his eyes intent on her face. "And for God's sake, Sheila, be careful."

"You too," she said.

It was a second or two before she realized she was alone. The wind swirled around her, and she shivered as she glanced at her watch and silently prayed.

•

Hank crept around the house to the front porch. The oak door looked solid; it would take too long to break through it, so he would have to unlock it.

Moving back to the side window, he raised his head enough to see into the living room. Santo faced away from the window, his head visible above the back of the chair. The volume on the television had been turned up so high that Hank could hear the commercial outside.

The glass door leading to the foyer was closed. The frosted glass was etched with an intricate floral design, making it almost opaque. With the sound from the television and with the door as a buffer, Hank should be able to get up the stairs and across the porch without detection.

It was risky but it had to be done.

He took one more peek through the window. The station break was over. The smiling face of the anchorman from Madison appeared on the screen.

Ducking below the window, Hank made his way to the front stairs. He took out his gun, putting it in his left hand as he pulled out the keys. The gold house key glinted in the moonlight as he put his foot on the first step.

He gritted his teeth as he climbed the stairs but made it to the top without a sound. He set his foot down, shifting his weight slowly, then took a wide stride forward. The floorboards squeaked only once before he reached the door.

The oak door had recessed panels and two small beveled windows at eye height. It opened into a small foyer, and beyond that was the wood-framed glass door that led into the living room.

Fritz had told him the lock was new and should turn easily. Hank hoped he was right. With his fingers he found the slot for the key and inserted it. He lowered his head to the lock, listening over the sound of the TV for the bolt to shift as he turned the key. He felt more than heard the distinctive click. The doorknob turned in his hand, and he could sense the movement of the latch. The door was unlocked.

By the time he had retraced his route, Hank's body was coated with sweat. He shivered in the chill air.

From his vantage point beside the front window, he could see Warren Santo leaning forward in his chair, his eyes trained on the TV screen. According to Hank's watch, Sheila was in the house. Her entrance must have been flawless, because Santo's attention hadn't wandered from the news.

Hank hated the fact that Sheila was inside. He no longer had control of the situation. His next move would be determined either by the discovery of the break-in or by any sign that Santo was going upstairs.

Staring at the back of Santo's head, he tightened his grip on the gun. The temptation to shoot through the window was overwhelming. He resolved that before the night was over, he would put an end to Warren Santo's crime spree.

•

Sheila stood in the back hall with her back against the outside door. Straight ahead the stairs faded upward into darkness. A railing was attached to the wall on the right side of the staircase.

She had ten minutes.

Before she could lose her nerve, she took hold of the wooden railing and placed her foot on the bottom step. She wedged it close to the wall and pulled herself upwards, trying to keep most of her weight on the railing. Her fear of what she might find upstairs was so great that she could barely hear the TV over the roaring in her ears.

As she approached the top of the stairs, she pulled out her flashlight and, shielding the beam, flashed it across the hall, identifying the doorways as she pictured the map in her mind. In her brief glimpse, she noted the slick finish on the wood floor.

The house was old. The floor would creak if she attempted to walk across it. She pulled her shirt out of her pants, tugging it down to cover the metal on her belt buckle and her holster. Opening the top buttons of her blouse, she shoved the flashlight into the V of her breasts, held tight by her bra.

Time to move.

Leaning forward, she lay down on her stomach at the top of the stairs. Using her hands and arms, she pushed her body forward. The only sound was the brush of cloth across the wooden floor. She moved along the wall until she touched the first doorway on the right. She pulled out the flashlight and directed the beam low on the floor.

A long table ran along the outside wall of the room. A sewing machine, piles of fabric, and open boxes of buttons and spools of thread littered the table. The room was small and smelled musty. Probably untouched since Santo's mother died.

Meg wasn't in the sewing room.

Slanting the beam across the hall, she located the master bedroom and slid over to the doorway. She could smell the odor of fresh paint, and the wallpaper of cabbage roses looked new. A four-poster bed stood against the far wall. She lifted the beam to the mattress and drew in a sharp breath at the sight of her missing nightgown draped across the foot of the bed.

Meg was not on the bed or anywhere in the room.

She glanced at her watch. Three minutes left. Moving quickly now, she propelled her body to the bathroom doorway. The only place Meg could be was in the bathtub, but in the beam of light she could see that it too was empty.

Only one more room.

Her arm muscles strained as she moved to the final doorway. She stared into the darkened room, afraid to look for fear Meg wouldn't be there. Oh, please God, please God, she chanted.

She was out of time. She flicked on the flashlight.

A large canopy bed dominated the small room. A floral bedspread covered the bed, and from her position on the floor Sheila could only see the edge of one of the pillow shams. She pushed up to her hands and knees so she could see the top of the bed.

Aside from the two pillows, the bed was empty.

Chapter Twenty-Two

The bed was empty. Oh God! Oh God! Where was Meg?

Sheila sagged down onto the floor. She pressed her forehead against the cold floorboards and couldn't hold back a moan of despair.

Like an echo, a faint whimper cut through the silent room.

Instantly alert, Sheila swept the light around the room, almost missing the small bundle beneath the window. Swinging the light back, she caught the glint of terror-filled eyes above a slash of silver tape.

Meg!

In her elation at finding her, Sheila fumbled the flashlight, catching it just before it hit the floor. Stuffing it back into her bra, she scooted across the floor. Her fingers touched the rough wool of a blanket, and she searched until she found Meg's shoes. She ran her hands along the girl's body, feeling the rope tied around her feet and her hands. Finally she reached a thick braid of hair and leaned over to whisper in her ear.

"It's OK, sweetheart. Mommy's here."

A silent sob shook Meg. Sheila cradled the trembling body against her own, using precious seconds to rock the frightened child. Her own tears mingled with Meg's as she rocked her and offered up prayers of thanksgiving.

Sheila ran her hands along the girl's body in search of injuries. Fingers caressed the long-sleeved knit shirt and the blue jeans, moving down to the anklets and sneakers. Meg didn't react to any of the pushing and prodding.

"Are you hurt?" she whispered.

She could feel Meg shake her head and released the breath she hadn't realized she was holding. She cupped Meg's face with her hands, her anger rising as she felt the duct tape across her daughter's mouth. Wiping the tears from her cheeks, she kissed the girl on the forehead.

Keeping her voice low, Sheila said, "I'm going to cut the ropes, but leave the tape in place until we're outside."

The little head nodded against her shoulder. She released Meg and reached to the small of her back for the hunting knife. Gripping the flashlight between her teeth, she directed the beam at the ropes and slipped the knife between Meg's ankles.

The blade was newly sharpened and sliced through the rope with ease. Moving the light to Meg's hands, she carefully cut the rope at her daughter's wrists.

A muffled cry came from Meg as the circulation returned to her hands and feet. Stuffing the knife back in her waistband, Sheila held Meg tight as she squirmed in discomfort.

When Meg had quieted, Sheila turned the light on the window.

It was a new double-hung window, the wood frame painted to match the trim in the room. She prayed that it wasn't sealed shut by the paint. Setting the flashlight down on the blanket beside Meg, she pushed herself to her knees and reached up to unlock the window. She grasped the window handles and tried to raise the sash.

The window didn't move. Shifting her position, she placed the heels of her hands just beneath the wood trim on the lower pane of glass and pushed upward. At first nothing happened, then inch by inch, the window rose. Fresh air filled the room, and greedily she sucked it into her lungs. Below her she could hear Meg doing the same thing.

She pressed her face to the screen and looked out. The sky was clouding over, blocking the moonlight for short periods of time. As it brightened again, she looked down at the roof of the front porch directly below, probably no more than two feet beneath the window.

It was far too risky to take Meg across the hall and down the back stairs. One sound and Santo would be waiting at the bottom. If she took Meg out the window, there was a better chance of getting away without alerting him. She bit her lip, wondering if the roof was strong enough to support their weight.

"We're going out the window," she whispered to Meg.

Running her fingers around the edges of the screen, she found the latches to release it. She scrabbled at the metal, breaking her nails, but finally the screen pulled away from the frame. She lifted it out and, careful not to bang it against the sill, set it on the floor, leaning up against the canopy bed.

Using the window frame for leverage, Sheila pulled herself upright, planting her feet slowly so the floor wouldn't squeak. When she had her balance, she reached down to lift Meg to her feet. Too late, she remembered the flashlight and caught her breath in a gasp of horror as it rolled off the blanket and hit the floor with a sharp thunk.

•

Santo's head jerked up, and he tipped it back to stare at the ceiling as if he had heard something. From the outside, Hank could see the expression of astonishment on the man's face. Santo was rigid only for an instant, then he slammed his fists on the arms of the chair and leaped to his feet.

He knew!

Gun in hand, Hank raced for the front stairs. He had two doors to get through, and Santo would hear him coming. It couldn't be helped. No matter what, he couldn't let Santo get near Sheila and Meg.

He took the steps two at a time. He charged across the porch, turning the doorknob the instant his hand touched it. As the door opened he squeezed off several shots at the glass door directly ahead. In the small room, the sound was deafening.

The glass in the door exploded.

He ducked his head, squinting in the shower of glass that peppered his face and body. Santo was crouched halfway between the kitchen and the living room. Hank didn't see the gun in Santo's hand until a bullet slammed into his shoulder.

The impact spun him sideways, and he fought to maintain his balance. He tried to squeeze the trigger, but another shot seared his leg, throwing him onto the porch. As he landed on his back the gun flew out of his hand, skidding across the floorboards and disappearing into the darkness.

He struggled to get to his feet. The longer it took for Santo to kill him, the better chance Sheila would have to get Meg out of the house. A dark stain was spreading across the front of his shirt. On his face and hands, he could feel the trickle of blood from the glass cuts.

His strength was seeping away. With a final effort, he managed to sit up. The pain was gone. His eyesight blurred and he blinked to clear it.

Santo smiled as he raised his gun. He pointed it at Hank's head and fired.

•

Sheila had frozen when she heard Hank charging up the front stairs onto the porch. The gunshots galvanized her into action. She had to get Meg to safety.

She grabbed the flashlight and jammed it back into her bra. Lifting Meg, she thrust her, feet first, through the open window. She braced herself against the window frame as she lowered Meg to the roof of the porch. It seemed strong enough, but she trembled as she let go of her child.

Sitting down on the window sill, she swung her legs outside. She flipped over on her stomach and placed one foot at a time on the shingled roof. Her arms ached as she held the window frame and carefully shifted her weight onto her feet.

Downstairs two more shots were fired.

Back flat against the wall of the house, Meg stared up at her. In the moonlight, the band of silver tape resembled a mouth opened wide in a scream. The light began to fade as clouds again moved to cover the moon. In the darkness, Sheila could feel Meg's body jerk as another shot ripped through the night, directly below them.

Then, nothing but silence. Sheila tensed, waiting for Hank's all-clear signal.

"Donna. Donna."

Sheila crouched down at the eerie cry from downstairs. Pain ripped through her at the realization that Santo was alive. Hank? Oh, God! Was Hank injured? Please God, not dead! She pressed her fist against her mouth and rocked back and forth in agony.

"I know you're upstairs, Donna. Come down here."

Santo's voice brought her back to the reality of their situation. The sound faded as he moved toward the kitchen. Knowing he was heading for the stairs, Sheila pushed away from the window and hesitated only long enough to ascertain that the roof would hold her weight.

Lying down on the shingles, she took a firm hold of Meg and crawled across to the edge. In the darkness she couldn't see the ground. She looked around wildly for another means of escape.

Light spilled out the bedroom window as Santo turned on the hall light. Kissing Meg for luck, she took the girl's hands and lowered her over the edge of the roof. Remembering the bushes that ran along the side of the house, she stretched out as far as she could without falling off the roof.

Meg's face was a mask of fear, and Sheila had to force herself to release her grip and let the girl drop to the ground. Crawling farther along the roof, Sheila lay down on her stomach and slid her legs over the side.

"Donna, where are you?" Santo's voice was sharp with anger.

Sheila inched backwards, dangling over the edge of the roof. Praying she wouldn't land on Meg, she pushed off into space. She remembered to bend her knees, but even so she landed badly. A streak of fire shot up her leg, and she closed her eyes, afraid she would black out.

"Hurry, Mom, hurry."

From a distance she could hear Meg's frantic whisper, and she focused on the girl's face until the wave of lightheadedness passed. The duct tape clung to the corner of Meg's mouth, and impatiently Meg yanked it, gasping as it tore away from her skin.

"Damn it, Donna. Where are you?"

Santo shouted the words, his normally deep voice shrill. Meg cringed against Sheila. Over their heads they could hear the banging of doors and crash of overturned furniture as the madman searched the second floor.

The moon was totally covered now, and there was no break in the cloud line. Light poured out of the windows of the house, illuminating the area around the house with bright patches. From above, Santo would be able to see them if they attempted to reach the gardens and sunflower fields.

Sheila's ankle throbbed, and she shifted her weight, sucking in her breath as her foot touched the ground. She would never be able to make it back to the car. She pulled out her flashlight and ran it along the edge of the bushes beside the house until she found an opening.

"In there," she said.

She held the light steady as Meg wriggled into the thick shrubbery. Santo's ranting grew louder, and she knew he was approaching the front bedroom. Dropping to her knees, she flicked off the light, tucked it back in her bra, and crawled into the opening.

She kept her head down to protect her eyes, using her arms and the top of her head to force her way through. Her hair tangled in the branches, and she yanked it free. She broke through to find Meg huddled against the concrete foundation of the house.

"Are you all right, sweetheart?"

Meg nodded and Sheila pulled the girl into her lap.

"Oh Mom. It's Dr. Santo."

Sheila heard the heartbreak in the soft wail. She closed her eyes and tightened her arms around Meg. She could only imagine the terror the girl must have felt when she woke up. She was bright enough to know she'd been kidnapped and why. Hearing the noises in the hall, she must have thought Santo was coming to kill her.

Anger solidified in Sheila, and she ground her teeth to keep from cursing. God! How she hated him! She promised that he would pay for what he had done to Meg and the other children. And what about Hank?

Santo must have heard the flashlight drop on the floor and started to come upstairs. With his heroic charge through the front door, Hank had sacrificed his life for theirs. She couldn't let his death be for nothing.

A cry of outrage cut through the night air. Santo had discovered the open window.

Setting Meg on the ground, Sheila stood up, her head just above the bushes. In front of the porch, she could see a bright rectangle of light from the bedroom window. Suddenly Santo's shadow darkened the grass in the reflection. His silhouette was elongated, huge fists pounding the wooden frame as he shouted out the window.

"Bring her back, Donna! You can't have her!"

Sheila wanted to cover her ears as he screamed Donna's name over and over. He shrieked, his words unintelligible as he slipped into dementia.

With her injured ankle it would be impossible to get Meg to safety before Santo spotted them. It was still a half hour before Fritz would call the police. They needed help now. With Meg well hidden, Sheila would have to locate the backpack with the flare gun.

Where was Hank? He had to be either on the front porch or inside the front door.

She would make her way between the bushes and the house until she reached the porch. She'd climb over the railing and find Hank and the backpack. After she fired off the flare, she would draw Santo farther away from Meg. Maybe she could stay ahead of him until help arrived.

She tried not to think about the gun Santo had used to shoot Hank as she ducked back down to the side of the house. She put her arms around Meg and rested her cheek on the top of the girl's head. The familiar scent of strawberry-shampooed hair brought tears to Sheila's eyes.

"I have to leave you to get help, Meg," she whispered.

Against her cheek, the little head shook violently and small hands clutched the front of her shirt.

"Don't go, Mom. Please."

Meg's voice was tinged with panic. Sheila tightened her arms and whispered words of encouragement.

"You have to be brave, darling. I have to go and you have to stay. Someone has to tell the police about Santo. If I can't, it will be your responsibility. Will you stay here?"

Sheila caressed Meg's cheek, wiping away the trail of tears with her fingertips. Leaning over, she kissed the wet face.

"I love you with all my heart, Meg," Sheila said. "Promise you'll stay here no matter what happens?"

With a whimper, Meg nodded her head.

"You can't hide from me, Donna."

Meg gasped. Santo's voice came from the front of the house. From the sound of it, he must be standing in the doorway, Sheila thought, as she pulled Meg into the shadowy base of the bushes and sheltered her against her bosom. Footsteps pounded across the front porch and down the stairs.

"If you come out now, Donna, I won't be angry."

Sheila's heart gave a lurch as a beam of light played across the top of the bushes. Beneath her, Meg quivered like a wounded bird. The light didn't penetrate to the ground and passed quickly overhead.

"Do you hear me?" Santo yelled. His voice began to fade as he moved away from the house.

"Stay here," Sheila whispered.

She crawled to the base of the house, sliding upward until she could see above the bushes. The beam of light swept across the gardens in front of the house, stopping at each one as Santo searched for them. When he got to the last one, he trained the light on the field of sunflowers on the far side of the house.

"I see you!" he shouted.

The beam of light bobbed across the ground as he raced toward the field and disappeared inside. He must have seen some animal, she thought, watching the light filter through the stalks as he worked his way along the rows. While he was occupied searching the field, she'd have to try to reach the flare gun.

She pulled out the Beretta and limped along between the house and the bushes. Pain shot up her leg in waves like electric jolts. She was panting when she reached the end of the shrubbery at the corner of the house.

Light from the front windows and the open front door lit up the porch. The night silence was eerie, and it frightened her that she could no longer see the flickering beam among the sunflowers. Taking a deep breath, she stepped into the open and moved to the side of the porch, where she could see through the pillars of the railing.

Hank lay on his side, his face in shadow. Fingers of blood trailed through his blond hair from the wound at his temple, and the front of his khaki shirt was stained dark from his shoulder to the center of his chest. She could see rips in his clothes where the bullets had smashed into his body.

Turning her head away, she covered her mouth to stifle her sobs. Oh God! How could you let this happen?

She gritted her teeth, knowing she had no time to mourn. Her first duty was to get the flare gun. The backpack lay beside Hank. The straps were torn as if it had been ripped from his body when he fell.

One last time she scanned the area in front of the house, but there was no sign of Santo. She'd have to risk it. Gun in her right hand, she reached up with her left. The tips of her fingers touched the railing. She opened her hand, stretching until she had a solid grip on the top.

"Mom!"

In the silence that followed Meg's terrified cry, Santo's voice rang out.

"You can come out now, Donna. I have the child."

Sheila knew that if she obeyed his order, she would sentence both of them to death. Ignoring the pain in her ankle, she crouched down, limped along the front of the porch, and hurried past the stairs. If she could reach the far side of the house, she could go around the back of the house and come up behind Santo. It was their only chance.

She had almost reached the corner of the house when the flashlight beam caught her. Her shadow spread out ahead of her across the grass. She stopped, knowing it was pointless to continue.

"Turn around!" Santo shouted.

Keeping her gun hand hidden in the material of her slacks, she turned. Unwilling to let Santo see her fear, she raised her head as she faced the blinding light.

"Drop the gun, Donna, or I'll shoot the child."

Sheila could hear the loss of control in his voice. He wouldn't hesitate to shoot Meg if she didn't obey him. Despair washed over her, and she raised her arms out to the sides, so that he could see them. Grinding her teeth, she opened her fingers and let the gun fall to the ground.

She waited. She realized he didn't know about the knife. Her heart kicked in excitement. She would have one last chance to save Meg.

Santo slanted the beam toward the ground, and Sheila could see him in the reflected light. He was standing directly behind Meg, the arm with the flashlight resting on her shoulder. She appeared to be frightened but unhurt.

He nudged Meg and the child moved forward, her movements wooden. Flashlight in one hand, gun in the other, he followed her. They walked to the edge of the stairs and stopped about ten feet away from Sheila.

She barely recognized the fastidiously neat Dr. Santo in the disheveled creature before her. His curly brown hair was sticking up around his head as if he'd been running his fingers through it. Lighted from below, his face was painted with nightmarish shadows, and his darkened eye sockets looked empty.

She wondered how much of a grip on reality he had. He had called her Donna. Had he regressed back to some childhood fantasy? Could she reach him by taking on Donna's identity? Taking a deep breath, she stared directly at Santo.

"Nino?" she said.

For a moment she thought the use of his nickname might have been a mistake. The flashlight jerked and the beam caught her full in the face. She closed her eyes.

"It is you, isn't it?" Wonder filled his voice.

"Of course it's me, but I can't see you with the light so bright."

Sheila spoke in the petulant voice of a spoiled child. She brushed at her clothes and tucked her shirt into her pants. When he lowered the beam, she gripped the bone handle of the knife and eased it out of the leather sheath.

"How are you, Nino?"

"Now that I've found you, I'm fine." His nervous giggle turned into a hiccup.

"How did you know it was me?"

"I saw you on television and you were so beautiful. I always knew you would be beautiful when you grew up. I was right. Then you came to the hospital with the bird, and I recognized you immediately."

"You were always so clever," she said. "Did you plant all the beautiful flowers for me?"

"Yes. Especially the sunflowers."

Sheila heard the pride in his voice. "I've never seen bigger flowerheads. You always had a magic touch with them."

"Just wait until you see them next year."

Santo's tone was calmer. Sheila spoke in a matter-of-fact voice, hoping to keep him that way.

"You have to let the child go."

"No!" His anger erupted and he chopped the air with the edge of his hand. "As long as I have her, you'll do whatever I tell you to do."

"If you don't let her go, I won't stay here. I want it to be just you and me."

"Please, Donna. Let me keep her."

Santo's words chilled her. He spoke as if Meg were an object, a possession.

"You can't keep her!" Sheila stamped her foot. "She's ready to leave."

Meg's eyes widened and Sheila could see that she understood the message. Tightening her fingers on the knife, she started walking toward Santo.

"Stop where you are. Don't come any closer!"

His voice rose until he was screaming the last words. He raised the flashlight, shining it into her eyes. Squinting in the glare, Sheila limped across the open ground until she was only two feet from the raging man.

"Run, Meg," she shouted.

Meg broke away, dashing into the darkness as Sheila raised her arm. She lunged, putting all her weight behind the knife. Santo sensed her movement and swung his arm up. It connected with her forearm, deflecting the point of the knife. He bellowed as the blade sliced into his shoulder.

Sheila's forward thrust knocked him off balance, but as he fell he dropped the flashlight and made a mad grab for her. His fingers caught in her hair, and he pulled her down on top of him.

The fall broke his hold and jerked the knife out of her grasp. She rolled away, pushed herself to her feet, and ran to the spot where she'd dropped the gun. Just as she spotted the glint of metal, her ankle buckled and she fell to her knees.

Santo rose to his feet. One hand gripped his injured shoulder; the other held his gun.

"You're trying to run away from me again, Donna. I'll make sure you never trick me again."

"Don't shoot her! Don't shoot her!" Meg screamed.

Sobbing wildly, she ran out of the shadows, flinging herself into Sheila's arms. Santo raised his gun. Still on her knees, Sheila grasped Meg and tried to cover the little body with her own as she turned her back to him. She tensed, waiting for the impact of the bullets.

From the porch came a loud pop. She heard a shrill whistle and the night lit up with a bright red glow. Behind her, Santo screamed. Jerking her head around, Sheila looked over her shoulder.

Santo lay on his back, writhing and howling in agony. A burning flare was buried in his stomach.

At the top of the stairs, Hank clung to the railing. His arm hung at his side, the orange and white flare gun dangling from his hand.

With a cry of thanksgiving, Sheila picked up Meg. The child covered her ears to block out Santo's shrieking, and Sheila turned until Meg's back was to the horrible scene. The screams faded to a long keening wail, then trailed off into silence. He gave one bubbling gasp and then lay still.

Warren Santo was dead.

Sheila shuddered in relief. The smell of burning flesh gagged her as she carried Meg around his body to the bottom of the stairs. She raised her eyes and found Hank staring down at her. In the fading light of the flare, his eyes glittered and she caught the touch of a smile on the blood-streaked face.

"Time for the cavalry," he said.

Meg gasped at the sound of Hank's voice. She raised her head and Sheila could see the relief on her face as she realized he wasn't dead.

He dropped another flare into the gun, pointed it toward the sky and fired. A streak of light shot upwards, the whistling sound cutting through the silence. The flare exploded, illuminating the area brighter than before.

When her vision adjusted, Sheila saw that Hank was again lying on the floor of the porch.

She set Meg down and the girl scrambled up the stairs. Leaning on the handrail, Sheila followed her. At the top, she knelt down beside Hank. She pressed her fingers under his jaw and cried out in relief when she felt his pulse. It was rapid and strong.

"Is he going to die?" Meg asked.

"Not if I can help it." She pulled the flashlight out of her bra and handed it to Meg. "I need light."

In the thin beam of light, Sheila eased Hank onto his back, looking first at the wound on his head. Just above his left ear was a two-inch groove caked with blood. It wasn't bleeding anymore, so she left it alone and reached up to unbutton his collar.

The shirt was saturated with blood, and when she couldn't unbutton the rest of the buttons, she grasped the material in both hands and ripped it open. Despite the amount of blood on his shirt, the wound didn't appear to be too bad. It was at the top of his shoulder and looked as if the bullet had bounced off his collarbone. Hank groaned and opened his eyes.

"Are either of you hurt?"

"I'm not," Meg said, "but Mom has a twisted ankle."

"Is it bad, Sheila?"

"In comparison to you, I'm in perfect condition."

"Thank God Santo was a rotten shot," he said, his voice weak.

"How many times did he hit you?"

"Three times. There's one in my leg."

"Does it hurt a lot, Chief Harker?" Meg asked.

"Not too bad," he said. "Can you find the backpack, Meg?"

Sweeping the flashlight across the floor, Meg shouted when she spotted the canvas bag. She crawled over and dragged it back. Sheila reached inside and pulled out a large first-aid kit. While Meg held the flashlight, she opened the top. Nestled among the first-aid supplies was a bottle of Johnny Walker and a cigar.

Laughing, she unscrewed the cap and raised Hank's head so he could take a drink. Then, after a momentary hesitation, she took a quick drink herself.

In the distance Sheila could hear the thin wail of sirens. Tears of relief filled her eyes as she looked down at Hank.

"I thought you were dead," she said, her voice breaking on the last word.

Hank reached out and took her hand, holding it tightly.

"I passed out after Santo shot me. It was Meg's scream that revived me." He turned his head to smile at the girl. "You're a brave young lady, Meg. I can see why your mother's so proud of you."

"Thanks, Chief Harker."

Sheila sighed as the girl's expression lightened. Meg was obviously pleased by the compliment and curled up next to Sheila. The sirens were getting louder. Hank shifted, his face grimacing in pain. Sheila leaned over him in concern.

"Give me that cigar," he said.

She could see the flashing lights as the police cars sped down the road and turned into the driveway. Shaking her head in mock disapproval, she pulled the cigar out of the first-aid kit and handed it to Hank.

"It's a disgusting, nasty habit," she said.

"You sound just like my mother."

"Is that how you see me?"

"I think you know damn well how I see you," Hank snarled as he bit off the end of the cigar and jammed it between his teeth.

At his words, Meg lifted her head and stared at Sheila.

"Oh, Mom," she said. "Not Chief Harker!"